PRAISE FOR *WALK ME HOME*

"*Walk Me Home* is a delightful, delicious recipe for second chances."
—Fresh Fiction

"Funny, tender, and full of heart, *Walk Me Home* is a delightful read that had me rooting for the hero and heroine on every page. Liza Kendall has penned a second-chance romance that was as compelling as it was entertaining. I can't wait to visit Silverlake Ranch again!"
—*New York Times* bestselling author Jenn McKinlay

Hometown Hero

LIZA KENDALL

JOVE
New York

A JOVE BOOK
Published by Berkley
An imprint of Penguin Random House LLC
penguinrandomhouse.com

Copyright © 2020 by Elizabeth A. Edelstein, Karen A. Moser
Excerpt from *Walk Me Home* by Liza Kendall © 2020 by
Elizabeth A. Edelstein, Karen A. Moser
Penguin Random House supports copyright. Copyright fuels creativity, encourages
diverse voices, promotes free speech, and creates a vibrant culture. Thank you for buying
an authorized edition of this book and for complying with copyright laws by not
reproducing, scanning, or distributing any part of it in any form without permission.
You are supporting writers and allowing Penguin Random House to continue to
publish books for every reader.

A JOVE BOOK, BERKLEY, and the BERKLEY & B colophon are
registered trademarks of Penguin Random House LLC.

ISBN: 9780593098042

First Edition: July 2020

Printed in the United States of America
1   3   5   7   9   10   8   6   4   2

Cover image of Couple by People Images/Getty Images
Cover design by Vikki Chu
Book design by George Towne

To Kat and Redwood,
who have read everything I've ever published.
Thank you for the support. Love you!—L.

To my late mother-in-law, a.k.a. "Young Lois,"
for being a mom when I lost my own,
and for enthusiastic support of my books.
I will always love you.—K.

Chapter 1

THE RADIO WAS STILL PLAYING. THAT WAS THE SUR-
real thing. Andrew "Ace" Braddock, second base-
man for the Austin Lone Stars, was suspended upside
down, hanging by his seat belt . . . and AC/DC was still
blasting.

Back in black . . .

"Pete?" he said urgently. "Pete? Are you okay?"

Nobody's gonna get me on another rap.

A moan came from the driver's seat, where shortstop
Pete Bergsen hung next to him. "Frannie's . . . she's gonna
divorce me."

The first thing Ace felt was sweeping relief. Pete was
alive.

The next thing he felt was agony. "Son of a bi—*aagh*. I
think my ankle is broken."

"My car. Oh, man. The *car*!"

"Yeah, the car. Sure. Did you hear me, buddy? My ankle. Is. Annihilated." *The pain.* The pain was like white-
hot lightning, streaking up from his ankle and then

colliding somewhere inside his nervous system in an explosion that left him breathless.

But the pain was better than panicking—giving in to flashbacks of a different crumpled car, years ago. *Don't go there. Don't* go *there. Deep breaths. Stay calm.*

"Your ankle. Really?" Pete's voice anchored him to the present mess.

"Yeah," Ace managed. "Really."

They hung there for a moment longer, absorbing the unholy mess they were in: wrecked in pitch-black darkness, out on the winding roads surrounding Austin's Lake Travis. Courtesy of a moment of stupidity by his buddy.

"Pete, you're *such* a piece of crap." Ace said it without heat.

"I know."

"You paid enough for the Maserati—you should know it has its own lighter."

"I like my lighter. Frannie gave it to me."

"Next time, leave it on the friggin' floor of the car when you drop it."

"Hindsight."

"Don't run us off the friggin' road and *into a live oak* and flip the car."

"Ace, you gotta switch places with me. Say you were driving."

"Switch . . . ?" If they hadn't been hanging upside down, his jaw would have dropped open.

"Just how many beers did you have, Pete?"

"Please, Ace. Frannie's gonna leave and take the kids with her. She *will* do it this time. She was serious. You gotta switch places with me, man."

"You have got to be kidding. Are you *nuts*?"

"C'mon. You're Easy Ace Braddock. You're a walkin' *Enquirer* headline. Nobody will be surprised that you're in the papers again. But Frannie warned me. She will walk and take my kids and then take me to the cleaners."

"You are such a *tool*."

"I know."

"I cannot believe you're asking me this."

"Please. Switch places with me, Ace? I'm beggin' you."

Maybe it was the excruciating pain. Maybe he was just a chump. But Ace thought about it for a moment. He thought about Pete's kids.

He didn't have much to lose in comparison. Then he unbuckled his seat belt with his left hand and folded his head and shoulders, followed by the rest of him, onto the roof interior of what had once been a very sweet car. It hurt. A lot.

He shoved open the door—which was an amazing feat in itself, since it was crumpled like a tissue from slamming into the tree. Not to mention the fact that it didn't work so well upside down.

Then Ace, cursing royally with each movement, hauled his sorry butt out of the car and fell into the grass.

His first thought was that it was way too quiet. No lights, no sirens, no witnesses—wait, that last part was good. *If* he was going to honor Pete's crazy request to switch places with him and say he'd been the one driving the car.

His next thought was: *Get Pete out of the vehicle,* now. *In case the gas tank explodes.*

Now.

Oh, damn, it hurts.

Now! On your feet, Braddock. Don't even think about wussing out. Pro athlete, and you can't take a little pain? Up! It was Coach's voice, as always. Ace might have left Silverlake High behind, but he'd always hear Coach Adams in his head.

Ace used the car to pull himself to his feet—it was like someone had poured acid over his ankle. He didn't want to think about what that meant for his career with the Austin Lone Stars.

He hopped around the Maserati, reaching the driver's side door with another blue streak of cuss words, none of which made him feel any better. "Pete, buddy, unbuckle your seat belt. We gotta get you out of there."

There was a pause as Pete fumbled. "Can't find it."

"What d'you mean, you can't find it? Look down—or up, actually, at your lap. Press the button. Prepare to land on your head."

Pete mumbled something unintelligible.

"What?"

The window was open, since Pete had rolled it down to smoke.

Ace winced again at the pain but lowered himself to the grass and stuck his head in, coming face to groin with his disoriented friend. "Get your junk out of my face."

"Can't help it," said Pete, his voice now more slurred.

"Did you hit your head or something? Unbuckle your seat belt and get the hell out of the car."

Pete hung there, silent. It wasn't like him. Was he concussed? Or drunk? Or both? Ace had been so hell-bent on getting away from that rabid baseball bunny that he hadn't noticed Pete was in no condition to drive.

Ace did his best to ignore Pete's crotch and fumbled around until he found the buckle to his seat belt. He pressed the button, and Pete dropped into a heap on the roof's interior.

Cussing a blue, green, purple, and black streak because of the pain, Ace lay on his side and hooked his arm under Pete's armpit. He braced his good foot on the crumpled car's frame and hauled with all his might.

Pete popped out like a cork, and they both fell backward to the uneven terrain.

Ace dragged him farther away from the car—it really could go up in flames at any moment—almost howling with the pain. "Pete? Buddy? What's wrong?"

In answer, his teammate puked all over the grass.

What the hell had he been thinking, to get in a car with Pete? What had *Pete* been thinking, to get behind the wheel?

Answer: Neither of them had been thinking at all.

Ace slid his cell phone out of his pocket, since one of them had to call 911 and explain their predicament. *Great.*

He checked Pete's pulse. It was steady, thank God. "Pete, can you hear me? Did you hit your head?"

Pete wiped his mouth on his sleeve. "N-no. Hit the tequila . . ."

Just as Ace had thought. Well, he guessed it was better than a concussion. But there was one big, Texas-sized problem. If Ace called 911 and revealed to the cops that Pete had been driving this way, then his friend was going straight to jail.

If, on the other hand, Ace told the police that *he'd* been the one driving . . . well, he'd ridden in the notoriety rodeo before. Pete was right—nobody'd be shocked that Easy Ace had gotten his face splashed across the scandal sheets or the gossip sites.

He'd go to PR hell, for sure. But he'd only had two light beers over the course of the whole evening, so he wouldn't go to jail.

Ace spun the story easily in his head: He'd spotted his friend's condition and he'd taken Pete's keys once they got out to the car. He'd been driving Pete home.

The team would thank him for salvaging the situation and being a good wingman. Frannie would thank him and not divorce Pete. Ace would serve as an example to the youth of America: Friends don't let friends drive drunk.

See, he wasn't a blithering idiot. He was a hero.

❦

Unfortunately, Ace's agent, Lucille Dunn, did not agree with this assessment when he woke three hours later in a hospital bed with his ankle still on fire. Upon opening his eyes, he took in the ugly green pattern of his hospital gown first, and the fact that under it, he was buck naked.

Then his gaze traveled to the white blanket on the bed and the beige walls. Overhead, he saw the black rectangle of a muted television. Only then did he glimpse a flash of satanic red. The ridiculously expensive sole of a stiletto shoe.

That was when Ace knew he was in deep, deep voodoo-doo-doo. He winced. He'd rather face a flesh-eating zombie at the moment than his agent.

She was sitting next to him, checking two smartphones and an iPad all at the same time. Lucille was a six-foot-tall, no-nonsense, smoking-hot blonde and one of the top sports agents around. She busted balls before breakfast and could outcuss a sailor. And he was pretty sure that she carried a switchblade, a shovel, tarps, and lye in her oversized Chanel handbag.

"Howdy, Luce," mumbled Ace, woozy from pain and whatever drug they'd given him for it. "What're you doing here?"

"Emergency management," she said crisply, tossing one of the phones at his head.

"Ow." Ace felt around on the pillow for it, and then took a look at the screen.

"Which I don't have the time, or the inclination, to do. Especially under these circumstances."

His eyes focused on an image of Pete's crumpled Maserati, underneath a blaring headline: *Braddock's Latest Line Drive*. Now that it was all over and he wasn't pulsing with adrenaline, looking at the car made him want to vomit. It wasn't a minivan, and he wasn't thirteen years old, but still. His stomach lurched. And then shadows, whispers, and ghosts filled his mind. The ones he expertly ducked, but that always somehow found him. "How . . . ? No press was there."

"Are you that stupid, Ace?"

"Someone on the inside sold the photo."

"Photos, plural. Ace, I told you to keep a low profile because of the contract negotiations."

He closed his eyes. "I know."

"Keeping a low profile does not involve drunken carousing or getting your name and face splashed across every news outlet in America!"

"I wasn't carousing, and I wasn't drunk," Ace protested.

"You're lucky your blood test came back under the legal

limit," Lucille said. "Or you'd be in jail. But this is a PR nightmare: You could have killed yourself *and* Pete Bergsen. And we have to show the public that you take that very, very seriously."

He swallowed and looked away.

"What aren't you telling me, Ace?" Lucille homed in on the tension inside him, as if she had x-ray vision. She probably did.

"Nothing."

"Ace. I will give you one chance to come clean. One."

"I didn't put peanut butter out for the grackles."

Lucille rolled her eyes. "Those birds are so gross. But this has nothing to do with your ridiculous superstitions. Now spill."

Ridiculous? He didn't pee on his hands, like Moises Alou. He'd never worn a gold thong, like Jason Giambi. Or women's stockings, like the Babe. In the great arena of weird baseball-player superstitions, grackle appeasement really wasn't that odd.

Lucille got up. "Fine. We're done."

"Okay, okay! I wasn't actually driving," he confessed. "Pete was."

Lucille closed her eyes and dropped back into her chair. "Are. You. Kidding. Me."

Ace just looked at her. "He would have gone to jail."

"You should have let him!"

"He's my friend. My teammate. My brother."

Lucille said a few choice words that almost made the white hospital blanket over him blush. Then she threw up her hands. "I could just kill you, Ace Braddock." She skewered him with her smoky green assassin's gaze. "But what's done is done. And if you're dead, I won't make my luxurious commission on your next Austin Lone Stars contract. By the way, *none* of this, especially not the fracture in your ankle, is going to help me in negotiations on your behalf."

"I know. I'm sorry."

"Save your apology for someone who cares." Lucille drummed her fingernails on her iPad and then slipped it into the monstrous black quilted bag with its entwined Cs. "The team's attorney, Larry Litman, is already threatening to pull the moral turpitude card. So this is what you're going to do. You will release a statement to the press. You'll thank fans everywhere for their concern and good wishes. You will be voluntarily going on the wagon and the team will hire a sober companion for you while you heal from your injuries in seclusion. Got it?"

Ace groaned. "I don't need to 'get sober' and I don't need a *companion*."

"Well, your public image does. And if Larry is going to scream moral turpitude, then we're gonna milk any dubious advantage out of it that we can—meaning they can pay gobs of money for your babysitter so that you don't have to. You're going to suck it up, Ace, or I'm done with you as a client. Talent, charm, and good looks are not going to get you out of this, and I have my own reputation to maintain."

"Lucille—"

"Don't even try to *Lucille* me. Not interested. And stop sabotaging your career. What is that about, Ace? You need to figure it out—before it's too late."

She held up her manicured hand and shot a meaningful glance at the phone that still lay on his chest.

He tossed it to her, and she caught it neatly. "See you on the other side of this mess." She shut the door firmly on the protests that he hadn't even begun to make.

Ace stared at it.

Stop sabotaging your career. What is that about?

He closed his eyes again, but the image of Pete's crumpled Maserati was burned into his retinas. And the image of a pale blue 2003 Dodge minivan came after it: front end mangled, windshield smashed in. No survivors.

Nothing would ever chase that image away. Not Coach Adams's affectionate mentoring. Not stellar stats, or league championship wins. Not beautiful baseball bunnies or bar fights.

It would follow him forever.

You will be voluntarily going on the wagon and the team

will hire a sober companion for you while you heal from your injuries in seclusion. Got it?

Yeah, he got it. It was good advice, if unwelcome advice.

But where, exactly, was "seclusion"? Where could he go to get away from the celebrity scene and the photographers and the reporters?

The last place anyone would expect.

Silverlake. His hometown. His family still owned a ranch there, and he had as much right as any of his siblings to stake a claim. Well, at least to one of the bedrooms. Never mind that he'd hardly seen any of his family in person for years.

He was the local kid made good in the major leagues. He couldn't think of one single person in the town of Silverlake, Texas, who wouldn't want to welcome back Andrew "Ace" Braddock—the hometown hero.

Chapter 2

MIA ADAMS STARED AT THE COLORFUL, GILT-FRAMED print on the wall next to her boss's desk; a painting of an idyllic cobblestoned street somewhere in the Mediterranean. She wished she could be sucked into it and transported there, onto the island. She'd inhale the warm sea-salt breeze and the scent of bougainvillea; wander to a café for a chocolate gelato; encounter a tall, dark, handsome gentleman who'd fall instantly in love with her. He'd turn out to be a shipping tycoon or a secret prince . . . the answer to all her problems.

"Mia?" her boss said. "You look exhausted."

Damn. Why wasn't life a romance novel?

"Would you like a cup of coffee, hon?" Phyllis was in her early sixties, comfortably and unapologetically graying and padded. She wore a lilac pantsuit over a crisp white blouse and pink lipstick that offered evidence of the soft heart under her businesslike demeanor.

"Oh," Mia said. "No, thanks. I've already had four."

"Four?"

"Yes. I was up a little late last night." She'd gone from her shift here at Mercy Hospital to her second job, taking care of three elderly patients in their homes. Then she'd hit her own kitchen to gulp a cup of soup and make another batch of Bee Natural Honey Lip Balm to sell in town. And finally, she'd collapsed in front of her laptop to track her dirtbag ex, Rob Bayes. Following his trail of unpaid debts (in her name) was almost a full-time job in itself.

"No wonder your hands are shaking, Mia."

She looked down at them. "Are they?" True: Her fingers were vibrating.

"Good thing you're not drawing any blood today."

"Yeah, I guess so." Oh, she'd love to draw some blood all right: Rob's. But not in a medically professional way.

"Mia, I asked you to meet with me this morning because I'm genuinely concerned about you. You look run-down; you have huge blue circles under your eyes, and you've lost at least fifteen pounds in the last couple of months."

"Oh, great—my diet is working." Mia produced her signature cheerful *I got this* grin.

"Look—I realize that I'm your supervisor and not your mom, but—"

Mia adored her boss. People were supposed to either hate, fear, tolerate, or grudgingly respect their bosses, but Phyllis was a peach in every way. Mia couldn't have gotten luckier than to get her as a supervisor.

The only problem with that was the strong urge to climb into her lap, cry on her shoulder, and spill all of her problems. And no matter how tempting that might be, Mia would shoot herself first.

Shooting Rob was a better idea . . . but she had to find the rat to do it. And when last spotted, he'd been cavorting on a beach in Buenos Aires, with some young, hot, and mostly naked company.

"But?" Mia said brightly. *But I have seventy thousand dollars in IVF debt to pay off? But the bank is going to foreclose on the monstrosity of a house that Rob mortgaged our souls down to the soles for? But I can't even afford the copay for a therapist to help me work out my fantasies of murdering him?*

"But I truly care about you, honey. And you won't like this, but I'm going to suggest that you use some of your banked vacation days and take some time off. You have over six weeks' worth, and you're going to lose them if you don't take them."

Mia blinked at her. *How do you say to your boss that you're saving those vacation days so that you can take off for South America, stalk your ex, make a Molotov cocktail out of his vodka bottle, and shove it up his . . .* "Oh, Phyllis. That is so sweet of you. Really. But I'm fine."

Her boss sighed. "I was afraid you'd say that."

"Never been better," Mia lied. "Able to leap tall buildings in a single bound." *Especially if Rob is on the roof and I can drop-kick him into heavy traffic below.*

"Honey, you're not Wonder Woman."

No kidding. Wonder Woman had an invisible plane that would get her to Argentina in a heartbeat—not to mention a lasso that would find Rob like a guided missile, drop a noose neatly around his neck, and bring him to his knees. And then there were those boots . . .

Mia looked ruefully down at her not-so-sexy Crocs. Well, you couldn't beat them for hospital work. "I'm sorry, what did you say?"

Phyllis laughed, but the sound was way too empathetic for Mia's liking. And if there was one thing she absolutely could not handle right now, it was empathy. She was spoiling for a really good, no-holds-barred fight.

Empathy? That would destroy her. She'd melt into a puddle of unshed tears, countless tubs of fudge brownie ice cream, and a morass of self-pity.

She couldn't afford empathy.

Just like she couldn't afford to shop anywhere but the dollar store, even though she lived in what was arguably the biggest house in Silverlake, Texas.

Phyllis said, "You are burning the candle at both ends, Mia. When was the last time you took a day off? Went to a spa?"

*Oh, I went to several spas last week—if you count all
the ones I visited at that Dallas trade show, trying to sell
my honey and beeswax products.* But Mia shrugged. "Spas.
Not my thing. Days off—I get bored. I have to be busy.
Darn that sick Scottish Protestant work ethic."

But Phyllis wasn't giving up. "Look, Mia. I can't force
you. But will you do me a favor, as your friend? Will you
take a long weekend off?"

Mia hesitated. She had been wanting to branch out into
goat's milk products, ever since she'd spied the three goats
from Lila Braddock's former petting zoo. Mia already har-
vested her honey from the bees at the Braddock ranch . . .
and what was Deck doing with the goats, other than com-
plaining to his sister that they were a destructive nuisance?

Attractive nuisance, Lila had said. A magnet for children and their parents. *Paying* parents. Who also held
events and weddings on the property—or used to, until the
Old Barn had burned down a few months ago. After that,
she'd switched her focus to events in town, and they'd
closed the zoo. But they still had the goats.

Being the thrifty student of agriculture he was, Declan
had suggested that somebody do something with the goat's
milk . . . sending Lila into peals of laughter. *I don't milk
anything on four legs, bro. I only milk brides!*

"Will I take a long weekend?" Mia repeated to Phyllis.
Her boss lifted her eyebrows, waiting.

"Sure. I guess I could do that." Mia smiled. "Thank you."

It wasn't Phyllis's business how she spent her time "off."

༄

Silverlake Ranch was better known for cattle and a few
crops, not goats. And yet here Mia was, at Declan Braddock's invitation, facing down an annoyed goat. It was a
true testament to Deck's good nature that he allowed the
critters on his ranch.

Silverlake Ranch spread out around her in a patchwork
of green and gold, white-fenced paddocks, the sparkle of a

stock pond, and then, in the distance, the liquid silver of the lake itself, which bordered the Braddock land. Mia's hair lifted on the breeze, and she soaked up the sunlight and the goodness of the blue Texas Hill Country sky.

"*Meh*," said the goat, interrupting her appreciation of it all. Bringing her back to her financial woes and the fact that her dirtbag of an ex had skipped out on them.

Goat's milk soap. Goat's milk hand cream. Goat's milk bubble bath . . .

The new product options were endless and fabulous, and almost guaranteed to make Mia extra money, like the beeswax and honey products—now, if only she knew what she was doing.

Mia held the goat's halter lead in one hand and her iPad in the other. The goat eyed the device as if it wanted to check Instagram.

"Not gonna happen," she told it. "And you can't keep up with your favorite Kardashian or play solitaire, either. Sorry."

"*Meh*."

"I need this for instruction."

The goat stomped its hoof.

"I have to say that you smell pretty rank, but you're cute in a homely sort of way."

"*Mehhh*."

"A backhanded compliment, you're right." Mia tucked the iPad under her arm and tied the goat to a mesquite tree. She did an Internet search. "Aha. Yes. Here it is: *How to Hand-Milk a Goat.* Hmmm."

She consulted the excellent article.

"Yeah. Strike one: no goat 'stand.' And what the heck is a stanchion?"

"*Mehhhhhhh*."

"Don't call me stupid. You're a goat."

The animal snorted at her.

"You have an attitude problem, you know?" she told it. "You're supposed to be encouraging to beginners. Supportive."

This the goat utterly ignored.

Mia continued to read.

"I've washed my hands. Well, twenty minutes ago. But . . . strike two. I have never even heard of Milk Check Teat Wipes, and I certainly don't own any. But I do have Wet Ones. So we'll use those."

The goat pulled on its halter lead, trying to get away from the tree.

"Cut that out. Okay, now . . ." Mia reached under the goat and tried to grasp the relevant parts to sterilize and then milk.

The goat tossed its head and stepped firmly onto her foot.

"Ouch! Well, I know— I should have at least bought you a drink first. But can you work with me here?"

Far from being compliant with her wishes, the animal began an elaborate dance of keep-away, and Mia could swear it was laughing. And not with her, but *at* her.

"No! No dancing! And no ki—"

The goat quite literally kicked the bucket. Not that Mia wasn't ready for it to be shot up to goat heaven, at this point. But it was just an expression.

She sure wished she herself had some spilt milk to cry over . . . but it seemed that was not to be.

"Listen, you goat from hell! I'm about ready to pull your beard. I need this free milk, kid. I really, really do. And Declan said I could have it. So stand and deliver!"

The sound of soft male laughter came from behind her, and Mia whirled to find none other than Deck Braddock chuckling at her expense, along with the blasted goat.

"Having fun?" He looked like the damn Marlboro Man in his snug denim, plaid shirt, and that ten-gallon hat. Deck was strikingly handsome and had a heart of gold. They were both single. Mia only wished there were an ounce of chemistry between them. But unfortunately, there wasn't. He'd always been sort of a brother.

"No, I can't say that I'm enjoying myself. How the heck does anybody do this?"

"Let's just say I'm mighty pleased that with you taking care of it, I don't have to find someone to do it anymore. I consider this a favor. Not to mention that a lot of that milk was just going to waste."

If Mia had a dime for every time Declan claimed *she* was doing *him* a favor, she wouldn't need to milk this darn goat at all. "Well, do you know how?"

"I do." He grinned.

"Would you be willing to teach a girl?"

"Sure. I need to talk with you about something, anyway." Deck walked over to the goat, which gazed up at him adoringly. Sickening. "How ya doin' there, Pansy?"

"Mehhhh."

"Pansy? Really?"

"Yep. Her sister's Petunia."

"No . . ."

"I kid you not." He smirked.

"I'd already thought of that one, Declan."

He shrugged, righted the bucket under the goat, and commenced milking her. Just like that. The goat even leaned into him and nuzzled the back of his neck.

"Slut." Mia folded her arms across her chest. "So . . . what did you want to talk about?"

Deck sighed and stopped milking for a moment while he gathered his thoughts. "I wondered if you'd like a job."

"What kind of a job? I already have three, if you count my side business."

"Yeah. No wonder you've got those purple bags under your eyes."

"Thanks for noticing those."

"You're welcome. Anyway—this gig would still allow you to create your products. And it would make use of your nursing degree."

"So . . ."

"It pays a lot. A whole lot."

"Deck? Why are you laying out all of the great things about this job, kind of like a used-car salesman on a slow weekend?"

He laughed, but the humor didn't reach his eyes. "You're nothing if not perceptive, Mia."

"So . . . what's the downside? What aren't you telling me while you butter me up?"

"Yeah. That. Well, you see, Ace has been in an accident."

Mia drew in a sharp breath. "Oh, Deck—" Everyone knew that the Braddock parents had been killed in a car wreck years ago.

"He's okay," Deck added quickly.

"Good." Relief flooded her.

"Just a little banged up."

"I'm sorry to hear that."

Ace. Andrew "Easy Ace" Braddock. Declan's trouble-making younger brother and onetime thorn in her side. Actually, that thorn never had gotten quite pulled out. She'd imagined him having *extreme* bad luck—about as bad a fate as you could wish on a ballplayer, according to her dad—but she'd never imagined him getting hurt. Declan must have been terrified when he got the call.

"Yeah. Well, Ace needs—"

"No," said Mia, as she realized what Deck was about to ask her. "Not a chance in hell."

"I haven't finished telling you what he needs."

"I don't care what Easy Ace needs. Never have, never will."

Declan leveled his dark gaze on her. He didn't sigh. Didn't try to reason with her. Didn't point out that in spite of the "favors" she did, such as milking his goat, it was more that she owed him, since she got the materials for her products from the Braddock land.

Deck was too decent a guy. He was also smart enough to see that she'd eventually loop back to that fact all by herself.

So she was the one who sighed, while Deck reached his big, competent, gentle hands under the goat again and produced a nice quantity of free milk for her. Then he got up.

"I'll get Petunia," was all he said, while Pansy flicked her tail at Mia as if it were a middle finger and followed

Deck adoringly back to the goat pen. Her funny little udder swung between her spindly rear legs as she skipped along behind him.

Mia stared at Deck's broad, receding back. Kind. Solid. Great-looking. *What's wrong with me? Fall in love with him already. Why can't I?*

And why did just the barest mention of his brother Ace give her the sensation of red-hot ants sprinting up and down her skin? Three different areas of her chest prickled, as if she were developing hives. She lifted her shirt collar and blew under it.

What a ridiculously over-the-top reaction to a guy she'd never been able to stand. And he wasn't even here.

She heard her father's voice, out of nowhere, cheering on Easy Ace.

Way to paint the corners, son! You are one five-tool player!

Watch for the steal . . . Yep, you got 'im. Nice, Ace, nice. Couldn'ta done it better myself.

Coach Adams had always been encouraging to his students; he was a gifted instructor. But it was the pride in his voice when he spoke of "his" Ace that was so hard to take, that got under her skin like a chigger, set up camp, and refused to leave. Made her itchy and borderline crazed as she thought about herself, as a little girl, trying to salvage even a scrap of his attention.

Dad, will you play catch with me?

Not now, Mia. It's time for dinner . . . It's time for a bath . . . It's time for the nightly news.

Dad, will you help me with my algebra?

Now, honey. I'm trying to read the paper. You're a smart girl. You can figure it out.

Dad, when's Mom coming home?

I don't know. Whenever she's done with her trip.

But there was always another trip.

Deck interrupted her musings as he came back with a recalcitrant Petunia and introduced her to Mia.

"Hello," she said cautiously.

The goat tossed her head.

"Got some milk you want to donate to my cause?"

"Mehhhhh."

Declan chuckled and tied the goat to the tree. "Okay. Want to learn?"

"Uh . . . it's just that it feels really weird."

He shot her an amused glance, and she felt her face heat. *What's your problem, Mia? You're a nurse. You've handled worse things than a goat's teats.*

"You think I'm better qualified?" he asked.

She all but choked. "Just how do you think I'm supposed to answer that, Deck?"

He shrugged, his mouth working.

"Move out of the way," she ordered. "Please." Weird feeling or not, if he could do it, so could she.

"Be my guest," Deck said, still trying to hide his smile. He waited.

Mia eventually came to an understanding with the disgruntled goat and got a stream of milk going into the pail. "So what kind of an accident did"—his name stuck in her craw, but she forced it out like a cat hacking up a hairball—"*Ace* get himself into this time?"

"Well," Declan began in measured tones. "It involved a Maserati."

"Of course it did."

"And a teammate," he said.

"And as many baseball bunnies as you can stuff in the back seat, trunk, and glove box?"

"None of those."

"Because the Lone Stars' PR gal got to the scene before the cops and hustled them off, after getting nondisclosure forms signed by every one of them?"

"You have a deeply suspicious mind, Miz Adams."

"I have a rightly suspicious mind, Mister Braddock."

"I repeat: According to all reports, it was a bunny-free zone."

Mia merely lifted an eyebrow, but she must have tugged a little too hard on Petunia.

"Mehhhhhhh!" shouted the annoyed goat.

"Sorry," Mia said. "Let me think: The incident also involved alcohol and loud music."

"It did. But Ace maintains that it was his teammate who was drunk, not him."

"Who was driving?"

"Now, that's a little complicated . . ."

Mia leaned her forehead against Petunia's fuzzy little goat shoulder—or whatever it was called—and rolled her eyes.

"Mia, Ace claims he took the rap for his teammate. Switched seats with him."

"What do *you* think?"

Declan shoved his hands into his pockets. "I've known Ace to color, bend, distort, and pull the truth somewhat inside out . . ."

Mia snorted.

"But I've never known him to outright lie. Besides . . ." Declan took a moment. "I find it hard to believe that Ace would drive drunk given our family history. So I'm gonna give him the benefit of the doubt in this case."

Mia bit her lip and said nothing, but in her experience, history tended to repeat itself, so she wasn't feeling as generous as Declan. Deck didn't know about a few little things in the past: random beer cans in her dad's trash that Ace always claimed were someone else's. Riiiight.

"The thing is," Declan continued, "the team won't be giving him the same courtesy. And there's the small matter of his contract. Since Ace took the rap, he also gets the slap."

"Spell it out, Deck."

"He needs a sober companion for the next eight weeks."

"A . . . ?" Mia stared at him, her jaw slack.

"Someone extremely well paid to keep him out of trouble and kick him in the pants, as needed. In short, he needs *you.*"

The magnitude of the Technicolor *NO!* that reverberated throughout her brain was staggering.

Deck bent forward and retrieved the pail of "free" milk from under Petunia before either woman or goat could kick it over.

And as Mia stood up and backed away from him, shaking her head, he advanced calmly upon her and handed it over. "They're willing to be very flexible with your schedule. I did say 'extremely well paid,' right?"

"You did," she managed.

He curled her fingers around the handle of the bucket and then patted her hand before releasing its weight into her custody. Gave her that charming and truly decent smile of his. "So you'll think about it, right?"

Mia nodded dumbly, dubiously, darkly.

Money. Cabbage. Kale.

Green stuff that her wallet and bank account desperately needed.

His ace in the hole . . .

And she couldn't even damn Declan. He was too nice a guy . . . unlike his brother.

Chapter 3

ACE CAUGHT HIS REFLECTION IN THE TINTED-GLASS window of the limousine, taking in the under-eye bags, the hair sticking up all over the place, and the grim set of his mouth. He looked like a rumpled rock star at the end of a long world tour.

His heart hammered in his chest as the car wove in lazy arcs through an achingly familiar landscape that looked like something out of a movie. Trees loaded with apples and still a few peaches? Check. Horses frisking about in pastures? Check. Fields of amber waving grain? Check.

He'd raced dirt bikes after school for years with Mick Halladay on that stretch beyond the cemetery. Holy crap. The Nash Mansion used to be just there, where a massive black scourge stained the ground. When he'd made his pregame call to Jake before the last playoff game, his brother had said he and his girl, Charlie, were gonna do something about that now.

Now that they were back together. In love again. The sweetness of that thought felt foreign to Ace himself; he was too jaded, too corroded by fame to deserve it.

He slouched down in his seat and stopped looking out the window as a mess of memories came roaring back like an angry sea. Instead, he stared at his hands. They looked average: large, with neat, squared nails at the end of tapered fingers. He looked down at his body, which had once been any other body. Nothing that screamed *Hot Stuff* or *Insured by Lloyd's of London for Obscene Premiums.*

In the silence of the car, without the distractions of a city, without the constant presence of teammates, coaches, trainers—fans, his pain was harder to ignore. His ankle hurt, and the other pain, the constant one he usually pushed into the shadows, felt louder than anything in the world.

Hi, Deck, long time no see, big brother. You ever gonna come to the big city and see one of my games? VIP ticket, all the way . . .

Naw. Too flip.

Hi, Deck, thanks for letting me crash . . .

Lame.

Hi, Deck.

Declan, I'm sorry for how I left things . . .

Just . . . no. No, no, no . . .

And suddenly the achingly familiar black iron gates of Silverlake Ranch appeared in front of him: the familiar silhouette of the bronco and its rider that symbolized a classic human struggle to survive and thrive. To stay on top.

The gates opened, the limo turned in.

A dog erupted out of nowhere, barking wildly. Did Deck have a dog? Ace stared out the window at it: a wild, hairy gray mutt with a curiously wide jaw. The damn thing looked like Oscar the Grouch from *Sesame Street*, it really did.

Ace lowered the window and barked back, just to mess with the dog. Oscar didn't like that one bit. He really let Ace have it, in dogspeak.

"Yeah, yeah, yeah," Ace told it. "I've heard worse, little guy."

"That your family?" the driver asked, as he brought the limo to a halt.

"Grab the luggage first?" Ace said instead of answering. He looked through the tinted windows at the porch of Silverlake's main house. One by one, his siblings came out to greet him. Jake, Lila, Rhett, Declan.

It was kinda overwhelming to see them all at once. Not to mention, Rhett had *sworn* that he was never coming back here. Just like Ace had sworn he was never, ever coming back here.

How times had changed.

The limo bounced a little as the driver slammed the trunk shut. Ace stayed behind the tinted glass for a moment longer. As if it would protect him from the memories.

Well, look at that—everyone was an adult. Jake he'd seen regularly on video chat through the years. But not the others. Only a couple of short phone calls at Christmas with everyone on speakerphone at once.

They were all grown up. Lila. Little Lila. He'd seen her pictures on social media, but he hadn't seen Declan.

His eyes shifted back to Deck, who looked like a postcard for the state of Texas, with his jeans and plaid and even a cowboy hat. He hadn't seen his big brother since the day he'd left town. How had that happened?

Well, yeah, he knew exactly how that had happened.

Ace stared at the stranger who looked a little like his mom, a little like his dad, and just thinking about them made him want to punch the leather seat in front of him.

At which point the driver flung open the back door without ceremony and stared expectantly at Ace.

Ace flipped his sunglasses down to cover his eyes, grabbed his crutches, and wormed himself out of the back seat. Whereupon Oscar-the-hairy-grouch-dog sprang at him, still calling him names in dogspeak. He planted two big muddy paws on Ace's thighs, growled, and actually bit one of the crutches.

"Grouchy!" Declan called. "No! *Friend*, buddy."

Friend? Nice.

Ace let one of the crutches fall so that Grouchy—funny

name—could inspect it. He sniffed it from one end to the other, then growled again.

"Yeah, little guy, I don't like it, either. Come say hello." Ace bent down and extended his hand for the dog to smell. Grouchy gave it a casual once-over, clearly not agreeing with Lloyd's of London that he was worth insuring. He shook his hairy head and snorted out the Ace scent. He looked him up, he looked him down, he cocked his head as if to say, *You're not all that.* But then, finally, he wagged his tail.

Ace grinned. "Well, this is better. Not exactly a celebrity welcome, but better. Do you fetch?"

"Does he fetch?" Declan said. "Yeah—he's got a real disgusting habit of fetching roadkill and bringing it home for our 'supper.' Can't seem to understand when it doesn't go right to the table, with a place set for him at the head."

Ace finally looked back up at his siblings and conjured up his signature sparkling smile. Some part of him registered that there weren't any cameras or phones pointed at his face, which was different, and another part of him registered that Declan stayed on the porch as Rhett and Jake rushed down the steps to mess around with the wheelchair that had just come out of the trunk. The one he refused to use.

Lila made a beeline for him.

"Oooh, I want to hug you so bad!" she yelled as she planted a giant kiss on Ace's cheek. Okay, this felt more normal.

"Hey, sis," Ace said, waving off the wheelchair and limping toward the porch steps on the one crutch. He left the other in the dirt, figuring someone would get it.

He caught a glimpse of Jake's face—that arched eyebrow—as Ace left his brother to handle all of his luggage.

"Welcome back," Declan said, finally moving down the stairs as Ace started up. Ace looked over his shoulder and watched him assist Jake and Rhett with the bags. *Huh.* He kinda thought Declan would be all over him, mothering and smothering, as he remembered. But Declan seemed more interested in doing that to the cat he was now petting—an unfamiliar gray cat with golden eyes and a mangy-looking tail—than stepping down to greet him.

Lila reached out and messed with Ace's hair. "You look like a rocker!"

He threw his arm around her shoulders and squeezed a little harder than he should have. "Missed you, too, baby," he said automatically, realizing with a kind of cold horror that he was programmed for the snappy comeback.

She gave him a funny look. *"Baby?"*

"Yeah, you know. Baby sister."

She shot him a knowing glance that said she didn't buy his amendment for a second. "Maybe think about coming home for the holidays this year? We'd love to—"

Ace's pulse raced. He dropped his arm. "I just got here. Lay off."

The look on her face made his own burn with shame, but instead of apologizing he focused on being super careful climbing up the stairs.

At last he was inside, taking a good look around, wincing at the large portrait of his parents over the fieldstone fireplace in the great room. It had been there as long as he could remember. It belonged there. A horrible sensation pooled in his gut. *But I don't belong here. I don't belong anywhere.*

His brothers burst through the door and dropped his bags in an unceremonious pile.

"Hey!" Ace said. "Careful with those. They're Gucci."

Rhett shot him a look. "It's friggin' luggage, hotshot." Ace flushed; Rhett was a billionaire now. He knew perfectly well they were Gucci.

Being unable to lean on being a celebrity made Ace feel even more awkward and out of place. He'd been gone so long he'd forgotten what it was like here in Silverlake, but standing in the foyer of his family's house, the memories came roaring back. The truth was, probably nobody in Silverlake cared if he had designer luggage or not. Back when he was just a kid playing catch in the grass, the people in this town hadn't been too impressed by fancy labels. They were impressed by grit and character and honesty.

He took another look at the portrait of Mama and Pop. Grit, character, and honesty were the same values they'd tried to teach their children. He took in the worn leather club chairs and sofas, the bookshelves in the great room, the wide, wooden-planked floors. The vast expanses of glass that Deck had added to open up the space and invite the trees inside, making the house one with the land and sky.

It was familiar—and yet it wasn't.

It smelled the same, at least. He could still pick up notes of Mama's cooking from long ago. Funny how the friendly ghosts of stews and casseroles and pies and cookies could hang in the atmosphere to provide comfort for decades.

He swallowed hard at the sight of one of Mama's hand-knit afghans slung over the arm of the sofa. And the fire-place tools that had been Pop's, along with the battered brass-handled log carrier. On a shelf in the corner stood his collection of beer steins.

It was easier to focus on all of these objects from the past than to face his brothers and sister in the present. Why was that?

"Gonna head over to the market and pick up some steaks," Jake said with a grin. "We can grill outside, fix a real meal. Jules and Charlie might even make it back from Dallas in time."

Jules and Charlie. Julianna Holt was Rhett's wife, now. The first of the Braddocks to marry. Ace had missed the wedding . . . just as he'd missed all the big milestones in Silverlake. And now Jake was back together with Charlotte Nash. Ace looked away. If they got married, he'd probably miss that, too.

"There's cake!" Lila said exuberantly. "Kristina brought it over this morning."

"I'll start prepping," Declan muttered, picking up Ace's suitcases again and heading straight through the living room.

"No, thanks," Ace said, maybe just to knock them all as off-balance as he felt.

Rhett gave a low whistle. Declan stopped in his tracks and turned around. Jake propped the folded wheelchair against the wall and dusted off his hands, his teeth biting down on his lip.

Lila's smile seemed to melt right off her face.

The five of them stared at one another with nothing but the grandfather clock making the slightest bit of noise.

Ace's heart pounded. He did what he always did. It worked every single time. Got him out of every scrape, every mess, every argument.

He smiled his megawatt smile, shrugged his shoulders, and said like the celebrity he was, "I had a big fancy steak in Austin before I headed out."

Something Ace couldn't read flickered in Declan's eyes before vanishing. His big brother nodded. "Well, great. Your, uh . . . companion will handle things when she gets here. For now, call me if you need anything." He tipped his hat to Ace and walked out the door.

Dismissal: It wasn't what Ace remembered. Not at all.

The moment stretched on and on.

Rhett finally pulled out his phone. "Guess I'll tell Jules and Charlie not to hurry back from their girls' trip to see you."

"You ready to head out, then?" Jake asked Lila.

Lila stared at Ace, a little wrinkle in her forehead. "I thought we would all . . ."

Ace waited for her to finish.

"Declan was really hoping . . ."

She didn't finish that one, either.

"I'll meet you both at the truck in just a sec," Jake said.

Lila heaved a sigh. She took a step forward to maybe hug Ace, but he'd forgotten to ease up on the don't-touch-me vibe that he generally used when fans got too enthusiastic. She pulled up short and said, "Have a good night. Call if you want to meet for breakfast . . . or something."

Jake gave her shoulder a comforting squeeze and then

Lila followed Declan's path out the door. Rhett hung up his phone, gave Ace a courtesy wave goodbye, and went the same way.

"You wanna explain what the hell is eating you?" Jake asked. "We're all grown up now and you don't have an excuse for treating Declan like crap anymore."

"That's fine coming from you!" Ace exploded.

"I've made my peace with him."

"I don't have any beef with him," Ace said.

"I should hope not! But that's not a very high bar for a brother who cares about you."

"Thanks for getting my luggage," Ace said between his teeth.

Jake stared at him and seemed to realize it was hopeless. After another moment of painful silence, he nodded. "I'll see you when I see you, I guess," he said in tones so low that he seemed to be talking to himself. "Welcome home, *Drew*."

Short for Andrew. Nobody called him that these days, and only the family ever had. The family that didn't feel like his; the family he didn't know what to do with—nor they with him. Ace watched as the front door slammed.

It didn't hit Jake on the way out.

Ace hobbled up the stairs to his old room and sat on the bed. Blue flannel sheets. Boyhood comforter covered with baseballs, catcher's mitts, and bats. Goofy to him now, but Mama had done her best to make the room his. He looked around, weirdly embarrassed by the rows of his baseball trophies and signed baseballs; there were some old wooden racecars and a mangy stuffed dog with floppy ears, only one eye and threads hanging where the nose should be.

The Gucci luggage looked utterly idiotic in this room. Mama's suitcase and carry-on had been Samsonite. Pop had used an army duffel. What exactly was Ace trying to prove?

The bustle and excitement of his arrival had left the house along with the rest of his family, and now he was just sitting on a guest bed in a guest room with the fading light casting a gloom.

Why did I behave like that? Why did I say those things? Why did I chase them all away?

Well, maybe because you're an embarrassment. And maybe because when you look at them, you feel like they're just waiting for the right moment to blame you for why our family fell apart. Declan had some nerve, though, standing there on the porch like a principal waiting to mete out some discipline.

Ace's gaze followed the last ray of light out the window and he had to choke back a wellspring of emotions. *That* looked the same. The view. Running out there with his brothers and sisters, asking Lila to be the catcher just one more time, making Jake fetch the good hits, Rhett pretending to announce the game, and Declan on a makeshift pitcher's mound with wildflowers poking up around his shoes . . . Pop smoking a brisket and Mama making the best jalapeno-cheddar cornbread in all of Texas.

Ace lay down on the bed and covered his face with his arm, seeking the oblivion of sleep. If only he could travel back in time. If only he hadn't made them drive that night. If only he could get the twisted wreckage of the minivan out of his mind. *Please, God, why can't I hit the rewind button?*

Chapter 4

ACE AWOKE DISORIENTED, WITH THE MORNING SUN searing through his closed eyelids. The harsh light was a single dangling bulb in an interrogator's cell. He blocked it with his arm and rolled over, his ankle screaming in pain.

Someone was using a blowtorch on it.

What was your purpose, Andrew Braddock, in forcing your parents out that night?

I plead the Fifth.

Whose needs consumed you at that moment?

I plead the Fifth.

How will you ever pay for what you've done?

I can't . . . I can't! Get the hell out of my head!

Ace opened his eyes, realized that he was in his childhood bedroom, and yanked the shade down with a curse.

He sat up, bleary and shaken after a night spent tossing, turning, and running in his sleep.

Not a sound came to him from the rest of the house. A bird chirped somewhere outside. A gust of wind rattled some branches against the window. Some kind of critter scrabbled around on a section of roof over his head.

No sign of any human here to fuss over him.

He told himself that was fine. In fact, it was great.

But then he wanted coffee. And it didn't appear that anyone was going to bring it to him, ask if he wanted sweetener or cream.

He was also starving, after his refusal of the steak dinner planned for him the night before. And that didn't make him feel too bright.

His ankle mocked him.

He shot it a rude gesture.

Then he swung his legs out of bed, located his crutches, and hobbled painfully downstairs.

Where was everybody?

Guess they have jobs, genius.

He crutched himself into the renovated kitchen. Blue walls, updated appliances, Mama's basket collection still on top of the refaced cabinets. That made him swallow hard.

Where was Declan? He hadn't even left him a microwaved breakfast burrito before going out to work on the ranch? *Nice. I'm injured!*

Ace fumbled some lukewarm coffee into a mug and slid it into the microwave.

He poked through the freezer and came up with a couple of stale toaster waffles. No syrup to be found anywhere in the kitchen. What kind of moron had waffles but no syrup?

Cranky, Ace ate in the kitchen nook and fed half of one of the waffles to Grouchy, since he was the only family member here to give him the time of day. He checked news and social media, but not for long, since everywhere there was lurid speculation about the circumstances surrounding the wreck of the Maserati and whether he, as a celebrity, was getting special treatment.

So there he sat, the silence stretching on and on, the ghosts of memories knocking to get into his brain and haunt him.

Finally Ace shoved his phone back into his pocket, his

ankle protesting enough to make him wish his painkillers weren't buried in his luggage upstairs. He crutched out of the kitchen and settled himself on the distressed leather couch in the great room, eyeing all the improvements Declan had made to the house.

Ace missed the older version of the house, but he had to admit that it looked spectacular.

And he'd had no part in renovating it—nobody had even asked his opinion, even though it had been his home, too.

Annoyed and feeling even more disrespected, he turned back to his phone.

Under Favorites, he hit the button for Pete, but it rolled right to voicemail. "Hey, Pete. I made it home . . . So, yeah, this is all crazy. Uh, call me." He scanned his contacts and then hit the button for the center fielder, Manny. Nobody home there, either. *"Oye, amigo. Yo soy . . . soy . . ."* He sighed, muttered, *"Esta situación es loco. Llámame."*

He scanned his contacts again, nearly threw the phone down, and then hit the button for his agent. Lucille picked up. "Are you in Silverlake rehabbing?" she asked brusquely.

"Yeah, I'm, uh, a little . . ."

"Is your ankle worse?"

"No, I—"

"You do something stupid?"

"No, it's—"

"Great. Thanks for checking in."

"Luce!"

"Kinda busy, Braddock. Focus on getting better so you can get back in the game," she said in that tone he hated. The one that meant, *I'm your agent, not your damn mother.* The screen on his phone blanked out when she disconnected the call.

Ace threw his phone clear across the room this time, only slightly disappointed when it landed on a cushioned chair and didn't dramatically smash into a million pieces.

"I need a drink!" he yelled at the top of his lungs.

"Oh, wow," said a woman's voice, as she stepped into the room. Except it wasn't "Oh, wow," the way the baseball bunnies always said it, usually in reference to a hand on his jock. And it wasn't "Oh, wow," the way the announcers always said it, usually in reference to Ace's mitt curled around a game-saving out.

It was kind of the opposite.

Ace tried to process what the girl was wearing. He started at the shoes from hell, enormous plastic-looking things with air holes; moved up to a set of green scrubs splattered with a couple of different stains, probably none of which smelled good; took in the pile of messy red hair piled atop her head; and then settled on her face.

He took longer with that face, because she was beautiful and, luckily, he had all the time in the world to enjoy those full pursed lips, the freckles dusting her nose and cheeks, and the long, long lashes framing her eyes.

"Well, *hello*," Ace said in his failproof bedroom voice.

The woman cocked her head, staring at him. Huh. Okay, failproof minus one somewhat surly medical professional with cinnamon freckles that looked kinda lickable.

Wait a minute. Medical professional. "Are you my babysitter?" He was tempted to add an obvious come-on, the charmer he would have tossed her way if this were a bar and she were a groupie.

His question went unanswered but did reveal that she must have been taking lessons from the Jake Braddock School of Eyebrows because that left one was cranked way up to Level 8—*Are You Kidding Me?*

"Hi, Andrew," she said, very professionally. "Declan recommended me to your team manager. I've been hired to be your sober companion during your time in Silverlake."

Aside from the fact that he didn't actually need a sober companion, there was something odd at work here. You'd think she'd be trying to conceal her excitement; she actually looked as if she thought he was one rung away from cow dung on the ladder of disgust. And it wasn't clear whether his rung was above or below said dung.

"You do realize that 'sober companion' isn't a licensed occupation," he said. "It's not a real thing."

"It's real enough for someone to pay me to do it."

"I can't think of one woman who wouldn't sober-companion me for free," Ace said.

"I'm the luckiest girl in the world," she said, totally deadpan.

Ace stared at her, completely nonplussed. This wasn't how women normally reacted to him. He racked his brain. She looked extremely familiar. Damn, maybe they'd already run the bases together. It wasn't his MO to call the next day. "Did we ever sleep together?" he asked.

Her eyes widened.

"I mean, I can see why I would. I'm really sorry if I don't remember—"

"You don't remember if we *slept* together?" she asked. "You do know who I am, right?"

"Uh . . ."

Shaking her head in disbelief, she tore her eyes away from his and looked down at the piece of paper in her hand. "Okay, let's get this first part over with. On your feet, Braddock."

On your feet, Braddock.

Some kind of muscle memory had him grabbing his crutches and standing. For a minute he was back at high school baseball practice, Coach Adams barking at him, saying that exact thing in that exact tone . . .

Holy sugarbritches. Of course. She said it just like her old man. This was *Mia*, all grown up. The high school coach's daughter. He stumbled back, his palms up. "Whoa. No. Mia Adams. You're Coach's daughter. Noooo. No way. We did *not* sleep together. I one hundred percent stayed out of your infield. I am sure of that. I would never . . ."

For a moment as Ace backpedaled like a crazy person, Mia looked as if she might laugh.

"Coach has always been like a father to me," Ace added.

Her expression instantly shuttered. "Yes. I know. But he isn't."

"Lucky, right?" Ace said, regaining his balance. "Because that would mean you'd be my sister. And you're *defi-*

nitely not my sister." He hadn't meant to say it with the same kind of sexy growl he reserved for the bunnies, but something about her made it come out like that.

Her cheeks colored just slightly, and she cleared her throat. "Back to business. Look, I have to say, I don't personally approve of this part, but it's on the checklist the Lone Stars sent me, which you initialed. So if you don't mind . . ."

She wasn't gonna . . . Oh, she was! *Okay, then . . . you want to play ball? Let's play ball!* Ace grinned as she approached him, her chin up in a kind of official professional-detachment stance.

Ace's grin widened as she attempted to force her hand down the front pocket of his snuggest pair of jeans.

"Looking for something?" Ace purred, thrusting a little while pretending to give her better access.

"Drugs," she said in a clipped tone. "Don't you read what you sign?"

"Actually," he said. "It's all kind of a . . . misunderstanding. I don't have a drinking problem. Not a drinking problem, not a drug problem. But, by all means, see if you can find something recreational down there."

Mia paused and looked him in the eyes. Her expression was completely blank.

Huh. "No, really, this is media spin. I mean, yeah, there was a car accident, but I'm telling you, I don't have a problem." *At least, if I do have a problem, it has nothing to do with alcohol and drugs.* Details and specifics would help, but he couldn't trust her not to spill that the real reason he was lying low was a worse-than-it-looks ankle injury that could impact his career. She'd just have to believe him. It really should not be that hard to get her on his side.

With that in mind, Ace smiled.

Mia smiled back.

There. On my side.

"Denial is very common," she said in a matter-of-fact tone. "Have you hired a counselor to see during your stay?"

Ace sighed. "Is that on the checklist, too?" Mia hugged the clipboard to her chest. He couldn't recall ever having felt jealous of a clipboard before now. "Well, no," she said, "but it's an important step, don't you think?"

"Mmm. That thing I said about this being a misunderstanding?"

"Yes. Not a misunderstanding after all?"

Ace really didn't like that condescending look she was giving him. "When I said that, what I meant was, I didn't drink as much as they thought I did. Look . . . did you see the press? They didn't arrest me, did they? If I'd been drunk they would have arrested me."

"I *did* see the press," Mia said, a little too pleasantly. "I saw all kinds of speculation about what did or did not happen."

Ace didn't like the look on her face. "What is that supposed to mean?"

"Celebrities get special treatment all the time. You used to get special treatment here in Silverlake before you were even famous, so . . ." She shrugged.

He knew what she was talking about. The articles that suggested that maybe wild-child Ace had been drunk driving, but that he'd gotten off scot-free due to his celebrity. That maybe he'd signed a couple of baseballs for the local police in exchange for favorable Breathalyzer results. His mouth dropped open at such an offensive idea.

"It doesn't matter, anyway. What matters is that you're required to have a sober companion, and that's me. Shall we move on?"

It doesn't matter? Is she kidding? Mia Adams had to know very well that whether he'd been drunk driving mattered. But Ace thought about Lucille's words. He was on thin ice with the Lone Stars. So he crossed his arms over his chest and kept his mouth shut.

"Listen," Mia said. "You may not remember me very well, but I remember you. I know that you're used to getting what you want, when you want, however you want it."

Well, that's more like it. "Great!" Ace said with a grin. "We're on the same page."

"Uh, no. It's the opposite," she said a bit primly. "My job is to make sure you *don't* get what want. I'm going to make sure you get you what you *need*."

They stared at each other in silence for a moment, Ace's smile getting wider as Mia's face turned redder. "Is that so?" he finally asked.

She cleared her throat, but it didn't help her with the blushing. "That came out wrong."

"Oh, sweetheart, that came out *so right*."

"Ugh! You're *gross!*" she blurted.

Ace laughed. "I definitely remember you now. You said that to me once before, right?"

"More than once," she muttered, her gaze skittering all over the checklist as if she was trying to find a foothold back from this disaster of a conversation. Then she closed her eyes, as if psyching herself up for something.

She took a deep breath, opened her eyes, and said, "I feel that we got off to a bad start. I apologize for being less than professional. I think we can tolerate each other for the duration of your rehab stay here, and I'd really like to start over."

Okay, now Ace was really confused. "Tolerate each other? You think it's going to be hard to *tolerate* me?"

"Well, I . . ." She wet her lips, looking nervous. Ace focused on the tip of her pink tongue as it slid across her lower lip.

"I'm gonna be honest with you," he said. "I've got people lining up for hours just to spend a couple of seconds in my presence. That's the reality of celebrity. Then there's the fact that I'm young, rich, handsome as hell, and can get free tickets to the World Series. So you having trouble *tolerating* me makes me wanna know . . . what's your problem with me?"

She didn't answer him, but wait a minute . . . *No, oh no.* "Are you going to *cry?*" he asked in horror.

"What?!" She blinked rapidly. "Of course not. That would be really weird."

"Yeah, it would," Ace said suspiciously.

He stared at her in disbelief as that devastatingly sad look in her eyes vanished in the wake of a fake, cheery smile. "And there's no crying in baseball," she said. "Everybody knows that."

"Everybody knows," he repeated slowly. *Huh.*

He racked his brain for their history together, but that didn't get him anywhere. His history was with her dad, with Coach. He remembered Mia vaguely behind the scenes, but he'd never hassled her, never bothered with her at all. In fact, if anybody had ever made it known that somebody was messing with the Coach's daughter, he'd have stepped up just as if he'd been the Coach's own son and fixed that situation right up. Baseball bat meet windshield, problem solved. "I'd really like to see your dad while I'm here," Ace said.

"He's recovering from the flu," Mia said.

"Oh, yeah? Well, maybe I could go to his place."

"At his age, it takes a really long time to get over the flu."

Ace cocked his head.

Mia smiled.

"Look," Ace said, doing his best to sound more friendly than he was feeling at this point. His charm offensive wasn't usually so offensive. "This doesn't have to be so hard. You show up a couple times, check those boxes on that list of yours, go about your business, and I'll go about mine."

"That's sweet but I don't work like that," Mia said. "Your team has hired me to keep you safe, sober, and to the extent it's necessary, secret. So it's more the opposite, with me around a fair amount. I've got a rough schedule of when I plan to be on the premises"—she unclipped a piece of paper and stuck it on the side table—"but I have a flexible schedule, and you should know that I won't always give you a heads-up before I come over. That's intentional. I've been asked to make sure that you don't aggravate your injury, that you stay away from narcotics and alcohol, and that you stay out of the limelight. Which basically translates to you lying low and not creating trouble for yourself. I'd suggest you just stay on the ranch the entire time. I can go into town whenever you like, do all the shopping, whatever needs to get done."

She must have correctly translated the annoyed look on his face because she said—in a misguided attempt to appeal to his better nature, "Try to keep in mind that if something bad happens to you, something bad happens to me."

"Why do I suddenly feel like I'm having a conversation with the mafia?"

"I'm sorry. I didn't mean it that way. The truth is that I really need this job, but believe me when I tell you that I take my career as a nurse very seriously. I care about all of my patients."

She leaned forward, close enough for Ace to tell that she smelled like honey, which became, effective immediately, his favorite condiment. And in a voice to match that sweetness, plus a look that made him believe 100 percent that she wasn't BS-ing him, she added, "I really don't want anything more to happen to you, Andrew Braddock. It's my obligation to look out for you, and I'm going to do whatever it takes to keep you safe. All right?"

All right? Keep him *safe*? As if he were five years old? Ace shot her a smile. "Beautiful."

He turned, picked up her schedule, and stuffed it in his pocket, taking no pains to keep it from crumpling into a ball. Then he grabbed his crutches and deliberately headed for the stairs, ignoring her attempts to help him get to the second floor or talk him out of it.

There wasn't a snowball's chance in ever-lovin' hell he was going to stick around the ranch for his whole stay, trapped with the one nurse in the world who didn't want to play doctor with him.

Chapter 5

UNBELIEVABLE. EASY ACE BRADDOCK HADN'T EVEN recognized her. Thought she was some groupie he'd slept with and discarded like a fast-food wrapper. Cat looked at Mia sympathetically from his spot on the chair by the door.

Ace might be hot. He might be famous. But he was just as loathsome as ever. Convinced that no woman could resist him and his panty-melting, white, toothy grin. His deep baritone. His rock-hard, six-foot, three-inch physique. His fame and his money.

He can shove all of it where the sun don't shine. Ace Braddock was a cow patty in a Tiffany box.

She took a moment to look past him at the massive fieldstone fireplace, above which hung a portrait of his parents, Steven and Beverly Braddock. She vaguely remembered them from her childhood, mostly because of the shock waves in Silverlake after their deaths. Steven Braddock looked confrontational and challenging—a lot like Ace, in fact, but without the easy humor in his eyes. Beverly seemed a little mysterious, as if she harbored a secret.

Did you raise Ace to think he was the center of your world?

Somehow, Mia didn't think so. Fame and easy money and easy women must have gone to his head.

The house itself was stunning, with soaring ceilings since it had started life in the 1840s as a barn, and then undergone remodeling and renovation various times until it was a showplace of rustic timber mixed with modern glass that welcomed in the sky and the Texas landscape. Declan had outdone himself—he had all the instincts of an architect—and Lila had decorated with the same mix of old and new.

Outside the house, Grouchy began to bark enthusiastically, and wheels could be heard rolling over the gravel drive. Then the slam of a car door; boots on the porch.

The doorbell of the big house rang. Nobody else was there to answer it—Declan's truck was around, but he wasn't.

She padded in her Crocs to the heavy oak double door, opened it a crack, and peered out to see Mick Halladay from the firehouse, a foil-covered rectangular pan cradled in his arms like an aromatic baby. He wore oven mitts decorated with mugs of beer.

"Mick?" she said.

"Howdy, Miz Sober Companion." He grinned. "How are ya?"

"Hey." She grimaced. "Nice oven mitts. What is that?"

"Mick's Maestro Meatballs is what this is. Surprised that you have to ask, darlin'."

They did smell like Italian heaven. She opened the door all the way. "Come on in."

"I figure poor Ace needs real food to keep up his strength and heal."

Poor Ace? Please. But Mia reached for the pan.

"Too hot. You think I wear oven mitts as a fashion statement? Let me take it into the kitchen and put it on the stove to cool."

"Sure." She led Mick down the hallway and into the cool blue kitchen where Declan microwaved his dinner every night.

He set the pan on the stove, carefully smoothed the aluminum foil, and then produced a Ziploc bag of grated cheese from his jacket pocket. "Fresh grated, imported from Bologna."

"I thought they imported baloney from Bologna."

Mick grinned. "So, how's the patient?"

Still an entitled jerk. "He's doing okay."

"Can I say hello?"

"Sure, as long as you don't have a bottle of Jack Daniel's in your other pocket," Mia said. "The Lone Stars are paying me an obscene amount of money to make sure he stays sober."

Mick laughed. "Okay, fair enough. You sure Ace is up for visitors?"

"Yes, he is. He seems to miss having a stadium of adoring fans."

Mick eyed her. "You seem kinda grouchy. You all right?"

"I'm fine," she said. "Sorry. Haven't had a lot of sleep lately."

"Yeah, I can tell. You've got huge blue circles under your eyes—"

"Thank you. If one more person tells me that, I'll—"

"Hey, hey, hey. You're still a knockout—"

There was a thump and then a curse from the vicinity of the stairs. "You hittin' on my sober companion, Mick?" Ace called.

"What the—" Mia sprinted for the hallway, closely followed by Mick, still wearing the oven mitts.

Ace had hopped down the stairs on his good leg, thumping both crutches down in his left hand and using his free hand to lean on the banister. "Mickey, my man! How the hell are you?"

"What do you think you're doing?" Mia snapped.

"Isn't she gorgeous?" Ace jerked a thumb in her direction. "Did I luck out, or what?"

"I realize you've got a surgical boot on, but you shouldn't be moving around like that," Mia said. "Not to mention, you could have pitched down the stairs on your face! Why did you even go up them?"

"Wouldn't you like to know? Wanna search me again?" Ace grinned and bumped down the remaining two stairs. "Pitched, she says. Get it?"

Mick groaned. "Yeah, we get it."

"I am bored outta my skull. What do you say we go for a ride in Big Red?"

"That will happen over my dead body," said Mia through gritted teeth. "Do you understand the concept of keeping a low profile?"

"She's too pretty to kill," Mick said regretfully. "Why don't we stay here?"

"It's silent as the grave around here—where the hell is Deck?"

"Deck actually works the ranch, dude."

"Oh. Right. Well, the walls are closing in on me," Ace said.

"Tough. Let's get you to the couch. In front of the fireplace." Mick grabbed the crutches and slid an arm around his buddy's back to help him into the great room, giving Mia an apologetic glance in the process.

Men. They were such—

The doorbell rang again, and Mia went to answer it.

This time, Sunny from the Sunny's Side Up diner stood on the porch, holding a huge pan of fresh-made cinnamon buns dripping with warm, gooey icing. They winked enticingly at Mia through the clear lid. "Sunny! How did you get away from the diner? Hi."

"Hi, hon. Aw, it's just for five minutes. Good grief—you look soooo tired."

"Thanks," Mia said, with a sigh.

"Oh, I didn't mean it that way—you look great—just like you could use some sleep. So I heard that poor Ace is recuperating in Silverlake. Figured he could use some of these."

"Um, yeah. They look amazing! I know how good they

are . . . Come on in and say hello to him. He and Mick are in the great room."

She led the way. "Ace, you remember—"

"Sunny!" he boomed. "Long time no see! How are you? Damn, but you don't look a day over twenty-nine."

"You lie like a dog on a porch, sweetie."

Ace grinned unrepentantly.

Sunny was closer to fifty, comfortably padded, but still very attractive. Mia always thought that the lines radiating out from her eyes looked like rays of sunshine. Her name fit her perfectly. "How are you feeling? How's the ankle?"

"Oh, nothin' but a thing. What's in the box?"

"Can't you smell them?"

"I can." Ace's grin widened. "I wanna do more than smell 'em. Thank you."

"Well, of course. Least I can do. The recipe was originally your mama's, you know."

His insouciance faded a bit. He nodded.

Sunny set down her tray of pastries. "Hi, Mick. Are those your meatballs I'm getting a whiff of?"

"Yes, ma'am."

In the meantime, Grouchy heralded the arrival of another vehicle. There were high heels on the porch. And unbelievably, the doorbell rang *again*.

"Hello, Mia, dear!" It was Mrs. Crispin from the knitting circle that used to meet in the Old Barn. Accompanying her was Mrs. Potter from the First Presbyterian Ladies' Auxiliary. And bringing up the rear was Dottie from the Grab n' Go.

"We heard poor Ace is home recuperating from that terrible car accident in Austin," Mrs. Crispin said.

"So lucky that they escaped with their lives," Mrs. Potter said. She leaned forward and whispered, "When I first heard, I thought it was history repeating itself. So glad our boy is okay."

"No kidding," Dottie chimed in. "Those cheap papers have some nerve. It's absolute nonsense. No way Ace Braddock would use his celebrity to get out of a drunk driving charge. I remember the past all too well; he'd never do such a thing."

Nodding her agreement, Mrs. Crispin held out a platter of homemade chocolate chip cookies. "I believe the kids at the high school are already circulating a petition in his defense."

"Poor Andrew. Such treatment!" Mrs. Potter offered something green and foamy in a bowl. "Seven-Up salad."

Dottie extended a frozen pizza in a box. "Everyone knows I can't cook worth a darn."

The two other ladies exchanged glances.

Dottie raised her chin and ignored them.

Grouchy danced around all of them, sniffing ankles and pocketbooks and wagging his tail.

"That dog looks like the old *Sesame Street* character," Mrs. Crispin said. "The one who lived in the trash can."

"Oscar the Grouch," said Mrs. Potter.

"He sure does!" said Dottie.

"Come on in, ladies." Mia held open the door. "Ace is in the great room down the hall."

She heard a rumbling out by the road, and Grouchy took off like a hairy flash to greet more visitors. Cat flinched and did the opposite, heading for the back rooms. Had someone sent out party invitations? This was ridiculous.

This time it was an F-350 work truck, emblazoned with Vic'll Do the Trick on either side. On the rear of the truck, as everyone in Silverlake knew, were letters spelling out PLUMB AWESOME, along with his phone number and a promise of a free estimate for any plumbing job, no matter how big or small.

Grouchy was delighted to welcome Vic Andrews, since he'd brought a platter of his notorious Hellfire Wings. He was incredibly proud of them, drowned them in melted margarine mixed with Tabasco and some secret ingredient, and had no idea that they gave anyone who ate them indigestion for days at a time.

"Hi, Vic!" Mia greeted him warmly. "Thanks so much for taking care of that backup at the hospital, and so fast, too."

"My pleasure, doll." Vic blushed from one muttonchop sideburn to the other. "Any time. Brought our Ace some chicken wings. Figured he can use 'em. How long's he gonna be laid up?"

"Hard to say." Mia held the door open yet again. "He's in the great room. Go say hello."

It couldn't have been fifteen minutes before Vic was followed by Aimi Nakamura—an old girlfriend of Jake Braddock's—with a gorgeous healthy salad, and then the entire cheerleading team—really?—from Silverlake High. They came bearing cupcakes frosted with the Austin Lone Stars colors and performed a custom cheer, to Ace's great delight.

> *We are the girls of Silverlake High*
> *Here to cheer on our favorite guy!*
> *The other team will score a zero*
> *'Cuz you're Ace, our Lone Star hero!*
> *We're so happy to have this Braddock*
> *Right back in his very own paddock.*
> *May your injuries heal without a trace—*
> *'Cuz you're our favorite hometown Ace!*

If the girls themselves hadn't been so earnest and cute, Mia might have had to puke. But they were. And it wasn't their fault that their "hero" was an idiot. An idol who'd sucked all of her dad's time away from her, used him to get to the major leagues, and was now blowing his big-shot career due to irresponsibility and partying.

So she welcomed them in, smiling, and got them lemonade and iced tea and Diet Coke. She asked about their classes and their mothers and fathers. She sliced up apples and celery because they were one and all watching their perfect figures and wouldn't touch anything else, not even Sunny's cinnamon rolls. They all sat at Ace's feet and got autographs and worshipped him.

Just when Mia thought the caravan of well-wishers had dried up, an actual school bus—just as big and yellow and black as she remembered—pulled into the drive. Grouchy went absolutely nuts as, one by one, the entire Silverlake baseball team, both JV and varsity, got off, each bearing a homemade casserole, cake, or pie.

Where would they put all this food?

In marched tuna casserole, green bean casserole, chili and cornbread, franks 'n' beans, barbecued brisket, smoked ham, deviled eggs, red beans and rice, chicken enchiladas, cheese enchiladas, chile rellenos, flan, red velvet cake, apple pie, cherry pie, peach pie, pecan pie, ambrosia, and blueberry Jell-O pretzel salad. Mia eventually lost count, though she tried to write everything down so that Ace could write thank-you notes.

Right. As if.

It was a party, and Ace beamed. He was once again the center of attention, Silverlake's golden boy. The hometown hero.

Mia ran around playing hostess and waitress. Getting everyone more drinks—nonalcoholic, of course. And she kept an eagle eye on Ace to make sure that he didn't have any mini bottles stashed on him to tip into his iced tea. She wouldn't put it past him.

"Look at her," Ace said proudly. "Mia and I go way back, as you know. We're old friends from high school."

She aimed the fakest, brightest smile in her repertoire at him. *We've never been friends, Easy Ace. I used to dream about shoving my dad's autographed baseballs down your throat.*

"And now she's my private nurse."

Sober companion, you mean.

Mia greeted yet another well-wisher at the door. "Well, hello, Mrs. Ramirez! Oooh, barbacoa . . . Ace will be thrilled. And tortillas. Thank you! Won't you come in? Can I get you something to drink?"

The party showed no signs of waning when Declan himself walked through the back door, blanched at the sight of all the people, and looked as if he'd rather run out again. "What in the Sam Hill?"

"All of Silverlake is here to welcome back Easy Ace, baseball's hottest face."

Deck laughed. He pulled a bandana out of his back pocket and mopped his forehead with it before stowing it away again. "What are we gonna do with all this food?"

"I think you'll have to buy a freezer."

"I'm not buying a freezer. Ace'll be here all of six weeks before he clears out again and goes back to his own, over-privileged life."

Mia agreed. "I'll bet you Ray Delgado would give you some space in his meat locker."

"Yeah, Ray's a good guy.

"Yo! Mia?" Ace hollered. "Can I get a beer, darlin'? And Mick and Vic can use one, too."

Declan shook his head.

Mia took a deep breath and went to do battle. "Ace, we don't have any beer."

He stared at her from across the room, clearly perplexed. "Why not?"

She hesitated, not wanting to publicly embarrass him. "The *carbs*," she said. "Remember?"

He squinted at her and rubbed his chin. "Right. I forgot. The carbs."

"You've got to stay in training shape."

"Yeah . . . but I don't see how just a few carbs and re-freshing bubbles could hurt. This is, after all, a party, Mia."

"No carbs. No bubbles. No exceptions. Sorry." She turned on her heel to head back to the kitchen so she wouldn't have to look at his too-handsome, overworshipped face. At those blue eyes that seemed so guileless.

"Now, don't go all Nurse Ratched on me, sweetheart."

Mia stopped. Turned back around. Narrowed her eyes on him.

"Just a couple of Lone Stars, honey. Is that too much to ask?" he wheedled.

"No. You're on pain medication, Ace. Declan," she called. "Can I have some backup, here?"

Deck emerged from the kitchen. "Hi, everyone. Welcome." Then he looked at his brother. "You're the only Lone Star here, and it's going to stay that way," he said firmly.

Mia nodded her thanks. "And I'm not easy, Ace."

❧

Ace smiled at the last couple of cheerleaders tugging at his sleeve for an autograph, but his attention was still on Mia Adams. She did one of those slow exhales you do when you're either exasperated or tired, and then she looked at Declan so gratefully that Ace felt a bolt of shame for giving her a hard time. "Thanks," she said to him.

Declan chuckled. "You heading over to see your dad today?" he asked her. Ace stared as his brother removed a green sprig from Mia's ponytail.

Mia smiled at his brother. "Just a quick check-in and then I'll be back again. And I'll put a call in to Ray on the way."

"Thanks. You take some of this food over to your dad, you hear?"

Still mothering everybody. Instantly Ace realized that thought was a reflex left over from a long, long time ago. Maybe Jake was right to ask what the heck his problem was, because Declan wasn't acting like anybody's mother or father. He was just being decent.

So far Declan hadn't gotten in Ace's face, ordered him to do anything, or played the I'm-in-charge-here card. In fact, he seemed to have vacated the main house entirely and apparently planned to sleep out in the fishing shack by the lake. Other than avoiding him, Declan was behaving like a mature grown-up, which was (a) apparently what he was, and (b) more than Ace had ever managed.

Unexpected jealousy shot through Ace as he took in Mia's easy smiles and Declan's hand on her shoulder. *Were they . . . ?*

He caught Declan's eye then, as Mia finally agreed—after some pretty savvy negotiation on Deck's part—to take one plastic container of blueberry pretzel salad and a pastrami sandwich home to Coach Adams. Declan seemed to read his mind, giving Ace a hint of a smile and a little shake of his head as if to say, *Nah, Mia and I are just friends.* And even though it was such a little thing, Ace suddenly remembered a feeling he'd long forgotten even existed: just a look and a nod and the knowledge that someone knew him so well that he didn't need any words to communicate what he was thinking or feeling . . .

Ace forgot about his ankle and stepped back, stumbling in the awkward surgical boot, as a rush of emotions swamped his senses.

Both the smile on Declan's face and the hand on Mia's shoulder slipped away. In a daze, Ace watched Declan move forward. All Ace could do was stare at his big brother's hand reaching out to him.

"Whoa there, hotshot," Mick said jovially from behind, propping Ace upright. Declan's arm dropped away, and the moment was gone as quickly as it had arrived.

"Thanks," Ace said to Mick. "Lotta people here. Getting a little tired, is all."

Mick nodded. "I'll start moving folks along."

"And I'll be back in a little while," Mia said, heading through the living room on her way to the front door. She hoisted a brown grocery sack. "Thanks for sharing. Dad will be thrilled."

"You tell him to finish getting better. Maybe I'll stop by tomorrow," Ace said.

Maybe it was his imagination, but her smile seemed a little tight.

Chapter 6

MIA PULLED HER TINY BLUE SMART CAR INTO THE driveway of the one-story brick ranch house where she'd grown up. Her dad's white Chevy Tahoe was parked dead ahead, freshly washed and waxed, as always. She could probably safely eat off the hood.

Her dad had always been neater than her mom, who was so busy traveling with her work that she was never home more than a few days, which were a whirl of unpacking, laundry, and repacking. Maybe it was the secret of how they'd stayed married for so long—they were simply never around each other long enough to argue.

Mia stacked the pastrami sandwich on top of the blueberry pretzel salad container, grabbed her purse and a Griggs' Grocers bag, and slid out of the tiny car. She knocked on the white front door, scooped a faded silk flower off the porch—it had dropped off the old spring wreath that hung on a hook—and then let herself in with her key.

Immediately Stetson, the adorable little Yorkie her dad had accidentally adopted, set up a ruckus.

"Hey, Stets." Mia stooped to greet him and scratch his head. "You getting excited for your birthday tomorrow? Calm down. Just me."

Inside was the same plain, sturdy furniture they'd always had, in beiges and browns with touches of rust and slate blue. Same fake rubber plant in a porcelain pot in the corner. Same terrible family portrait from some long-ago reunion over the sofa. Dad's eyes were half-closed, Mom's glasses were crooked, and Mia had a chocolate smear on her chin. Grandma looked as though she'd been sniffing glue, Grandpa looked like an owl, her aunt and uncle stared out as if from a *Wanted* poster, and nobody had noticed that three-year-old Cousin Clay was picking his nose.

As Mia averted her eyes from it, a horrific sneeze came from the back bedroom, followed by a croak.

"Dad?"

The house smelled a little sour, of garbage too long in the can. And musty. It needed airing out, but it was too hot outside to even think of opening the windows.

"Dad, how are you feeling?" She set the grocery bag down along with her other things, scooped up Stetson, who was pawing at her calves, and made her way to her father's bedroom, where she could hear the TV going. A ball game, of course. She heard sports commentators in her dreams, along with the muted roar of crowds. She smelled phantom hot dogs and pretzels at times.

Mia knocked lightly on the door frame as Stetson wriggled wildly and licked her face. "Hi!" she said, brightly. "How're you doing?"

Coach—even she thought of him that way, all too often—lay sprawled on top of the bedcovers, his pajamas soaked in sweat. He raised a hand in a weak hello. His reddish-gray eyebrows clashed unfortunately with the shade of hair dye he'd begun using. It had a distinctly maroon tinge that she found unsettling, but she didn't have the heart to say anything to him about it.

His pale blue eyes were pink-rimmed and watery, and his nose was red and swollen. There were wadded-up tissues scattered all over the bed, and a Chinese food take-out container sparred with a can of cola on the nightstand.

"Dad." She sighed. "Listen: Grease, MSG, and sugar are not going to make you feel better. You need chicken soup, orange juice, clear fluids, and no nasty chemicals not made by nature."

Coach sneezed again in answer to this advice.

"Bless you," Mia said automatically.

The sneeze triggered a hellacious coughing fit.

"Oh, boy. You're just miserable, aren't you?" She got a wastebasket out of his bathroom and swept all of the disgusting used tissue balls into it, and then deposited Stetson back on the bed with him. "I'm sorry you're feeling so bad."

"Wait, shh." He held up a hand. "I need to see this replay."

Mia tamped down her irritation at his dismissal of her—as if she were a hired hand—and took the wastebasket back into the bathroom. She unearthed a can of Lysol from under the sink and hosed the place down, wiping the counter, sink, and toilet clean.

Then she grabbed her dad's dirty clothes hamper, which was overflowing, and hauled it off to the laundry room to sort. She started a load, washed her hands, and then returned to the kitchen and shoved the pastrami sandwich and the Jell-O pretzel salad into the fridge. From the grocery sack, she retrieved a big jug of orange juice, a rotisserie chicken, an onion, carrots, and celery.

She poured Coach a glass of OJ, stowed the jug in the fridge, then unearthed her mom's old Crock-Pot. She chopped the chicken and vegetables, tossed them in the slow cooker, and added water and bouillon. Then she plugged it in and turned the dial to low.

She took the OJ back to her dad, who was now shouting at the television. "Butterfingers, you couldn't catch a cold! You idiot!"

"Want some orange juice?"

"And what kind of BS call was that?!"

"Dad?"

"What? Oh. Sure. Thanks, hon."

"We need to take your temperature. You're definitely running a fever."

"Yeah, so . . . it'll break when it breaks."

"Dad. Open up." Mia brandished a thermometer at him, and he let her slide it into his mouth, closing his thin, chapped lips over it.

He continued to gesticulate at the TV screen.

Gee, Dad, I'm fine. Thanks for asking. I love you, too.

"I started a load of wash for you," she said. "But you'll have to put it in the dryer. Will you remember?"

He nodded.

"And I may not be able to make it over here as often for the next few weeks. I have an unexpected job opportunity." She couldn't bring herself to mention that it involved Ace Braddock.

He nodded again, his eyes glued to the game, where a player stole second base.

She waited for a couple of minutes, idly following along. Then she bent over and took the thermometer out of her father's mouth. "Yikes. You're running a temperature of a hundred and two degrees."

He shrugged, then shivered and pulled the covers back up over his sweaty body.

"No, no, no," Mia said. "Let's get you clean pajamas, Dad. And you really should consider taking a cool shower to bring your body temp down."

"Mia, I'm freezing," he barked. "I am not going to get under cold water."

"Okay, okay. Do you want clean pj's?"

"No." Then he belatedly added, "Thank you." And finally the kicker. He brightened and sat bolt upright in bed. "Hey! Did you hear that Ace Braddock is back in town for a spell?"

The old hurt flared up, along with a vicious bout of heartburn. Mia pressed her hand to her stomach. "Yeah. I heard."

"I can't wait to see that boy!"

"I'm sure he'll stop by, as soon as you're feeling better."

"Aw, I'm fine." But he shivered again under the covers. "Don't suppose you'd get me another blanket, would you, sweetheart?"

She sighed. "Sure."

"Yeah, so Ace. He texted me a picture of the Maserati after the wreck. Damn lucky he's alive. Almost gave me a stroke to look at it—he's like a son to me."

She felt that like a kick in the stomach. *The son you never had. Instead of the daughter you don't notice.*

"He's lucky he didn't kill anyone else, either," she said tartly.

"Aw—the media's makin' a huge deal outta nothin.' Ace doesn't have a drinking problem. He explained it all to me."

"Did he, now?" So Ace wasn't the only person in denial around here. Mia spread the second blanket over him and Stetson wriggled around underneath it before burrowing his way out again and making a nest in it. "What should we get Stets for his birthday this year, Dad?" she asked, changing the subject. "It's tomorrow. Remember?"

Coach offered a weak grunt.

She rubbed the Yorkie's little belly. "Do you want to be a cowboy this year? A little cowboy outfit, maybe? What do you think, Dad?"

He pointed to the folded newspaper on his nightstand; it was creased, the sports section facing up. "Lot of nonsense about Ace in the news. He's going to have to clear that all up."

Mia stared at her dad. Dressing Stetson up for his doggie birthday was a long-standing tradition. Her dad usually insisted on having a say. They'd take pictures, give Stetson special dog cookies, and have a big laugh. It was silly. And it was also one of the few bonding opportunities they still seemed to have.

"The team's gonna park him with some silly 'sober companion' until it all blows over."

"Is that right?" Mia murmured.

"Ridiculous, if you ask me. Getting a babysitter for a grown man."

"Yes, it sure is." She kept her voice even. "A grown man shouldn't need one."

"All a lot of PR spin and media management." He snorted.

"Dad, I've started a pot of chicken soup for you, okay? But it won't be ready for hours. In the meantime, there's a pastrami sandwich and a dessert in the fridge. Do you want them?"

"No, no. I'm not real hungry. Thank you, honey."

"All right. Don't forget to put the washed clothes into the dryer."

"Sure thing. I tell you what, I sure can't wait to see Ace!"

Mia nodded and headed for the door. She popped three Tums from her pocket on the way. "Feel better soon, Dad. I'll call you later."

Mia got into her car and sat there for a long moment. How was it so easy to drive a vehicle, but so hard to drive her own life? Coach—her dad—didn't even realize how much he hurt her with his constant obsessing over Ace, and she couldn't seem to tell him. She'd never been able to.

Coach took her love and care for granted, because in his mind, that was what daughters did. Especially if a wife wasn't around.

Mia knew he was proud of her in his way—proud that she was pretty, that she'd gotten her nursing degree. He'd been proud, too, in an abstract way, that she'd married the town's most eligible bachelor and become a member of the country club . . . for a while. Until Rob had stopped paying the dues, along with all of their other bills.

Mia hadn't felt that she had any real friends there, so she didn't really care that she could no longer go. It seemed a lifetime ago that she'd ever sipped cocktails by the pool or played terrible tennis in a tiny, flirty skirt. Been ogled by some of Rob's pals who recreationally cheated on their wives. *Ugh.*

Coach had walked her down the aisle and given her away to Rob, but Mia didn't really feel that she'd been his to give. He treated Ace more like a son than he treated her as a daughter. He had a closer relationship with Stetson than he did with her.

And she still couldn't figure out what she'd ever done to make him push her away.

But Ace, the golden boy, could do no wrong in Coach's eyes. *Boys will be boys.* That was her father's fond attitude when it came to Ace.

A scandalous party, busted up by the cops? That got a chuckle and a shake of the head.

Another bar fight, ending with Ace arrested but not charged because of his celebrity and his expert handlers? Coach might sigh, but never a word of disapproval crossed his lips.

A minor injury from some stupid hijinks? This elicited a cuss word or two.

Her dad had gone as far as to call and lecture Ace on his attitude when he got into a scuffle with an opposing teammate and mouthed off to a ref. But that was it.

Otherwise, her dad followed Ace's every move in every game as though it were his own. As though he were a young Ace Braddock himself, dialing back time to before Mia had even existed. It gutted her, but she'd gotten past it. She was in the habit of emptying her feelings on the subject as she might empty a bedpan.

But with Ace in her face . . . those feelings eddied again, deep inside her.

So did a growing anger that felt like the acid in her stomach. Andrew Braddock seemed to take for granted everything her father had done for him. He'd climbed to the very top with Coach's help, and now he was doing his best to throw himself off the peak of his career. How dare he?

How dare he put his multimillion-dollar physique into a car, drunk, and endanger not only his own life but his teammate's? How dare he even think about breaking Coach's heart that way? Mia wasn't sure she could forgive him.

Chapter 7

*THIRTY-THREE HOT DISHES, TWENTY SALADS (USING THE
term loosely), and seventeen desserts. And all I want
to eat is a grilled steak. The one I told them not to make
yesterday.*

Now that all of Ace's well-wishers were gone, it was a
lot quieter. He hobbled over to the back door, opened it, and
looked out over the Braddock land, which stretched as far
as the eye could see until it met the horizon and the heart-
breakingly blue Texas sky.

He could see some of the cattle near the stock pond and
a swarm of buzzards circling something far afield. In the
distance, the lake shone like a vast silver mirror. A few
dark dots on it were probably ducks.

He hobbled to the porch, wondering with some amusement which threshold constituted a jailbreak in Mia's world.
He decided it was probably the steps leading down from the
porch to the ground, and then he decided he didn't care.

Without anybody watching him, without the weight of
expectations, without the competitive vibe that seemed to

run through all of his interactions in the sports world, Ace felt light. Almost free, standing in the breeze and staring out at Silverlake Ranch's wide-open spaces.

He had room to breathe, which was good. He had room to think, which was . . . not bad, but something else. Sometimes when it was too quiet, things from the past took up space in his head, trapping him. While he wanted a break from being "on" around people all of the time, he was afraid of what might enter his mind when he was on his own.

He didn't always want to bring a girl back to his bed. But it was better than being alone, wasn't it?

Grouchy appeared, galumphing across the back yard like a crazed comic Muppet. He hurtled toward the porch, scrambled up the steps, and made every attempt to flatten Ace.

"Good try, buddy," Ace told him, bracing himself against the wall and then easing down to a seated position on the steps.

Delighted, Grouchy put both front paws on Ace's shoulder and slurped on his face.

"Dog, you have the breath of a steer's butthole. I don't wanna know what you've been eating." But Ace tolerated it, a laugh unexpectedly rumbling up from deep inside his chest. Dogs were so uncomplicated in their love. They didn't overthink anything. They didn't agonize over memories from a decade ago. If they liked you, they licked you. Simple as that.

Ace scratched him behind the ears and roughed up the fur on his chest, as Grouchy's tail wagged a mile a minute. "Just don't expect me to lick you back, you mangy mutt."

Grouchy barked, as if to say, *Why not?*

The twin thuds of the screen door opening and closing behind him had Ace looking over his shoulder. Lila headed toward him with two seltzer bottles, handing him one and taking a seat next to him without a word.

"Thanks. Where'd you come from?" Ace asked.

"Just drove up with Jake. We thought you might need some lunch."

Ace unscrewed the bottle top and took a swig.

In another moment, a similar soft bang brought Jake

with a plate of cold cuts, which he placed on the step below Ace's feet.

Grouchy headed toward it eagerly.

"No, Grouch. No."

The corners of the dog's mouth turned down in dismay. It was comical how expressive he was. But he sat obediently and didn't attack the cold cuts. He just stared at them, unblinking, as if he could use the Force to will them into his snout.

Ace was impressed. "Somebody's trained him well."

"Declan. He's had better luck with the dog than with the four of us."

Ace snorted and took a look inside Jake's red party cup. "It's just OJ," Jake said.

Ace shook his head in disgust and adjusted his injured leg on the steps.

"It isn't true what some of those papers are saying, is it?" Lila asked softly. "I just want to know. You weren't driving drunk, were you?"

Ace took a moment to press his teeth together. "You gonna believe what I say?"

"Yes," Lila said.

He looked at Jake. His brother nodded seriously.

Ace kicked the toe of his good foot into the dirt. "I think driving drunk is pretty much the last thing you'd catch me doing in this lifetime, given that it's what killed our parents."

"So it's not true. You didn't drive drunk?" Lila asked.

Ace shot her an annoyed look. "I actually have to say the words?"

"Yes," she whispered. "You do. Tell me the truth, and I will believe you."

"Lila, I didn't drive drunk. I won't drive if there's even so much as a question about how much I've had. But I wasn't paying attention, and I didn't know *he'd* had too much. Don't even think about telling anybody this, because if you do, it's all for nothing. But Pete asked me to take the rap, and I did. That's all. I swear. I was just helping out my brother . . ."

Jake and Lila shot a glance between them. Jake looked away so Ace couldn't see his face.

"Do you believe me?" Ace challenged Lila.

She looked him right in the eyes. "Yes. I do."

"Okay, then," Ace said defensively.

Jake muttered something under his breath that sounded like part swear word, part the word *stupid*.

"I'm so glad I finally came home," Ace quipped, rolling his eyes.

Lila grabbed his arm and gave him a genuine smile. "Me too. Seriously. Maybe you could learn to make it a habit?"

"I don't think so," he said, making a show of rolling up a thick wad of salami and provolone and chomping down. "It's just not real comfortable here."

There was a moment of silence. "Are we talking about a mattress or a mental state?" Lila asked.

All at once, the three of them started laughing, and as dumb as it was, it felt really good. But as with all good things, the laughter eventually died out and Ace shifted on the steps. "Maybe I should go inside and lie down. Put my leg up or something," he said.

Jake put his hand on Ace's shoulder. It was a firm grip, and if it hadn't been his own brother holding him so hard, Ace would have had something to say about it. "Please don't go yet," Jake said. "I know this stuff is hard. It's always been hard. But you're in Silverlake right now, and it might be the only chance we get to talk things through."

Ace eased himself out from under Jake's grip and leaned against the railing, as if back support was the reason he pulled free. "Listen, Jake, I think it's really great that when you get together with your firefighter buddies, it makes you feel good to hang out and hold hands and talk about your broken hearts."

Ace pressed his palm over his heart and gave his siblings a ridiculous moony look. "Mick, Grady, Tommy— man, it warms *my* heart to think of all of you guys I only ever get to see on video chat wearing those big suspender pants and fireman hats, just huggin' it out."

Jake's eyes narrowed.

"But that's not what we do on *my* team, okay?" Ace continued. "We show up, we play hard, we go out, we play hard, and we go home. Nobody's having a heart-to-heart. Nobody's revealing their soul and sharing their innermost thoughts over a bowl of chicken soup. And I like it that way . . . Lila, will you *please* stop looking like you lost your stuffed bunny?"

Jake looked at their sister. "It's not as if we didn't know he had an attitude problem."

"Whatever," Ace said in disgust.

"Don't make it worse," Lila said. "Both of you." She stood up, her hands on her hips. "Okay, Drew, here's how it is. We miss you. If there's any part of you that wants to try to be a family again, I think this our chance. You haven't been home in years. If you leave without fixing things, I don't think you'll ever come back. And that makes me . . ." Lila choked up for a moment. "That makes me so very, very sad for all of us. So can you please just *try*?"

"Try what?" Ace said, a little more forcefully than he'd intended. "I don't belong here."

"People in town sure think you do. There must be a hundred casseroles in there, welcoming back our hometown hero."

Ace slapped his hand down on the porch. "They're welcoming back some celebrity. A claim to fame. They don't even know who I am, underneath the uniform and autographs and the BS."

"You're hurting," Lila said.

"Yeah, I'm hurting. My ankle."

"Drew! You're *hurting*," Lila repeated.

He stared at her, suddenly beyond furious. He raised his arms out to his sides. "Hey, wow. Y'all just spilled your guts and nothing's better. Whaddaya know." He grabbed his crutches. "I'll see you guys later."

As he pushed through the door, Grouchy left the plate of cold cuts to follow him. Ace was ridiculously touched. "C'mon, boy. Let's you and me hang out."

As the screen banged shut behind them, he heard Jake say to Lila, "Nothing wrong with the friggin' mattress."

Chapter 8

JAKE WAS RIGHT. THERE WAS NOTHING WRONG WITH the mattress, especially when a man had a dog on it with him. And a dog didn't require any effort, any flirtation. He didn't stare adoringly at Ace with a weird kind of covetousness—as if he wanted to mount him on the wall as a trophy. That was the way most baseball bunnies eyed him.

Grouchy just hung with him, stretched out next to Ace with his paws in the air. He didn't want an autograph. He didn't want box seat tickets. He didn't want even a nugget of Ace's celebrity. He did sniff the boot and lick it, as if he wanted to heal him. He did keep him company.

"Why haven't I gotten a dog?" Ace asked him, idly.

Grouchy cocked his head. Then he yawned, as if to say, *Because you're dumb, and it's too complicated to explain to you.*

"I may have to take you back to Austin with me, Grouch. If you had a bath and a trim, you could be quite the chick magnet."

Ace could have sworn the dog rolled his eyes.

An hour or two went by, and the quiet started getting to Ace. He tried calling Pete again, but it went straight to voicemail. He thought about shaving the scruff off his chin and cheeks, but why bother?

And he wondered where his surly but stunning sober companion was. Mia was supposed to be here, babysitting him, wasn't she? Making sure he didn't touch a drop of alcohol. He remembered she'd left him a schedule. And then he remembered that he'd used a knuckleball to dispose of it in the kitchen trash after she'd left.

Ace rolled over and fished his phone off the nightstand again. He'd programmed in her number at her insistence, so he punched it now. This call, too, went straight to voicemail. Why wouldn't anyone take his calls?

"Mia. Ace here. Listen, where the heck are you? I could use a shave. And I gotta tell ya, there's a bottle of Tanqueray callin' my name. Would you bring me some tonic and lime for it? Thanks, sweetheart."

He grinned. There. That should rile her up. She'd be here within five minutes to tear him a new one.

But another hour went by, and she wasn't. He could have been halfway down the mythical bottle of Tanqueray by now.

He pulled himself up, grabbed his crutches, and hopped back down the stairs. Declan sure had made himself scarce. Ace tried turning on the news, only to see a recap of his accident on a local Austin station with the headline *ACE CAN'T SHOW HIS FACE*.

A brunette with tortured, sprayed-stiff Medusa locks and an avid expression spoke into the camera. "Andrew 'Ace' Braddock is conspicuously missing from recent team events. Where he's hiding out is anyone's guess—but he's clearly got a lot to answer for, given the wreck of his buddy Pete Bergsen's Maserati. Both are lucky to be alive. We've ascertained that Pete is recovering at home with his wife and three children. But where is Ace? Austin Lone Stars coach Ricky Masterson and the rest of the team remain tight-lipped. Rumor has it that he's in rehab, where he belongs. This is Lena Harding, from Austin's Channel 9 News. Now back to you, Tom."

Ace hurled a few choice cuss words at the screen, clicked it off, and threw the remote against the wall, successfully knocking the batteries out of it.

He next tried reading the mangled copy of the *Silverlake Reporter* that had been hurled onto the porch by some disgruntled paper boy.

Huh: Kingston Nash had gotten a permit from the town council to rebuild his old mansion. And as usual, a Lundgren hog had won first prize at the county fair—the damn things were monstrous in size. And . . .

Ace wrinkled his nose. Silverlake's Little League baseball team was second to last in the entire state? That wasn't how it was in *his* day. Okay, it was Little League. But seriously? That was just embarrassing and unacceptable. Clearly they needed Coach to come out of retirement.

Speaking of Coach. Ace palmed his phone again and called Coach's number. He missed the old man. But it went straight to voicemail.

He tried Pete again. No dice.

Ace almost threw the phone after the remote. His best friend wouldn't take his calls? What the—? As if on cue, a text from an unknown number suddenly chimed:

> Ace. It's Pete. On my daughter's phone. After the wreck, I had to promise Frannie that I would cut off contact with you. Sorry.

Ace stared at the message. Cut off contact? After he'd taken the rap for Pete? And he was such a coward he had to text from somebody else's phone?

Ace's pulse kicked up and thundered at his temples.

> Nice, dude. When you get your balls back out of the jar on her dresser, let me know.

As expected, there was no response. A slow, roiling anger seeped into Ace's veins. He hobbled over to the couch, braced himself against it, and then beat the hell out of some cushions with a crutch while Grouchy retreated, alarmed, to the hallway that led to the kitchen.

"What're you looking at?" Ace growled at him.

Grouchy cocked his head as if to say that he was pretty sure the guy in front of him had escaped from a lunatic asylum.

After a few moments, Grouchy hesitantly thumped his tail.

"I'm getting out of here," Ace announced to the field-stone fireplace, the books, and the now-silent television. "Right now," he said to the portrait of Mama and Pop.

They didn't answer. They just stared back at him, as if to say, *Bad idea.*

Ace avoided their gaze. He really didn't care if it was a bad idea. He was leaving. Before the quiet killed him. Before the guilt brought him to his knees.

He grabbed his crutches, jammed an Austin Lone Stars cap backward on his head, and hobbled toward the big oak double front doors. He threw one of them open and slammed it, startling poor Grouchy, who was hot on his heels. He needed beer, buddies, bunnies, and song. In short, he needed Schweitz's Tavern.

But how exactly to get there?

Not even his sober companion was taking his calls. Not that she'd drive him to a bar.

He scanned the driveway: no cars, no trucks, no ATVs—not even a golf cart.

His eyes narrowed on the barn, and a mischievous grin spread over his face. Inside that barn, if he remembered correctly, was a perfectly good moving vehicle: Pop's old John Deere tractor. And Ace knew exactly how to fire it up.

Grouchy barked wildly from inside the house, scolding him in advance. But Ace just laughed and hobbled toward the barn.

Conveniently, it was open, the big machine parked at the back. Wow, look at that, it was a newer version of Pop's. A model 6930, Deck kept it spit-shined, and its front link arms seemed to reach out to embrace Ace. He took a moment to admire the sunny yellow deep-dish rims on the massive tires, dubbed it the Green Hornet, and then awkwardly clambered aboard, hauling his crutches up into the cab with him. He'd have to use his left foot on the gas, but that wasn't such a problem if he sat a little sideways. And hell, he'd always been a little sideways. So that was nothing new.

Under the disapproving gaze of a couple of horses he didn't remember, he popped the tractor into neutral and used the key start to fire her up. He flipped her into high gear, where she'd remain for the duration of his jaunt. And then he took the wheel and eased her right out of the barn.

The steering was light and responsive, surprising on a beast this big and heavy. Ace whooped as he headed down the gravel drive, savoring his freedom as he approached the highway and turned toward downtown Silverlake. He pressed the pedal to the metal, and he got her to twenty miles per hour in short order.

This was fun! He cruised past the fields and mailboxes and driveways of the properties outlying town, and then took the turnoff that eventually led to Main Street and the square where Schweitz's stood opposite the grand Hotel Saint Denis.

Ace approached the bar, scanning for any open parking spaces. He paused at the two handicapped ones, hesitating. He might have balls but he also had principles. He'd never use his celebrity as an excuse for better parking. But he *was* technically handicapped. So he eased the Green Hornet into one, then popped her into neutral and killed the engine as people on the sidewalks around him stopped and stared.

❧

Mia finished changing an elderly home-healthcare patient's disposable underwear, put her in a clean nightshirt, and made sure she had a few meals prepped and waiting in the fridge. Then she kissed the old lady's cheek and headed out to Silverlake Ranch, where her next few hours belonged to Ace Braddock. Oh joy.

Grouchy and Cat greeted her as usual, Grouchy with bouncing exuberance and Cat with lazy disdain. Cat allowed her to scratch his head. Grouchy galloped inside the house after her, tail wagging a mile a minute.

"Ace?" she called, slipping the key Declan had given her back into her pocket.

No answer.

Mr. and Mrs. Braddock still stared back silently from where their portrait hung over the huge fieldstone fireplace in the great room. She remembered how their deaths had rocked the community—their minivan hit head-on by a drunk driver. They hadn't had a chance.

How could Ace have gotten behind the wheel in that condition, given what had happened to his parents? It was inexplicable and unforgivable. Except somehow she seemed to be the only person in town who believed the rumors were true.

"Ace?" she called out again.

Silence.

Maybe he was taking a nap.

Mia climbed the stairs and stuck her head into his room, wryly noting the baseball trophies and signed baseballs that still littered the shelves, the unmade bed, and a neat pile of get-well cards from fans that Declan must have brought up. But no Ace. Strange.

He wasn't anywhere else in the house, either.

Mia checked her cell phone to see if he'd left a message, and relaxed slightly when she saw that he had. Then she actually listened to it.

Mia. Ace here. Listen, where the heck are you? I could use a shave. And I gotta tell ya, there's a bottle of Tanqueray callin' my name. Would you bring me some tonic and lime for it? Thanks, sweetheart.

He could use a shave? Who did he think she was—his personal barber?

And Tanqueray? Bring him tonic and lime . . . The top of her head almost blew off at not just the obnoxiousness of his message but the smug entitlement that accompanied the words.

As if she, Coach, and everyone else on the planet only existed to serve him, grant his every wish, and entertain his every whim.

What a . . . what a narcissist!

And evidently, his addiction had driven him from the house in search of alcohol and mixers. He had to have had help. But who would he call? And where had he gone?

Mia called Declan's cell phone.

"What do you mean, he's gone?" Deck's tone was even, but she could sense his irritation beneath it. "Call Jake or Rhett . . . or Lila. I'm sorry, but I'm working with the boys and the cattle clear on the other side of the ranch."

"I'll find him, Deck. That's my job, not yours. Sorry to bother you."

Mia called Rhett next. Nothing doing.

Lila didn't answer her phone.

Jake suggested Brogan's BBQ or Schweitz's.

"How would he get there? As far as I know, Uber doesn't exist in Silverlake."

"Maybe he got a local to pick him up, give him a ride," said Jake.

So Mia zipped off in her car, fuming. Ace was bad enough without this. Now he had not only insulted her and made her look like an idiot to his siblings but was further endangering his career and the one truly lucrative job she had—because the only person he cared about was himself. If he'd gone drinking and word got back to the team, she was done.

Chapter 9

ACE GRABBED HIS CRUTCHES AND USED THEM TO brace himself as he slithered down from the tractor, then aimed his biggest bad-boy grin at the passersby.

A teenage girl clutched at her friend's arm. "It's *him*."

The friend squealed and fumbled for her phone. "Selfie, selfie!"

And was that . . . yes. Pullman Duff. Silverlake's accountant and the cheapest man alive ambled toward him, raising an eyebrow at the tractor.

The dude looked exactly like a catfish escaped from a pond, and Ace, with a shudder, remembered that he'd had a thing for Mama.

"Howdy! Andrew, is it? I mean, Ace. You've come home to pay a visit?"

Ace nodded, raising a hand weakly and then doing his best to escape into Schweitz's before he had to chat. No such luck. The teenage girls ran him down.

"Ace! Ace! OMG, will you let us take a selfie with you?"

His ego fluffed its feathers and preened. "Sure, girls. It would be my pleasure."

The squealer squealed again. Ace winced, pretty sure she'd shattered his eardrum.

"OMG, Deirdre is going to just die!" said the other one.

They jostled up on either side of him and started snapping away with their phones as he contorted his face into various versions of his megawatt smile.

"Thanks, girls," he said, drumming his fingers on top of Schweitz's notorious garden gnome and thumping his little red cap. "But this is thirsty work. I'll catch you later."

"How long are you staying? Are you okay after that horrible wreck?"

But he just winked at them and hobbled inside, a little disconcerted that Pullman Duff held open the door for him. "Thanks, man."

"No problemo, Andrew."

Inside, Schweitz's was still the same, and Ace let out a sigh of relief. The interior was lined with reconstituted barn wood. The seating was a mix of picnic tables and benches or round tables made of whiskey barrels with hammered-copper tops. Black-and-white historical photos of Silverlake hung amid wagon wheels and the requisite neon beer signs. And there were at least two mirrors framed by rusty horseshoes.

Stevie Ray Vaughan played on the sound system, proof that all was right in this corner of the world.

Duff followed him to the bar, where a few regulars had gathered to shoot the breeze. There was Vic the plumber, with his muttonchop sideburns. And Ray Delgado, the butcher. And Dottie from the Grab n' Go—all of them had brought out food for him to the ranch, making him feel welcomed and cared about.

Funny how they all looked the same as they had when he was a kid, just a little older and . . . wider. Instinctively, Ace ran a hand down his six-pack. He hadn't exercised much since the accident.

Better get on that, so he'd be ready by the time he moved off the IR list. Ace didn't want to give management any further excuses to put him out to pasture, and the fallout from taking the rap for Pete was turning out to be more than he'd bargained for. He could hear his agent 'Lucille' in his head; he might make a show of waving away her concerns, but he always heard them: *No career lasts forever. You're getting older, too.*

Everybody turned to stare as Ace settled himself onto a stool. "Hiya."

"Well, if it isn't Silverlake's hometown hero," Dottie exclaimed. "Hope you enjoyed my pizza."

"Will you hate me forever if I tell you it's still frozen, Dot?" Ace asked, with his most hangdog, charming smile.

"Not at all," she said with a laugh. "You know I didn't make it. Stouffer's did."

"Still tastes good," Ray mumbled, smiling at Dottie.

"Thanks for the storage, man. I can't believe the caravan of casseroles and desserts that came out to Silverlake Ranch," Ace said. "Incredible. Almost makes me feel like moving home."

Almost. If the ghosts would leave him alone. If there was any way to forget . . .

Ace's jaw tightened. He wasn't going down that path.

Just smile a little brighter, like you always do.

"Ace Braddock. I'll be damned," said the guy behind the bar, who looked vaguely familiar.

"Well, I'll be joining you down in the hot place, for sure," Ace said easily, meaning it. "Wait . . . you're . . ."

"Otto."

"Otto! Otto from high school. Been a long time! Working for your uncle, now?"

"Naw. He works for me," Otto said, chuckling.

"I hear zat!" Schweitzie yelled from the kitchen. It had to be him—same warm growl, same German accent.

"We got ourselves a bona fide see-lebrity in here, Uncle Steffen," Otto called.

Schweitz came barreling out, wiping his hands on his white apron, and then on his graying blond beard. "Eh?" His face changed when he saw Ace, split into a grin.

"A Braddock! Back in ze paddock, so to speak. *Wilkommen!*"

"Thank you."

Schweitzie turned to Otto. "What you waiting for? Get ze man ein beer! On ze house."

Pullman slung an arm around Ace as if he were his long-lost brother. "Make that *zwei*?"

Schweitz narrowed his pale blue eyes on him. "*Nein.* You 'forgot' to pay last tab, Duff. So now? I 'forget' to serve you, eh?"

Those catfish whiskers quivered in outrage. "I have no recollection of—"

"A round for everyone on me," Ace said, before things got heated. "How's that?"

"Well, that's mighty generous of you," Pullman said, parking himself on the stool next to Ace's. "Dang, boy. You remind me a truckload of your mama."

"That so?"

"That *is* so. Dag jiggety, but she was one fine filly, back in the day."

From behind the bar, Otto shot him a glance, his eyes brimming with laughter as bile rose in Ace's throat. Otto slapped—what else?—a Lone Star down in front of him, and the same for Duff.

Ace took a hefty swig.

"You know," his new pal mused, "I was out fishing one afternoon, and I seen her and your dad out in his johnboat. She was wearing the tiniest blue polka-dot bikini, and lemme tell you, son . . ."

Ace felt his face growing red.

"But that was before you met Molly, Pullman," said a throaty female voice. "You know: the love of your life."

Ace would know that voice anywhere. "Bridget!" Attorney Bridget Kelly. He'd had the hots for her in high school, but she'd liked his brother Jake better. No accounting for taste. He'd bumped into her once or twice in the city, but he'd usually extricated himself pretty quickly to avoid talking about Silverlake.

She smiled. "Hi, darlin'—we've missed you around here."

Pullman's gaze dropped from his beer to her incredible legs.

Ace couldn't help but notice them, too. He took another pull on his own beer. "Have you?"

She nodded, anchoring a hot-pink leather portfolio more securely under her arm. "Pullman, honey, would you be a doll and slide over? I'm just dyin' to catch up with Ace."

Pullman nodded, without taking his eyes off her legs. "Sure thing, Bridge." Clutching his free beer, a Gollum with his precious, he hopped down and then up again, leaving Ace some breathing room.

"Thanks for the rescue," Ace said under his breath.

She smiled again. Bridget still seemed to be something of a princess in Silverlake. From what he'd seen in Austin and Dallas, most men would do her bidding gladly and without question. She was one of those women who looked . . . perfect. Not a hair out of place. Everything color-coordinated, down to the nail polish. Designer bags and shoes. She looked, in fact, like a lot of his teammates' wives and girlfriends. They were all stunning.

Bridget also had a whole boatload of brains.

After Jake broke up with her, he used to joke that despite her glossy surface, there was a lot more to her than met the eye . . . but one of the reasons they didn't work out was that he never figured out what it was. *Ouch.*

Ace studied her face. Back in high school she was just a hot girl to him—in the days when he was just a cocky baseball star to everybody else. The way the crowd at the bar treated him, it was as if he hadn't changed a bit. Ace liked to think there was more to him, now, too, and if any woman ever figured out what *that* was, he was going to make it a point to fall in love with her.

Otto set down a Pearl and a frosty-cold glass in front of Bridget.

"How are you still getting those, Otto?" Ace asked, gesturing at the Pearl.

"We keep a stash on hand. Just for this beauty." Otto winked at Bridget.

She almost managed a blush.

"Meaning nobody else will drink that stuff," Ace said, razzing her.

"Hey, hey!" Bridget swatted his arm. "This is the champagne of beers."

"More like the Thunderbird of beers," Otto muttered.

Ace laughed as she glared at Otto.

"Otto, honey, I can always choose somewhere else to review my billing," she said, tossing her hair and tapping her nails against her pink portfolio. "It's not like I can't afford to go across the street and drink prosecco instead at Jean-Paul's."

He leaned forward, wrapping a bar towel around his wrists and holding them out to her as if he were handcuffed. "You're so hot when you're menacing, Bridge."

Ace snorted Lone Star out of his nose.

Bridget leaned forward toward Otto. "Then don't insult my favorite beverage."

"Never again," Otto said hoarsely, a slave to her beauty.

"That's a good boy, Otto." Bridget smiled and straightened as the door to Schweitz's flew open.

Ace turned on his barstool to behold two hulking off-duty firefighters.

"Easy Ace Braddock! Again!" yelled Mick Halladay, launching himself forward and pounding Ace on the back.

"Been a long time, knucklehead," said Grady Holt, who caught Ace in an elbow lock, flipped off his ball cap, and proceeded to give him one hell of a noogie.

"Hey! Cut that out," Ace said, trying to defend himself with his crutches. "I'm injured!"

Both Mick and Grady had been friends of his brothers' in high school. Mick had run around with Jake; Grady and Rhett had been inseparable until Rhett had been packed off to Deerville Academy. Mick, Grady, and Jake now worked at the Silverlake firehouse together, and if there was one fan group who'd always had his back, it was these guys.

"*You're* looking fine, Bridge," Mick said, suddenly oozing charm.

"Hi, Bridget." Grady nodded at her, as if she were encased in a suit of armor and had the same level of sex appeal.

This seemed to annoy her. "Hello, Gray."

"Gray, huh." Mick winked. "Is that all fifty shades, *Gray?*"

Was it Ace's imagination, or was Bridget turning slightly pink under her perfect makeup? "As usual, the baseball star gets all the hot chicks." Mick rolled his eyes, but he and Grady turned away.

"Chick, Mick?" Bridget called after him. "I am a *goddess.*"

Mick grinned. "True."

Grady rolled his eyes.

"But since both Jake and Rhett are now off the market, I have to flirt with Ace—the dregs." Bridget winked.

"Ouch! I may have to rethink buying you that Pearl," Ace told her, feigning hurt.

Bridget pulled it toward her, mock-protectively. Then she winked and raised it. "A toast! To the return of yet another Braddock brother: Ace."

"Hear! Hear!" The clink of bottles followed.

"Hey," Ace boomed to the entire bar. "And speaking of returned Braddocks, I missed the original toast, so let's all raise a cold one right now to my brother Rhett and Julianna Holt!" He raised his Lone Star. "To Grady's sister!"

Grady and Mick turned back toward him. Grady squinted at him but reluctantly raised his own beer; Mick did likewise.

"To Jules and Rhett," they both said.

"God help her," added Grady, with a scowl.

"Another round on me to celebrate!" yelled Ace.

"I'll drink to that," Pullman Duff said, happily. "Just keep the boy away from any stray Maseratis in town."

Duff had never been one for social graces.

"Wow, that was in poor taste," Dottie told him, acidly.

Pullman blinked, clueless. "Huh?"

Bridget leaned over and said into Ace's ear, "Need a lawyer? Because I don't buy that you were driving that night."

"No," Ace said between his teeth. "But thanks."

"So how did they railroad you into taking the blame?"

Ace slid off his barstool. "Excuse me."

"FYI, you *do* need a lawyer. Or, failing that, a good PR professional," Bridget said.

"Covered," Ace said desperately. He slid off his stool and hobbled off to the men's room.

As he hopped and thumped back from the men's room, two calamities occurred.

First, a bunch of patrons had gathered in front of the window. "Hey, Ace, you gotta see this!" someone yelled. Ace crutched himself closer. Outside the bar was a tow truck with a large flatbed trailer on it, lowered so that—

"*Son of a bi—*" Ace pounded one crutch on the floor.

So that the Green Hornet could be driven up on it and hauled away out of the handicapped spot.

"No, no, no, no, no!"

Deck was gonna kill him.

Chapter 10

ACE LUNGED FOR THE DOOR AND WRENCHED IT open. "Hey!" he yelled at the massive, bearded tow truck driver. "Don't tow my ride. I *am* handicapped." He waved a crutch and pointed to his surgical boot.

"Got a permit?" the guy called back.

"No."

"Then you're SOL."

"Dude, c'mon . . . do you know who I am?" He hated to pull that card, but this time he had to.

The guy whipped off his sunglasses, stared him down, and then spat on the pavement. "Sure do. A jerk who illegally parks in handicapped spots. Just one with a lotta zeros after his name."

Ace swore under his breath and reached awkwardly for his wallet. "So what'll it take?"

"My sister back. Killed by a drunk driver. Keep your zeros, Zero."

That knocked the breath out of him. Stricken, Ace opened his mouth to publicly deny that he'd been the one driving, and then shut it again as he realized that he couldn't. He hopped back inside Schweitz's, let the door close, and leaned against it for a moment. So much for rest and relaxation in Silverlake; this place was just begging him to think about things he thought he'd put behind him.

"The truth hurts, doesn't it?" a too-familiar voice called out. Ace looked up to discover the second calamity, and her name wasn't Jane.

The old adage is true: When it rains, it pours.

She must have come in from the back entrance. About five foot three inches' worth of beautiful, red-headed, freckled Mia Adams was staring at him furiously. "Ace, you are such a *child*."

Child? He'd been called many things. But not that. How dare she call him a child. *First a zero? Now a child?*

He did his best to stalk toward her, but the crutches did not lend him authority or dignity. Still, he managed to get within two inches of her and look down his nose and flex his biceps. "What did you call me?"

His biceps seemed to have no effect upon her. Neither did his famous pecs, when he threw his shoulders back. Or his six-pack abs, when that maneuver tightened his T-shirt against his body.

"A child," she repeated. Loudly. So that everyone in Schweitz's could hear her.

Ace's jaw tightened, along with his temper. He drilled his gaze into those cinnamon-brown eyes of hers. "They don't hire children to play in the major leagues, sweetheart."

"They do if they don't see past the disguise," she snapped. "You get left alone for what, like two seconds? And you can't behave like a normal adult. You have to *steal a tractor—*"

"Declan wasn't using it!"

"And ride it into town to a *bar*."

She lowered her voice, stepping close to try and make things private. Her hand slid up his arm, delicate fingers trailing heat across his skin. She didn't even notice but Ace sure did, and if there hadn't been a bunch of *blah, blah* coming out of that lush mouth of hers, he might actually have been worried about how complicated it could get if he was attracted to her.

"What part of 'stay away from substances' do you not understand? What are you thinking?"

"I'm *thinking* I don't need to hide in my own hometown," Ace said, raising his own voice on principle. "That's the point of coming here. Yes, there was an *accident*. No, I don't have a problem with alcohol."

"Was I, or was I not, hired to be your sober companion? My job is to keep you out of trouble." Her voice dropped even more, to a mere whisper, but she might as well have been yelling because every person in Schweitz's had tuned in to the drama unfolding in front of them: *As Silverlake Turns*.

Ace snorted loudly.

"Oh, I see how it is," Mia said at normal volume. There was a long pause as they glared at each other, and damn, but did she look good when those cinnamon eyes flashed like that. "Let me make something clear. I'm not your team's PR wizard, sweeping all your bad behavior under the rug and then rolling it up around any bodies you've left behind—and burying them for you."

"Bodies?" He gaped at her, stricken. The reference half killed him, but he wasn't going to let her see that. Unfortunate choice of words—or deliberate?

"What I am is your babysitter. Because you cannot regulate your own behavior or stop falling off your tricycle, so you need one. And guess what, Ace? I happen to need this *job*. So you are going to come with me and climb back into your Pack 'n Play and stay there."

Mia was way out of line, and she was shredding his man card.

Ace poked his tongue into his cheek and surreptitiously checked the reactions of the witnesses to this scene.

Otto had fled to the other side of the bar to studiously wipe down glasses.

Pullman Duff's catfish whiskers quivered, though he'd ducked his chin as far into his beer as possible.

Bridget looked uncharacteristically stunned.

Dottie's orange eyebrows had climbed into her hairline to hide.

Vic the plumber and Ray the butcher were *waaay* too fixated on a TV ad for denture cream.

Mick and Grady looked at each other, whistled, then looked at Mia. Then they raised their beer bottles, grinning, and clinked them together.

The beers that had been put on *his* tab!

His comeuppance was complete.

Except Easy Ace Braddock didn't get bested. Not by coaches, cops, or the best players in baseball. And certainly not by a diminutive redheaded psycho who had absolutely no right to talk to him this way.

"You're fired, Mia." Ace said it with a pitying smile. Then he turned his back on her and settled once again onto his barstool. "Otto, I need a new beer. This one's warm."

"Sure thing."

"Oh," Ace said, as if it were an afterthought instead of a carefully calculated curve ball. "And Mia may need one to cry into."

Presto! He had his man card back, intact.

Mia nodded, then began to clap slowly. "Great performance, Ace. I'm sure you're wondering why I'm not fleeing Schweitz's with my tail between my legs."

"Is she still talking?" Ace asked the room at large. "Or is that a dog barking outside?"

"But here's the deal," she said, ignoring this fresh outrage. "You *can't* fire me. My contract is with the Lone Stars, not you."

He froze with his beer midway to his lips. His back stiffened.

"Oh, boy," said Bridget. "I would *love* to see that contract."

❧

Mia tried to get a handle on her anger. Where was it coming from? It didn't only stem from the inconvenience of having to track down Ace, or the threat to this job with the team. No, it was far more than that. She was in a rage on behalf of her dad. Coach Adams had expended all of his energy and time and affection on this man-baby. And Ace had chosen to disrespect that by drinking, pulling shenanigans, and jeopardizing his career—not to mention his life and Pete Bergsen's. Pete had a wife and kids. Had Ace thought even once about them?

What a loser.

It was bad enough that he'd stolen her father from her, but at least it had better mean something. To toss away his incredible opportunities—the ones her father had *gifted* to him—that was the cherry on top of the cow-patty sundae.

She was also extremely angry at herself for finding him hot.

He was, though. No denying it.

She tried to remain steadfastly immune to Ace's broad, muscular shoulders and biceps; his cut forearms—one of which still held a Lone Star aloft in the vicinity of his incorrigible mouth.

"I'd set that beer down if I were you," she said. "Unless you'd like me to call your team manager or your agent. I've got both of them on speed dial."

After a long pause, the Lone Star rose instead of lowering. Tipped back. Half of it disappeared in two swallows. Only then did the bottle hit the bar. Without turning his head, Ace said in deadly tones, "I don't respond well to threats."

"That is abundantly clear," Mia retorted. "Since the Maserati incident and your resulting injury is the biggest threat yet to the career you are *throwing away*—and you're responding about as well as a manatee would to wings."

"Woman," said Ace's back, now ramrod straight. "You are really starting to annoy me."

"The career you clearly do not deserve," Mia blurted.

A hot flush swept across her face. *Oh, wow. All this time, and I'm just . . . so not over it.* But Ace had gotten every shred of her dad's attention for so many years, all the encouragement and instruction and support Coach had possessed—and all for the sake of sending this overgrown brat to the majors. This *ungrateful* overgrown brat, who didn't even appreciate what he had enough to hang on to it.

A low whistle came from Mick's direction.

"Hey," Grady said. "That's a little harsh—"

"You two are clearly going to need mediation," Bridget put in.

Ace stared them all down. "Thanks. But I don't need anyone's help to fight, or mediate, my battles." He looked at Mia. "Maybe you had the right idea before; you *should* keep your voice down. Maybe throw caution to the wind and try *mute*."

A communal flinch went through the bar. *"Oooooh."*

Vic the plumber choked.

Ray Delgado hooted in disbelief.

"Don't think you want to take that tack, buddy," Grady murmured, shaking his head.

As Mia's blood hit a slow boil, Ace fished his wallet out and tossed a platinum card onto the bar. "Otto, the check, please. Add everyone's next round and then a twenty-five percent tip for yourself."

"Hear, hear!" Ray Delgado called. "Thanks, Ace."

Others joined him.

"Don't mention it." He grabbed his crutches and slid off the barstool, turning back to Mia once more. "Now, if you'll excuse us, my nanny and I need to have a private conversation about her job description, her mouth"—his blue gaze settled insolently on her lips—"and her parameters." With the last word, his gaze roamed all over her body, stopping at the curviest places.

"Oh, boy," Mick muttered. "It's on."

"My parameters?" Mia repeated. "As your *nanny*?"

Ace didn't bother to answer, since he was signing the credit card slip Otto slid to him.

She turned to Bridget. "You know the law, Bridge. Tell me, is corporal punishment still legal in Texas?"

The whole bar went silent, then exploded in laughter.

The attorney smirked. "Well," she said slowly. "It's not popular with everyone. But . . . yes, it's legal."

Mia bared her teeth at Ace. *Let's see you come back from that, hotshot.*

He looked up, unruffled. "Mia, sweetheart, you can spank me any time. Bring it." A delighted collective gasp came from their audience.

As Mia looked around for something to hit him with, Ace's cell phone rang.

"Yeah?" he barked into it.

"Really?" said the voice on the other end.

Declan Braddock was so angry that the entire bar could probably hear his end of the conversation. "Really, Ace?" he yelled. "Grand theft *tractor*?"

Small towns. Someone had already dropped a dime on him. Ace's shoulders slumped. "Deck, I—"

"Are you friggin' kidding me?! And you drive it to a bar and leave it in a handicapped spot?"

"I *am* handicapped!" Ace protested.

"Make up your mind, little brother. You either have a problem or you don't. Can't just be when it's convenient."

Ace cracked his neck as Mia took her turn to smirk. "You know, I'm really tired of—" he began.

"You don't get to say anything else," Declan said. His voice was more measured now, which was actually a little scarier. "You *do* get to pay the ticket and get my tractor out of the impound lot."

"Fine," Ace muttered.

"And?"

"Sorry," Ace growled.

"And?"

"And . . ." Ace rolled his eyes. "I promise I will never steal your tractor again?"

"Any tractor!" Mia called, loud enough for Deck to hear.

Ace squinted at her with loathing. "Any tractor," he agreed.

"At least I know that since you're a Braddock, your word is good," said his brother.

Both of the Braddock boys went quiet for a moment. Mia watched a bittersweet smile soften Ace's face. *Oh, he's beautiful like that.*

Ace took a deep breath, the wind apparently knocked out of him. Then his expression shuttered once more, the cocky grin back in place. "Yeah, my word is good."

Maybe Declan felt it, too. He cleared his throat before adding brutally, "Now, if you plan on staying out at Silverlake Ranch, you need to have Mia bring you back, do what she says, and grow the hell up."

With that, Declan hung up on him, leaving Ace staring at the phone.

Mia ran her tongue over her bottom lip, walked to the door, opened it, and crooked her finger at him. "Heel, boy."

જી

Ace refused to look at her as they exited the bar.

"What's the matter, Skippy?" Mia asked, slapping him on the back. "Not used to having your older bro open up a can of whoop-ass on you?"

"Look: I may have to put up with you contractually, but you don't get to talk to me that way. And did you really just say that I *don't deserve my career*?" Ace muscled his way in front of her and turned to stare down at her, his gaze the blue inside a flame.

He looked almost . . . hurt? Mia shook off her surprise. "You tried to fire me!"

"You called me a child. You're going around making people think I've got an alcohol problem."

Mia poked him in the chest. "I'm not making people think anything. I was hired after you already made people think a whole lot of things. But you *do* have a problem. And part of that problem is not taking responsibility for what's gotten you into this situation."

Ace's mouth clamped shut and he looked up at the stars as if they might give him a clue. Finally he said, "You've never even seen me drunk."

"I don't need to. There are plenty of articles about your behavior. The fact that the Austin Lone Stars hired me says it all."

"Declan told you what happened. I know he did, but you don't believe me," he said through clenched teeth.

"Declan loves you a lot," Mia answered.

"Right . . . I didn't—" Ace dragged a hand down his face.

Mia waited, tapping her foot. When he said nothing further, she started walking again. Her little blue car was parked behind Schweitz's in the alley.

Ace let out a string of curses and then followed. He pulled up short as she stopped in front of her car. "You've gotta be kiddin' me."

"What's the problem?"

"There is no way in hell that I'll fit—"

"Get in."

Ace seemed speechless. His jaw worked.

Mia opened the door for him, raised her eyebrows, and waited. "I'm sorry . . . is this not the limo you're used to?"

"It's tiny. It's a clown car!"

"So get in, clown." She smiled cheerfully.

Ace stumped toward her, looked into the car, and then glowered down at her, his hair lifting in the early evening breeze, his eyes a completely unfair and underhanded shade of blue, the five o'clock shadow on his face doing funny things to her insides.

Mia refused to admit it, even to herself, but the man *was* hot. Way too hot for his own good. Way too hot for her to handle—not that she'd ever want to.

"I won't fit in that thing."

"Oh, c'mon, Ace . . . you've fit into much tighter spaces. Judging by the number of baseball babes you've banged."

His jaw dropped open yet again. And then, of all things, he laughed. *Laughed.*

It was genuine, deep from the belly, out-and-out man mirth. And it completely transformed his face, washing away the arrogance, the worldliness, the boredom, and the entitlement that normally played out in his expression.

She stared at him. He looked like a different person. Almost like a nice guy.

"You," Ace said when he caught his breath again, "are something else."

Whatever that meant.

"The things that come out of that mouth of yours . . ." His eyes settled on her lips and stayed there, making her uncomfortable and then too warm and then somewhat breathless.

Mia fought the urge to lick her lips, because that would be entirely wrong in this situation. It would feel like . . . a tease. But her mouth had gone dry, and her gaze had flown to *his* lips, of all things. Which was the exact wrong place for her eyes to go. Because it made her want to— *Don't be ridiculous, Mia. What is wrong with you?*

His blue gaze locked with hers, and she couldn't look away even if she wanted to. Which of course she did. Of *course*.

His head bent toward hers, then lowered . . . which didn't make any sense at all . . . not that she'd know what sense was even if someone came along and knocked some into her.

And *then*. She, Mia, was *kissing Easy Ace Braddock*, of all the Worst People to Kiss on the Planet. Or he was kissing her. Or something. Somehow.

She didn't pull away; she didn't want to. Her mind knew better but the rest of her wasn't behaving at all. Ace pulled her even closer.

Electricity sparked between them, and he smelled like heaven: a hint of some gazillion-dollar aftershave and laundry soap and baseball and apple pie and just a hint of beer.

His arm slid around her and pulled her firmly against the rock-hard wall of muscle that was his chest. He delved into her mouth expertly, over and over. He stole every last particle of oxygen from her body, and she found herself utterly boneless.

At last he lifted his head.

Mia blinked and braced herself on the Smart car's door, feeling anything but smart. "Wh-what was that?"

"Proof," Ace said.

"Of what?"

"That I'm no child." He cupped her chin and then held it between his thumb and forefinger as she stared dumbly up at him. "Got it? One hundred percent man, darlin'. You should remember that."

She wasn't sure she remembered her own name. But his words lent her total recall as to what a pig he was. "Move."

"Huh?"

She jerked her thumb backward, so he shrugged, and hopped to the open passenger-side door.

"Seat yourself." She gave him a light shove and he fell back comically, his bad leg barely fitting into the footwell even with the knee bent. His crutches were another story; the tiny amount of space behind the two seats was packed with crafting supplies and boxes from her last trade show. "How is this gonna work, exactly?" he asked with a huff.

"Stick 'em out the window," Mia ordered, chuckling as he rolled down the window and stuck his crutches through it. She shut the door, wedging his substantial athlete's frame into the tiny space.

"This is not comfortable," he called as she rounded the bumper.

"And I care about that why?"

"You're a nurse. Devoted to your patients' well-being."

"You're not a patient. You're a pain in the butt."

Ace grinned. "Correction: I'm a professional, *major league* pain in the butt. Consider how good that's going to look on your résumé."

"You won't be a major league anything for much longer if you don't pull yourself together. And I'm not here to stroke your ego, Andrew Braddock."

Ace was clearly about to make the obvious joke, so Mia suddenly palmed his face and shoved him back against his seat. "You're disgusting."

She fastened her seat belt and started the car. "And don't touch me again, Ace." She hit the accelerator too hard, bumping them over the gravel perhaps a little more carelessly than usual.

They navigated the rest of the trip in silence.

Ace's skull nearly collided with the door frame as another hard right brought them through the black gates of Silverlake Ranch, then into the paved driveway at the main house. It was lit warmly from within behind the ominous dark figure who threw open the door.

Beside her, Ace groaned and muttered, "Great."

Mia forced herself not to smile.

"Where's my tractor?" Declan growled.

"You know," Ace called through the open window, "technically, I'm not sure it's all your tractor. I mean, doesn't the rest of the family have a share in . . ." He let his voice trail off as Declan crossed his arms over his chest.

"Okay, yeah. It's pretty much your tractor. We'll, uh, get it back tomorrow."

"Before or after I break your other ankle?"

"Ha ha. Say, Mia here would love to come in for a cocktail and dinner once she's figured out how to get me out of this tin can."

"No, Mia would not," she said, putting the car into neutral and slipping out. She went around the side and deftly extracted Ace's crutches through the open window before swinging open the door and pressing them into his chest. "But thanks."

Ace made a show of having trouble extracting himself from the car. At last he'd crutched far enough from the wheels that she couldn't "accidentally on purpose" run him over.

"See you tomorrow, hotshot," she said, hopping back into the driver's seat.

"Don't leave me alone with him," Ace wheedled.

Mia slammed the door on his plea. Only once she'd turned the car around did she let herself smile.

Chapter 11

ACE SLEPT FITFULLY, FINALLY WAKING A LITTLE BE-fore noon like the celebrity slacker he apparently was. The rest of the world had already gotten up and gotten down to business just fine without him; Declan was probably out being super productive. Mia was, no doubt, out doing a hundred things at once. She'd said her hours were flexible. How flexible? He wished he knew where she was. Or at least when she'd be coming back.

Last night's shenanigans kept replaying in his mind. He saw Mia Adams's face in his dreams, and at least one of them had her reaching out to him in the sort of way that made a man wish he had company in bed.

A little worked up, Ace took a shower, threw on some clothes, made a call and threw some money at the tractor-retrieval problem, then considered his options. Well, glory be. Waiting for him was a text from Coach Adams. The man was no longer contagious, and he wanted Ace to meet him at Sunny's Side Up for a cup of joe. Sweet. But without the tractor to hijack . . .

Ace scrolled through his contacts. He wasn't sure who to call, and it didn't sit well with him that asking one of his siblings for a favor felt like such a stretch. Real brothers and sisters wouldn't make you feel like you were asking for a rocket ship to the moon when all you needed was a simple ride.

He looked at the whole gang lined up next to one another.

Braddock, Declan
Braddock, Jake
Braddock, Lila
Braddock, Rhett

He finally decided Lila would give him a minimal amount of lip and pressed his finger to her name.

"Ace!" Good choice. She sounded happy to talk to him.

"Declan's pretty heated about my grand theft tractor," Ace said. "You probably heard about it already."

"Oh, I heard." She chuckled. "I heard last night."

Small towns. Ace sighed. "I'm afraid I'll bump into him today and just by looking at him I'll set his hair on fire. You wanna do something in town?"

There was a pause. "You want me to come pick you up. So you can avoid Declan." It didn't sound like a real set of questions, and she didn't sound pleased.

"You hasslin' me?" Ace asked.

"You're lucky you were born with more charisma than the rest of us put together or you'd be alone the rest of your life," Lila said.

Ace flinched, his face heating up, and he was glad she couldn't see it.

"I guess I am hasslin' you. You probably don't get enough of that."

"Am I that bad?" Ace asked tightly.

"Kind of. But you have many other fine qualities."

"Right. I'm not going to ask you to tell me what they are, in case nothing comes to you right away."

"That would be embarrassing," Lila said.

"It would," Ace said.

"I actually don't have enough time for a sit-down lunch today."

"Fine," Ace said, even though it wasn't.

"But I'll take you into town if you like."

"That's perfect. Gonna see Coach Adams today. Can you drop me at Sunny's Side Up?"

"You ready now?"

Ace brightened. "Yup." Stupid superstition or not, he put out a dish of peanut butter for any stray grackles, and about twenty minutes later, Lila pulled up in her Suburban. Ace was sitting on the porch swing, waiting for her. He hopped down the stairs as Lila got out of the car and opened the passenger-side door for him.

"Thanks," he said, sticking his crutches in the nice, big back seat.

"Did you leave a note?" Lila asked.

"Deck doesn't care," Ace said, flailing his arm out to try and reach the door handle. Lila didn't push the door closed.

"I meant Mia," she said.

"Oh, I don't think we're doing notes." He shrugged and made a grabby hand gesture toward the still-open car door.

Lila smiled. "She didn't ask, 'How high?' did she? Atta girl."

"What do you mean?"

"You said 'jump' and she didn't ask how high." Her smile widened. Ace slumped back in his seat, grumpy now, giving up on shutting the door.

"What?" Lila said.

"Nothing. Can we go, already? It's not nice to keep an old man waiting."

"Sorry, geezer."

"I was talking about Coach!"

Lila casually hip-checked the door and it slammed shut. She went around and hopped into the driver's seat, finally, blessedly turning the key in the ignition.

She started down the road toward the ranch gates, and Ace relaxed a little.

"You have no idea how to adult," she said.

"Neither do you."

There was a silence. And then Lila said, "Yeah."

"You attempting to school me on being an adult is like the blind leading the blind." He snorted. "Leave a note? 'Dear Mia, I'm in the bathroom taking a piss.' Please."

"Leaving a note is just being polite. Mia's got a lot on her shoulders. She doesn't need to wait around for you, thinking maybe you're injured on the property after stepping in a hole in the pasture."

"Why aren't Mia and Declan together?" He'd meant it as a casual question but once it was out, Ace didn't feel so casual.

Lila blinked. "Where did that come from?"

Probably from the part of my brain that hasn't stopped thinking about her since I kissed her.

"They are really close friends," Lila said, "but—"

"I saw him touching her."

"What?" Lila failed to swerve for a pothole and they both bounced up and hit their heads on the roof of the car.

"That is not good for my injury!" Ace yelled. "I'm healing here!"

"Sorry, but Declan and Mia are *finally* getting it on?"

"I did not say anything remotely like that." *Not to mention, as if it was inevitable or something!*

Lila looked over again, and Ace gripped the sides of the seat. "Eyes forward," he barked.

"Explain yourself and be precise," she said.

"I saw him in the kitchen with her when I first got here."

"Yeah?"

"He took stuff out of her hair."

Lila didn't answer at first. "You saw Declan taking stuff out her hair. What kind of stuff?"

"It was green herbs. Parsley, maybe."

Lila didn't answer for another long moment. And then she looked over.

"Eyes," Ace warned.

She looked at him again.

"Eyes!"

And then she burst out laughing.

"What? I mean, he was like a gorilla picking nits. It's a mating thing. He said he didn't—well, he didn't *say* he didn't have a thing for her, but he telegraphed that he didn't—but I bet he does. I think if she ended up seeing somebody, and he hadn't made a move, he'd really regret it."

Lila eventually stopped choking on her laughter. "You got all this from a ten-second display of Declan taking parsley out of Mia's hair? Are you jealous?"

"Jealous?" The word exploded out of Ace's mouth. "I don't see us together," he said flatly. He looked away from his sister to roll down the window.

"You've actually thought about this? Drew, you just *got* here. What are you doing?"

"We didn't really discuss it. We just . . . sorta . . . kissed. And . . . you know . . . we don't really make sense. Mostly because she thinks she hates me."

"OMG," Lila said, drawing out each letter as far as it would go. Her car did a weird stuttering thing that made Ace nostalgic for the tractor. *"You and Mia kissed."*

Lila's reaction made him nervous. "Don't go around talking about it, though. It wouldn't make a ding in the side of my reputation, but Mia's another story. This is not Silverlake phone-tree material."

"Aw, listen to you. That's sweet. But just so you know, what happens in the Suburban stays in the Suburban. It's in the vault," Lila said, making a zipping motion over her mouth.

Ace reflexively checked his seat belt.

"I know how to keep your secrets," Lila continued. "Kept plenty of them growing up."

True that.

"So it was terrible?" she asked.

"What was terrible?"

"The kiss! Seriously, Drew. You're killin' me."

"Are you joking? No, it wasn't terrible. I don't know how to do terrible. If there's one thing besides baseball that I'm really good at, it's kissing women."

Lila made a gagging noise. "Why were you kissing her?"

"We were . . ." Ace stared through the windshield, his mind going back to the evening prior. "You know, we were . . . kinda . . . flirting . . . and arguing . . . and she was trying to tell me what to do, and the whole time she was looking at me like she woulda kissed me herself if I hadn't made the play."

"Are you sure you read it right? Maybe she was looking at you like she wanted to kill you."

"Lila, I'm sure. No offense, but I don't have to try real hard."

Lila rolled her eyes. "But maybe you like things that don't come easy. And Mia Adams is not one for being easy. You were arguing and flirting and then you were kissing?"

"Well, yeah. Pretty much. I mean, I was trying to tell her where she could stuff her orders . . . and then she just . . . looked, so . . . I guess you could say lightning struck."

"Just like in the movies," Lila said, sounding a little bewildered. "Why does this never happen to *me*? Anyway, keep going. What *did* Mia look like?"

Ace blinked. She'd looked so beautiful. She'd looked so full of sass and spirit and can-do. She'd looked like frustration and desire and someone who cared about stuff in a world where a lot of people just didn't care.

For a moment, she'd looked like she cared about *him*, even if she didn't want to.

Ace's mind went back to that moment and the electricity that had struck him last night, as he took her mouth with his, shocked him again. He gripped his shirt over his heart, trying to make sense of the fact that he was feeling stuff that was supposed to be squarely outside his strike zone.

Because most of all, Mia Adams had looked like someone who deserved better. Better than Easy Ace Braddock.

"We were supposed to be talking about Declan," Ace said. "Declan is the better choice. He's the one who makes sense. I mean, Mia and I were just goofing around. But Deck makes sense for the long run. He's a solid, solid guy. And if Deck has a chance to be happy, I'm not gonna mess that up just because I wanna—"

He stopped short, not wanting to say out loud to his sister what he'd like to do with sweet, sweet Mia Adams.

"We're talking about *Declan*, so why don't I feel like we're talking about Declan?" Lila eyeballed Ace.

"Hey! For the love of all things sacred, Lila, watch the road."

"Don't change the subject."

"I'm just trying to keep us alive."

"I drive this road all the time. Stop being such a man."

They huffed at the exact same time, realized they were completely in sync, and then grinned at each other. Ace felt that same almost-forgotten blip as his heart registered the bonding moment.

"Okay, let's back up. Declan deserves somebody great," Lila said. "Mia is great. But if it was gonna happen, it would have."

Ace had to wonder what had happened with Mia's first marriage that would make her so gun-shy she'd say no to a saint like Declan.

"So if what you're asking is if you'd be standing in Declan's way by having a fling with Mia," Lila continued, "then as a loving sister of you both, I can tell you that there is nothing and nobody standing in your way. Other than the decency to not start something that's going to break her heart."

"I wasn't asking about any of that," Ace said. What *was* he asking about?

"Whatever you say. But since when are you so concerned about Declan's love life?"

"He needs a family."

"He *has* a family."

"He has family *members*. It would be good if he had his own family to focus on. You know, so he wouldn't always be in our business."

Lila sighed heavily. "I don't see him in your business, Drew. I think you're thinking of a version of him that's long gone." She paused and then added, "You've been away for a while."

"Give him time," Ace cracked. "He'll be telling me to brush my teeth and say my prayers soon enough. Mothering and smothering."

"Isn't that what your team is paying Mia to do?"

"Feels like it," Ace said darkly. "She's a right pain in the—"

"You really saw something between them in the kitchen?" Lila asked. "Maybe he just wasn't ready before. Maybe he is now. 'Cause it sure is a nice thought."

Ace was starting to wish he'd never brought up the idea of Declan and Mia together; from what he'd heard, Lila was an active participant in trying to help her brothers find love.

She glanced over at him. "I mean, if you're actually worried about him under all your moaning about this nonexistent overbearing version of Deck, then, well, that's nice."

Ace took a long time before answering. "I didn't leave Silverlake on a high note, Lila. Not with the family. You know that."

"Do you feel guilty?" she asked.

I am *guilty.* Ace looked down at his "winning" hands.

After a while, Lila said softly, "You don't have to answer that."

"Seeing someone in person is a lot different than seeing them on a phone screen," Ace finally said. No way he could go on without making a fool of himself, so he shut up. He felt Lila's eyes on him for a second. *Don't ask me anything else like that. Please.*

"That's for sure. You look *way* shorter in person," Lila cracked.

Ace chuckled and then asked, "What about you?"

"What *about* me?" Lila made an exaggerated detour around some roadkill.

"Are you happy being single or are you looking for somebody?"

Lila heaved a sigh. "The last guy I dated turned out to be married. That one stung. I hope there's someone out there for me. I-I've never felt lightning."

Her voice cracked and Ace looked over in alarm. Her

jaw was tight but she looked resolute. "You've always been really strong. As a kid and now," Ace said.

"Yeah." She shrugged.

"It's a big deal."

"It doesn't matter."

"Maybe stronger than Deck," Ace said.

Her eyes widened.

"Because you haven't given up," he explained.

Lila brought the Suburban to a stop outside the diner's front door. She looked over at Ace. "I think we should be more worried about you than me, bro. You're in kind of a mess."

"There's no mess," Ace said with a shrug. "That's what this fake rehab is for. Rehab is awesome for fixing stuff like this. It's like a celebrity Magic Eraser. It'll be fine if I don't go crazy from boredom."

"Just . . . be careful. You're still in the news a lot. Those rumors about the police covering up you blowing over the limit are still floating around. If it gets out where you are and what you're up to, we might get some reporters."

"The cheerleaders at my little welcome party told me that the phone tree has that locked down. Word went out to keep me the town's favorite secret."

Lila rolled her eyes.

Ace continued, "Besides, nobody really cares that I'm out resting in the country, do they? It's not like I'm in rehab for sex addiction. Hmmm," he said pensively. "Now that'd be interesting."

Lila winced, putting up a palm to stop further oversharing. "Maybe they care and maybe they don't. If it doesn't bother you when they do, great. Just make sure you also don't mind when they don't."

Ace did not like where this conversation was going. "Old man. Waiting."

"See ya, geezer."

"See ya, midget." Ace eased out of the car, grabbed his crutches from the back, and headed for the door of Sunny's Side Up.

Chapter 12

MIA GRINNED EVILLY TO HERSELF AS SHE AP-
proached Silverlake's newest boutique business,
Paws for Applause. She'd asked Sabine, the owner, for a
favor: to groom Stetson in a special way for the little dog's
birthday. In a *Yankees* kind of way. Dad, a die-hard Red
Sox fan, would be fit to be tied.

And sure enough: When Sabine brought Stetson up to the
front, he wore not only a tiny Yankees shirt but a Yankees
cap, placed backward on his tufted, furry little head. He
seemed to know somehow that this was deeply disturbing,
because he barked at her once, refused to wag his tail, and hid
under one of his paws as she slipped Sabine her credit card.

"You promise me that Coach won't have a stroke?" Sabine asked, chewing on her bottom lip. "I don't want his
death on my hands."

"He won't," Mia said cheerfully. "Because the damage
isn't irreversible."

"So you say. He may not ever get over this."

Mia chuckled diabolically. "Well, it'll get his attention,
anyway."

"Happy birthday, Stetson," Mia said, kissing the Yorkie's

head. Dad hadn't registered an official opinion about Stetson's birthday look. He'd forgotten to buy the special biscuits. He'd forgotten to bring out the camera.

The one thing he hadn't forgotten about was meeting Ace Braddock for coffee at Sunny's diner. Apparently, tradition only mattered when you didn't have something better to do involving your "son."

Well, she could get mad. Or she could get even.

She popped Stetson into his sporty blue pet carrier and strolled over to Sunny's Side Up, the diner where Sunny had been slinging omelets and hash browns for as long as Mia could remember. Dad's fever was gone, and he'd insisted he felt up to meeting Ace there.

Sunny's featured a U-shaped bar for customers eating on their own, but also a number of tables and padded booths with red and white checked vinyl tablecloths. In the center of each one was a ceramic rooster planter that held silverware and napkins. The atmosphere felt like someone's oversized kitchen, cheerful, bright and comforting.

Mia could see the two men sitting in the back, leaning in toward each other, coffee mugs almost touching, faces lit up like kids at Christmas. Something in her stomach slid sideways, something disquieting.

She pulled open the door, sending the bells jangling, along with her nerves. It was good to see the guys enjoying each other's company.

Sunny saw her immediately and swung by with her coffeepot. "Hiya, hon."

"Hey, Sunny." It was impossible not to smile in the face of her relentless good cheer.

"Look at those two," she said fondly. "Just livin' it up together."

The thing in Mia's stomach curdled. "Yeah."

Sunny was nothing if not perceptive. She tilted her head, evaluating Mia. "What's wrong? You're looking a little peaked these days."

If one more person tells me how tired I look, I am going to scream. "Nothing. Coach got his favorite kid back."

Unwelcome comprehension flickered over Sunny's face.

"And I've brought him his dog. It's Stetson's birthday."

Sunny squinted into the mesh that didn't hide Stetson very well. Her eyes widened. "You didn't!"

Mia grinned.

"Oh, Lordy." Her eyes crinkled at the corners. "Now, because of the health department, I would ordinarily not allow you to remove that animal from its carrier inside my restaurant. But seeing as how there aren't any officials from the H.D. here at the moment, I think that Coach is in sore need of his furry friend and should see Stetson in all his glory—along with everyone else—because this is gonna be good." She winked.

"On your orders, Sunny." Mia kissed her cheek and unzipped the carrier as she strode toward her father and Easy Ace. *Sleazy Ace.* Ace who had kissed her.

Stetson growled as she slid her hand under his little body, as if he knew full well what she was doing. She plucked him out and held him aloft like Liberty with her torch as the entire restaurant fell silent.

Coach looked up. His mouth dropped open and a piece of bacon fell out of it and down onto his plate again. "WHAT HAVE YOU DONE TO MY DOG?!"

"Hello, Dad. Happy birthday to Stetson!" Mia handed Stetson over as he whined with his tail between his legs, seeming to know that he'd been transformed from an object of pride and affection into an object of shame. "How're you feeling?"

On the opposite side of the table, Ace held a napkin over his mouth and quite literally choked as he beheld the Yankee Doodle Dandy.

Stetson evidently didn't like the sound of that, because he bared his teeth at Ace and barked maniacally.

"Hush, boy. Hush, sweet boy," Coach crooned as he cradled the Yorkie, though he was clearly nauseated by the dog's attire. He pulled the cap off Stetson's head, but not before Mia had snapped a picture of him holding Stetson in all of his Yankee glory.

"What is that?" Ace finally managed to ask, as he put his napkin back into his lap.

"This here's my dog, Stetson," Coach said.

"*This* is Stetson? And he comes with a . . . *a man-purse*? For a dog?"

"It ain't a purse," growled Coach.

"You tight with Paris Hilton, or something?"

"You mockin' me, boy?"

"Not . . . exactly," Ace said somehow with a straight face. Mia was impressed with his self-control.

"I think it's your daughter who's mocking you, Coach."

"Don't I know it!" Her old man glared at her. "What is the meaning of this?"

"Meaning?" Mia asked innocently. Then she let herself laugh in both of their faces.

The rest of the diners in Sunny's did, too.

But her dad refused to play along, and the laughter morphed into an awkward silence with everybody watching.

"Here, you hold my dog, while I get that jersey off him. This is animal abuse!" Coach snapped.

"No, it's not." Mia slid into the booth next to her dad. "He's fine. He's freshly bathed, shaved, and combed."

"He'll survive," Ace said. But her dad still wasn't playing.

"He's been . . . tortured. Humiliated!" Coach pulled the hated shirt off his pet and threw it under the table. Then he kissed Stetson on the head and put him back into his carrier.

"Please. You're the only one who's been humiliated," Mia teased.

But her dad wasn't laughing. "Why would you do this to your old man?"

Her smile faded. "It's a joke, Dad."

"Not a funny one!"

"Um . . . it *is* funny."

"Not to me." He folded his arms on the table, refusing to look at her.

Mia's breath caught in her throat. Was he serious? Her gaze slid to Ace's. Underneath the horror that his manly mentor and coach owned a tiny dog, and under the general outrage over having to see Yankees insignia, his eyes held . . . sympathy. For her. Which was intolerable. She didn't want or need his sympathy.

Not to mention that she was crushed at her dad's refusal to play along. "It's hilarious to everyone in this diner except for you, Dad."

"And why do you think that is?" he shot back.

She shook her head. "Because you're not being a good sport?"

Across the table, Ace made an urgent chopping gesture across his neck—an *oh no, you did not just say that* gesture.

"I'm not being a *good sport*?" her dad repeated woodenly. "Did you actually just say that to me?"

What? she mouthed back to Ace, uncomprehending.

Ace shook his head and stared up at the ceiling, as if to say that she was beyond his help.

The silence at the table was deafening. Granted, her dad was the king of the good-sportsmanship speech. She just hadn't realized that it was such a point of personal pride. It was always embarrassing when a joke fell flat. This was rapidly turning into something much, much worse.

Mia felt disappointment, mortification, anger, and shame building inside her. It didn't feel good. Her throat clogged; her eyes stung.

Coach aimed a tight smile at the folks in the diner who were still rubbernecking at their table. But for her, he had nothing. Not a laugh, not an *atta girl*, not even a grudging acknowledgment of the brilliance of her joke.

She sat there with her face burning, petrified, wanting to run. Afraid to move, though—because if she did, she might shatter into a million pieces.

And the whole time, Ace looked at her with that unexpected streak of empathy and understanding that she could just kill him for . . . because she wanted it from her dad, not from him. And because he was witness to her crashing and burning with the old man, yet again.

Sunny appeared at her elbow, seeming to know uncannily when she was needed. "That would have been a good one for Fool Fest," she said, switching the subject.

God bless Sunny.

In the continuing silence, she turned back to Mia. "How's Jules?"

Ah, Jules. Her loyal and devoted best friend . . . who was struggling through the pregnancy that Mia had so desperately wanted for herself. "She's good. Really good. Things are easier on her now that she's through her first trimester. She's actually in Dallas with Charlie for another day, whoopin' things up before becoming a mom, I expect." It was hard not to feel jealous about the baby, the money the women were probably spending, and the fact that sometimes it felt as if she were losing her best friend to Charlie . . . and Rhett Braddock.

"Glad to hear it. Now, can I get you something to eat, Mia? A nice, juicy burger or maybe something lighter?"

Mia shook her head. "I'm not hungry. Just stopped by to—"

"Pull your prank." Her dad supplied the words.

She took a deep breath and slid out of the booth. "To say hello and to celebrate Stetson's birthday. Like we've always done."

"Coffee to go?" Sunny asked.

"That'd be great, thanks." Time to pull up her big-girl panties and be an adult. Mia smoothed down her scrubs and looked at Ace. "You're okay under my dad's supervision?" she asked pointedly.

"Yeah," Ace said, in a quiet tone.

"Coach?" She looked at her dad, who still refused to look at her. He gave a single nod.

"Great." Mia produced the smile that she saved for when she had to clean up a particularly unpleasant mess at the hospital. "Then you two go ahead and enjoy yourselves. Call me if you need a ride back to the ranch, Ace. Otherwise, I'll meet you back there at five to make sure you've got dinner squared away and whatever else you need to get settled."

Cheeks burning, Mia walked out of the diner and got back into her hot, airless little car, feeling suffocated. Mia had planned to be sitting there at the table, enjoying the joke with her dad, when Sabine came in with the Red Sox replacement gear she'd also ordered. But it didn't matter now. Because her bid for his attention in the face of Ace had backfired . . . badly.

That was what it had been, even if she hadn't wanted to admit it.

She'd messed up his reunion with his most famous student. And she'd made folks in town laugh at his expense, when he traded on respect in Silverlake: He was Coach, the guy who'd trained up Easy Ace Braddock, sent him to the majors, and made Silverlake famous.

Mia rested her forehead on the steering wheel for a moment.

Well, her mom always said that the best way to feel better about yourself was to do something for somebody else. And that somebody else was, in fact, waiting for her. She had exactly four minutes to get to her next regular eldercare patient's house.

Mrs. Dooley was at least 179 years old. She had been the British bride of a Texas oilman who'd met her in London and swept her off her feet. She was paradoxically tiny but had three chins and four bellies stacked on top of one another, because she had once been large. It was all skin. And because she was deaf herself, she shouted—at awesome decibels. She sounded exactly like Winston Churchill giving a radio address.

"Helloooo, Mrs. Dooley," Mia called, letting herself in with her key. Knocking was always fruitless. "How are you today?"

There was no answer, as usual.

"Mrs. Dooley?" Mia closed the door behind her, then straightened the crocheted, cheerful saying under the peephole: *Bless This Mess*. It must have been a gift from someone, because it was way too Southern a saying for Mrs. D.

She turned, wincing. The mess needed blessing—that was for sure. Newspapers had exploded all over the floral couch. Two cardboard dishes from frozen entrées sat on the coffee table, with forks stuck in the hardened goo. A martini glass winked at her from nearby, a bit of lemon rind drying in the bottom. Mrs. Dooley's cat, Simon, had been productive lately, judging by the smell.

"Mrs. D?" Mia picked her way through the mess, collecting trash items as she went. She dropped them in the garbage in the small kitchen, where a collection of grandchildren peered out from their frames on the refrigerator at a small café table set for four. It was always set for four, with blue and yellow place mats, starched yellow cloth napkins, lovely blue and white bone china, silver, and crystal. A small pot of yellow roses perched in the middle of it all. And Mia had never seen anyone sit there for as long as she'd known Mrs. Dooley. It made her sad.

She found Mrs. D ensconced on the throne, as she called the toilet, where she'd fallen asleep. This was normal. "Mrs. Dooley?" she prompted her gently.

"Hell's bells, woman!" the old lady roared, her eyes flying open in alarm. "What are you trying to do—finish me off?"

Even though she'd steeled herself for this, Mia still jumped. It was hard not to, because of the sheer volume of her voice. "Hi," she chirped. "How are you feeling today?"

"My bowels won't cooperate."

"Sorry to hear that."

"It's better than the trots," Mrs. Dooley said, looking on the upside.

"I suppose so. Would you like to take a bath?"

"Yes, that I would."

A copy of *Flea Market Marvels* had fallen off Mrs. D's lap, so Mia handed it back to her while she started running hot water for Mrs. D's bath, which she had agreed not to take unless Mia or another attendant was there to help her.

She helped the old lady stand up, got her undressed, and then settled her on the side of the tub, which could be tricky for aged, arthritic bones. Then on the count of three, she lowered her into the water.

"Divine!" shouted Mrs. Dooley into Mia's left ear, all but shattering it. "There is simply nothing like a bath."

Mia smiled at her. "I know, right?"

"One emerges reborn! Ready to frolic."

Er, frolic? Sure . . . okay.

"I am delighted that you've come today," thundered Mrs. Dooley, "for I'd like to learn something new."

Mia's heart warmed. Even if she couldn't connect with her own father, she could help other people in need. She was here on the planet for a reason.

"Of course, Mrs. Dooley. What can I help you with?"

"I should be much obliged if you'd help me set up a profile on something called . . . eh . . . what the bloody hell is it? *The Little Match Girl* . . . told myself to remember that to jog my senility . . . *ah!* Yes! *There* it is. I should be much obliged if you'd help me set up a profile on something calling itself Tinder."

As she made this pronouncement, Simon the cat stared at Mia, unblinking and deadpan, from his chosen spot on the bathroom counter.

Simon smirked at her. *It is funny*, he seemed to say.

Not to me.

"Mrs. Dooley," Mia said at last. "Tinder isn't . . . that is to say . . . why don't we try Match.com instead?"

"No," insisted Mrs. D. "I want to go with the fun one, the wicked one."

There was no way Mia was putting Mrs. Dooley's information up on Tinder for strangers to mock. It wasn't going to happen.

Simon yawned, indifferent to Mia's squirming. *Looks like* this *joke's on you.*

She glared at the cat. "How about Bumble, Mrs. D? Tell you what: I've been meaning to set up a profile on that one, too."

"Bumble? Who wants to *bumble*? I want to sail, swagger, flourish! Not bumble. Tinder sounds much more exciting."

Mia sighed. "Got it. I'll explain later. For now, let's just get through your bath, okay?"

"Splish-splash, my dear."

Mia smiled and reached for a sponge. She prayed that Mrs. Dooley would just forget all about Tinder. She had no desire to see Ace's profile pop up on it . . . and she was almost certain it would.

Chapter 13

THE WIND HAD GONE RIGHT OUT OF COACH'S SAILS after the painfully awkward dog-tastrophe at Sunny's. Mia was already gone when Sabine came into the diner with a special delivery: a replacement Red Sox uniform for Stetson. But it was too late.

Coach had stared sadly down at the red and white doggie uniform in his hands as if it were a puzzle that had no answer. He looked older than his age all of a sudden, and Ace didn't want to see that, so he quickly paid the bill and suggested they head to the nearby park where Ace used to stretch after running conditioning miles all over town.

While Ace crutched along, Stetson trotted happily at Coach's ankles; it might have been his imagination but it seemed that the dog was throwing Ace some disapproving looks. He'd have to get Grouchy to explain that Ace wasn't really *trying* to give Mia a hard time.

Two blocks behind Main Street was a strip of grass that turned into an oval-shaped field behind the First Baptist

Church. It was still there, and well maintained, with pots of yellow and purple flowers around the border.

It used to be that Ace and Coach could run miles around that oval for hours, side by side. Now Coach was old and Ace was broken—and in danger of getting a little soft, courtesy of his hiatus.

Not that Coach said anything about it. Part of Ace wished he would; Coach Adams always gave him the truth and after his parents were gone, Coach was the one Ace listened to. Not Declan, that was for sure.

"Given how rusty my body is right now, this should not feel this good," Ace said, as Coach protected his right leg while he did sit-ups.

Coach grunted.

"You're awful quiet," Ace said. "Used to be advice a mile a minute."

His mentor smiled. "You're a professional now, boy. You know more than I ever did." He signaled the end of the count, and Ace moved on to the next stretch: He didn't have to focus much on Coach's adjustments and corrections. The old routines were so ingrained he could let his mind wander.

He lay in the grass, working hard, as he always did—he might be known for partying and getting into trouble, but that never affected his work ethic. Baseball was his life, his escape, his world. Whatever else happened, his coaches were never going to be able to say that he gave less than 100 percent in the gym or on the field.

Coach muttered something under his breath, reaching out a free hand to rub Stetson's tummy; the dog was lying on his back in the grass with his paws sticking out at all angles. If the dog had displayed even one iota of respect for Ace, Ace might have admitted that he'd never seen anything cuter in his life. The cap had fallen off but the Red Sox jersey was still in place.

"Hey, I saw the Little League stats in the town paper," Ace said. "Holy moly, that's bleak. Why aren't you coaching anymore? What that team needs is some experienced leadership. You could turn the whole thing around." He scoffed. "Second-to-last place? Silverlake? It's a disgrace."

"That's too much work for an old man," Coach Adams said.

Ace rolled his eyes. "I'd do it myself if I knew I was sticking around. It's a matter of town pride."

Coach looked thoughtful. "Maybe you should. That'd be the first good press you've had in a long time."

"Hey, that is not true."

His mentor just gave Ace a woeful look. "When you go back," he said, "promise me you'll keep better company. Know who cares about you and who doesn't, out there. When the money and fame is gone, you might find yourself looking around and wondering who your true friends are. Don't end up like me."

"Aw, I'd be honored to end up like you."

His mentor snorted. "You can do better." And then hastily added, "Except for Mia. Best thing I ever did." He looked a little misty all of a sudden.

"You should have seen your face when Mia brought that Yankees crap into the diner. That was messed up," Ace said. "I kinda didn't know which one of you to feel worse for. You gonna make that right, Coach?"

Coach sighed. "I don't know what to say to her. Never did. So I don't say anything. And then it just goes on like . . . How could she think I would find that funny?"

Coach looked at Ace, outraged. And then the two of them cracked up.

"Poor Mia," Ace said.

"You can say that again. Stuck with me, her mama never around." Coach shook his head. "I don't know how that girl turned out so well, but I can't take any credit for it. It was her grandmothers."

"Aw, jeez, Coach. That's not true."

"She didn't choose me; she just got left behind by her mama." Coach shrugged.

"You're a great dad. Mia's lucky."

The pained expression on Coach's face was not what he expected.

"I was a better dad to *you*," Coach said.

Ace finished the last set of reps and lay back in the grass, feeling guilty.

"Well," the older man said. "I guess that's all just water under the bridge. What's done is done and nobody's figured out how to turn back time."

Ain't that the truth. Ace closed his eyes and breathed in the scent of the freshly mown lawn. Somewhere to the left, a couple of birds were having a conversation in one of the big live oaks. The sun was shining down, but thanks to the shade of the trees, it wasn't killer heat. Instead it warmed Ace's face, making him drowsy after the diner food and a warm-up that made him feel almost whole again.

Stetson kept making a point to ignore Ace in favor of Coach. The little dog stood in the circle of Coach's crossed legs, his paws up on the man's stomach and his tongue trying to reach his daddy's nose. "Truth is, since that day you lost your folks, I've always thought of you as my son. I guess I felt some guilt. Some responsibility. And some . . . well, you know."

Ace shifted uncomfortably in the grass, both surprised and unsettled that the man would go there. They'd never talked about it. Not in all these years, not once the funeral was over and the Braddock kids went home alone. Thank goodness Stetson was between them because Ace felt his eyes get watery.

He swung his body up to a sitting position and then grabbed his crutches and stood up. "I oughta get going, Coach." As if he really had somewhere to be. One thing was for sure, he was not talking about his parents dying on the way back from a baseball game.

He held out a hand to help the older man up, but Coach Adams didn't let go. Ace didn't know what Coach wanted to hear, but he said, "I don't guess we need to make ourselves feel worse about the past than we already do. On the plus side, Mia's right there in front of you. You still have time to do things differently if you want to."

"Andrew."

"What?"

"Mia and I don't have a lot of places where we meet in the middle. We don't have a lot in common. But you and Declan . . . heck, the whole lot of you Braddocks, you were so close."

Until the accident.

"Where are those friends of yours on the team?" Coach asked. "You said nobody was in touch. Where are they, Ace?"

Ace shrugged as if he didn't know, didn't care.

"I see Jake, I see Rhett, I see Declan . . . all your mama's boys running around making peace and putting the family back together again. Lila's there, too. Everybody but you. I know I taught you to aim for the top outside Silverlake, but you got to the top. You did it. Now take a moment to breathe and look around you." He pointed a trembling finger at Ace. "You and Declan *are still here.*"

Ace cleared his throat. "Well, uh, yeah, I can see that. Everyone's still here in Silverlake."

Coach sighed, but he didn't push it further. "Come by soon and watch a game with me."

Now that was something Ace could get behind. He clapped Coach Adams on the back, more than a little relieved when a couple of fans who'd been waiting for him to finish came forward with pens and paper.

If he was lucky, one of them would have transportation.

Chapter 14

AFTER WORKING OUT WITH COACH, ACE HITCHED A ride home with a couple of cute girls. He arrived back at the ranch and was disappointed not to see Mia's little blue car. She wasn't there. And it struck him that he was more disappointed than the situation deserved.

After his fans headed out, Ace spent two hours drawing caricatures of various townspeople, which was fun, but now he was over it. He'd propped up the sketches on the mantel of the huge fieldstone fireplace: Coach with Stetson the Yorkie in Yankees wear; Schweitzie backward on his own mechanical bull; Pullman Duff swimming along the bottom of a river, whiskers waving, full-on catfish. Bridget looking like Jessica Rabbit, shaking her finger at a befuddled judge in black robes.

Ace was officially bored and lonely, while Declan was apparently making a point of staying outside and working, clearly aggravated with his younger brother and giving him the silent treatment. Fine.

The TV news and the *Silverlake Reporter* were both full

of more crap and innuendo about the Maserati incident and whether Pete was planning to sue Ace for the loss of his car and his injuries.

That was rich—if they only knew the truth. And Ace had never thought, not once, about suing *Pete* for his own injuries. Muckrakers.

To top it off, there was a snotty quote from Frannie, Pete's wife: "Easy Ace Braddock is a Lone Star wife's worst nightmare." *Really, Frannie? You have no idea.* That stung.

He was so pissed off that he was climbing the walls, crutches and all. He wanted a hefty pour or three of Macallan 25. And he wanted another go-round with his bossy, annoying nanny. A good verbal spar session would off-gas some of his frustration. Where *was* she?

Ace glanced at his watch. She was twenty-seven minutes and forty-three seconds late. If she didn't get here in the next two minutes and seventeen seconds, he had a good mind to dock her pay. This was downright unprofessional. And it gave him something to razz her about. He hit her number on his phone, but it just rang and rang before going to voicemail. *Huh.*

This was very unlike her. Ace wondered briefly if she'd had an emergency or she'd fainted or she'd quit on him. Unacceptable: She'd have to quit to his face.

Except she *didn't* have to. She only had to tell the team manager.

Had she walked on him? Ace felt a surge of anxiety. Nah. She'd said she was going to be here at five P.M. That was pretty specific.

Where did Mia live, anyway? He found the address easily. But was it weird for him to go there? Stalkerish?

Nah. Ace Braddock didn't need to stalk anyone. He had crazy fangirls stalking him all the time. One had literally been removed by security from the second-story balcony of the team crash pad in Austin, trying to break in so she could have her wicked way with him.

He was just checking up on Mia. That was all. A concerned friend/employerish person. Right? Right.

But how would he get to her place?

Declan might need his truck for work, and Ace had sworn not to steal a tractor again. He couldn't think of any other piece of farm equipment that would make the journey, and that he knew how to operate. *Hmm.*

But! An idea began to form in Ace's head . . .

A horse was not the same thing as a tractor. That was something on which most people of reasonably sound mind could agree. So if he, say, borrowed a horse, by no means, under no interpretation, was Ace breaking his promise not to steal anybody's tractor ever again.

Ace had a lot of experience dodging managers, over-eager fans, and babysitters of one sort or another on the road. As he crutched toward the stables, he cast a glance toward the path leading to the fishing shack and then made a thorough review of the property as far as his eyes would take him. The wind shifted and the acrid scent of burned wood coming from the ruins of the Old Barn wafted under his nose.

Declan was still nowhere in sight. If the tractor was back, Ace'd never know it. Declan would probably keep it out of sight for the rest of his stay. Make that the rest of his life.

So Ace crept toward the stable door and slipped inside, falling through a time warp of over a decade. The sweet smell of hay hit him first, and then the old weathered wood and leather. The rich, loamy, musky scent of the horses inside came next, along with the more pungent stink of their by-products and the sawdust that covered the cement floors of their stalls. Liniment and saddle soap and saddle oil.

The horses nickered, sensing his presence, and Ace found himself nickering back. "Hi, guys. How you been?"

It was just as he remembered. "Which one of you characters is gonna be my partner in crime?" Ace asked.

Silence.

"Aw, c'mon. You guys must be as bored as I am."

A dun, a tan horse with black mane and tail, poked his

nose forward over the stable door and sneezed his opinion of Ace onto the floor.

"Gee, thanks. I am really not used to being turned down. First Mia, now *you*. Y'all are starting to hurt my feelings." Ace crutched down the center aisle of the stables and decided to be practical, for once. He chose the horse closest to the tack room, where the halters and bridles hung on the back wall. A carefully carved wooden sign spelled out his name: Rowdy. *Perfect.*

"I haven't ridden a horse in ages," he said to Rowdy, "but your name speaks to me, and they say it's just like getting back in the sack."

Nobody in the entire stables laughed.

"Tough audience," he muttered, and grabbed Rowdy's bridle off a hook. His hand froze when he saw the old picture posted above the row of hooks, though. The photo was faded and the frame was splintered and chipped at every corner. The whole family looked out at him, lined up on horses as if they were ready for a Braddock cattle roundup. Mama and Pop, both grinning so wide they might've exploded from happiness. And then all five Braddock siblings, small to large. Little Lila in pigtails on her pony. Rhett and Declan in the new cowboy hats they'd gotten that Christmas. Ace leaning over to goose Jake's horse—the photo couldn't show the five seconds afterward, when Jake's horse took off running as if it'd seen a ghost, coming close to taking out the photographer. Ace had nearly fallen off his own pony because he was laughing so hard.

Ace reached up and pressed his index finger first against Pop's image and then Mama's.

I miss you.

I'm sorry.

When he pulled his hand back, it was covered in dust. He brushed it off on his jeans.

The gray horse on his left nickered, and Ace looked over. "I know, right? This is no time for sad. This is time for another first-class jailbreak!"

He slipped the reins over Rowdy's head and bridled him.

It would be extremely awkward to try to saddle him properly with his injury. He admitted to himself—and to the occupants of the stables—that he had no business riding at all. If he fell, it wouldn't be pretty. So he wouldn't fall. Simple as that.

Ace led the horse out of the stables to the mounting block outside.

It was embarrassing to have to use the mounting block, but in his condition, he had to. Frankly, if anybody had seen the disgrace that was him attempting to mount Rowdy, he'd probably be kicked out of Texas.

At last, after a few tries, Ace was up, Rowdy pawing at the ground with his hooves and tossing his head a little. "Yeah, boy. An evening ramble. Aw, how could Declan *possibly* mind?" Ace asked, patting the horse and taking the reins in his right hand. He hauled the crutches up and laid them awkwardly, diagonally across his lap. They weren't even close to secure there, so he ended up looping his belt through them. It was only after he'd done so that he noticed his cell phone lying under the mounting block. Ace groaned and left it there. Then he gave the animal a gentle kick with his heels to get him moving. A slight twinge ran up his bad leg.

Not caring that he made quite a peculiar sight, Ace turned Rowdy's head toward Mia's property. He inhaled the shadowy night air, redolent with cedar and mesquite, and grinned.

Chapter 15

GIVEN THAT MIA'S PROPERTY BORDERED THE BRAD-dock land, it didn't take long to get to the front of Mia's place. Ace was busy apologizing to his unhappy balls for riding bareback after so many years, so he didn't quite register the size of the house at first.

House? Make that palace. Ace sat atop Rowdy, staring at the ostentatious mansion. It was nice, but it looked as if a tornado had plucked it out of a ritzy Dallas development and dropped it down here, in the middle of nowhere. Built of pale gray brick with white trim and double doors, it sported a grand façade with steps leading up to a white-columned portico that looked as if it could easily welcome the governor and first lady of Texas. Ace half expected a butler in tails to throw open the doors, look down his nose, and tell him to use the service entrance.

How could Mia worry about where her next paycheck or meal was coming from when she lived in a place like that? She'd need a full-time housekeeper just to keep it clean.

And her tiny car looked like a matchbox toy parked in the driveway. It was downright comical.

There didn't seem to be any obvious place to leave Rowdy, so he guided him across Mia's front lawn and slipped down, using the crutches to cushion the landing. He looped the reins around one of the massive urns that framed the front entrance and struggled up too many stairs to count. He knocked. Nobody came.

Rowdy seemed uneasy. He sidestepped and snorted, pulling on his reins.

"Hey. Behave yourself."

But Rowdy clearly didn't want to be there. He seemed to smell trouble in the air.

"Dude, the only trouble here is the kind we're making."

Rowdy sidestepped again, his eyes rolling back in his head.

"Calm down."

Ace rang the doorbell and laughed out loud when he heard the chime from inside: It played "The Eyes of Texas." While any self-respecting Longhorns fan deeply loved the song, it was a bit pretentious as a doorbell. Finally it subsided, but nobody came. Ace put his ear to the door but heard no footsteps, no sign of life from inside.

He tested the front door and it opened, so Ace pushed it wider and called Mia's name. She didn't answer, but he thought he heard her voice. Had she called for help?

If she had, she didn't repeat the plea.

But Ace's arms erupted in goose bumps, and every nerve in his body went on high alert.

Under Rowdy's unhappy gaze, he stepped inside.

Weirdly, he saw not a single stick of furniture.

He moved slowly, silently, aware that it was extremely uncool to trespass or eavesdrop on Mia, but no one ever said that Ace Braddock had manners.

A whimper came from deep inside the house, which was also unbearably hot and humid; musty and dank, too—as if the air-conditioning hadn't been run in months, even in the sweltering Texas heat.

A whimper and then a low sob. Then, "Get away from me!"

Mia's voice, for sure. Trembling. Hanging on to the final vestiges of authority by a thin thread. Who could be threatening her?

Her ex.

It came to Ace suddenly. She'd been married, but the guy was no longer in the picture. Bridget had gossiped about it over a drink in Austin once. Mia's man had disappeared—there was some intrigue or scandal about it. He'd been a jerk. She'd been trying to hunt him down . . . what the hell was his name? Rob. Robert Bayes.

Ace remembered him now: tall, dark, smug. Way too much hair gel.

Ace'd once beat the living crap out of him for saying that he couldn't wait until Lila got old enough to—

He simmered, just thinking about it.

Something smashed in the other room. Mia screamed, and this was followed by a low growl that didn't even sound human.

Ace sprinted, crutches and all, toward what looked like the kitchen. If Rob was hurting her, he was going to friggin' kill him. He'd knock his skull clean off his neck and outta the park.

It all happened very suddenly: Ace burst into the kitchen, separated from the family room by an eat-in bar. He gave about a nanosecond of attention to the fact that there was no Rob, a nanosecond to the fact that it was really not okay for there to be a live, pissed-off coyote in Mia's living room, and a lot more than a nanosecond to Mia, who'd crawled up on the bar at the kitchen island and was cowering against the wall.

Coyote. What the—?

It was huge. Lotta teeth. Turned from Mia and growled at him, instead. Crouched as if to spring at him.

Ace hurtled forward before it could, and wound up tight with his crutches doubled up as if he were at bat. Then he unpacked the swing.

Thwack! He delivered the blow straight to the coyote's head.

HOME RUN!

The coyote yowled and recoiled, heading like a shot back out the . . . out the . . .

Ace gaped. There were no walls at the back of Mia's perfect mansion.

"What the hell?" was all Ace could come up with as he processed the fact that the coyote had run off into the night through a hole in the plastic sheeting that was stapled from floor to ceiling—over the two-by-fours that framed out the structure.

Over the kitchen island and bar hung an expensive-looking modern light fixture. And in the living room: cheap lawn furniture.

But Ace didn't take more than a second to evaluate the decor. It was Mia he was concerned about.

Mia's panicked breathing was loud enough to wake Declan on the neighboring land next door. She was still huddled on top of the marble kitchen island, trying to become one with the only finished wall in the rear of the house.

On the backside of the adrenaline that had driven him, Ace leaned on his crutches, wincing at the fresh pain he'd managed to gain himself. He looked at Mia, who was clutching the front of her skimpy tank top in two balled-up hands. Then he looked again at the disaster of what wasn't quite a house. "Hey. Mia. You okay?"

"Thank you," she managed in a shaky voice.

Never had a girl looked in more need of a hug.

Ace remembered clearly that she'd palmed his face and shoved him away the last time he'd tried to get close to her, but this was different. Still, he hesitated. Then he went for comic relief instead. "You know, there are better ways to get rid of your dad's yappy little Yorkie. You don't have to lure a rabid coyote into your house."

"Heh," Mia said. Not much of a laugh. Then, "I love that little dog. I'd never feed him to a coyote."

"Ah. So . . ." Ace spied a pair of familiar-looking pans

on the stove near where Mia was crouched. Was that from the caravan? He reared back: tuna. *Ugh.* "You were heating up dinner and an unwelcome, hairy guest stopped by. I mean, one other than me."

She followed his gaze. "Oh, one of those is for Mrs. Baxter. I shouldn't have swiped them without asking," she said miserably. "But I knew you couldn't eat all that food, and I just don't have much grocery money this week. I was going to replace them with something fresh. I swear."

He tried to bend his mind around the fact that she was apologizing for heisting a pair of lousy frozen casseroles she knew he'd never eat, after she'd just been almost eaten herself. It took a few moments to process.

"Mia. Forget it. I had no idea you were living like this."

"Nobody does," she said in a small voice.

"I want you to take all of the damn casseroles out at Silverlake Ranch. And I'm doubling your salary for putting up with me."

"Stop it. You don't even pay me."

"I do now. I will personally bankroll doubling your salary if you'll let me."

Mia shook her head no . . . and then she sniffled.

His heart rolled over. Or at least it felt like it did. Which was an uncomfortable feeling, one that he wanted to avoid at all costs.

Ace crutched around to take a look at the plastic tarps and the staples and the frame-out that had been abandoned before ever being introduced to concepts like insulation or stucco. He looked through the slats to the next room, also framed out with two-by-fours. The would-be palace had lots of nice, big rooms. Well, lots of nice big spaces, connected together into what could possibly be rooms one day.

What a nightmare for Mia.

"Huh," he said. He rounded the kitchen island and approached her as she eyed him warily.

"Just say it," Mia challenged him, mortification written all over her face.

"You had me for a while, but it turns out you're something of a hot mess, Mia Adams," Ace said softly, bending toward her, a little awkward with his bad ankle.

She was still trembling; tears rested on her cheeks. And she looked as if she'd rather crawl into the microwave and nuke herself than have him see any of this. "Fair enough."

Ace put his weight on his good leg and brushed the tears away with the pads of his thumbs while she sucked in a breath. He'd rather kiss them away—in fact, it was all he could do not to—but there was that whole face-palming thing, and the adjective *disgusting* that she'd applied to him. And it hardly seemed fair to take advantage of her under these circumstances.

Still. Ace pulled her into his arms and gave her an honest-to-goodness hug, no strings attached, rubbing her back for good measure. She froze at first, then slowly relaxed against him, trusting that he wouldn't push for more and was only there to comfort her.

Something unknotted deep inside him and came undone in response to her trust.

"I guess you've gone from being my biggest pain in the butt to being my hero," she muttered ruefully against his chest.

"Wow," Ace said into her hair, which smelled like jasmine and sunshine. "That may be the most grudging compliment anyone's ever paid me. Therefore, I hold it dearest."

He was rewarded with a peal of laughter, and then punished again when she wriggled out of his arms. He felt the loss immediately.

She sighed and rested her head against the wall, as if all the fight had gone out of her. "I honestly don't think I've ever been so scared—and now so tired, in my life. I'm sorry I didn't make it back to work."

Ace's ankle ached. He backed up to the wall and slid onto the one barstool in the place, which looked as though it had been around since 1847 and salvaged from a saloon. It was totally out of place under the pendant lighting. He sat next to her, staring out at the night through the rip the coyote had graciously made in the tarp. "So Rob left you with this mess?"

"Yep," Mia said, staring straight ahead.

"I wanna punch his face," Ace said. Actually, he wanted to do a lot more than that. Crunch his bones. Rip out his liver and feed it to him. Stuff like that. Primitive, satisfying, bloody stuff that the guy really deserved for treating Mia so badly.

That got him a soft smile. "I don't condone violence."

Ace raised an eyebrow.

After a moment of silence, Mia said, "In general. I do make exceptions."

"I'm relieved to hear it."

"In fact, I'll cop to having at least three fantasies per day that involve Rob losing limbs, which is sort of embarrassing since I'm sworn to heal and comfort people. But according to one article I read, three out of five therapists approve and find these thoughts healthy—as long as you don't act them out."

"Good to know. Acting them out could be fun, though, don't you think? It was fun the last time I did it."

Mia looked alarmed.

"I guess you didn't know I punched him out back in high school," he said.

"Why?"

Ace cracked his knuckles. "He made a very disrespectful comment about my little sister."

"So you went caveman on him?"

"Yep. And I'm not apologizing."

"Hmmm."

"So?" Ace grinned unrepentantly. "A penny for your violent fantasies."

Mia laughed. "Fine. I have drop-kicked him off a building into heavy traffic."

"Cool. Give me more."

"I have lassoed him from Wonder Woman's invisible plane and dropped him, totally naked except for his ostrich-skin cowboy boots, into IRS headquarters."

"Oooh. Good one."

"And I have velcroed him to a wall in a freezing-cold room at a convention of supermodels, then unveiled him like a statue so they could point and laugh at his shrunken, um, tiddlywink."

Ace hooted.

She looked happy for the first time since he'd arrived back in town. And that made his heart turn over again—or whatever it was doing when it felt like that. He didn't really want to know, because it felt vaguely . . . squishy. And Ace refused to have anything about him be squishy.

They resumed looking pensively at the plastic sheeting and the general disaster that was Mia's home, hidden behind the ridiculous façade.

"You try to sell it like this?" Ace asked.

Mia squirmed. "I can't even show it to a real estate agent. Word would get out . . . I can't have that."

"Why not?"

She didn't answer for a moment and then mumbled, "It's complicated."

"But you can't live like this, either," Ace said gently.

"I *do* live like this, because I have to pay the mortgage until I can hunt down Rob and make him cough up what he owes me—which is a *lot*."

"Wait. He just up and left you with nothing?"

"*Less* than nothing," Mia said bitterly. "Cleaned out the joint accounts and walked on all the joint debt—and more, that he fraudulently ran up in my name, which I didn't know about. He also sucked all the equity out of the house and there's a *balloon payment* due soon that—" her voice cracked. "That I knew *nothing* about and cannot possibly handle." Then she clammed up for a moment, seeming to regret what she'd shared. "I really can't talk about the details. Especially not to *you*."

Ace blinked. "Um. I'm going to ignore that last bit."

"Sorry," she muttered.

"Where's the furniture?" Ace couldn't help asking.

"Everything we own is in storage because of the renovations to the house. And now I'm getting 'past due' notices from the storage facility . . ."

"I like the layout," Ace said. "And I can see what it could be. You could make this house a home, for sure. I know where *I'd* start."

"You planning to stay in Silverlake?" Mia asked.

"No way," Ace said with a laugh.

"Well, then," Mia said. She shrugged.

Ace's wandering gaze fixed on a long utility table in the room behind the kitchen—the "family" room?—on which was a whole mess of tiny plastic jars with screw-on lids, and a big jar of pinkish goo. Next to that was a mess of colored crystals and charms, a bunch of glass containers, and a huge metal pot of waxy stuff. Weirdest of all were some molds and an anatomical drawing of a goat's udder with arrows and what looked like instructions.

"Mia, what is that?" He pointed.

She sighed. "That's my side business. Lotions, lip glosses, candles."

He gaped at her. "You have three jobs *and* a business?"

"What do you want me to say?"

"I'm doubling your salary," he repeated.

"No. I'm not taking charity."

Ace blew out a frustrated breath. "Fine," he said. "You ready to get out of here?"

Mia looked up, worry in her eyes. "Drew, I'm so sorry I never made it back to help you with dinner and get you settled, but now I'm late for a client."

He knit his eyebrows. "I thought *I* was your client."

"Well, my contract specifies certain conditions and hours, and I have the right to maintain my existing clients. I'm supposed to be at Mrs. Baxter's in fifteen minutes."

"Mrs. Baxter?" Ace asked. "I-know-what-you-did-last-summer Mrs. Baxter?"

"The very one," Mia said, standing up and brushing off her clothes. She was still a little unsteady on her feet as she went to grab her purse. "Except she's more like I-know-what-you'll-be-doing-*next*-summer Mrs. Baxter."

"Yeah. Crazy psychic lady."

Mia swatted him. "Don't say that!" But her swat came with a tiny laugh. Wasn't a big deal, but it felt good to have a hand in cheering her up.

"On the plus side, she's my last errand today."

Ace watched Mia. She was clearly still shaken, clearly running on empty. "Can you tell her no, just for tonight? You said yourself you're beat. I wouldn't say this if I didn't really feel the need, but darlin,' you're done. Understand?"

"I can't be done," she whispered. "I need the money, but also, Mrs. Baxter is counting on me. She's alone and half of my job is showing up and showing her that someone cares about her. I don't want to disappoint her—and she probably didn't eat enough today, either."

Ace stared down at the floor for a minute, trying to decide which was getting to him more: the fact that Mia was in a financial disaster that seemed insurmountable for someone who was getting paid what she was getting paid. Or the fact that she cared about other people so much that she'd go without sleep and work herself to the bone just to avoid disappointing someone who wasn't even a close friend. Because that didn't go without saying. Not in his line of work where big talk, big bucks, and big at-bats ruled all.

"You can't call her and tell her you'll come by tomorrow?" he asked.

"No. I just can't." Outside, it had started to thrash in a good, old-fashioned Texas thunderstorm. A wet gust of wind blew through the tarp. Mia shivered. Ace wished he had his baseball jacket with him, so he could wrap it around her.

"Well, then I'll go with you. Let's find you a rain jacket and get out of here once there's a break in the weather," Ace said.

She stopped in her tracks. "Wait. Who drove you here?"

"I managed it myself."

Mia's gaze shot from the boot stabilizing Ace's ankle to

his face. "How is that even possible? Without Declan's tractor, I mean."

Ace put his arms out, palms up, directing her attention to his entire body. "Anything's possible, if you set your mind to it."

Her expression hardened. "I wish that were true." She slung the strap of her purse over her shoulder and headed for the door.

Ace cocked his head. "Uh, Mia. Where's your stuff?"

She gestured to her purse.

"Your other stuff."

"I don't have anything else. I'm coming straight back after Mrs. Baxter."

"Are you kidding me? You're not coming back here tonight," Ace said.

"I'm the one who tells *you* what to do, remember?" Mia asked, her chin hiked.

"You're the one who makes it *look* like somebody's telling me what to do," Ace answered with a grin.

She rolled her eyes, but she smiled.

"Go stuff enough into a bag for at least a week. There's no way you're staying here."

"*Excuse* me?"

Okay, not smiling now. "You're gonna fight me on this? I can't believe Declan lets you stay here!" Ace said.

"Declan doesn't know how bad it is," Mia said, and then winced, probably realizing she'd revealed too much. "Besides, he doesn't get to make that decision."

Would you like him to? Ace quickly pushed that thought out of his head.

"You're just being stubborn because giving up a run to me is worse than anything else you can think of," he told her, exasperated. "It's unsafe. A coyote just tried to eat you, he may come back with several friends next time, and from what I can tell, you don't have more than half a roof up there, either. Pack up. You're moving to the ranch for a while."

"Absolutely not! I won't impose on Declan that way."

"Declan's moved out to the fishing shack to avoid my company. So you'd only be imposing on me. Which is kind of your job. Go. Pack."

"Bossy, aren't you?"

"Thanks," Ace said cheerfully.

Mia glowered back.

"Well, I don't remember Mrs. Baxter being especially patient," Ace said, "and the last thing I need messing with my career is a hex. Let's go."

"She doesn't do hexes," Mia said wearily.

"A curse, then."

Mia paused. "She *does* do curses. But I think she'll forgive me for being late since I'm bringing her the other tuna casserole." She looked up, wide-eyed. "I really hope you don't mind about that. I know you hate tuna, but I should've asked. I'm sorry."

"Enough about the casseroles. But . . . how'd you know I hate tuna?"

She laughed. "Dad stopped letting me make it in high school because he was afraid you'd come over and have nothing to eat."

Ace paused, remembering. Feeling pretty sheepish. "You sure took good care of me," he said. *And I was oblivious.*

"Thank my dad," she said briskly, as she started down the hall.

Ace followed her into her bedroom and reached over her head to grab a duffel bag at the top of her closet. He threw it on the bed and then followed her to the bureau, where she was grabbing socks and underwear.

Looking around, he could see that Rob had really and truly cleared out. Or maybe Mia had cleared him out. Either way, there wasn't so much as a stray man's dress sock to be seen. "Do you miss him at all?" Ace asked, leaning over her shoulder and watching her try to hide a wad of colorful, lacy panties under some beige shorts that looked like a bandage with leg holes.

"No. Um. Do you mind?"

"You think I haven't seen sexy undies before?"

"On the contrary. I think you're probably eighty-seven percent *made* of sexy undies. You're a human male entirely composed of hot air, baseball, and sexual conquests."

Ace hooted in laughter. "You must read all of my press."

Mia gave him a look. "It's hard to avoid. I think my dad *bathes* in your press." She scooped up half of her underwear and sock drawer and quickly jammed it in the duffel. It looked like it would last a month, not a week. Unless somebody kept taking it off her. Somebody who wasn't him, though, since he was pretty sure she still mostly despised him.

She'd moved on to what appeared to be a drawer for scrubs and T-shirts. "Hot air, baseball, and sexual conquests," she repeated. "Where does that leave you if you can't play baseball anymore?" she asked, stuffing several more handfuls of clothing into the bag.

Ace stilled. Her question sucked all of the oxygen out of the room. *You don't ask something like that.* She didn't know, but she couldn't ask. "What makes you think I can't play baseball anymore?"

Mia looked over her shoulder with a funny look on her face. "I didn't say you couldn't, only what *if.* I mean, I assume you've thought about the future."

Ace's mind went utterly blank. "Right," he said. "You ready to go?"

Mia dashed into the bathroom and came out with a travel bag full of makeup and toiletries, which she added to the duffel. "Ready."

Ace grabbed her bag in one hand, slid the handle over his wrist, and then gripped his crutches.

"Give me that. You're injured." A brief tussle ensued, which he won easily, even one-legged and in a level of pain that he would never admit. She settled for grabbing the tuna casserole.

They were halfway down the path toward the road when Mia stopped in her tracks.

A pile of horse manure sat on the front lawn. Rowdy, however, was gone. Couldn't really blame him, what with the coyote and the thunderstorm. He'd have made his way back to Silverlake's barn.

"Well, I guess that solves my logistical problem," Ace said.

"*Tell me you didn't*," she said, her voice dripping with horror. "Andrew Braddock, just because something is possible doesn't mean you should do it."

"Really?" Ace asked. "Go figure. Well, thanks—now I know."

"If you hadn't just saved my life with those crutches," Mia said, "I'd beat some sense into you with them."

"Thought you didn't condone violence, and all that?"

"As I said before, there are exceptions," Mia ground out, "to every rule."

Chapter 16

MAIN STREET WAS STILL LIT UP AS EVERYONE BUStled to their cars to head home for dinner. Mia parked in front of Piece A Cake and went around the car to see if Ace needed help getting out.

Mrs. Shelley Baxter lived in a tiny apartment in the building sandwiched between Piece A Cake and Amelie's dress shop. This allowed her to use what had once been a very large coat closet downstairs to double as a place of business. About ten years ago she'd hung a neon sign out her window, which regularly put Jake and Mick over at the firehouse in a cold sweat, because no matter how many times they told her not to, she still ran the frayed cord under the window sash and had it plugged into an ancient kitchen outlet.

In good weather, the neon sign said PSYCHIC SHELLEY, and when the air was on the humid side, it often just said PSYCHIC HELL. Luckily, the line underneath, Know Your Future, never wavered.

The building didn't have an elevator and Mrs. Baxter

wasn't as mobile as she used to be, so she'd hired Mia to come by a few days a week to help clean, act as handywoman, and keep her company. As a bonus, sometimes Mia would get her tea leaves read, sometimes her palm, maybe a little tarot. Once, when Mia stopped by on a Saturday night, she'd helped with the ingredients for one of Mrs. Baxter's mysterious "tonics."

Mia never asked to have her fortune told, because *be careful what you wish for*, and all that. But whenever Mrs. Baxter suggested it, she sat down with a cup of tea for both of them and went with it. Because when Mrs. Baxter suggested this, she seemed to have something to say that Mia either wanted or needed to hear.

"She's still at it?" Ace asked, pointing up at the sign.

"She sure is," Mia said, smiling.

She wasn't quite sure that "Mrs." B had ever actually been married. Rumor had it that if she had, she'd disappeared her husband into a bottle, like an unfortunate genie. Maybe she kept him in the pantry along with the blackberry wine and various tonics she mixed for people's dreams or woes.

She wore colorful hippie scarves and wraps over a black dress, always a pair of crazy dangling earrings, and often a pair of socks with individual toes. Young children loved her. So did cats.

Mrs. Baxter was humming and opening a lot of cabinet doors in her 1930s-era kitchen when Mia and Ace walked in. The countertops were composed of small white hexagonal tiles ringed by graying grout. She'd painted the cabinets purple, and along the tops of them marched a collection of Depression glass. "Hello, Mrs. Baxter, it's Mia. I hope you don't mind I brought company. Andrew Braddock. Do you remember him?"

"Evening, ma'am," Ace said.

"Hello, dears," she said, giving them both a distracted wave. "Now, where do you reckon I put the Windex?"

Mia set down her purse and the casserole and went to the sink, reaching underneath. "It's probably just tucked behind . . . Here it is." She pulled out the blue bottle and a clean rag. "What do you need? I can do it for you."

Mrs. Baxter nodded toward her black lacquered dining room table. There weren't any windows over there. Just a silk runner and a . . .

"Oh." Mia went to the crystal ball sitting on the table and gave Ace a warning look when he threatened to laugh.

Mia sprayed cleaner on the rag and gently began to freshen up the crystal as Mrs. Baxter lowered herself creakily into an easy chair upholstered in orange velvet with gold fringe. Mia caught Ace steadying the elderly woman by the elbow when she teetered before landing in her seat, but he didn't look up at Mia and it didn't seem to be for show. Which could only mean he was being helpful. Again.

Frowning, Mia went back to cleaning. "I think I got all the fingerprints. What else is on your to-do list? Oh, let me do the kitchen window. It looks a touch greasy." As she sprayed and wiped, she looked over. "Your hair looks lovely, Mrs. Baxter, but if you want, I'll help you give it a wash."

Mrs. Baxter touched her hair and smiled at Ace. "I'm all right for today."

Mia finished the job and then turned on the water in the sink to scrub a couple of teacups and plates sitting there. Mrs. Baxter stared at the crystal ball.

"Now wait just a minute," Mrs. Baxter said. Her sudden excitement was palpable.

Mia and Ace both looked at her and then looked at each other.

"You okay, there, ma'am?" Ace asked.

"Oh," Mrs. Baxter said, her eyes lighting up. "Ask a question," she said to Mia. She gestured for Ace to help her up again, so he did and the two of them went up to the ball. "What do you want to know? And say it loudly so the ball can hear you."

"Well," Mia said, playing along. She set a teacup painted with delicate pink rosebuds into the drying rack. "I'd like to know where Rob is. I'd like to know if he's coming back to Silverlake before they take all our belongings out of storage and put them up for auction." Her face flamed with embarrassment as she realized a moment too late she'd said those personal things in front of Ace.

Mrs. Baxter did not seem fazed. Ace's face reflected the same angry expression he'd worn when she'd explained why there wasn't more than half a house.

The look softened something in her, and in the split second before Mrs. Baxter closed her eyes and started to moan a fairly unnerving tune in a minor key, Mia thought how lovely it would be to have a champion. If only Ace wasn't *Ace*.

"Aaaaaaaaaaaaaaa, ooooooooooooooooooooooo . . . mwwwwwaaaaaaalaaaaaaalaaaaaaaa."

Ace's lips twitched. Mia tried to give him a stern look, but her own lips twitched, too.

Mrs. Baxter raised her hand high in the air and then dropped it quickly, pinching her fingers together and ceasing her wailing very suddenly.

She sat down at the table, pushed her glasses higher up on her nose, and peered into the center of the crystal ball. "Hot tamales!"

Both Ace and Mia flinched.

"Beware of moving staircases!"

Moving staircases? What on earth was she talking about?

Mrs. Baxter released a very long, slow exhale. She shook her head. "It's very murky in there. Very murky." She cocked her head. "Maybe it's the algae in the water."

"I understand," Mia said, even though she didn't. "Perhaps another time—"

"A boat!" Mrs. Baxter shrugged, sat back in her chair, and pushed her glasses back atop her head. "And that's all."

"A boat?" Ace asked.

"It's red, and I see the word 'cobalt,'" added Mrs. B.

Mia went a little cold.

"And the bill of sale—oh my—it cost a mint."

Yes, it had. Rob had borrowed the money for it in her

name—without mentioning it, or that he'd forged her signature on the paperwork.

"Well, Rob has a boat," Mia said, forcing a laugh. "But he left that in storage, too."

"I didn't know Rob had a boat, dear," Mrs. Baxter said. "It would be very pleasant to take a boat out on that lake by your property, Andrew."

Sure, you didn't know. Mia smiled at Mrs. Baxter indulgently. "Well, why don't we—"

"I don't need any fussing over me today, Mia," Mrs. Baxter said. "But, Andrew, I am going to need your hand. Sit down."

There was a silence as both Mia and Ace processed the request.

"Come now, young Braddock," Mrs. Baxter said, reaching over and tugging on Ace's arm. Ace gave Mia a *help me* look, which she ignored, and then he sat down. Mrs. Baxter took Ace's hand in hers and began to smooth her index finger over the lines across the palm.

"Ohhh . . ." she said.

Ace's eyebrows flew up. "What?"

"Mmm . . ." Mrs. Baxter replied.

"What?"

Mia pressed her lips together to stop herself from laughing.

"Well, well, well . . ."

"What?"

"Baseball players are a superstitious lot, Mrs. Baxter," Mia said. "I think you're scaring him."

"I'm not scared," Ace muttered. "I put the peanut butter out for the grackles."

"You did what?"

"Nothing," he said hastily. He took enough grief for the grackle snack.

"You look petrified," Mia said.

"No, no. Just . . . a little freaked out. Is something wrong?"

"Not at all. Mia, darling, come here." Mrs. Baxter appeared to be keeping Ace's hand in an iron grip, but with her free hand she patted the cushioned seat next to her.

Mia wiped her hands on the little flowered dish towel next to the sink, went over, and sat down. Mrs. Baxter stared at Mia's palm. And then she stared at Ace's palm. Mia's palm. Ace's palm.

And then, she stuck Ace's palm against Mia's palm and pressed their hands together. "Stay like that," she ordered, and then got up.

"I'm not—"

Mrs. Baxter pointed her index finger at Ace's face. He blinked but kept his mouth shut. Mrs. Baxter left the room. Mia snickered.

"Did she put a hex on me?" Ace asked.

He looked legitimately nervous.

Mia stared at their palms pressed together like they were praying. Ace's fingers shifted, entwining with hers just slightly.

"This is ridiculous," Ace said.

"You didn't take your hand away," Mia teased.

"Baseball players are a superstitious lot," he echoed.

"Is that why you're ranting about grackles and peanut butter?"

He shrugged. "Maybe."

"Oh jeez. Are you one of those guys who does a naked dance at midnight before games?"

"Maybe I am," Ace said, waggling his eyebrows at her. "Care to join me?"

She snorted.

"Hey, it could be worse. I could be like the Detroit Tigers manager Jim Leyland, and not change my lucky winning-streak boxers for weeks."

Mia made a retching noise.

A loud thump came from the back room. "Mrs. Baxter, are you okay?" Mia called. "Do you need any help?"

"I'm fine, dear," she called. "Just stay right there."

"This is weird," Ace said. "I'm bored."

"Just relax," Mia said.

They sat there in silence until even Mia had to admit this

was really weird—and she was really tired. "Mrs. Baxter, I really have to be going. I put a tuna casserole in the refrigerator, okay?"

"Just another moment, dear. I'll be right out!"

"Your button," Ace said.

"What?" Mia looked down at her shirt. "Oh, thanks." She fixed it with her left hand.

"You always had a baseball cap on," Ace said suddenly. "Hiding under the brim. And you had this funny way of looking down or away or whatever, when I was talking to you. Like you couldn't wait for it to be over."

He was talking about when they were kids. Teenagers. Mia smiled. "Baseball cap, true. Waiting for you to be over, only sometimes true."

"Always true. Wondering if it's still true," he said. His gaze shifted from her face to their hands.

"I think we can let go now. It won't hurt her feelings," Mia said, suddenly feeling hot.

"I can't take the chance. But if *you* drop *your* hand, I guess that's all right. I hope. I mean, there's nothing I can do about it."

"I'm not going to drop my hand alone! You'll never let me hear the end of it. You'll hit an out at your next at-bat and blame me!"

Ace studied her face. "Then I guess we hold on until she gets back."

His gaze swept her face, landing a couple of times on her mouth. Mia blinked, hyperaware of the prickle of desire sweeping her skin. How was this even happening?

Okay, don't panic. You are not truly attracted to Easy Ace. It's just his natural charisma. The same natural charisma that ends with him boning strangers in hotels around the country. You are not special in his eyes. He's a sexy man with a big drive and you are what's available. Kissing him again would be incredibly dumb. Dumber than driving a tractor with a bad ankle and crutches at dusk on a busy road. Dumber than riding a horse in the same condition. And just remember how awful he's always been.

As Ace looked at her with fire in his eyes, unconsciously moistening his lips as he stared at her face, Mia tried to remember all the awful things he'd done. But all she could come up with was that her dad had loved him more. She couldn't actually remember Ace actively trying to make that so.

"Hey, Mia," Ace whispered. "You're beautiful."

His fingers curled down, turning their pressed palms into a kind of embrace. Ace squeezed hard and leaned forward.

Mia's heart pounded.

"You can let go, dears," Mrs. Baxter said, suddenly hovering over them. Ace sat back, looking as dazed as Mia felt.

"She's a very healing woman, our Mia," Mrs. Baxter said. "You'll be playing baseball again in no time."

Ace's expression brightened.

Mia was pretty sure hers didn't. Because for the first time in her entire life, Mia realized she wasn't 100 percent wishing Andrew "Ace" Braddock would just go away.

Chapter 17

ACE WAS GOBSMACKED BY WHAT HAD HAPPENED AT Psychic Shelley's. The old lady was clearly off her rocker, and yet he'd felt a sort of benign, amused truth and wisdom emanating from her . . . oh no. Had he really been about to even think the word *aura*? He shuddered. He'd make sure to give the grackles extra peanut butter tomorrow. Maybe even some tonight.

She'd said he'd be back to playing baseball in no time. And he damn sure wanted to believe that. But Mrs. Baxter was truly unsettling.

Maybe Mia was rattled, too, because the ride back to the ranch in that clown car of hers was mighty quiet. When he'd first arrived, he'd seen in Mia the same lush curves he'd seen in a lot of women; he'd indulged in quite a number of them in the past. He'd always known he'd be near impossible to tame.

Why, then, did he get the feeling that Mia was different? He squirmed in the passenger seat as he considered the notion of actually getting attached to a woman. Attached enough for a night to mean something.

That would sure be different. Staring out the window at the darkness as they drove the old familiar route, Ace took a deep breath. He thought about the moment he'd decided to take the blame for the accident. How Pete's life seemed to matter so much more than his. Pete had people counting on him. Loving him.

Ace didn't have all that much. Or so it had seemed. Maybe if he'd come back to Silverlake sooner, he'd have given Pete a different answer.

Ace snuck a glance at Mia, driving so responsibly with both hands on the steering wheel, her eyes narrowed slightly so she could pick out details in the dark. That same tight feeling in his chest when he looked at her came over him again. He averted his gaze, spooked.

She finally pulled up at the big house, helped him out of the car, and they both trooped up the steps with her duffel bag. The clanking sound of dishes and water met them in the hall.

Declan was at the sink when Mia and Ace entered the kitchen. Ace steeled himself, because his brother looked like thunder when he turned, his tense gaze flicking between the two of them.

This was beginning to feel like a habit.

Mia made a soft sound of dismay and set her bag down on the kitchen chair. Deck leaned against the side of the sink and exhaled, his eyes now locked on Ace's. "You call Jake before every game."

"Yeah?" Ace said, feeling real off balance.

"One of your pregame rituals is to make sure that your brothers and sisters are still *alive*," Deck said pointedly.

Ace shifted his weight.

"So I would *think* that you would understand that I—"

"You think *that's* weird?" Ace said. "Our catcher does this thing to his bat involving butter and a live chicken—"

"Ace!" Declan barked.

Beside him, Mia flinched.

"I find you gone. Then Rowdy shows up, bridled, spooked as hell, and soaked. Can you put yourself in my shoes and imagine what I thought might have happened?"

Ace flushed. "Declan—" he began.

"Shut. Up. I make it a point to stay out of your way, but you gotta know that I'm still looking out for you."

"Don't waste your time. That's what I have Mia for," Ace said with a grin.

Declan looked wrecked. "Mia didn't answer her phone."

"Oh, Deck, I'm sorry!" she exclaimed.

Through gritted teeth he continued, "I was about to call Bode and get a search party together. Do you have any idea how worried I've been? Do you?"

"I love you, too, bro." Ace said it flippantly, jauntily.

Mia sucked in a shocked breath.

Deck swore. "Don't take it for granted, Ace. Ever."

Ace cracked his neck. "I, um, left my phone under the mounting block. It fell out of my pocket."

The two men stared each other down for a long, awkward moment. Then Declan wiped his hands on the red and white checkered dish towel and left it carefully folded beside the sink.

"I was planning to do those dishes, Deck," Mia said, obviously seeking to change the subject.

"I know, but . . ." He shrugged.

Ace followed his brother with his eyes, waiting for Deck to say something more or give him a little more hell, but nope. The tension was painful. Ace thought of the one subject that could keep things under control. Mia. "So, if it's okay with you, Deck, Mia's going to crash here for a while. Her place is . . ." Mia was blushing and Ace couldn't think of a word that represented what he thought of her place that wasn't a cuss word or just plain embarrassing.

Then he remembered that Declan didn't know how bad it was over at Mia's, and she obviously didn't want him to. "It would be easier for her to . . . sober-companion me," he finished.

His brother smiled at her. "You're welcome here as long

as you want, Mia. And it'll make your harvesting easier, right?"

"Harvesting?" Ace asked.

"Mia didn't tell you?" Deck shoved his hands in his pockets. "She, ah, helps me out by milking the goats and harvesting honey from the bees. I don't have time for that stuff."

Declan was helping Mia with her side business. Of course he was. The extent of his older brother's heroic nature was really beginning to chafe. "We have goats and bees now?"

"Yeah, *we* do," Declan informed him. "Mostly thanks to that crazy sister of ours." His wary expression dissolved into a grin, which he tried to hide.

"I guess I don't mind the manual labor as long as it puts a smile on Deck's face," Mia said. She left out the fact that she got the milk and honey for free.

"What about *my* face?" Ace asked, his hand clutched dramatically to his chest.

"The opposite," she said, dropping her purse on her luggage. "I'm waiting for *you* to start taking yourself *seriously*."

"Me too. On that note . . ." Deck nodded at the two of them and headed for the door.

"Wait," Mia called. She met Declan on the threshold and gave him a hug. "Thanks for letting me stay here. Thanks for everything you do."

Declan managed a fraction of a smile. "Thanks for taking such good care of our boy," he murmured. "He doesn't make it easy."

"That's just not his way, is it?" Mia said.

"Contrary to his nickname," Deck muttered.

"Uh, Mia?" Ace called, glowering. "You can stop hugging Deck now."

All three of them chuckled. Deck gave his brother a warning look and an exaggerated tip of an imaginary hat before heading out into the night—probably to the fishing shack.

Mia closed the door and leaned on it. "You two really

are a mess. Do something before you go, will you? It's absolutely tragic that two great guys should be so at odds."

Ace stared at her. *You think I'm a great guy, do ya?*

"What? What did I say that wasn't true?"

He took a moment and then just shook his head. "Nothin'."

"So, as long as I'm here, what can I do for you?" Mia asked Ace once Declan was gone and the tension eased.

Ace's eyebrows flew up.

"Drop a pencil and need me to pick it up?" Mia laughed.

The joke stung a little, and Ace found himself wondering when her good opinion had started mattering so much. Sure, he'd sign up for a dance in the bedsheets with her anytime, but everybody knew that you didn't need to like each other to have a good time in bed.

Mia leaned against the kitchen counter and studied his face, as if she was waiting for his comeback. To his surprise, he didn't have one. Or didn't want to throw one.

"Actually, if we're being serious, now . . . thanks." She looked down, her arms crossed against her chest. "Thanks for making me leave the house. It's awful living there. Declan has offered before, but I guess my pride just wouldn't let me."

"What happened with Rob?" Ace asked. He studied the high color in her cheeks; she looked so lovely, her hair falling out of that messy ponytail.

She looked up and caught his eye and they held gazes for a moment before she cleared her throat.

"It turns out that Rob just wasn't that into me," Mia said. "He was into a vision of what our life would be like. He wanted the biggest, fanciest house in Silverlake, the fastest car, the most accomplished kids, the most beautiful wife . . ." She studied her fingernails.

"Well, he got close," Ace said. *Especially with the wife.* "He got a lot more than a lot of people." When Mia didn't answer he added, "But it wasn't enough?"

"Nope. I guess he didn't feel special enough. And that's what Rob needs. A messy nurse struggling with infertility issues didn't make him feel special enough, no matter how he tried to dress me up."

Ace stared at Mia. She didn't look cowed. Just tired and matter-of-fact. "Fertility issues?"

"I don't want to talk about it."

"Okay. But . . . where the hell is he?"

"Rob . . . met somebody else. He doesn't live in the US anymore."

Ace tried to wrap his brain around what she was telling him. "Well, how . . . how did he get away with not leaving you anything?"

She flushed and looked away. "Drew." She shook her head.

Yeah, he was getting too personal, but *man*. "Rob just skipped town," Ace guessed.

Mia didn't answer, which was answer enough.

"Where is he?" Ace asked again.

"Oh *my*." Mia cracked a smile. "You look like an avenging angel right now. It's a good look on you, but really. This is not your problem."

"You don't know where he is."

"Not yet. I'm looking. Rumor has it that he's in South America."

"Who's helping you?"

"I've hired someone to track him down, but it's expensive. Declan helped me with the retainer. He insisted. He's always there for me if I need a hand," she said. "You Braddocks are good stock."

That crazy jealous feeling welled up for a moment before Ace remembered that none of this was his business. But the urge to kick Robert Bayes's butt was growing in him to epic proportions. What a lowlife.

Mia sighed.

"You should go lie down and chill," Ace said. "I'm good."

"You ever so tired you're too wired to even relax?" Mia asked. "I think I still have coyote adrenaline in me." She headed into the living room and sat down on the couch, kicking off her shoes.

Ace chewed on his lower lip. "Mind if I hang with you

for a minute? We don't have to talk if you don't want to."
He looked around and waved in the direction of the couch.
"Just, uh, you know. Companionable silence and all that."

She looked amused but not as prickly as she normally
was around him. So Ace eased onto the couch on the opposite side and rested his booted leg on the ottoman.

"Music?" Mia suggested.

"Sure. Whatever you want."

She grabbed her phone and put on a laid-back country mix.

"Perfection," said Ace.

∽

They sat on the couch, at opposite ends. Mia tucked her
legs up on the cushions; Ace folded his hands behind his
head, staring up at the rafters while he spun his fantasy of
what her home should be.

"That back room, you know, by the family room? It
would make an awesome rec room. Pool table, Ping-Pong
table, widescreen TV for movies . . . and in the other room,
that huge one in the corner, you could do an amazing mas-
ter bedroom suite. Put in a soaking tub the size of a small
swimming pool, with a fireplace, even. Can you see it?"

Mia listened, her gaze on the intriguing swath of skin
that exposed a set of muscular abs where his shirt was hik-
ing up. She must be losing her mind a little—sleep depriva-
tion and all—because Ace wasn't annoying the crap out
of her.

On the contrary. The way he talked about turning her rag-
gedy mansion into a home with such boylike enthusiasm—
she'd never known he could be like this. There was something
gentle here, something almost pure in him that she'd caught
glimpses of in their school days, before his parents died and
he'd become a fixture around her house. Of course, they'd
never really spent time together.

In part, because she was always flouncing away from
him in a snit about her father.

Huh. This might be the first time she'd ever taken even an ounce of responsibility for her behavior. She'd always just blamed Ace. For being there, being in the way, sucking up all Coach's time and attention.

"You know what else I'd do?" he was saying, his face aglow, eyes on the ceiling but mind far away. "I'd cut a little winding dirt road between your place and mi . . . this one. You could get to the lake in less than five minutes." Ace went silent for a moment. "Imagine that. Living right next to my brother. That'd be . . . That'd be somethin', anyway."

"Why Andrew Braddock, you almost sound homesick," Mia said softly. "Like a boy looking for a nest."

Ace looked startled at her words, then displeased. He reached over and grabbed her foot, pulling her down the couch toward him as she gave a squeal of protest. "Nest? Me? You're the one in need of a nest."

She laughed wildly as he pulled her feet right into his lap.

"What are you—whoa! What are you doing?"

She tried to free them for a second but gave in almost immediately. His big, capable hands were warm, so warm they almost burned through her socks. And then he started to rub the arch of one foot, skillfully, right where it hurt her at the end of a long day. "Ohhhh. That feels . . . so . . . *good.*"

"A coyote-proof nest," Ace added, working his way over every tiny muscle of her foot, blazing a path of pure bliss.

"What?"

He took over her other foot, and she didn't even try to pull it away. His hands were pure magic, and he seemed to know instinctively just where and how to touch her.

Mia lay back on the couch next to him, closed her eyes, and tried not to moan. She must look a sight. Her crazy red hair was loose and uncombed, she wore not a smudge of makeup, and she was too tired to care. "I can't let you do this," she managed to murmur.

"Sure you can," he murmured right back. "This is Easy Ace's Traveling Massage Parlor."

Mia wrinkled her nose. "That sounds really sleazy."

"It does, doesn't it?"

She waited for him to add something vile about providing happy endings, but he didn't. Shocker. Who was this guy? And what had he done with Ace?

"Okay," he said instead. "This is Drew's Foot Spa. Access by invitation only."

"How many members are there?" she teased.

"Only one. You."

Mia opened her eyes to find him smiling at her. "Oh, sure."

"I'm serious."

"What are the requirements for membership?"

Ace considered this for a moment. "Almost being eaten by a coyote."

He seemed to expect her to laugh, but she shivered instead. "That was really, truly scary. I don't know what I would have done if you hadn't come along."

Ace's blue eyes darkened. He set down her foot and reached for her hand instead. He tugged her upright and over before she could protest, and then snuggled her under his arm. His extremely muscled, warm arm. "I'm glad I got there when I did."

She sat there with him, thigh to thigh and side to side, feeling ridiculously comforted and protected and . . . oddly cherished. By Easy Ace Braddock, of all people. Her childhood nemesis.

She also felt electric and alive in a way she hadn't in years.

Which scared the living daylights out of her.

Mia should have tried to move away from him, but the delicious weight of that rock-solid arm made her hesitate, especially given the way he was looking at her, as if he'd like to . . .

Oh, no. That was so *not* going to happen.

And then Ace utterly shocked her by sweeping her into his lap and then maneuvering her right between his thighs, her back to him.

"What are you—*ohhhhhhh*," Mia breathed, as those incredible, strong, knowing fingers began to move in skillful circles over her neck and shoulders. "Oh my . . ."

"Shh," Ace said, as her head fell helplessly forward and she succumbed. "Just relax."

Mia did moan then, unable to stop herself.

A strange creak came from the kitchen, but neither of them paid any attention.

"That feel good?"

"Mmmmmmm. Ohhhhhh . . . don't stop. Please don't stop."

"Wow! Sounds like you two are making a porn flick out there," a deep male voice called from the kitchen.

Ace cursed as Mia shot, with a shriek, from between his thighs and at least three feet into the air.

"Jake?" Ace called. "What the hell are *you* doing here?"

Ace's brother Jake came out of the kitchen, looked at Mia making an idiot of herself while trying to detangle her body from Ace's, and then glanced back over his shoulder. "Well, guys, I think we can safely say that somebody got their signals crossed. Uh, maybe we ought to put that six-pack in the fridge for another time." The refrigerator door slammed.

Mia froze in place as Charlie walked into the living room after Jake, trailed by Rhett and Mia's best friend, Jules. *This is the part where I say this isn't what it looks like . . . except it almost was.*

Charlie looked fantastic, tanned with her blond hair loose around her shoulders. Jules sported her usual tied-up rooster-feather hair, but was wearing actual lip gloss (shocker) and pricey-looking dangly earrings that could only have come from Rhett. Her belly was swollen from her pregnancy, and Mia had to avert her eyes to hide the raw envy she couldn't help but feel.

Love sure looked good on those two.

Jules and Charlie glanced at each other and then down at Mia, who immediately gave her rucked-up shirt a good yank downward. Ace stretched out on the sofa, looking as relaxed as if he'd been the one getting the massage.

The guy was never fazed. A slight sinking sensation pooled in Mia's gut; Ace seemed as far from embarrassed as you could get. He almost looked . . . pleased. Did he consider her one of his conquests? Was that massage one of his techniques for getting women into his bed?

Charlie's eyebrows reached for the sky.

Jules mouthed *Sorry!*

"You didn't interrupt anything," Mia said crisply, smoothing her shirt.

"They don't look ready for Groovy Movie Motorcade," Charlie said to Jake.

"Well, they definitely don't look ready for a *G-rated* Groovy Movie Motorcade," Jake said.

Jules cocked her head. "Did you not get Charlie's e-mail?"

"I didn't send an e-mail. I thought you were going to," Charlie said. She looked at Ace. "We thought Mia might need help entertaining you, but . . . well . . . she, uh, seems to have things under control . . ."

Rhett coughed in a poor attempt to cover a laugh.

Mia's face went hot. Everybody was more dressed up than usual. Well, Rhett always looked dressed to kill when he went up to his office in Dallas, but the others were noticeably fancier than usual. Jules wore her good jeans, a silky sleeveless tunic top, and sandals with a hint of a *heel*. Charlie had on a floral summer dress and Jake had on a button-down with his jeans.

"You could have at least saved it for the back seat," Jules said.

"*We* get the back seat," Rhett said, giving her a suggestive look.

Jake looked at Charlie and tucked a strand of hair behind her ear. "Maybe we should all take separate cars," he murmured.

It finally dawned on Mia. The Groovy Movie Motorcade was a two-night event. Everyone got spiffed up for a date night and drove their cars and trucks out to a field outside town where the Silverlake City Council had set up a massive screen and a movie projector. Some of Silverlake's business owners dressed as old-school concessionaires and sold baked goods, popcorn, and drinks from trays.

Mia couldn't remember committing to that. Mia couldn't remember much beyond the sensation of Ace's hands working on her body. She looked at him, trying to figure out how much was Ace the man and how much was Ace the player.

Charlie's gaze flicked between Mia and Ace. "We can always go tomorrow . . ."

"I don't mind going twice," Jake said, tucking her into his side.

"Me neither," Jules said to Rhett. "As long as I can take off these shoes in the car."

"You can take off whatever you like," Rhett said.

"I definitely think you should take two cars," Ace said. "I think you should take them right now and get going because all this lovey-dovey is making my injury ache."

Even Mia had to laugh. "I'm so sorry there was a mix-up, but there's just no way I can go anywhere tonight. I'm beat." She gave Ace a smile, so grateful for the earlier rescue, and then realized too late how that must have sounded and looked to her friends.

Jules's eyes shifted from Mia to Ace, whom she examined with a weird intensity, and then back. She cocked her head in the direction of the back room. "Mia, could I have a word?"

Mia shrugged and followed Jules into the private area. "Is that a good idea?" Jules blurted, jerking her thumb in Ace's direction.

"Is what a good idea?"

Jules lowered her voice. "What's going on?"

A slow burn crept across Mia's face. "Nothing."

Jules crossed her arms over her chest. "I am so out of the loop."

"There's no loop!" But even as she said it, Mia knew that wasn't exactly true, and Jules had been her friend long enough to know the same.

"Ace was always a fun guy. A great guy, really."

He's been pretty great today.

Jules continued. "Obviously, I don't know him as an adult, but he's a Braddock, so I think it's safe to say that he's still a great guy."

Mia had to smile. Jules was so in love with Rhett Braddock and it hadn't worn off even a little since they'd married.

"But he's also a player."

"Jules—"

Jules raised a palm. "I know we haven't been as close lately . . . we're both so busy . . . but I'm still here for you. Always."

Mia put an arm around her dear friend. It wasn't just that they were busy, although that was certainly true. One of Jules's hands cradled her pregnant stomach. Jules had once asked if Mia wanted to adopt her baby. She obviously hadn't thought things through at the time, but the offer—and the near-instantaneous retraction—had changed things between them. It had been very painful for Mia, after her struggle for a baby with Rob.

So now Jules had Rhett, and a baby on the way. She was part of the Braddock family, and as close to Declan as Mia was, Mia wasn't a Braddock. She was an outsider. She was on her own, as always.

"We'll get together next week," Jules said earnestly, meaning it. But Mia was willing to bet they wouldn't. She followed Jules back into the living room. It all would have been so easy if she could only have fallen in love with Declan Braddock, instead of . . .

Whoa. Freudian slip. Mia looked at Ace, suddenly breathless.

He glanced up curiously, and then a slow grin spread over his face.

"Uhh . . . Sorry about the interruption," Jake said to Ace, pulling Charlie by the hand. Rhett gathered Jules in a protective embrace as Jules held her pinkie and thumb up to her ear. *Call me,* she mouthed, giving a somewhat too-obvious head thrust in Ace's direction. Mia smiled wanly.

And then in a bustle of giggles and smooches, everybody was back out the door.

"So, where were we?" Ace asked smoothly.

Mia stared down at him. "Don't do that," she said gently. "Just be you. I like you. I don't really know who that other guy is." She leaned over and kissed Ace on the forehead, wishing with all her might that she had the guts to press her lips to his, the way he'd done to hers after leaving the bar that night.

But he didn't move, just evaluated her with a thoughtful expression on his face.

"Good night, Drew."

"Night, Mia."

Mia grabbed her duffel bag from the kitchen and headed up the stairs, pulling it into the first empty room she found. Her dreams were not G-rated.

Chapter 18

MIA AWOKE WITH A START, UNABLE TO REMEMBER for a moment where she was. Then it came back to her: She was in a warm and comfortable bed at Silverlake Ranch. She was in what was clearly a boy's room, in a twin-sized bed that was made up with a quilt with bears and pine trees on it. The sheets were flannel and in coordinating colors of blue and green plaid. It looked mother-decorated. Who had occupied this room in the Braddock boys' youth?

She was so comfortable that she felt she could stay here forever. Except for her unexpected and very unwelcome attraction to Easy Ace. Her mind wandered back to the previous day—and night. So much had happened. So much had been said. It wasn't like her to reveal so much. Only Jules had known the full extent of her troubles with Rob and the reality of her awful living situation, and yet, suddenly . . . of all people, Ace now knew more than anybody! Mia weighed that fact in her mind. She'd thought he was just an empty-headed, ego-driven waste of space. But he'd rescued her, comforted her, listened to her, and made sure she had a safe place to stay. He'd reminded her to laugh.

Suddenly, life didn't feel quite so impossible. If she could just find Rob and get some of the money he owed her, life might very well feel like this all the time . . .

Except. This was what Ace Braddock did. He came in and he took over. He'd wrapped her father around his little finger and he was capable of doing the same to her if she didn't watch out. She happened to be on the winning end of his charismatic focus at the moment, but it wouldn't last. She'd be a fool to think it would.

The only person who could really make her life better wasn't Ace. She had to find Rob and free herself. Mia thought about Mrs. Baxter looking into her crystal ball. Finding Rob was her key to a better future.

She'd redouble her efforts, then. With that thought in mind, Mia slid out of bed. The floor was made of wide oak planks, cool under her bare feet. A simple, spare roll-top desk with a chair stood against one wall, a dresser against another. She put on yesterday's bra and dug into her duffel, which lay on a trunk at the end of the bed. She pulled out a pair of leggings, which she slipped on under the T-shirt she'd slept in. Then she went in search of a bathroom and coffee.

The bathroom was right next door and was also clearly mother-decorated for boys, in the same colors. Plaid shower curtain on an old-style tub. Stacks of navy and pine-green towels in open oak shelving, instead of a linen closet. A comic plush moose's head on the wall over the toilet, its antlers askew. It eyed her quizzically as she tried unsuccessfully to tame her riot of red hair before brushing her teeth.

She followed the smell of coffee down a hall framed with pictures of the Braddock children at all ages, stopping in front of one of Ace at bat. He was maybe twelve years old, with a terrible scraggly haircut under his cap, freckles dusting his nose, and an expression of fierce, unwavering concentration. Even though it was a full-length shot, the intense blue of his eyes was visible in that take-no-prisoners stare. It told every viewer that the ball would be his, that he'd hit it to the Milky Way and back.

Mia touched the outline of his firm young jaw with her index finger, wondering when Ace had gone from that player to a different kind of player: one who treated women as though they arrived in decks of fifty-two, ready to be shuffled.

Behind her, a floorboard creaked. She spun around to find a half-naked Ace lounging against a door frame, clearly amused. "Wasn't he a cutie pie?" he asked sardonically. He wore nothing but a pair of boxers.

Flustered, she went on the offensive. "*Was* being the operative word."

He adopted a tragic lost-puppy-dog expression. "You don't think I'm still cute?"

"You are many things, Ace," Mia said. "But no, cute isn't one of them." *You are so far beyond cute.*

"I'm devastated. You have to admit that I'm an excellent masseur, though." Ace grinned, stretched, and rubbed absently at his chest, which was . . .

Mia swallowed. No other word for Ace's chest: It was glorious. Bronzed, perfectly proportioned, framed by wide, massive shoulders that tapered down into biceps that could launch ad campaigns for a thousand workout supplements. Ace's chest was downright criminal in appeal. It did funny things to her insides that she absolutely refused to permit. She needed to look away from his torso right now, before she dissolved into a puddle of drool with only her lips floating on top.

"Mia?" Ace snapped his fingers. "You okay?"

She blinked. She was way too smart a girl to yearn after the likes of despicable Easy Ace Braddock. Because he was despicable—for many, many reasons. She just couldn't recall any of them at the moment. *Oh, Mia, you've got to tighten things up between the two of you. No more massages!*

"Coffee," she croaked. "Need coffee."

"So you're a morning person, then," Ace teased. "Let me show you the way to the kitchen."

"Could you . . . could you put on some clothes, first?" Mia asked, hating the note of pleading in her voice.

"Why?" Ace seemed genuinely perplexed.

"Because." Mia felt her face flame. "Because you and I have a professional relationship, and I think in the name of that you shouldn't be cruising around in front of me in your underwear."

"I have a professional relationship with my coaches and all the players on the Austin Lone Stars," Ace reminded her. "And that doesn't stop us from showering and changing in front of one another."

Mia desperately tried not to think of thirty hot, athletic, naked men in a major league locker room, and failed. "That's different."

"You're adorable when you blush," Ace noted.

"I'm not blushing," Mia muttered.

"You are."

"Coffee!" she said loudly, and lunged toward the stairs.

"I'd be happy to escort you, if you'll wait for me to find some pants."

"No!" Mia raced down the steps and followed the heavenly smell toward the kitchen, where she pulled up short at the sight of Declan, dressed for work already in faded denim, a T-shirt, and a plaid cotton shirt over it with the sleeves rolled up.

"Good morning," he said pleasantly. "Did you sleep well?"

"Yes, thanks." *Once I retreated firmly from the idea of Ace massaging more than my neck and shoulders . . .* "Did you?"

"Like a baby."

"In the fishing shack?"

Deck nodded.

"Um. Why are you sleeping out there?"

"Because Ace chaps my ass," he said matter-of-factly. He got a mug from a cabinet and handed it to her.

She nodded her thanks and approached the coffeepot, pouring herself a full cup.

"I know you understand," Declan added, "since he does the same to you."

She nodded silently, but then felt bad about that for some reason. Disloyal. Which was ridiculous and uncalled-for.

Deck took a sip of his coffee. "Ace is too big for his own britches, and he's definitely too big for Silverlake."

Ouch. Mia actually found herself wanting to defend him. She opened her mouth to do just that.

"Thanks so much, Declan," Ace said loudly behind her.

She jumped, sloshing coffee over the side of her mug.

Unperturbed, Deck just raised an eyebrow. "You're welcome. Did I say anything that's not true?"

"My britches fit just fine." Ace's voice was a little too even. So casual that it hurt. "And as for Silverlake, it's real nice paying a visit. Trippin' down memory lane."

"Too bad about the circumstances." Deck drained his coffee, rinsed the mug, and put it in the dishwasher, ignoring the tense atmosphere.

"We'll talk later," Ace promised him.

"Sure. Gotta get to work now." And with that, the older brother departed.

"So I chap your ass, do I?" Ace glowered down at Mia.

"I didn't say that."

"Yeah. I noticed that you didn't refute it, either." He grabbed a mug and poured himself some fuel.

"I didn't really have a chance . . ." But that was weak, and she knew it. "Look. I'm going to take a shower. And then I need to check on my dad. You want to come along?"

"Fine."

"Great." Mia took her coffee and all but sprinted back to the stairs.

❧

They went through the usual comedy routine of cramming Ace into the tiny car, with crutches sticking out the window. Mia got his door shut, then pulled out her phone and snapped a couple of pictures.

"Those better not turn up on any social media feed," Ace growled at her.

She grinned. "No promises."

"I mean it."

Mia ignored him and zipped out of the driveway, with Grouchy following and barking as though begging them to stay.

"Go play with Cat!" Ace called to him.

Grouchy looked less than thrilled with this idea but eventually stopped chasing them and went back to the porch.

Within minutes, Mia pulled into Coach's driveway, and it was time to get Ace extricated again.

"I have an idea," he said as she lifted the crutches through the window, opened the door, and offered him a hand he ignored. "Why don't I rent a comfortable car for you for the duration of my time, here?"

"Waste of money," she said. "My car is fine."

"Says you," Ace groused.

"Sorry I don't drive a limo. Suck it up and slum with me."

"I never said I needed a limo. And I'd hardly call your company 'slumming.'"

"Yeah, I guess it's not really slumming, since I'm the help." Mia handed him his crutches.

"You know, I was trying to be nice—but you ruined it."

"Don't be nice," she shot back. "It confuses me."

"We were getting along so well last night," he said provocatively.

"Last night I had almost had my face ripped off by a coyote. So don't read anything into that back rub, Drew."

"'Ohhhh . . . don't stop. Please don't stop,'" he quoted, smirking at her. "I believe those were your very words."

"And I just told you that my judgment was impaired. Coyote adrenaline. Now don't bring any of this up in front of my dad." Mia turned her back on him and headed for the front door, leaving Ace to hobble after her.

Stetson met her just inside, barking and showing off some Austin Lone Stars gear: a bandanna and a silver star dangling from his collar. "Hi there, boy," she crooned, picking him up. He wriggled and licked her face, making funny little grunting noises, while Mia tried not to be hurt that he wasn't even wearing the Red Sox gear she'd sent for him.

But then she smiled evilly as he put his paws on her shoulder and barked ferociously at Ace, who came in behind her. "Yes, you tell the guy exactly what you think of him, sweetie."

Stetson just cocked his little head, so Mia mentally filled in the blanks: *Protective. Sexy as hell. Unexpectedly sweet . . .*

Mia watched her father's face turn toward them, the way he lit up entirely when he saw Ace enter the room.

But also: *Intruder. Interloper. Father-thief.*

Even as she was starting to consider the possibility that she'd royally misjudged Ace, that maybe she hadn't given him enough credit for being a good guy, the moment he stepped into the living room of her father's home was like a trigger.

She wanted to take Ace away from here as quickly as they'd arrived, make up some excuse that he was tired . . . his ankle . . . anything! But she knew that her dad would want to see his boy as much as he could while he had the chance . . . and she felt torn between giving him what he wanted and trying hopelessly, once again, to *be* what he wanted. Her mouth twisted.

Her dad heaved himself off the sofa in the den and came to greet them. "Ace! What a nice surprise! And hello there, honey." He dutifully bussed her cheek before turning back to the Boy Wonder. "How's the ankle? You keeping up the workouts?"

"Yeah, sure. Almost good as new," Ace said. And then they immediately launched into a deep conversation about the latest major league stats.

Mia remembered how, at age fourteen, she'd rattled off

the batting averages of every Texas Rangers player just to impress her father. And he'd patted her awkwardly on the shoulder, while eyeing her as if she had three heads. "That's . . . just great, honey. You go get ready for ballet, now, okay?"

She'd hated ballet with a passion. And piano, too. Lessons that her grandmothers had enrolled her in during yet another of her mother's absences. Coach had agreed. Mom hadn't been around, as usual. And so that was the end of that.

Mia went into the kitchen to empty the dishwasher, glaring at the picture of her mother that had been on the counter next to the toaster for as long as she could remember. Since Mom had gone off on her first humanitarian trip with the children's medical aid group she'd helped found, and left the photo there as a poor substitute for her presence.

She'd cut her long brown hair short in preparation for the trip, leaving them speechless. Her eyes shone with excitement. She smiled out from the frame at them lovingly, which made it hard to hate her for being gone, leaving them both behind as she bounced from continent to continent.

Mia grabbed a stack of clean plates and put them into their cabinet with more force than necessary as the guys kept on blathering enthusiastically in the next room.

Why aren't you here to do this? she asked the photo of her mom. *Why do I always feel that I have to be you for Dad? Not me? Why isn't it good enough for me to be me?*

Not that he wanted her. He'd always wanted a boy.

What is so wrong with me that you had to leave us for more important things? she asked the silent photo of her mother. *Caring for hundreds of children instead of the two of us?*

But Mom didn't answer, and immediately Mia felt guilty. How could she hate a saint? As a nurse, she even understood the calling. Nobody she knew did more for needy kids than Moira Adams.

Just not her own needy kid.

Mia pulled out a jangling handful of silverware and

mechanically shoved each fork, knife, and spoon into its respective slot in the relevant drawer.

"Have you seen that new player on the Astros? The one out of Baylor?" her dad exclaimed from the other room.

"Martinez? Yeah—what an arm. They clocked him at ninety-seven miles per hour . . ."

Baseball. Always baseball. Their grand passion.

She pulled out a few coffee mugs and slid them home into their cabinet over the coffeepot. It was good for her dad to have Ace here. He needed something in his life since he'd retired.

Yeah, like a wife who was in the U.S. and in his life every once in a while. Not skipping around the globe trying to be the second coming of Mother Teresa.

She'd once asked him why he didn't divorce her mother.

Her dad had looked down into the depths of his Shiner Bock bottle as if it held the answers to the secrets of the universe. Then he'd looked up at her again, and there might have been a tear or two in his eyes. "Because I love her," he said gruffly.

"But she's never here!" Mia exploded.

"That don't mean I don't love her," her dad said simply.

"Well, she doesn't behave as if she loves *you*—or me." She hated the bitterness in her own voice. "Like a normal wife. A normal mother."

"Mia." Her dad sat forward in his La-Z-Boy. "Ain't nothin' normal about your mom. She's the most incredible woman I've ever met. She lives her ideals. She has oceans of love to offer continents of kids. She's . . . bigger . . . than this. This town. This life."

"But I don't want her to be! And you don't, either."

Her father shook his head sadly. "She can't help being who she is. When she feels she's done enough to make a difference, honey, she will come back. I know it."

Mia stared at him angrily. *You're lying to yourself.* But she didn't have the nerve to say it aloud. She didn't want to break his heart.

Dear Mom, she'd written that day.

Where are you? When are you coming back? We miss you. We need you. It's not fair for you to be gone all the time . . .

And this had resulted in a phone call.

"Mia. You know exactly where I am, and I sent pictures. I'll be back when I'm back. I miss you, too, sweetie pie. But you have been a hardy, pragmatic, and centered little soul ever since you were born. You came out of my womb wise. You came out self-sufficient. I know you: You will always be fine. You don't need anyone to coddle you."

"But it's not fair!"

Silence. And then, "Mia, do you imagine that life is *fair* to anyone? Let me tell you a little about fairness: You have a roof over your head to shelter you, and plenty of food to eat. You go to an excellent school and you live in a safe neighborhood. You have parents who love you. You live in the richest country in the world, and you go about your days without fear that a horde of people from the neighboring town will attack you and kill your family."

All this was irrefutable. Mia sniffled.

"So," Moira continued. "Your life is much more than fair, sweetie pie. The lives of the kids I help? Not so much. They're starving, malnourished, orphaned, and unschooled— often with nobody to care about them except for people like me. Do you understand?"

"Yes," Mia said after a long pause. Because it was clearly the thing she was supposed to say—not because she wanted to say it.

"Good," her mother said in tones of finality. Tones that said the discussion was now over, because she was done with it. "I love you, sweet girl."

"Love you, too," said Mia, feeling anything but sweet. Feeling angry still, and resentful—and also guilty for feeling those things. Feeling ultimately unheard, her emotions dismissed.

"Will you put your father on the phone now?"

* * *

Mia returned to the present because of male shouts from the other room; Dad and Ace were yelling encouragement to a player in a game on television who couldn't hear them.

Why couldn't anyone yell encouragement to her? *Go, Mia! Milk another goat. Sell another few candles and lotions to scrape up another lousy two hundred bucks to pay that mortgage! Dig out Rob from whatever rock he's under and squeeze him for his half of the money before the bank forecloses on the mansion that you never wanted in the first place! Yay, Mia! You do an awesome job of taking care of your elderly patients: bathing them, clipping toenails, changing dressings and diapers, wiping private parts . . .*

Wouldn't that be nice?

Stop it, she told herself. *You are in danger of succumbing to a bad attitude and becoming a grouch. Which only drives people away and makes life worse.*

She finished cleaning up the kitchen and went to check on the laundry. A putrid, moldy smell came from the washer. She opened the door to discover that her father had forgotten to put the wet clothes from the other day into the dryer. She sighed: They now had to be rewashed.

She started the load, then went to change the sheets on her dad's bed.

As she pulled off the comforter, her cell phone rang from her purse in the other room.

She had assigned a specific—and ominous—ringtone to contacts related to her search for Rob, so she sprinted for her phone and fished it out just in time. It was the PI she had tracking him down.

"Hello?" Mia said breathlessly, over the noise of the game. She flapped a hand at the guys to mute it. "Franco, is that you? Any luck?"

Both Ace's and Coach's heads swiveled in her direction. Ace's eyes widened slightly at the expression on her face, and he turned off the sound.

She listened to the brief update. "Rob is in *Costa Rica*?" she repeated. "Does the US have extradition or whatever there?" She slumped into the easy chair next to the sofa.

Franco explained to her that he could go down there and get documentation and photos of the house Rob had bought with money that was half hers; even try to reason with him and bring him back. But it would cost a mint—a mint she didn't have. It would be cheaper to get a local to try.

"Um. Okay," said Mia, miserably. What else could she say? "Thanks, Franco. Yes, please hire a local for the next step."

She hung up to find both Ace and Coach squinting at her.

"That turd is in Costa Rica?" her father asked.

Mia nodded.

"What's he doing down there?"

She sent him a speaking glance.

Ace's eyes widened. "Eating tamales?" he asked in a reverent voice, obviously thinking about Mrs. Baxter's prediction.

Mia pressed her lips together. If Mrs. Baxter really wanted to be helpful, maybe she could conjure up a handful of Costa Rican currency. Her mood darkened, if that was even possible. What was wrong with her? Her own mother hadn't stuck around to see her grow up. Her father wanted a boy, not her. She hadn't been able to hold on to her husband. And she couldn't even have a child of her own to love. She had clearly been made on a Friday at five P.M. on the way to happy hour.

"I never did like Rob," Coach announced.

"Neither did I," agreed Ace.

Great. Now these two lunkheads in the living room were calling her stupid for falling for him. *Stop, Mia. They're trying to be supportive—albeit in a pathetic lunkhead sort of way.*

"Hey," said Ace to Coach. "Wanna take a trip down to South America and kick his butt?"

"Sounds good."

"Excuse me," Mia told them politely. "Nobody is flying down there to do any such thing. I have an investigator on it, and I'm taking care of it myself—with the least amount of fuss and embarrassment possible. But thanks."

"It'd be so much more satisfying to go caveman on him, though." Ace gazed at her hopefully.

"Right," she said acerbically. "You're going to go skipping through the rain forest with your crutches, guided by a toucan, and Dad's going to wheeze and huff behind you, dragging his CPAP. This is a wonderful idea, guys. Really."

"Just trying to help," Ace said mildly.

"Thank you," Mia reiterated. "I appreciate the thought. But I'm a grown woman, and I don't need a rescue."

Coach cleared his throat, as if to disagree.

She shot him a warning glance.

With a shrug, her father hit the MUTE button and filled the room again with the baseball game.

He and Ace turned back to it, as if nothing more important on the planet was happening, while Mia swallowed her frustration and her sense of being an outsider in her family home.

Soon they were shouting again, reviewing the stats of different players, and placing bets on the outcomes of upcoming games.

Mia would have loved to join in, sit down right between them. But she knew from long experience that it ruined the dynamic—she didn't know why. If she had to guess, it somehow made Coach feel guilty for his emotions toward Ace the Wonder Boy, the son he'd never had. And it interrupted Ace's bonding time with the man he'd turned to in crisis, when he'd lost his own parents.

Stetson sat on her father's lap, occasionally looking up and baring his teeth at Ace, bless him. Mia decided that they didn't get the dog, too. She walked in, scooped him up, and snapped his leash on, while he went nuts at the prospect of a walk.

At least the Yorkie wanted to hang out with her.

Mia missed Jules. She thought about calling her, following up on their pledge to do something soon. But given how she felt, she wasn't sure she wanted to talk baby stuff right now. *Ugh. That is the last depressing thought I'm going to have today. I swear. I'm a terrible person. I'm mad at my mother for helping sick orphans. I'm jealous of an orphaned kid for spending time with my father. I'm sick with envy that my best friend is pregnant with the baby that I wanted more than anything in the world . . . What is wrong with me?*

As she went out the door with an ecstatic Stetson, she felt Ace's gaze on her.

What are you looking at? She turned and met his eyes.

His expression was thoughtful, even sympathetic. Which was intolerable. Ace was the last person on the planet she wanted to feel sorry for her. "Enjoy the game, guys," she said crisply. "Stetson and I will be back in a while."

Chapter 19

ACE FOUND HIS ATTENTION WANDERING FROM THE game, where the Orioles were soundly thrashing the opposing team, outstrategizing and outplaying them. He found himself analyzing some weird things, such as the defeated and resigned set of Mia's shoulders and the quick, I-don't-care tuck of her hair behind her ears before she hustled out Stetson and his little attitude problem, as if she needed him for comfort of some kind.

He even pondered the way she'd shut the door: It wasn't as angry as a slam, but it wasn't a calm, normal click of the latch, either. It was the firm placement of a barrier between her, outside, and them, inside.

He tossed around these signals in the primitive-lizard part of his brain while he also examined Coach's demeanor and his craggy, weary face. Coach's shoulders were a bit hunched, in a defensive sort of way. He kept tugging on his left earlobe as if it held the key to an inner voice that would respond with wisdom of some kind. And every once in a while, he'd gaze over at a picture of Mia at about age ten,

stuffed into a pink ballerina tutu and looking sullen—
which was terrifically hard for a freckled, sunny little redhead to do. She'd always been cute as a button, bright and
funny. But in this photo, she looked a little as though she'd
like to bite the photographer. She made no effort to suck in
her tummy, and Ace could tell that the wobbly smile she
wore had been very recently teased out of a scowl.

The picture made Ace want to laugh. But Coach's mouth
worked a little as he looked at it, as if it troubled him.

"Cute snapshot," Ace said.

"She hated ballet. But both of her grandmothers . . ."
Coach sighed. "I thought they knew best. What did I know
about raising a little girl?"

Ace found himself wondering what Declan had known
about raising kids at all. And yet he'd stepped up to the
plate. Swung and missed sometimes. Hit foul balls. And
they'd all sneered at Deck for trying to take Pop's place.
Resented him for it. Pretty unfair of them.

"Coach. I've never asked you this. It's none of my business. But why did, ah, Mrs. Adams—I mean, why *does* she
travel so much?"

He half expected Coach to bite his head off.

But his mouth only twisted.

They sat in silence for a moment, and Ace wondered if
Coach'd answer at all.

"We had one helluva fight about it one time," Coach
confessed. "About how she could leave us to go take care
of strangers. But Moira is a force of nature. It was like trying to stop a tornado with my bare hands. I'll never forget
what she said to me that day: *There are no strangers.* That
we are all connected, we are all bound by love that we cannot allow to curdle into hatred."

Coach's face was curiously, carefully blank. As if he
was willing himself not to feel.

After another long pause, he said, "She's right."

Ace thought about it.

"I miss her," Coach said next. "Sometimes I hate her for

being gone. But how do you hate a woman with a heart that big?"

Ace didn't know how to respond to that.

"What was I gonna do, divorce her for spreading love and hope? Providing medical aid to desperate people? Divorce her for being who she is? I couldn't do that—I *can't* do that."

"But what about Mia?" Ace felt the stirrings of unexpected anger in his gut. Outrage for a little girl who'd essentially been abandoned by her mother.

"Mia's never known anything different. This is her normal. She's so strong. So self-sufficient and competent. Taking care of other people, you know—like a different, more domestic version of her mama. She don't waste time crying. Never has." Coach shrugged. "Guess she got that from me."

No, Coach hadn't wasted any time crying. Ace could see that. But the woman he loved had gone to save the world instead of staying by his side. And maybe he'd tolerated that, resigned and bewildered, but he'd compensated by becoming detached.

Ace had a flash of unwanted insight. Coach seemed to love his daughter the same way: from behind a batting cage he'd erected to prevent injury.

He'd met Ace inside that cage—a smaller version of him, with the same interests and drive. The same bottomless need. Ace had lost his parents. Coach had lost his wife and couldn't risk losing his heart to the daughter who'd only grow up and leave him, too.

Insight sucked.

Ace tried to shove it away, back to wherever it had come from. But it wasn't budging.

Mia . . .

She'd grown up without her mother.

And he, Ace, had unwittingly taken her father away, too.

Dad! Dad! I can throw the ball as far as he can. Look! Mia at age eleven.

She'd had a great arm—truly, as good as his—until nature took its course and made him physically bigger and stronger than her.

That's awesome, honey. Now go on in the house and help Grannie Mel in the kitchen.

Ace recalled Mia's freckled face falling, her smile congealing. And his own unconscious smugness that he got to keep basking in the sunshine of Coach's attention.

He no longer felt smug. He felt guilty. And restless.

"Coach, I'm going to go out for some air."

His mentor looked up and gave him a little sideways squint. "O-kaay."

"Be back in a few." Ace grabbed his crutches and stepped out the door just in time to see Mia bending over to scoop Stetson's little by-products into a green plastic disposable bag, while Stetson scuffed his back legs proudly as if claiming praise for a major achievement.

But he whirled to hurl insults at Ace in high-pitched dog-speak, with comical ferocity.

"Thanks, little cowboy. I feel the same way about you." He shoved his crutches up under his arms and started gimping across the street to them.

Mia grimaced as she tied a knot in the bag. Then she wound up and pitched it perfectly all the way into Coach's open trash can, which stood next to his driveway. She still had her great arm.

"Nice," Ace said with admiration.

She sighed. "Don't patronize me."

"I'm not. Really." He stood there evaluating her stance and expression. The way she held herself: perfect posture that admitted to nobody that she carried the weight of the world on her shoulders, without complaint and without help. The warm, if challenging smile that stretched across her face and held self-pity at bay. Every freckle on her face reflected competence and cheerfulness, without a hint of the loneliness that his knowing her better now revealed.

He searched for the right words to tell her what he urgently wanted her to know. "Mia. I . . . You know how much I care about your dad."

Her smile went a little lopsided.

"He was there for me during the worst time of my life. He was my anchor. He kept me focused on something other than my total devastation at the loss of my parents."

She nodded. "I'm glad he was there for you," she said briskly.

"Stop it."

"Stop what?"

"Brushing it aside."

"I don't mean to do that, Ace. But . . . everyone knows this. How Coach took you under his wing, the orphaned kid. Everybody understands. You don't need to bring it up."

"I don't care about everyone. I want *you* to understand what that meant to me. To have a place to go after school. To have someone who cared."

"You had Declan," she reminded him, with an edge to her voice. "Your brothers and sister. They've always cared."

"Deck was learning on the job. He barely knew how to be an adult, much less a father."

"But he—"

"Just like you."

"*Excuse* me?" Mia's eyes flashed.

"You had to be an adult too young." Ace gave a chuckle devoid of humor. "I finally *see* both of you, after all these years. I'm a little thick, though. So it's taken me a while."

"See what?"

"That you were both . . . struggling."

She picked up Stetson and tucked him under her arm like a weapon, triggering the little dog to hurl more insults at Ace. "Thanks for your assessment."

"Mia—that wasn't meant as a hostility."

"Well, it's surely not a compliment!" She started to walk away.

"It's high praise, in my awkward, bungling way. I don't know a finer man in Texas than my brother Declan."

She stopped, her back still to him.

"He's a stoic. He doesn't run from anything. He's smart, he's tough, he's caring, he's damn near selfless. And all my

life, I've avoided his clear gaze, his judgment. He saw too
much and he asked for too little. He swallowed whatever
bitter pill life handed him—dry, without water. Like
you, Mia."

Her entire body quivered.

"I . . . I never realized what a bitter pill I must have been
to you. You didn't have your mom. And there I was, camp-
ing out at your house and eating your food and taking up
your space and stealing your own father."

Her head went down and she cradled Stetson. Then she
straightened her shoulders once again. "Ace, there's no
point in—"

"You choked it all down dry."

"I was a brat to you."

"I'm sorry, Mia." His voice went husky, without his permission. "I really, truly am."

❧

Mia didn't know what to do with this version of Ace Braddock. She preferred the shallow playboy she could scorn.
The one who strutted through his celebrity life without a
care or a thought for anyone else—much less a heartfelt
apology.

She opened her mouth to say what a reasonable person
does when apologized to: *It's okay.* But was it?

The two words simply wouldn't come out. It was as
though her mouth was paralyzed and couldn't form the letters. She chalked it up to shock and shut her mouth again.

Meanwhile, Ace seemed fixated on her lips, waiting for
her response: her forgiveness. His whole expression was
tense; those blue eyes, normally lit by easy humor, were
troubled.

She managed to clear her throat and find her voice. "I—
I don't know what to say, Ace. Thank you."

Disappointment washed over his face.

"The thing is . . . it's not just you. It was never just you.
It's my dad."

"Yeah," Ace said softly. "I know."

"He doesn't mean to, but he—he *lives* through you."

Ace swallowed. "Mia, I never intended—"

"I know you didn't, Ace." Tears prickled and stung in her eyes.

He noticed and seemed appalled by them.

Mia blinked them away. "You shouldn't apologize to me. You needed him, and he needed you. It's that simple."

"But if I hadn't been there, taking up all of his time and attention—"

She shook her head. "He would have directed it somewhere else. He can't bond with me. He doesn't know how to relate to a girl." She got the words out calmly, even though they felt like bricks in her mouth. She stacked them in front of Ace so that he'd focus on them, and not on the fact that she couldn't tell him that just because he'd apologized, everything was okay.

It wasn't.

But she didn't know what to do about it.

And she did appreciate him noticing and caring.

Who knew that Easy Ace had a conscience? It appeared that there was even a soul buried underneath his impossible good looks and good fortune and talent.

But Mia wasn't sure she could handle a discovery like that.

"I'm sorry," Ace said again.

She put her hand on his arm to acknowledge the words, and Stetson barked. "Stets!" she said sharply. "Stop it. Ace is a friend. FRIEND, Stetson."

The Yorkie looked up at her dubiously, but subsided.

"I *am* a friend," Ace said, but to her, not the dog.

She met his level blue gaze and knew he meant it.

Something shifted and softened in her as they went back inside to Coach and the blaring baseball game.

Her father was now sprawled back in his La-Z-Boy with his feet up. He nodded as they came back in and took a pull on his beer. Mia felt a rush of frustration and resentment toward him, as well as the affection she always felt.

Ace had figured things out, had felt remorseful, had hobbled outside and across the street to her in an attempt to make things right. But it looked as though her dad never would. And 50 percent of the problem lay squarely in his lap, on that ugly chair.

Ace settled himself down on the sofa again.

"I'm going to make a phone call," Mia told them. And she went outside on her dad's little screened back porch to call Jules.

"Hey, Mrs. Braddock," she said, when her friend answered.

"Don't call me that," Jules protested.

"Why? It happens to be true," Mia teased. "You did marry Rhett not so long ago."

"Because it's *weird*."

"Mrs. Ever-Rhett Braddock."

"Stop! And I don't think you get to give me a hard time, considering what we all walked in on last night. I was just about to call you."

"Jules, that's a total misunderstanding. Ace was giving me a back rub. That's it."

"Some back rub. You were practically having an or—"

"No, I wasn't! Leave it, Jules."

"Fine, Miss Prickly. But I also hear that you've *moved in* to Silverlake Ranch. What on earth happened?"

"Ace rode a horse to my house—" Mia began.

"With a fractured ankle? Is he an idiot?"

"Sometimes. But a coyote got in through a rip in the tarps. It was about to attack me. So it's a really good thing that he showed up when he did, idiot or not."

"He *saved* you? That's so romantic."

Mia snorted. "It was actually really scary."

"And then you rode off into the sunset with him on the horse?"

"No, you goof. It wasn't a Hallmark movie. The horse panicked and ran home in the thunderstorm. We fired up my car and drove."

"How did you get Ace into that thing?" Jules asked.

"Carefully."

Jules hooted. "And he refuses to let you go back there to the Half a House."

"Pretty much."

"That's really sweet."

Mia was quiet for a moment. "He's not all bad."

"Did I just hear you say that? And you let him give you a back rub, too? Seriously, what's going on?"

"Nothing. He's just . . . not like I remembered him. Not totally."

"How do you mean?"

"He just *apologized* to me. For stealing my dad." Mia said. "It was so out of character. And I can tell he means it. That's the strangest thing of all."

"Huh. So did you accept his apology?"

"I don't know."

There was a pause as Jules considered this. "How can you not know something like that?"

Mia sighed. "I'm thinking about it. I'm still shocked. I appreciate that he did it. But it doesn't change anything. He and Coach are inside right now, doing their male-bonding thing as usual."

"Why haven't you ever said anything to your dad?"

Mia squirmed and changed the subject, not subtly. "So how are you feeling?"

Jules gave a snort, making it clear she wasn't fooled for a second. Still, she followed Mia's lead. "Fat, tired, and spacey. With cravings for onion rings and strawberry ice cream at the same time, which is disgusting."

Mia laughed.

"And Rhett hired another hand because he doesn't want me digging out stalls in my condition."

"That's great."

"No, it isn't, because it makes me feel lazy and entitled when other people do my work."

"Jules, honey? You're pregnant." Mia said the word carefully, because it still held so much pain for her. "And once you become a mother, you won't have one second to feel lazy or entitled, because you will belong, body and soul, to your baby. So just accept the help."

Her friend was quiet for a moment. Then she sighed. "All right. But I have to do something with the other half of my day. Do you need help with your lip glosses or lotions or candles?"

"Always."

"Okay. Get your supplies together, and I'll be out to the ranch in the next couple of days. Any luck tracking down the dirtbag?"

"Sort of. I just found out he's in Costa Rica."

"That's progress!" Jules exclaimed.

"I suppose I should be more excited, but it's just the first stage. I'm going to have to hire a local guy to help."

"Help do what? Break his kneecaps?"

Mia forced a laugh. "Talk to him. Reason with him."

"Good luck with that. Hope you know that if it comes to murder, I have pitchforks and a lot of muck out at the stables to hide the body in."

"Jules."

"Just sayin'."

"I appreciate that," Mia said dryly. "But no. I need him alive and able to give me a cashier's check."

"What about the girlfriend? Can we off her?"

"Jeez. Pregnancy makes you bloodthirsty, Jules! No murders."

"Oh, c'mon. We could at least plot them for fun . . ."

"Trust me, I have."

Chapter 20

IT WAS A WEEK BEFORE FRANCO'S LOCAL CONTACT called Mia's cell phone. She glanced at it and then did a double take, bobbling the handset. "It's a foreign number." Her heart absolutely raced as a whoosh of adrenaline shot through her system. "Oh, gosh . . . hello? Please don't hang up. I'm here! Hello . . . I mean, *¿hola?*"

Ace stood up, his eyes searching her face.

A rush of Spanish came at her on the other end of the line. "Señor Azevedo? Señor, is that you? I can't . . . *por favor*, please talk slower. I can't . . . I don't speak Spanish, and I . . ." He might hang up on her before she could get the information. Racking her brain for the right Spanish words, she started to panic, but then her eyes suddenly locked with Ace's.

A rush of calm stopped her in her tracks.

Ace held out his hand for the phone, mouthing something: *Trust me.*

He wasn't ordering her around or trying to joke the situation away. He was just there, offering his hand like a lifeline. *"Un momento, señor,"* Mia said in broken Spanish, never tearing her gaze away from the man in front of her.

Ace cupped her cheek with one hand and put the headset to his ear.

"Buenos tardes, Señor Azevedo. Soy un amigo de Mia . . ." And a torrent of fluent Spanish flew from his lips like the most beautiful song Mia had ever heard. Ace grabbed a pad of paper and a pen, making notes as he talked and listened.

She'd seen Andrew Braddock take charge of things before. She'd seen him bring a town full of casserole-bearing admirers to their knees. She'd seen him make the craziest things happen. And she'd seen him full of unrelenting certainty that everything was going to be okay, even when everyone else doubted him. Mia thought about how many times his can-do, self-assured, almost over-the-top enthusiasm had seemed impossible to fathom. Now, she saw things differently. Life had knocked him down hard when he lost his parents. He could've stayed down. Instead, he'd turned himself into someone who looked for solutions. Sometimes those solutions involved tractors and a cocky grin. Sometimes, all he needed was words.

This was what it would be like if he were her man, on her side, boosting her up when she couldn't go on alone.

Before her stood a good leader. A good *man*.

Mia leaned on the back of the couch, shaking.

Ace turned toward her, still on the phone. His eyes met hers once more.

She took a deep breath, her hand over her heart.

Ace held out the notes to Mia. "I think I got everything you need for now. Is there anything else you want me to ask?"

She scanned the notes; he *had* covered everything. She shook her head, wanting to cry more now than she had when she had been frustrated.

Ace spoke for another few minutes; she saw him take out his own cell and plug in contact information, and then after confirming that Mia didn't have anything further, he hung up.

They stood silently for a moment. "I also gave him my personal phone number since . . . I speak Spanish . . ." He frowned. "Not trying to overstep. I just . . . Is that cool?"

"Is that cool?" Mia asked. She shook her head no. It was beyond "cool." It was beyond mere words. All at once she closed the space between them and grabbed a fistful of Ace's T-shirt. Stepping up on her toes, she kissed him with everything she had in her.

Beneath her lips, Ace experienced a moment of shock and then instant acquiescence. He took over, driving her backward until she hit the wall, and then deepened the kiss.

When they finally broke apart, it was only to take a deep breath and then Ace's fingers were tangled in her hair, his body pressing hard against her own.

He took her mouth again as she melted into him, her curves fitting perfectly against all the hard planes of his athletic physique. He slid his fingers out of her hair and cupped her face gently between his hands, his fingers warm and tender against her cheeks.

And then one of the wide oak front doors opened and Declan walked in. He froze when he saw them, and they both sprang apart.

Mia's face was flash-fried.

Ace looked stunned.

"I—ah . . . was just looking for Mia," Deck said in gruff tones.

Mia stared at Declan in a daze. "Oh, hi, Declan!" she said loudly and somewhat ridiculously.

Ace's eyes still looked glazed.

Declan looked between the two of them, his expression unreadable, which wasn't necessarily a good sign. "There's plenty of fresh beeswax for your candles," he said. "You'd mentioned maybe having a table at Founder's Day?"

"Great!" she said, overenthusiastically. "I'll just go get my supplies. In fact, I was just leaving. To do that." She lunged for her purse and cell phone. "No time like the present. I'll be back. Soon. Back soon with the . . . stuff . . ." She hurtled out the door that Deck hadn't even closed yet. "Bye!"

* * *

Ace gazed after Mia as she threw herself into her little car and fired up the three angry squirrels under its hood. If Declan hadn't been watching him so closely, he'd have allowed himself the luxury of looking as gobsmacked as he actually was. That kiss . . .

That kiss! What the hell was happening here?

His body felt electrified; his mind was reeling.

If there'd ever been a doubt that Mia wanted him, she'd erased in it in a second. No matter what she claimed, no matter what denials she was conjuring up right this very second, she wanted him as much as he wanted her.

More than that, Mia Adams was starting to forget how to hate him. Things between them were changing. Ace touched the pads of his fingers to his lips. That kiss was real. It was different. He felt different around her.

He watched Declan shut the door.

The reason it's different with her is because it's real. Those baseball bunnies aren't real. What was between them and me in bed wasn't real.

Declan cleared his throat; Ace focused on his brother, who shot him a long, thoughtful glance. "Drew. Let's you and me find something to eat among the current fifty casseroles that these fans of yours keep bringing, and have a talk."

Ace finally found his voice. "I'm not sure I like the sound of that."

"Humor me." Declan walked into the kitchen and opened the fridge, which was still exploding with every kind of casserole and dessert known to the great state of Texas. "Not gonna lie; I eat a lot better when you're around."

There was Tex-Mex spaghetti, Frito pie, enchiladas, steak chili, sausage-and-kraut bake, and chicken-fried steak over mashed potatoes with gravy. There was also something that looked so peculiar that Ace laughed and pointed at it.

"What in the Sam Hill is that?"

Deck squinted at it. "I'm not sure."

"It just looks plain *wrong*."

Deck slid it out and they stared as it quivered and shivered on its plate. It was alien green Jell-O with weird white and orange shreds in it. "I think it's alive." He shoved it toward Ace, who almost fell over backward trying to get away from it. The tension sloughed off his shoulders as Deck started laughing.

"Look, there's a tag on it," Ace said. "'Perfection Salad. Please return plate to Mrs. Dolly Dufresne.' Who's that?"

"Mrs. Dolly Dufresne is the widow of Elmer Dufresne, who used to be mayor of Silverlake about fifty years ago."

"Oh, right . . . I remember some kids calling him Elmer the Doof. Poor guy."

"Poor guy is right, if she used to make him eat this stuff." Deck stared at its glistening, quivering, unnatural green surface. And suddenly, he grinned. "I double-dog dare you, Andrew Braddock, to eat a big honkin' piece of this."

Ace shuddered, but he'd never backed down from a dare in his life and wasn't about to start now. "I will if you will."

Declan's dark eyes sparked with mischief, and suddenly they were kids again—the older brother egging on the younger. He pulled a spatula from a drawer, got out two plates, and cut each of them a hunk of the evil-looking stuff.

Ace limped over to the kitchen table and sat. Deck plopped a plate in front of him and sat down in another chair with the other one. They looked down and poked at the goop at the same time with their forks, then laughed. Holding each other's gazes, the brothers dug in and lifted the "food" to their mouths simultaneously.

They also gagged simultaneously. But both swallowed.

It was coleslaw—with sliced jalapeño!—inside lime Jell-O.

"What the—?!"

"That is *way beyond* disgusting," Deck said with a grimace.

"What kind of sadistic mind even comes up with an idea

like this?" Ace asked, reaching for a napkin so he could blot the taste out of his mouth.

"Can't tell you." Deck sprang up to get them both glasses of water. "Damn. I wouldn't even feed that to the Lundgren's hogs."

"You know, Gramma used to serve up some pretty weird Jell-O desserts, too."

"But this . . . this Perfection Salad stuff . . . it's not a dessert. Who puts coleslaw into any flavor of Jell-O?"

"Someone trying to get kids to eat their veggies?"

The two burst out laughing.

"That's it," gasped Declan. "Mrs. Dufresne wants our hometown hero to eat his veggies like a good boy and get back to bat."

"I don't care what Mrs. Dufresne wants. It was real nice of her to think of me, but we are scraping this down the disposal."

"Yes, we are. But you still get to write her a thank-you note on Austin Lone Stars stationery and tell her how delicious it was."

Ace moaned. "Lying is a sin. I'll go to hell."

"The tabloids say you're goin' to hell anyway." Declan grinned. "Write her the note."

"Fine."

Deck's grin faded and he took another gulp of water. "Listen, Ace. Normally it's none of my business who you . . . get cozy with. But Mia is different."

Whatever goodwill they'd created between them over the last half an hour vanished in an instant. Ace opened his mouth to tell his brother off, but Deck held up his hand.

"Hear me out. Mia's not like your baseball bunnies. She's good people. And she's had a really rough time of it. Don't mess with her. She doesn't need any more heartache."

"Are you finished?" Ace said, between his teeth.

"No. I look out for Mia as much as possible, since that bottom-feeder took off on her. As much as I can without hurting her pride. And underneath all that no-nonsense, I-got-this, I'm-in-control BS, she's at the end of her rope. She does not need to get mixed up with a guy like you, Easy Ace. And what's more, she needs this job. Badly. So don't screw it up for her."

Ace hoisted himself out of his chair. "And here I thought I'd pegged you all wrong. Thanks for the insulting and totally unnecessary lecture, *Dad*. You have no idea what you're talking about. And you don't get to tell me what to do. Mia doesn't need you stepping in to parent her, either. She's already got a father."

"No, Ace." Declan said it quietly. "*You've* got her father. And I don't think that's easy for her."

"Enough, Declan. Not another word." Ace glared at his brother, then stood up and grabbed his crutches.

"Don't run away from this conversation."

Ace froze, ran his tongue over his front teeth, and turned around. He propped the crutches against the wall. "I don't run away from anything."

Declan sighed, dumped the plates of goo into the sink, and turned to the fridge. He pulled out two beers and popped the cap off the first, but then he froze. He looked uncertainly at the beers and then at his brother.

Right. Deck, along with everyone else, thought he had a drinking problem. He was being kind. Getting rid of temptation. Ace grew angrier and angrier with his situation. "What's the problem? Is the beer flat?" he asked, his voice like a knife.

"How about some coffee instead?"

"I don't want any damn coffee." Ace shook his head in disbelief. "I told you I didn't drive under the influence. I told you I switched places with Pete after the crash. I thought you were giving me the benefit of the doubt."

Furious beyond reason, he crossed the kitchen on his booted foot, grabbed the open beer, and began pouring it down the sink. "That better? You think I'm some kind of drunk? You think I killed our parents?"

Deck reared back in horror, as if he'd been hit. "What do Mama and Pop have to do with this?" he asked incredulously. "Drew, do you think you killed them?"

"What? No!" Ace's face flamed, letting the can drop into the sink with a crash. "That's not what I'm saying." Actually, he wasn't sure what he was saying. And here, now, was Declan looking so much like Pop, calling him "Drew." It was what he'd always called him. Andrew or Drew. "Ace" came from Coach. Ace was the guy he'd become after the accident. Smiles for miles. Golden glove. A whiz at bat.

Declan's incredulous expression faded into confusion. He finally asked, "Why did you take the rap for Pete Bergsen?"

Ace shrugged, trying not to let on that his heart was pounding way too fast. "He asked me to. He was afraid his wife would divorce him and take his kids away if it came out that he was driving—if he got a DUI. She was already pissed about . . ." Ace realized that wasn't his secret to share. "About some other behavior of his."

Declan shook his head, blinking rapidly.

"What?" Ace asked. "*I* don't have a wife. *I* don't have kids . . ." His voice trailed off as he registered the dark rage on Declan's face.

"No," Deck said tightly. "You don't. But now you have a messed-up ankle, your career's on the skids, and your reputation is in shreds—"

"It already was," Ace said. "I didn't have as much to lose."

"What about *us*?" Declan roared. "Do we matter so little to you? That you'd get into a car with a drunk?"

It was Ace's turn to stare at his brother. He opened and then closed his mouth.

"And what about yourself?" Declan continued. "You had to know this would get you in trouble with the team."

"I didn't think about it," Ace muttered. "He begged me . . ."

"Only a selfish jerk would do that—"

"And he's like a brother to me."

Wrong. Thing. To. Say.

Declan's face had gone from enraged to totally blank in half a second. An ominous silence ensued. "Like a brother," he repeated, at last.

"Aw, Deck—you know what I—"

"Has this *brother* of yours even called once to ask how you're doing?" Declan's jaw was rigid.

Ace thought about the messages he'd left for Pete that had gone straight to voicemail. The goodbye text he'd gotten back from him on an unknown phone, explaining that he wasn't allowed to talk to him anymore. The blistering comments Frannie had made to the media.

"Yeah. That's what I thought." Declan took a deep breath. "I got one more question for you."

Ace didn't say a word, frozen with anticipation.

"Nobody could replace Pop. I get that. At the time, all I could see was that I was trying so hard and nobody was willing to give me a chance to succeed at taking his place at the table. I know that I failed at being a father to you. What I don't understand—what I still don't understand after all these years—is why you can't let *me* be your *brother.*"

A strangled laugh slipped out. Ace's mouth went dry. "You're still my brother. *Obviously,*" he said, going for a light tone. It sounded all wrong in his ears.

Declan wasn't fooled. He shook his head and raised his palms. His eyes were clear and his voice was calm when he asked simply, "Then why'd'ya give me up so easy?"

Ace's blood raced in his veins. Declan waited, but he shouldn't have; Ace was never going to be able to get the right words out.

In the silence, disappointment flashed across his brother's face. At last, Declan turned on his heel and strode down the hallway to the back door, slamming it on his way out.

Grouchy whined from under the table.

Ace just stared at the floor. And all of a sudden, he longed for Mia. Don't-get-mixed-up-with-her Mia.

Chapter 21

MIA JUGGLED TWO BOXES OF HER SUPPLIES WHILE attempting to press the latch on Declan's back door with her elbow. It didn't work well, so with a sigh she set everything down, opened the door, picked everything back up, and muscled it over to the counter as Grouchy barked and put his paws up on her backside.

All morning, nothing had seemed to be working quite as well as it should have been, which was bound to happen when one's focus was more on a certain sexy ballplayer than on the task at hand. Inappropriate to say the least, when the task at hand was saving herself from financial ruin.

She'd had all night—all restless, overheated night—to think about what had happened. And what might have happened if Declan hadn't walked in on them. "Down, Grouch. Good boy." Mia absently scratched him behind the ears. "Ace?" she called. No answer. Part of her was relieved. Part of her couldn't stop thinking about kissing him again. Part of her burned with embarrassment when she thought about throwing herself at him; part of her burned with desire.

All for Easy Ace. How ridiculous.

She took a deep breath, steeling herself, and then walked into the massive, timbered great room, expecting to see him sprawled on the couch, or in one of the leather chairs, but he wasn't there.

He'd promised not to steal any more tractors or horses, so where was he? And what was left for escape transport—a couple of goats tied to a wheelbarrow?

She hadn't seen him at all last night. He'd been holed up in his room when she returned and answered with a terse, "Nope, thanks," when she asked if he needed anything. This morning, she left breakfast in the warmer for both the Braddock boys and then zipped off to get her crafting supplies. He couldn't still be sleeping. Well, maybe he could.

"Ace? Ace, you here?"

No answer. Maybe he'd had a buddy pick him up to run an errand. But as his sober companion, she was supposed to know where he was. Her mistake was assuming he would actually tell her without her asking. Actually, her mistake was bigger than that. She'd assumed he'd be easy to keep track of, that he'd be happy to stay on the ranch the whole time he was here. The joke was on Mia. Well, she'd give him ten minutes before she started calling around.

In the meantime, Mia did some accounting in her head. She was short two hundred sixteen dollars for the mortgage again. That meant she had about a week to sell either forty-four lip glosses, twenty-seven lotions, eighteen large candles, or twelve gift sets (including lotion, lip gloss, and a small candle).

Her best bet was to have Lila Braddock pitch the gift sets to some of her clients, drop some more off at A Cut Above, the hair salon, and Glam Girl Day Spa, and then focus on the large candles. There was no way she could unload that many lip glosses or lotions in such a short time. But higher-margin candles made a lot of sense.

Grouchy took a break from sniffing her and went to dig in the corner for something. When he emerged, she saw that it was a baseball, and he was very excited to have it. Hmmm.

Mia thought about all of the women and girls in Silverlake, trekking out to the ranch to pay homage to Ace, their baseball hero. What if . . . ?

What if she figured out how to make baseball-shaped candles—and maybe even had Ace sign them? Cheesy, maybe . . . but kind of adorable.

"Hey, Grouchy," she suggested. "I don't suppose you'd let me borrow that for a second?" She approached him and tried to get him to drop it.

No dice.

She pried at his jaws, but Grouchy emitted a small warning growl.

"Well, fine. Be selfish, then."

He wagged his tail and then went running off with his prize.

Mia dug through her box of candle-making supplies and came up with a set of spherical silicone molds with one side just flat enough to stabilize a candle. She'd bought them just to try a new shape but hadn't used them yet. They'd be about the right size. And she could paint the candles white when they were dry, then add the red stitching.

She felt a little buzz of excitement as she went into the kitchen and began the process of heating her beeswax and prepping the molds. How much would people pay for an autographed-by-Ace-Braddock baseball candle? Maybe twenty dollars?

Mia checked her watch. It had been ten minutes, and there was no sign of her charge. She dialed him, half-surprised when he actually answered.

"Yep?" Ace said.

"You alive? Have you hitched a mule to a neighbor kid's Big Wheel to get to a bar?"

"I'm right here on the property," Ace said in surly tones.

"Where is 'right here'?"

"Look out the kitchen window."

Sure enough, there he was, swinging around on his

crutches about a hundred yards away. "What are you doing out there?"

"Why do you care?"

Mia sighed. "Ace."

"I decided to go for an invigorating walk. Sing with the birds. Buzz with the bees. Honk with the geese. Commune with nature."

"Don't you mean an invigorating *hop*?"

"Details."

"Okay, Ace. Whatever you say. Why are you in such a grouchy mood?"

"How can you tell?"

"It's not that hard."

"Well, let's see," said her patient. "I spent quality time with my brother last night. I guess that alone's enough to put me in a crappy mood, but the kicker was a lecture about not messing with you. Since you're not like my typical baseball bunnies, and you are above such worthless riffraff as myself."

Mia gaped at the phone.

"So I'm not to *get cozy* with you anymore, darlin'," Ace added.

Heat suffused her face.

She couldn't even croak anything into the phone.

"Got it?" Ace asked. "Just so we're clear. No more lunging at me and kissing the stuffing out of me—even though I know you couldn't help yourself."

"You—you—" She couldn't think of a word bad enough. So she hung up on him, flung her phone back in her purse, and splashed some water on her hot cheeks.

Just when she thought there might be a decent human being lurking under the disgusting surface of Easy Ace Braddock, something reminded her that such a thing was not possible. She hoped he stuck his crutch right into a cow patty, then slipped and fell into it, face-first.

She checked on the wax in her double boiler. It was thick, rich, and gooey. And it smelled like heaven.

Declan . . . looking out for her. Warning off his brother.

She was torn between being annoyed and being touched. She decided to be touched, since she was, after all, staying for free on his property. And milking his goats. And taking honey and wax from his bees. It was pretty hard to be annoyed at a guy when you considered all of that.

Ace, on the other hand. She grimaced. Had she actually told Stetson that he was a friend? Seriously? She was going to sic the Yorkie on him next time they were in the same vicinity.

Kissing the stuffing out of him? She had done no such thing. She'd . . . okay, she might have kissed him first. But he'd taken it from there.

If anything, he'd kissed the stuffing out of *her. Couldn't help myself?* The nerve!

Almost growling, Mia transferred the hot beeswax into a pouring pot with a spout; then she began pouring the candles into the molds, being careful to keep the wicks centered and immobile. She'd done five and had moved on to the last one when a disheveled Ace flung open the door, surprising her.

She whirled, pouring hot wax onto her left hand instead of into the candle mold. *"Aaaagh!"* She slammed the pouring pot onto the stove and lunged for the sink.

"What are you doing?!"

"What does it look like I'm doing?" she snapped.

"I have no idea. But that's gonna be a nasty burn." Ace crutched quickly to the fridge and slid out a stick of butter. He unwrapped one end of it, crutched over to the sink, and took her hand.

"Let go of me!"

"I'm trying to help you." Ace smeared the stick of butter onto the burn, which was sizable and hurt like hell.

Mia was surprised the butter didn't sizzle when it came into contact with her skin. And thankful when it almost instantly felt better.

"What's that goop on the stove? And why are you making grenades? Are those to toss at me?"

She had to laugh at the last question. "Yes."

"Seriously—what . . . ?"

"They're candles.

Ace looked perplexed. "But they're round."

"Yes. Your powers of observation are keen."

"Why?"

"They're going to be baseball candles."

If anything, Ace looked even more confused.

"Why?" he asked again.

Mia focused on the butter and her burn, and didn't answer.

He waited. She figured he was tired of saying the word *why*.

"I'm over two hundred short for my mortgage payment," she confessed at last.

"So you're making candles to sell." He looked pole-axed. "Baseball-shaped candles."

Mortified, Mia shrugged. "People in Silverlake seem excited by the presence of their hometown hero. I figured I could capitalize off that at the Founder's Day Festival."

"Seriously?" Ace flung himself into a kitchen chair. "Mia, I will give you the lousy two hundred bucks. You don't have to do this."

"No," she said evenly. "You will not. After all, you might be in danger if you did. Of losing your *stuffing*, and all." There was no way she was asking him to autograph the candles now.

Ace leaned back and cracked his neck as his color rose. "I'm sorry. Shouldn't have said that. I was pissed at Declan, not you. It came out wrong."

"Uh-huh."

"Please let me help, Mia."

"I don't need your help, Ace." She smiled sweetly. "And just for the record, the only reason I kissed you is that you spoke Spanish. It was a thank-you. Nothing more."

Ace said nothing, just leveled his blue gaze upon her. Knowingly. Insufferably. "Sure. Whatever you say."

"I did not *lunge* at you."

"No, of course you didn't," he said agreeably.

Her eyes narrowed.

"How's that burn doing?"

It still hurt. But it was better. "It's fine. Thanks."

"All right. When is the Founder's Day event?"

"You don't remember?"

He shook his head.

"It's this weekend."

"Okay. So what do we need to do to finish up these candles of yours?"

She raised her eyebrows. "We?"

"I'm bored. Let me help." He shot her a look that was half-pleading, half-mischievous, and wholly irresistible.

"You draw, right? Can you design a label for them?"

"Of course. What do you want to call them?"

"Home Run Candles. By You & Mia. That's my company name."

He grinned. "You & Mia. I like it. All right."

While she cooled the candles in the one free area she could find in the fridge, he located his sketch pad.

"What was in this spot?" She tried to remember. "Oh, the Perfection Salad. Mrs. Dufresne has been making that since the 1950s. Did you and Deck actually . . . ?"

Ace looked up. "He double-dog dared me."

Mia began to laugh. "What are you two, ten years old?"

He grinned. "And change."

"So you ate the entire . . . uh . . . salad?" It seemed criminal, an insult to salads, to call it that. A way to shame lettuce, tomatoes, and cucumbers. Mortify avocados. Humiliate radishes.

"Not exactly."

"Please tell me you didn't feed it to Grouchy."

Ace looked up with genuine horror on his face. "What do you think we are? Animal abusers? Of course not. That hole in the sink there got hungry."

"Poor Mrs. Dufresne. I'm going to tell her that you scorned her cooking."

"No!" Ace looked alarmed.

"I have blackmail on you now." She gave an evil chuckle.

"No, no. Anything but that. I don't want to hurt her feelings." He was sincere. "I have to write her a thank-you note. Jeez . . . a lot of thank-you notes."

Mia stared at him. "You're kidding me, right? Are you telling me that Easy Ace Braddock has manners?"

"No. Definitely not." He shook his head. "You are confusing him with some other Easy Ace. One whose mama brought him up right."

"I thought so." Huh. Just when she'd decided he was irredeemably repulsive, he wanted to help her and write thank-you notes to little old ladies.

"Hey," she said, lightly hip-checking him. "To be honest, I shouldn't be razzing you about manners." She couldn't quite meet his eyes when she added, "If I maybe confused things by trying to . . . thank you yesterday, I'm sorry."

"You're apologizing to me?" Ace asked, incredulous.

"Sure. I'm big that way," Mia said, grateful he wasn't going for maximum embarrassment.

He smiled. "Well, just don't let it happen again."

"Of course not."

They both chuckled and then stared awkwardly at each other. Ace's gaze dropped to her mouth and then he looked away. "I'm, uh, going to go get started on the label," he said, looking around for his crutches.

As Mia watched him go, she wondered why she was suddenly sorry that "it" would never happen again. And then she wondered if any part of him was feeling the same way.

Chapter 22

ACE COULDN'T EXPLAIN THE FEELING OF ANTICIPA-
tion he felt as he woke on Saturday morning. He'd
traveled and played in the most cosmopolitan cities in the
country, so why did he care about Silverlake's podunk,
small-town festival?

Maybe because his baby sister, Lila, was all grown up
and producing it.

Maybe it was because he knew he'd be one big fish in
this small pond, and that was always gratifying unless he
thought about it too hard—which he made a point of not
doing.

Or . . . maybe it was because he remembered Mama bak-
ing pies for the pie-eating contest: peach, cherry, and apple.
But especially peach, the fruit picked by them from the
trees in back of the house. And Pop had made hand-cranked
vanilla ice cream with rock salt . . . each one of them, even
Declan, clamoring to take their turn helping with it. There
was nothing like homemade ice cream. He smiled just
thinking about it.

The morning of Silverlake's traditional Founder's Day event dawned clear and bright, the Texas Hill Country sky true blue. Puffy white clouds hung in clusters like cotton candy. Colorful, patriotic bunting draped every business along Main Street, and signage pointed visitors to the grounds of Silverlake High, where most of the activities took place.

It was wonderful to see the town come alive and wave the banner of its history. Founded in 1839 by a few enterprising families, Silverlake had flourished as immigrants had forged west to seek their fortunes in the United States.

The festival was family-friendly and featured Silverlake's famous chili cook-off, the pie-eating contest—now sponsored by Sunny's Side Up—a bake-off judged by Kristina at Piece A Cake, the annual Fire and Rescue vs. police tug-of-war, and an art contest for the creative types. There were also sports events: flag football, volleyball, and a youth baseball game in addition to the family sack race.

And there were booths and tables set up for townspeople to sell their homemade goods. Mia had enlisted Jules to help her with her products and be her cashier.

Ace wandered over to say hello, still not entirely able to believe that his brother Rhett-the-Dallas-Suit was hitched to Julianna Holt, who was gorgeous in an all-natural way but was also usually mud-encrusted and looked as if she'd never met a comb. Today she wore overalls and a T-shirt, which almost hid her softly rounded belly. Her hair was scraped up on top of her head, as usual, and looked like a protrusion of rooster feathers.

"Hey, Jules," Ace greeted her. "So when are you making me an uncle? I missed the wedding, so there's no way I'm missing the christening."

"You'll get an invite, don't worry. Why does everybody want to rush this kid? There's so much to do! Rhett wants to build a brand-new house out at the stables, and he's already had at least ten architects out there. He's driving me crazy. I told him I don't care if we live in Aunt Sue's old trailer." She laughed. "But he's not having that."

Ace raised his eyebrows. "Doesn't he have a palace in Dallas?"

"He does. It gives me hives. Anyway, since you're here, what can I sell you?" She gestured at the array of Mia's products on the table in front of her.

Mia had brought all of them: the beeswax lip gloss and candles with colorful crystals set into them, the new goat's milk soaps and lotions . . . and the brand-new Home Run baseball candles they'd worked on together. They were beautiful with their hand-painted red stitching, and Ace had signed each one for her, in addition to designing the labels.

Back at the ranch with all of the supplies piled high and products scattered everywhere, it had been a little hard to see Mia's vision. But here, with the products packaged beautifully and displayed together, it was beyond impressive. Ace had absolutely no idea what to do with any of this stuff, but he sure admired and respected Mia's resourcefulness. Eventually, everything would sell.

But Mia didn't have that kind of time. She needed the money. "Tell you what, Jules. This is top secret, though—got it?"

She squinted at him suspiciously, but nodded.

"You sell what you can to the locals. And then I'll buy the rest."

"You?" Jules cocked her head, hair-feathers waving.

"Me," he said emphatically. "And I'll order another batch."

"Of . . . which product?"

"All of 'em."

Jules sat back in her folding plastic chair and crossed her arms across her chest. "Why? You've started wearing raspberry-honey lip gloss? You moisturize and soap up with goat's milk?"

"I—"

" 'Course the tabloids make it sound like you haven't showered alone since you got famous."

Ace shot her the most charming smile in his repertoire. "It's a new thing I'm trying. So yeah, I'll need a lot of Mia's products. But keep it to yourself, you hear? I don't want her to know who bought them."

"Whatever you say," Jules agreed. "You'll have to pay cash if you want to hide your tracks, though."

"Done."

Some chestnut strands of her hair had escaped the feather duster on top of her head and blew across her face in the September breeze. Jules tucked them behind her ear. "Huh," she said thoughtfully. "It's possible that you're not as loathsome as she's been saying."

That stung. *"Loathsome?"*

Jules grinned. "Well. Generally obnoxious and repulsive."

"Thanks. I hope that's not a recent saying of hers."

"Huh. Come to think of it, she hasn't said it in a while." Jules gave him a knowing look that he pointedly ignored.

"So, where is Mia, the great flatterer?"

Her friend waved a hand nonchalantly. "Dunno. She's out there somewhere. I made her promise to have a good time for me. Your brother will barely let me make coffee or open the refrigerator by myself these days—he's so overprotective because of my 'condition.' So I'm stuck here. No volleyball or sack hopping for me." She sighed. "The truth is, it's good to sit down."

"Want some iced tea or some ice cream? I'll get it for you," Ace offered.

"Hey!" Rhett said from behind him. "You trying to hit on my wife?"

Ace turned and winked. "You caught me. Jules here was just telling me that upon sight of the sonogram, the doctor crossed herself and the nurse fainted . . . because the baby is so ugly. The spittin' image of *you*, bro."

Rhett looked offended, but then realized his brother was yanking his chain.

Jules hooted. "Why's it taken you so long to come back to Silverlake, Ace? I can tell we're gonna get along."

"Ace is such a big-time celebrity that he hasn't had any time to spare for us," Rhett said dryly.

"Oh yeah?" Ace replied. "Well, Rhett is such a snotty banker that we're not in his social circle anymore."

Jules looked from Ace to Rhett and back again. "You are both full of it."

"Well, of course," they said in unison, grinning and slapping each other on the back. "We're Braddocks!"

Chapter 23

ACE HEADED TO THE BASEBALL FIELD, GAZING AT the familiar buildings that composed Silverlake High, his old stomping grounds. Where it had all started for him . . . Coach recognizing he had something special, the cheering crowds, the feeling that he'd finally found his place in the world and his unique calling.

The Founder's Day game was in progress. Not wanting to interrupt and draw attention away, he watched through the chain-link fence. There was something so pure about the dirty, sweaty faces of the kids and their intense expressions. He'd played right on that diamond himself, on more than one Founder's Day.

It was strange to be back. Everything about the school had once seemed so big. It had been his whole world. And now it belonged to a whole other crop of kids. Not him. It looked smaller, insignificant in the great scheme of things, just another high school dotting the vast expanse of America.

But it was still Silverlake High. The school he'd grown

up in. The place of friends, feuds, freshman pranks. The site of his first kiss (Molly Malone at a dance in the darkened gym), his first fight (when her boyfriend Darnell caught them), and his less-than-stellar SAT scores when he'd been unable to concentrate after the deaths of Mama and Pop.

But it was also the site of hundreds of practices and games during which he was a star. The kids had noticed him. Even now, they were nudging one another, gesturing in his direction, beginning to approach him for autographs. He signed a few, said some friendly words, and then went in search of Mia.

He found her dominating the opposing team in a volleyball game not far from the baseball field. Under his widened gaze, she lunged forward and spiked the ball over the net, hard, scoring a point for her team. She also landed on her stomach in the grass, red hair flying up in a cloud, her pale, slim legs bent behind her. But before anyone could help her to her feet, she was up again, poised and ready to defend her side of the net.

He'd never seen her play before. Come to think of it, he hadn't seen her in anything but unflattering scrubs of various colors since his arrival in Silverlake. Now she wore a pair of cut-offs with a snug T-shirt that highlighted her curves.

And damn: Mia had perfect, beautifully proportioned, toned legs—dotted with a smattering of freckles like her face. He found himself riveted by them as she moved into position and executed a killer serve, grinning triumphantly when the opposing team scrambled unsuccessfully to return the ball.

But the most attractive thing of all was just the sight of a carefree, high-spirited Mia having fun. She looked like a wholly different person.

She served again, and Ace cheered her on.

Mia shot him a startled glance and then gave him a small wave before returning her attention to the game.

Then he was distracted by a new gaggle of girls, asking

him to sign autographs and take selfies with them. "Sure thing." Ace obliged them. "But have you seen those Home Run baseball candles for sale over there? Handmade, hand-painted stitching. My signature on 'em. Those will make incredible gifts . . . or just mementos. And there are other cool things, too. By You & Mia."

He steered everyone he encountered over to Mia's products, telling them they'd sell out fast. Soon Jules had quite a line.

He wandered through the crowds, meeting new people, greeting old friends. Chatting with Dottie from the Grab n' Go and her partner Libby, even though they were die-hard Yankees fans. Shooting the breeze with Charlie and her granddad, old Kingston Nash. Flirting harmlessly with Sunny, who urged him to enter the pie-eating contest.

But it wasn't pie he craved. It was some good old-fashioned home-cooked Texas chili.

At least two dozen townspeople stood near the line of Crock-Pots and camp stoves at the cook-off site, the chefs behind them proud—and loud.

"Two-step up an' git yer chiiiiiili!" yelled one guy.

"Gotta try my No Beans, No Bullcrap variety!"

"Nah, his slop sucks! Have some o' mine: my famous Hoppin' Habanero Hot Stuff!"

"Shoooot, his is *nothin'* compared to my Flirtin' with Fire!"

"Or my Come On, Ice Cream Chili. Belly up and have a taste—anyone who's brave enough, that is."

Mick Halladay, representing the firehouse, sparred with them all. And even if Ace hadn't known him well, he was wearing an Austin Lone Stars cap with Ace's signature on it. So he was obligated to taste Mick's Burnin' Battery Acid chili—and he did. It was delicious, with a kick that came straight from fresh jalapeños.

"Compliments to Chef Mick," Ace said, meaning it, blinking watery eyes.

"Thanks. So how much longer you gonna stick around? Not that we want to get rid of you."

"Oh . . ." Ace gestured at his ankle in the surgical boot. "It's not fatal. Long as it takes the bad press to die down, I guess." Actually, that was a good question. One he hadn't thought that much about. He found himself looking back toward the volleyball game. To where Mia was probably still smiling up a storm.

Mick started to ask him something else, but they were distracted by a bunch of hooting and hollering.

Lila had commandeered a microphone. Ace took in her outfit: silver earrings the size of satellite dishes, a very low-cut, sprayed-on black dress that he would have enjoyed seeing on someone other than his sister, and black cowboy boots embroidered with red roses. She looked like a whole lotta trouble.

He fought the urge to throw a trash bag over her so that various men in the crowd would quit ogling her.

"Got us a Yankee judge, here! Mr. Sebastian Linland!" Lila announced, oblivious to Ace's protective feelings. "Friend of Jean-Paul's from New Yawk City. He's never been to a chili cook-off before. Let's give 'im one warm welcome, y'all!"

A startled man, wearing all black and fancy shoes, shoved his designer sunglasses atop his head. He was escorted down the makeshift aisle between the tables. As one, each chili chef raised his ladle and grinned maniacally.

"Get this guy a beer—he's gonna need one," Mick called.

Ace laughed under his breath.

"Ah, thanks," said the unwitting victim. "People certainly are friendly in Texas."

"Yes, we are," Lila said, smirking. "And we are excited to have a gourmet food critic from the Big Apple here to help judge our competition. Now, where are our locals? Mayor Gloria Fisk, please come on up. And Ray—Ray Delgado."

Silverlake's mayor stepped up in her long denim skirt, silver concha belt, and cowboy boots, followed by the town butcher. Jean-Paul hid nearby, peeking from behind an oak tree with a mischievous look on his face.

Apparently New Yawk had no inkling of what he was about to face.

"Okay. First up is No Beans, No Bullcrap," announced Lila, handing each judge a small bowl of the entry. Each judge took a bite while the audience waited.

"Not bad," Ray said. "Some kick. A little heavy on the onion."

"I love it," Gloria countered. "Perfectly spiced."

Big Apple took two large gulps of beer, then another. "My tonsils are scorched," he said at last.

"You all right, Yankee?" somebody called.

He took another sip of beer before nodding.

"Next," Lila called, "is Flirtin' with Fire."

"Smoky," Ray pronounced.

"Barbecue flavor," Gloria nodded. "But a little too heavy-handed."

The East Coast guy gingerly put the spoon in his mouth and chewed. By the time his throat convulsed in a swallow, sweat had beaded across his forehead and his eyes bulged. "You people cook with hellfire and sulfuric acid!"

Everyone laughed while he poured the rest of his beer down his damaged throat and looked around for another.

Lila handed him one before announcing the next entry. "And now for Hoppin' Habanero."

"Got a subtle kick to it," Ray said, nodding. "Good stuff."

"I think it needs more cayenne," Mayor Fisk said.

Big Apple gulped and eyed the bowl handed to him as if it were filled with hot coals.

"What's-a-matter, New Yawk?" a man called from the crowd.

Slowly, the poor judge slipped the spoon into his mouth, didn't bother chewing, and gagged. "Hhhhhelp! My tongue ith on fire!" He upended the second beer and sucked it dry without a breath. *"Aaagh!"*

This caused much amusement among the spectators. A

third beer was found for the northern gentleman and passed, hand by hand, up to him. He accepted gratefully.

"Next: Burnin' Battery Acid!" Lila declared.

"Yeah, nice kick to it," Ray said.

"It could be hotter," Gloria disagreed, while Mick's eyebrows snapped together.

The New York judge emitted a small whimper before subjecting himself to Mick's recipe. This time his eyes crossed and he began to choke.

Lila rushed over and smacked him on the back. "You okay?"

"That's not chili—it's *lava*!" he yelled, clutching at his throat.

Several spectators stepped back, alarmed.

"Lava. And—it's burning right through me!" the Yankee judge looked around, wild-eyed. "Toilets. Where are the *johns*?"

"Over there, honey," Lila said, pointing to a row of blue portables.

He sprinted.

"Wait!" one of the contestants called. "You haven't had the Come On, Ice Cream yet."

Jean-Paul stepped out from behind his tree, his shoulders shaking as he wiped his eyes. "*Merci, ma petite*," he said to Lila. "That is payback for ze Rocky Mountain oyster affair!"

Ace caught his sister's gaze and laughed until it hurt. *These* were some of the things he'd missed about Silverlake. You couldn't make this stuff up. It was home, and people had one another's backs. And Lila was absolutely priceless.

He looked around for Mia, wondering if she'd finished her game and made it back to witness the scene. But she was nowhere in sight. He wandered around looking for her.

At last he turned a corner and saw her eating an ice cream cone. If he had to guess, it was butter pecan—his favorite. She was flushed, her nose a little sunburned, her cinnamon eyes warm with laughter. And those legs . . .

Ace forced his gaze up, but he couldn't decently linger on the way her fitted T-shirt curved to her body, a little damp, still, from her workout. So he focused higher, which meant watching her mouth as she went to work on the ice cream cone. And that sent some pretty X-rated thoughts into his male brain. He discovered he was short on oxygen and tried to pull more air into his lungs.

"Hey, Ace," Mia said. "You all right?"

"Fine," he managed.

"You sure? You look as though you may have heat-stroke." She walked toward him and put a hand on his fore-head, which didn't help his situation at all. Now she was touching him?

"Here. Have some ice cream," she offered.

Ace looked down at the cone where her lips had just been. He looked at her mouth. And then he accepted the cone, which was a poor substitute, but better than nothing. He took a bite, and it was indeed butter pecan. Unbelievably good . . .

"Homemade?" he asked.

She nodded. "Kristina's been selling it, but word is that there's a new ice cream parlor coming to town: Get the Scoop. They'll also have fudge and other locally sourced homemade candy."

Ace smiled. "I like the name. Love the ice cream." He handed the cone back to her. "Thanks." His gaze dropped to her body again. What was wrong with him? "You're quite a volleyball player. Never knew that."

She raised an eyebrow. "I'm a mean softball player, too. I might be able to give you a run for your money, hotshot."

He chuckled, back to looking at those lips again: a per-fect pale pink, slicked with ice cream as she took another bite. She was going to give him a heart attack if he didn't walk away.

"You sure you're feeling okay, Ace?" she asked, evaluat-ing him.

"Yeah, yeah. I'm just kind of tripping down memory lane. It's . . . weird, to be back at Silverlake High." *And I'm this close to licking you like your ice cream cone.*

But he couldn't say that. Well, he could, but she'd never believe that it wasn't a standard Easy Ace the Player line. So he didn't. He started to ask her if he could get her something to drink, but Lila shushed the band and grabbed the singer's microphone.

"Listen up, everyone! Hellooooo! We have a very important announcement to make."

All of Silverlake turned, beers, chili, pie, cotton candy, or ice cream in hand.

"You ready for this?"

Mystified, everyone cheered anyway. Texans were always ready. For anything and everything that came along.

Lila turned and yanked Jake up onto the stage, who in turn pulled Charlie Nash up with him. Charlie blushed, her blond hair tucked behind her ears, while Jake looked as proud as a man could get.

"You all know my stinky brother Jake," Lila said, her face splitting into a grin. "Right? He fixes things, he does physical therapy, he hangs the holiday lights with the rest of the Fire and Rescue crew, he gets rid of hornet nests, saves cats, and brings idiot teenagers down from water towers—"

"He needs no introduction," someone called from the crowd. "So get on with it!"

"You sayin' I talk too much?" Lila demanded.

"Yes," Jake told her, wresting the microphone out of her hand. "And you meddle."

"Damn straight I do," Lila retorted. "And you should thank me, since it was my meddling that got you and—"

Jake hip-bumped her and slipped his free hand around Charlie. "I love this town more than anything . . . well, almost anything. That's why I wanted to tell y'all . . . Charlie and I are engaged."

As Jake's future bride looked up at him adoringly, cheers went up throughout the crowd.

Ace's breath hitched—at the words, and at the sheer happiness on his brother's face. A lump rose in his throat, and he unconsciously took Mia's hand and tugged her along with him as he made his way toward the happy couple. Somewhat surprisingly, she didn't resist.

"Congrats, you two!" called another person.

"It's about time!"

"When are you tying the knot?"

"Does old Kingston know about this?"

"Yes," Jake answered this last question. "He has given us his blessing."

"Miracles will never cease . . ."

Jake and Charlie both laughed, and she blushed some more. Then Jake kissed her, in front of God and everyone. And the crowd cheered.

So did Lila, right into the microphone, which deafened every person at Founder's Day and probably any cattle for miles around.

Jake wrestled the microphone back from her. "Ouch. Can I just say that for everyone in attendance? Ouch, Lila. Thanks. But I have a question for my brother Declan. Where are you, Deck?" Jake shielded his eyes and searched the crowd until he found him. Ace followed his gaze. "Charlie and I would like to get married out at the Old Barn at Silverlake Ranch."

The crowd fell silent as the smile dropped off Declan's face and into the dirt. The historic structure, as everyone knew, had burned down several months back.

"After the barn-raising, of course," Jake amended.

At this, all of Silverlake cheered, while Deck stood there looking stunned. Ace found himself with a case of nerves, worrying about what Declan really thought about that. He never talked about the Old Barn. Hadn't said a word about it to Ace, anyway, after the call letting him know it had burned. Rhett was taking care of the insurance issues and Ace had put it out of his mind. But it sure mattered to Declan. You could see it all over his face.

Jake grinned at his big brother. "We've been plotting. And the Fire and Rescue boys have pledged to make it happen."

With these words, he picked Charlie up and swung her off the stage as the crowd swarmed them.

Ace didn't have any chance of getting near his brother.

He stopped and watched the commotion, the excitement, gripping Mia's hand. And he realized how utterly strange it was to not have all the fuss be about *him*, the major league baseball player, the celebrity. Then he knew a moment of shame—what kind of egomaniac was he?

Beside him, Mia sighed, her eyes shining. "That was so . . . romantic. They're perfect for each other."

"Are they?" Ace asked. He suddenly felt, once again, like an outsider. A visitor. Someone of no account, with no inside knowledge of the kind of woman who'd make his brother happy.

"Yes, of course." Mia glanced up at him, and from this different angle, he saw that the shine in her eyes was because they were wet with tears.

"Hey," Ace said. "Mia . . . you okay?"

She nodded, biting her lip.

Ace realized he was still holding her hand, and she was holding his. "Do you . . . do you want to get out of here?"

Mia blew out a breath. Met his gaze uncertainly. Swiped a renegade curl out of her face.

She was so beautiful.

He almost didn't hear her say yes. And when she did, he wondered if he'd imagined it.

But then she released his hand, turned, and walked away, without looking over her shoulder to see if he was following.

He was.

Chapter 24

NOT A SOUL—EXCEPT FOR GROUCHY AND CAT—
was back at the ranch when Ace and Mia drove
through the gates and parked. Declan was still at Founder's
Day. The last time Ace had spotted him, he was having a
beer and chuckling at the pie-eating contest, which was
always a total disaster: contestants covered in smears of
fruit filling, whipped cream, and crust crumbs. Funniest of
all was the bidding to hit Sunny in the face with a banana
cream pie. It often went into the hundreds of dollars—all
donated to charity.

Grouchy came running and tail-wagged them inside,
while Cat yawned lazily and refused to stir from his spot
on the porch.

Mia helped Ace disengage from her Smart car, and they
went inside. Ace settled on the couch and patted the spot
next to him. Gingerly, Mia sat down on the edge of the
cushion.

"What were you feeling back there?" Ace prompted her.

"When my brother told everyone that he and Charlie are engaged?"

Mia avoided his gaze. "Just really happy for them. They make a great couple."

"And?"

"And what? Since when do you talk about feelings, Easy Ace?"

"Since I saw tears in your eyes."

She blinked and then the corner of her mouth turned up in a smile. "You being sweet seems like less and less of a surprise every day . . . it was just sentiment."

"Bull. Come on, Mia. You know it was more than that."

She sighed and sank back against the couch cushions. "Fine. I was thinking about back when I got engaged to Rob. I looked at him like Charlie looks at Jake—"

An electric charge of jealousy shot through Ace at her words.

"—and I had no idea what was coming down the tracks. I was dumber than a box of rocks."

"That's not being fair to yourself, Mia."

"Why not? I knew, even back then, that he was all about appearances. The perfect hair, the nicest clothes. Top of his class. The most exclusive fraternity. Sponsored by his parents, later, at the country club."

"He sounds so wrong for you."

She laughed, the sound tinny and bitter. "Yeah."

"So how did you end up with him?"

Mia gave him the saddest smile he'd ever seen. "Because he wanted me, I guess. *Him.* The guy all the girls in Silverlake would kill to marry. And he chose me. I was never really sure why . . ."

Ace shook his head. "Are you crazy?"

Mia raised her eyebrows. "What do you mean?"

She genuinely didn't know what he was talking about. "He chose you because you're gorgeous and sexy, for sure. If he had any sense at all, it was also because you're smart, you're sassy, and you're kind. You go out of your way to help people like nobody I've ever seen. You have this way of looking at people that's so warm and comforting . . . like cinnamon sprinkled on buttered toast."

Mia seemed to have trouble processing his words, as if he'd delivered them in a foreign language that she didn't understand. Then she swallowed hard and edged away from him. "That's really nice of you, Ace."

"I'm not being nice. I mean it. Don't you see who you are, Mia Adams?"

"I'm—I'm just me. Plain old me."

Ace shook his head. "There's nothing plain about you, woman."

But again, Mia didn't seem to be registering what he was trying to tell her. "It felt so . . . *incredible* . . . to be wanted— and by someone like Rob Bayes," she said.

Ace saw again, in hindsight, the lonely girl she'd been. The only child whose mother traveled the globe and whose father was preoccupied with a boy who wasn't even his kid. Was it *his* fault that she'd ended up as Rob's wife? He couldn't stand the thought.

Mia laughed again, the bitterness even more pronounced. "Pathetic, right? I mean, I know myself now. I've learned not to settle. I've learned not to allow myself to be treated badly. I've learned a lot in the last few years. But I've also learned to be really honest with myself: giving myself to Rob? Pathetic."

"No. You're anything but." Ace reached out, as he had the night of the back rub. He looped an arm around her and slid her toward him, pulling her into his lap.

Funny, this time she didn't protest. She just curled into him and laid her cheek against his chest. He bent his head and kissed her hair, breathing in its essence. It smelled like sunshine and laughter and sweet ice cream and . . . home.

Ace couldn't remember the last time he'd simply held a girl like this. Come to think of it, he wasn't sure he ever had. There'd always been an agenda, a base curiosity to see what a layer of clothing hid, a series of writhing and rolling and bumping, a chase after fleeting and meaningless pleasure.

Mia was different. All he wanted at the moment was to comfort her, to touch those sweet, soft lips with his own.

Ace tipped her chin up and traced them with one index finger, looking into her suddenly shy brown eyes. Without any further conscious thought, he kissed her, and nothing he had ever done felt so right.

Mia kissed him back, and there was wonder in the way she explored his mouth, a sense of discovery that he could feel in her fingertips as she traced his jaw and his neck. As if she was finding something she didn't expect and couldn't explain.

"I want to sweep you off your feet," he murmured against her mouth. "And carry you up the stairs to my bedroom. But with this bum ankle, I'd kill us both."

She laughed softly.

"So if I ask nicely and very"—he kissed her again—"enticingly, would you consider walking up in front of me so that I can admire the view?"

"I'll consider it," Mia said, looking into his eyes in a way that made his body tighten.

Ace cleared his throat. "Uh. How long do you need for this consideration?"

Mischief danced in her eyes. "Maybe another month or so?"

I won't be here in another month or so. How is it possible that I didn't want to come here and suddenly I don't want to leave?

The realization that for the first time in his life, his desire for a woman was matched by the depth of his feelings for her must have shown on his face. For Mia cupped his cheek with her hand and whispered, "Don't borrow trouble, Braddock."

Then she slipped off his lap and headed for the staircase, her hips swinging provocatively.

Ace almost forgot his crutches in his haste to follow. He wasn't nearly as graceful as she was in getting up to his room. But finally they were there, and he shut the door on the outside world, ignoring the dozens of baseball trophies on glass shelves for the true treasure in the room: Mia Adams.

Mia Adams sitting *on his bed*. Looking at him in what could only be called a very come-hither, sexy way. Waiting for him to undress her.

❦

Mia opened her eyes a couple of hours later to a softer evening light streaming through the windows. She registered that she was lying in Ace Braddock's bedroom, entwined in his blue sheets, held firmly in his muscular arms as he spooned against her. She'd fallen asleep there after the most sensual, scorching experience of her life. And a blush rose to her cheeks as she recalled losing every iota of control . . . to Ace, of all people.

Had she lost her mind, along with her panties?

He stirred against her, brushing her neck with his lips, kissing her bare shoulder, and causing her to shiver with pleasure. And fear.

Rob had been one thing. She'd gotten over his disappearance pretty quickly, her emotions limited mostly to anger and a sense of betrayal. Had she loved him? Sure. But if she was honest? Not truly, not deeply, not with all her heart and soul.

But Ace? God had broken the mold after creating him. Men like Ace were players and heartbreakers for a reason— they almost couldn't help themselves. Women threw themselves at the Ace Braddocks of the world.

And now that Mia had seen him naked, she couldn't blame a single one of them.

Why had she come upstairs with him? Why had she succumbed to his . . . his . . . *Ace*ness? His easy grin, his world-famous charm, and his notorious powers of seduction?

Was it, as she'd confessed to him regarding Rob, simply because Ace wanted her . . . and she wanted to be wanted?

Shame and doubt ignited in her veins, traveling through every inch of her. Was she following that old pattern?

No. If she was honest, Mia had to admit that she'd wanted *him* since he'd first set foot back in Silverlake, sassing and flirting that first day in this same room. The very idea of him had gotten under her skin before she'd even seen him.

But that didn't change who Ace was: a major league baseball player who was constantly on the road, in a gym, doing PR events, or otherwise at his team's disposal. In short, Ace was the most unavailable guy she could possibly find.

This had been a one-afternoon stand.

If he didn't immediately drop-kick her down the stairs now that he'd "had" her, then it wouldn't be long before he extricated himself from an awkward situation. At best, this hookup would last the rest of the sober companion contract. At worst, he'd have the team manager fire her tomorrow.

Idiot. Why, why, why had she even talked to him about her vulnerabilities, much less allowed him to kiss her? She needed to get out of here. She needed to think. She needed to make it crystal clear to Ace that she knew the drill: good time, no expectations.

He'd be relieved, more than anything. So that was okay. But there'd been that moment before he'd followed her up the stairs. A moment of doubt in his eyes. She'd remembered that Declan had warned him off her, and what had she said when he actually showed a moment of self-restraint? *Don't borrow trouble.*

Nice going, Mia. What was I thinking? He is trouble! She struggled to get out from under his arm, but it was made of warm, contoured steel and it refused to budge.

"Hey," Ace said sleepily. And then he nibbled on her earlobe, which sent all kinds of renegade nerve endings into overdrive as they clamored for more of his mouth. More of his touch.

Mia ducked, trying to slide down under the covers and escape.

But Ace took it as a game. He chuckled and flattened her onto her stomach with his big, warm, tender body. "Where d'you you think you're going?" He kissed the back of her neck through her hair. Then he ran his hands down her sides, propped himself up, and went to work on other areas.

Oh, that feels so impossibly good. Mia relaxed into his overtures but then tensed again. She couldn't allow this to happen again. She'd get addicted to him. To the way he worked her body until it no longer belonged to her. And then he'd shoot that gorgeous, carefree grin at her and leave town. Just like her ex.

Except if she allowed herself to fall for Ace Braddock, she might never recover. She didn't know how, but he saw a part of her and understood a part of her that was off-limits to everyone else. And if he took that from her and then stole it away with him, she'd . . . die.

Drama queen. Get over yourself.

But it was true.

She'd been operating beyond physical and emotional and psychological capacity for so long; she was stretched so thin that one more disappointment would break her. And Mia couldn't and wouldn't allow that to happen—especially courtesy of someone as transparent as Ace.

So despite what he was now doing to her body, which wanted to stay and play, Mia squirmed out from under him, somewhat breathlessly. "I have to, uh, use the bathroom."

Disappointment flitted across his face. "Okay. But come right back."

She disappeared into the adjoining facilities, put her hands on the sink, and stared at herself: flushed skin, beard-burn along her neck, swollen lips, sleepy eyes, mussed hair.

Nice, Mia. Some sober companion you are, getting drunk on Essence of Ace.

She ran the water in the sink and washed her hands while she tried to pull her thoughts together. Her instinct was to wrap herself in the bath mat and flee out the door, not even stopping to grab her clothes.

But she went back into Ace's bedroom, where he lounged quite shamelessly, nude and waiting for her.

"C'mere," he said, patting the mattress.

"I have to go," Mia told him, starting to gather up pieces of her scattered clothing.

"No, you don't."

"I have to be somewhere."

"Blatant lie." Ace looked at the clock. "It's way too early."

"Declan will be here any minute."

Ace shrugged. "And I care why?"

"*I* care," Mia said, desperately, climbing into her clothes.

"Stop that. I like you much better without those." He shot her a grin that almost melted her resolve. His hair was mussed in a very sexy way, he had two days' worth of stubble on his face, and his eyes were the deep blue in the Texas flag. "In fact, I'd rather you come to work from now on without them."

"Ha," Mia said. "That's not likely. Can you picture the headlines? 'Naked Woman Arrested Driving Smart Car.'"

Ace laughed, then grew serious. "Mia. What just happened between us . . ."

Oh no. Here it comes.

"Was incredible. I want you in my bed every night."

"Can never happen again," she said decisively, at the same time as what came out of his mouth.

They both stared at each another.

"What?" they each asked, simultaneously. And then, "Are you kidding?"

Mia, now fully clothed, backed toward the door as outside, Grouchy set to barking and the wheels of a truck crunched over gravel as it pulled through the gates and approached the driveway.

"Declan's here," she announced, which was unnecessary.

And then she fled down the stairs, taking full advantage of the fact that Ace was still naked, needed crutches, and therefore, couldn't catch her.

Chapter 25

ACE STARED AFTER MIA, TRYING TO PROCESS HER words. What the hell did she mean?

He stared down at his personal bat 'n' balls, then back at the empty doorway.

This had never, in the history of his life, *ever* happened. Usually women were instantly addicted to him. They called him. They texted him. They stalked him.

Judging by her reaction in the afterglow, as Mia lay tousled and smiling in the sheets, there was no way he'd struck out.

And he was serious. He did want Mia in his bed every night from now on. Mia Adams was . . . was . . . a keeper. He hadn't just had sex with her. He'd—Ace winced at the term—he'd made love to her. *Made love!*

That wasn't like making a bet. Or making a hamburger patty. Or even making a comeback.

Ace realized with a shock that he'd never—he winced again—*made love* to anyone else.

He'd, uh, banged. Screwed. Whatever term applied to

the mechanical achievement of mutual pleasure with a beautiful woman he didn't care much about seeing again— or at least not more than a few times. To his reasoning . . . why?

So many baseball bunnies. They came in all sizes and flavors, most of them delicious. So he'd never seen a reason to limit himself to one.

But Mia . . .

Ace stared at his bat 'n' balls again. "Really?"

They did not seem to feel the need to reply. Their mind was made up.

Mia was *The One*.

"I thought this was a mutual decision," he told his equipment. "I mean, shouldn't we talk about this?"

Nothing doin'.

"Have some high-powered negotiations, represented by my agent?"

Silence. Ace headed to the bathroom and turned on the shower, still holding up his end of the conversation. "Well, you're right. Lucille would never agree. She'd cut you off first and put you in a jar on her dresser. But this unilateral decision making is kinda galling for a guy like me." He stepped under the water and cleaned himself up, still replaying the morning in his mind. The hot water ran out before clarity set in, and just as he'd finished toweling off, his cell phone rang.

He tossed the towel aside and answered it. "Braddock here."

A torrent of Spanish flooded the line.

"Wait, wait. Slow down." Ace listened as the local investigator Mia had hired dropped his bombshell. "Uh-huh . . . *¿Qué?* . . . *Claro que sí.* Uh-huh . . . *Entiendo.* That's great news. Excellent news, in fact. *¿Dónde?* . . . Austin? What's the flight number? *¡Muchas gracias!* I will make sure you're paid. *Por despuesto. No problema. Adios.*"

Ace hit the off button on his phone and simmered. Robert Bayes was finally flying home, coming in under the radar—or so he thought. The creep was coming to snake his boat out of storage before it got auctioned off. The boat he'd bought on joint credit, but put only in his name. He cared not about Mia, but about his *boat*.

White-hot rage started to build. It was reminiscent of the feeling he'd experienced once or twice before when a bad call stole an important game.

That's my girl he's messing with. Ace's heart pounded in his chest as he quickly dressed in baggy shorts and a tee, then grabbed his baseball cap. *My girl.*

He scrolled to his sister's name in his phone and dialed her right up.

"My favorite brother . . . no, wait, is that really true?" Lila teased without even saying hello.

"I need a favor," Ace said.

"What else is new?"

"Lila, I need your help."

There was a pause. Ace knew his voice sounded strained.

In a less teasing tone, Lila said, "When I know Declan is right there and you ask me to drive all the way out from town instead, it makes me sad. Did you know that?"

Ace gritted his teeth. "I'll work on all that. I promise. But right now, there's something I have to do for Mia. And I have to do it *now*."

"Mia?" Lila asked. But all the same, he could hear her keys jingling in the background. "Did something happen?"

Oh, you could say that. You could definitely say that.

"She's fine. She's great." *She's way more than great.* "There's something I need to do for her. Will you drive me to the airport in Austin?"

"Oops," Lila said. The phone clattered against something. "I'm on my way. This feels like a secret. And yet it doesn't have that nice, light oh-Lila-help-me-ask-Jules-to-marry-me feeling I got when I helped Rhett." She turned on the engine and Ace relaxed a little. His sister was on her way, and for once, Ace was glad Lila drove like a bat out of hell.

With a ton of adrenaline flowing through his veins and the lack of a clear plan beyond *intercept Rob/fix things for*

Mia, Ace wished he could pace. Every second he waited until Lila's Suburban showed up felt like an eternity.

This can never happen again, Mia had said. Well, Ace didn't blame her for not believing in him—in the two of them together. He'd given the world plenty of evidence that he wasn't looking for something real, thanks to all those tabloid stories.

But not only did Rob deserve to be put in his place and be forced to treat Mia fairly, it was the best way Ace could think to show her just how special she was to him.

No, *more* than special. Necessary. He'd been breathing in cigarette ash and pickup lines way too long. He needed air. He'd needed air for a long, long while now. Mia was the fresh, clean Silverlake air he'd been missing all this time.

Lila pulled up in a cloud of dust, and he was already at the door, scrambling in. "We gotta go, sis."

She didn't say a word, just peeled back out toward the ranch gates, her lips pressed in a tight line. "Declan's going to kill me, isn't he." It was more a statement than a question. "Are you sure you want to be leaving Silverlake right now? You don't even have sunglasses on."

"This isn't about me," Ace said.

Something resembling a snort came out of Lila's mouth. "Sorry, I don't know what that was just then. I think it was shock."

"Shut up," Ace said, finding it hard not to smile along with her.

They drove in silence for another while. "You're not the same," Lila suddenly. "There's something different about you. Either I just couldn't really know you through the phone the way I know you now. Or something's changed you while you've been here."

Or both.

"You gonna tell me what you're up to?"

"Better not," Ace said. "I'd like to keep this visit under the radar."

Lila goggled at him. "Seriously?"

Ace kept his mouth shut.

"What're you doing taking a plane to go help Mia even though, far's I know, Mia's sittin' pretty in Silverlake, which is where you're supposed to be?"

She wasn't "sittin' pretty," which was why he was doing this. "I'm not taking a plane. I just . . . I have a meeting at the airport."

"Uh-huh. And?" Lila looked over a couple of times, then sighed when he didn't give her more information. "Are we parking? Am I coming with you?"

"I appreciate it, but this is all me. Drop me at the curb. I'll call a car service for the drive back." He didn't want Lila getting involved in something with Bayes any more than he liked Mia in such a tangle.

"You're a little low on public sympathy at the moment. I don't know if 'under the radar' really works for you."

"Lila?"

"Uh-huh?"

"Thanks for coming to pick me up. You didn't make me tell you why. You didn't make me do anything. You just showed up when I asked you to. I'm lucky you're my sister."

She kept her eyes on the road for once. And then she swallowed and said, "See now, what you've been missing by staying away all these years?"

"I'm seeing a lot more clearly than I used to, that's for sure," Ace said.

Lila smiled and hit the gas.

Ace's heart raced a mile a minute during the rest of the drive to Austin. He could feel his sister's eyes on him; he was definitely aware of her insane driving. His thoughts were in kind of a pregame state, and it was a feeling he hadn't experienced in a while. He kept seeing Mia in his mind's eye—it was as if he was dedicating a game to her.

He had all the same jitters he'd have if he'd been waiting to head out from the locker room into a crowded stadium, and even though he was preparing for an undoubtedly less-than-pleasant confrontation with Rob Bayes, Ace was struck by a very strange and sweet sensation that had nothing to do with the man at all: He was reminded how much he missed playing baseball.

It wasn't about wanting to go back to work after an injury. It was more as if he'd suddenly remembered what it was like to play for the pure, sweet love of the game.

When he thought about his last season—the one that wasn't so great, the one where he'd really turned it on for the tabloids—he knew that much of his behavior was about him acting out for lack of a better purpose. He'd done what he did for Pete because he didn't think he was worth as much as him, as a family member, even as a man.

Mia. It all connected now. If he could do this for Mia, get Rob to stop affecting her decisions in life because of this financial mess he'd created, he'd be able to give real meaning and purpose back to her, too.

Lila dropped him at the arrival-level curb with a nervous smile on her face. She wished him good luck and waited until he was through the door.

Fully inside the terminal now, Ace pulled the bill of his baseball cap down lower to avoid recognition and successfully crutched through the crowd without having to provide any autographs—or explanations. He scanned the screens for Rob's flight information and saw that a baggage drop-off number had been assigned. He took the escalator up and headed to the area where arriving passengers funneled after disembarking.

You had to love an airport that served awesome Texas barbecue and cold draft beer and sported giant guitars in the baggage claim area to represent Austin's renowned music scene. Ace made a couple phone calls, one to his usual car service—and one to the team's local police contact. But right now, he had a rendezvous point and a plan. This was Game Day now. He'd be on the field soon, according to the neon glow of the screens above. Rob was finally coming, and Ace's mind was focused. He felt clearheaded and certain of himself.

Mia had tried to tell him they didn't have a future. *This can never happen again*, she'd said. Didn't she know that anything was possible?

Especially after he dealt with Rob. Ace's knuckles itched with the urge to knock him down, but he had no plans to actually do that. He would be diplomatic and reasonable, but firm. He wouldn't take no for an answer. And thanks to his calls, he also had insurance.

Rob, he'd say. *Been a while, man. How ya doing?*

And Rob would be pleased to see him—after all, Ace was a star and in the majors, now. He'd probably want his autograph.

Ace would offer to buy him a beer for old times' sake. And then, man to man, he'd tell him that Mia was a friend of the family and that everyone makes mistakes, but Rob now needed to square things with her, make them right. Give her what he owed her.

Rob would hang his head, and then meet Ace's gaze and nod. *Yeah,* he'd say. *It's time . . . I screwed up. What I did wasn't fair.*

This was going to work. Balancing on his crutches, he craned his neck as passengers surged forward. Rob must be all the way at the back of his plane or at a far gate. Ace shook his arms and hopped a little on his good foot, mimicking the stance he'd normally take at second base just before the first pitch.

He was in the zone, suddenly all kinds of zen. *I got this.*

When he was done with Rob, Mia would be grateful enough that she'd fall irrevocably in love with Ace. Coach would be thrilled! The old man could even marry them himself . . . after all, he had done the honors for Rhett and Jules.

Ace cracked his neck, adjusted his crutches, and leaned against a nearby wall. Finally, Rob Bayes came ambling down the corridor, a distinct red tint indicating he'd spent a lot of time in the sun. He wore a heavy gold Rolex, and he checked over his shoulder more than once as he waited for his bag.

"Rob," Ace called. "Rob Bayes."

It took the sleazebag a moment to register who Ace was under the baseball cap. His eyes widened and his brows shot up. "Ace Braddock? What . . . what're you doing here?"

In Ace's peripheral vision, he saw a couple of interested parties perk up at the sound of his name. Keeping his own voice low and even, he said, "Funny you should ask. I'm waiting for you."

Rob's eyes narrowed, and he tensed. "Why?" But then he took in Ace's surgical boot and the crutches. He visibly relaxed.

"Ace Braddock," said one of the onlookers in a dreamy voice. "Can I have your autograph?"

Ace pleaded lack of a pen but agreed to a quick selfie to get it over with and then stepped aside. "Hey, man. Can I buy you a beer?" he asked Rob. So far, so good. It was going according to script, more or less.

"No can do," Rob said. "Some other time. I've got a thing. Followed by a thing. But great to see you, and all."

"Five minutes," Ace said, not posing it as a question. "And then I'll have my driver drop you off wherever you need to go." The selfie-taker was too generous; she'd alerted other travelers in the airport that Ace was there, and some had begun to take video. People were starting to jostle the two men trying to get to Ace; Rob took a step back out of self-preservation and bumped into a woman applying lipstick in preparation for what Ace suspected would be another selfie request.

He knew he'd be in public—he was always in public— but somehow he'd thought Rob and he would be able to talk alone. Ace could feel his anger rising, and it was already a small miracle that he hadn't shown this guy who'd treated Mia so poorly what he *really* thought of him.

"Your driver," Rob repeated, flashing his teeth. "Of course. I hear—and see—that you need one these days, Ace. Shame about the Maserati."

This was how it tended to go. Other men were either his new BFF or they decided to be hostile because his fame made them feel small. Ace gritted his teeth. "Insurance covered it."

"Yeah? Does insurance cover your ankle, too, bud? Got a policy on every muscle, joint, and bone? How long will you be sidelined?"

Ace's knuckles started to itch again. "Remains to be seen," he said evenly. "But I'm healing well, thanks to Mia. You do remember marrying Mia Adams, right?"

Rob began to walk alongside the conveyor belt as if he thought he saw his bag coming out.

"Mia would appreciate it if you'd take care of your obligations, Rob."

"And I'd appreciate it if you'd mind your own damn business."

"Mia *is* my business." Ace gimped in front of the man and turned, leaning forward on his crutches. There was no mistaking the warning in his tone. "And you left her high and dry, with no funds, all of your mutual debt, a half-built house, and a ridiculously unaffordable mortgage with a balloon payment set to kick in real soon. That's not cool, Bayes. Not cool at all. You also skipped the country so that she couldn't file suit and have your wages garnished or your assets frozen."

"What the hell?" inserted the lipstick lady, now staring at Rob in outrage. Ace could only sum her up as a caricature of a woman, tottering on five-inch stilettos, paired with sprayed-on jeans and a top cut so low as to be just shy of illegal. She dropped the lipstick into her bag and put both hands on her hips. "You did that?" she asked Rob.

By this time, at least eight other travelers were avidly aiming their phones at the scene. Ace—used to this, and more focused on controlling his temper—put out a palm and said, "Hey, guys, please don't." But they faded into the background as Rob laughed loudly, shaking his head.

Rob was too loud to notice the low, growling-like sound coming from Ace's throat. Nothing was going to stop him from fixing things for Mia. If Rob remembered anything from high school at all, he should remember that he couldn't beat Ace.

"You've been misinformed," Bayes told him. "Mia's

telling everyone a pack of lies. She's hormonal and crazy—she ran up a bunch of debt that I didn't even know about, and I was gentleman enough to leave her a mansion in her name. All I want is my boat. Now, if you'll excuse me." Rob stepped back around Ace and hightailed it in the direction of the escalators.

You unbelievable lowlife. Absently, he noted that his fingers had curled up against his itchy knuckles. "Yeah, the mansion," Ace said, limping forward and keeping pace. He caught up within two feet of the moving staircase, turning Rob by the shoulder and looming over him from his superior height. "The place with no back walls, full of wildlife and friggin' lawn furniture? What a showplace. Mia was cornered by a coyote in the kitchen!"

Rob had the nerve to laugh. "Puh-lease. What a sob story!" His smug, entitled, contemptuous expression was bad enough. But then he rolled his eyes—the last straw.

Ace's itching knuckles could no longer help themselves. He let go of his right crutch and coldcocked Rob, knocking him to the floor right in front of the down escalator. Unfortunately, he then had to step down hard on his already destroyed ankle, and hissed with the pain. He didn't like that slight crunching sound, either.

"I was *there*," he said between his teeth. "It was no sob story."

Rob lay there stunned. Then he struggled up on his elbows and compounded his first mistake. "So you're balling my ex, Easy Ace? Then *you* can pay her bills."

Before the words were out of his mouth, Ace had retrieved his crutch. He used the end of it to poke Rob in the chest, hard enough to push him backward onto the escalator, like a dead fish floating belly up in a pond. From there it was a foregone conclusion: Rob yelped and took a ride down, headfirst, cussing all the way.

It was horrible, humiliating, and hilarious all at once. Most of the onlookers cheered. Despite the excruciating pain now radiating from Ace's bum ankle, he followed behind Rob, trailed in turn by the lipstick lady. He rode down standing, admittedly some part of him enjoying Bayes's comeuppance, but mostly, more than anything, just wanting to go home to Mia. Several more bystanders were avidly taking videos on their phones—not that Ace cared.

"I'll sue you!" Rob shouted, finally landing in a heap at the bottom.

"Bring it," Ace said coldly. "But you'll have to do it from jail, because there is now an active warrant out for your arrest, and you've demonstrated that you are a flight risk. Not to mention that attorneys are expensive."

Rob continued to bluster and curse as he scrambled to his feet.

"Oh, look!" Ace pointed, more than happy to see his police contact had shown up as requested. "There's your ride. That officer, there, with the badge and the gun? Say hello, because he's the one with the warrant. And I'll have Mia get in touch to make sure you're comfortable behind bars, okay? Welcome home, Bayes."

"This man assaulted me!" Rob yelled to the officer. He turned to the woman with the scarlet lipstick as she and Ace got to the bottom of the escalator. "You saw him."

She folded her arms over her ample chest and glared at him. "I saw nothing. Besides, this guy's injured. You can't defend yourself against a man on crutches? Please." She smiled flirtatiously at the officer. "Would you like to take my statement?"

Ace watched with a grin as the cop took a raving, spitting Rob into custody. If he noticed all the phone cameras pointed his way, well, that was just a typical day in the life of a celebrity, wasn't it?

༜

Ace hobbled to the car waiting for him at the curb, feeling as if he'd just found out the team was going to the World Series. He was euphoric, despite the pain. Therefore, the fact that Lucille was suddenly calling didn't seem strange in the least.

He took the call just as the airport vanished from sight and relaxed back into the plush seat. Whatever he was expecting, he wasn't expecting Lucille shouting a stream of obscenities into his ear.

He put his phone back to his ear. "Lucille? How ya doin'?"

"So of all the absolutely stupid things you could do, you picked the *most* stupid, didn't you? Of course you would. Arrogant, young, too much money, all those women . . . *What the what*, Braddock!"

It wasn't the first time he'd gotten an earful. No, ma'am. But an uncomfortable feeling prickled across his skin, because it was the first time he'd heard a note of absolute coldness in her voice. Well, not directed at him. He'd seen Lucille go cold on a client before. Before she dropped them from her roster. It was the sound and tone of someone who was ready to stop believing.

"Lu—" he began.

"No. Absolutely not. You don't talk right now. I talk. Let's start with facts. The fact is, you're one lousy hero. I don't know what's going on with you, but you're terrible at it. You need to stop pretending you're a stand-up guy. Stop doing this helping-people thing. It gets you into trouble, it's taking money out of our pockets, and everybody knows you're not that guy. You're Ace Braddock, star ballplayer. You sleep around. You drink too much. You get in fights. But you never break the law. And all that works because everybody loves a bad boy who just can't help himself . . . until he *can't. Play. Ball!*"

Ace's hands suddenly felt like ice. And his ankle was cussing at him even louder than Lucille.

"You're supposed to be recuperating on your childhood ranch. It was a great story! Small-town community, a pretty nurse, cheerleaders bringing you smoothies and get-well cards. It looked fabulous on paper. What the hell are you doing at the Austin airport *punching* people? Pushing them down escalators with your crutch? You're getting into *real* trouble. Again! Nobody wants *real* trouble."

"How did you—" How did she know? She was worse than Mrs. Baxter.

"I'm not done. You don't talk. *I* talk. Because you know who isn't playing ball right now? The guy with the *real* injury. The guy who everybody thinks was one swallow short of a DUI. The guy who coldcocks people in airports when he doesn't get his way. *He's* not playing ball anymore because his team only wants the version of Ace Braddock who's a *real* hometown hero, the bad boy with a heart of gold. But for some reason you've decided to stop being that guy! They just want you to seem a *little* naughty, a *little* dangerous. They don't want a bad boy who's *actually* bad. Don't you know that? Unless you're the Greatest of All Time, no team is going to pay for the legal hassles that come with that."

For one of the few times in his life, Ace didn't know what to say. He could say what was in his heart: *Those guys you're talking about aren't real. I just want to be myself. I want to be the guy Mia saw when we were lying in each other's arms.* Lucille wouldn't understand what he meant; she'd laugh in his face.

Mia would understand.

Lucille finally wound down and huffed. "I'm headed out to Lone Stars HQ as we speak. I don't have to tell you what happens if they decide you're not worth it anymore."

His head had started hurting about one minute into Luce's rant, and now he was looking at a migraine. Worse, the shiny-new, stabbing pain in his ankle suggested he'd put a crimp in his recovery when he'd manhandled Rob.

Ace exhaled slowly, but the pain wasn't going away. Now that the adrenaline of besting Rob was gone, that pain, yep, it was loud and clear.

Sweating now, and nauseated, Ace could barely think straight, though it was doubtful Lucille had anything new to say anyway.

But all he could think about was Mia. The look on her face when he told her that her problems were going away.

She would understand why he'd done it.

Wouldn't she?

A double shot of pain tore through his ankle.

Lucille went abruptly silent. "What is it, Braddock?" she asked.

"What?" Ace managed.

"That was not a good sound."

He hadn't realized he'd made one. "My ankle . . ."

If he thought Lucille had cussed a blue streak before, this was something else. "Give your phone to the driver. You're turning around and getting checked out again at the hospital."

Ace opened the window in the divider and handed his phone over along with some unintelligible words. And then he slumped back and waited to pass out from the pain.

Chapter 26

MIA WAS AT MRS. BAXTER'S WHEN HER PHONE started going crazy. Given Mrs. Baxter's powers of prognostication, the woman could have warned her what was coming, but no. The texts started coming fast and furious, from her nursing buddies to the firehouse squad to Sunny over at her diner. All of them shared the same link: a video of Ace doing everything in his power to mess up Mia's life. Telling the entire world the intimate details of her life. Punching Rob in the face and knocking him down. And then using his crutch to shove him down the escalator, flat on his back, like a Twinkie in a production line.

So there Mia sat at Mrs. Baxter's kitchen table, with an unsampled square of chocolate walnut fudge in one hand and her phone in the other, pressing PLAY so many times, Mrs. Baxter started reciting from memory the dialogue between Ace and Rob.

And there, where the video was posted on social media, the comments started flooding in. People trying to figure out who Mia was. Mia from Silverlake. *A nurse . . . is this her? It is! She looks . . .*

Mia turned her phone facedown on the table doily and pressed down with her palm as if that would make it all go away. She shoved the fudge in her mouth all at once.

She couldn't even figure out what she was feeling: Shock, mostly. Horror? Definitely some enjoyment at Rob's humiliation. Fury at Ace for his interference and his indiscretion.

Mrs. Baxter reached over to rub her back, and the two of them sat there for a while as Mia chewed and thought about that amazing experience in Ace's bed and then wondered nervously if Mrs. Baxter had the power to read her mind. It would be the last time she'd ever see his bed, so did it matter?

Her feelings began to overwhelm her.

"I have to go now," Mia said, resolute, if a bit wobbly. And then she got up and hugged Mrs. Baxter, rushed out to her car, and turned on the ignition.

If Mia thought she could slip into Silverlake Ranch and slip right out again, she had another think coming. The wagons had circled; parked haphazardly next to Declan's truck were Rhett's, Jake's, and Lila's vehicles. Dust was still swirling in the air; at least one of them had only just pulled up.

Her first feeling was pure envy—no matter what, those Braddocks had one another's backs through thick and thin. Her second was embarrassment. She hadn't done her job well enough, had she? But she wanted to make a clean break, so she squared her shoulders and walked up the steps to the porch and let herself in. A crack of disbelieving laughter and a curse word from someone shot down the hall from the direction of the dining room.

Grouchy met Mia at the door but couldn't decide whether to stay and sniff or head back down the hall in the direction of the noise. Cat peeked around the corner and made a firm decision to run away.

"Ace, is that you?" Declan called.

Mia swallowed nervously and moved into the doorway. The Braddock family—minus Ace—was huddled at the dining room table in front of a laptop, watching the same video Mia had just seen.

It continued to play toward its embarrassing conclusion, even as all four Braddocks turned and stared at her. "Wow," she said, forcing a smile. "That's the fourth time I've watched that, and I feel like I see something new every time. Rob used to be a boxing guy."

Lila snorted.

"So I guess this means it's really, thoroughly all over Silverlake, huh?" Mia asked.

"Oh, honey," Lila said. "It's all over the planet."

There was a pause and then Jake said, "Yeah. And heads up. It triggered the community phone tree. But, you know, most things relating to Ace do that."

Rhett pushed the laptop away. "Just so you know, everyone has your back."

"Jeez, Rhett, I never pegged you for the sort who'd be indulging in phone tree gossip unnecessarily, so dare I ask how you know this?" Mia asked.

Rhett cleared his throat. "I only just got here. I was out getting stuffed olives, watermelon Jolly Ranchers, and tamales for Jules, and . . . people were out and about."

Lila put her arm around Mia's shoulders. "Honestly, as I pulled out of Main Street about ten people stopped me to ask if they could do anything for you. Nobody's judging."

Mia groaned. "Only ten?" she asked sarcastically.

"Well . . ." Lila winced. "I'll admit I'm being conservative. I've been asked to chair your fund-raiser."

"My . . . *fund-raiser*?!"

"I said I'd have to ask you first."

"Anything else I should know?" Mia asked.

The Braddock boys suddenly looked at anything but her. Mia looked at Lila. "What?"

"Um, well . . . there's been a bit of speculation about something Rob said on the video about you and Drew . . . together . . . but, you know, it's Rob, so . . ."

Mia's head throbbed. She grabbed the back of the nearest dining room chair to steady herself.

Declan stood up. "Are you okay?"

Mia's face burned. "Um . . ." She wanted to cry, and there was no way she was going to do that right here, right now, in front of all of them.

Lila stood up so fast she knocked over her chair. "I have to make a confession. *I* drove him to the airport. He said he wanted to help you, and—"

Mia gasped. "*Help* me? How could he possibly think any of that would *help* me? How could he think I'd want that? He didn't ask me what I wanted. He just does whatever he wants to do. That was *my* private business. *Mine*. Well, it isn't mine anymore. It seems to belong to everybody with an Internet connection now. I don't even know if I'm still going to have a job after this!"

The Braddocks looked at one another. "I'm sorry," Lila whispered. "I-I didn't know."

Declan strode forward and offered a chair. "Why don't you sit down."

Just when you think you can't be more tired, something blindsides you and you go down a little deeper. There didn't seem to be a bottom to the hole Mia had fallen into. She slumped into the chair and looked at Declan. "I thought he knew me. Deck, I . . . messed up. I thought he knew me."

Looking into Declan's face, she saw the moment he figured out she really had slept with Ace. A flash of anger passed across his features, but he schooled them, as he so often did.

"He never listened to me, that's for sure," Declan said bitterly. "How bad is it?"

Lila, Jake, and Rhett looked at one another, trying to catch up.

Mia shrugged. *He means my heart. And the answer is, bad. Drew's broken my heart into so many pieces I think some of them will be stuck between the floorboards of this house for the rest of my life.* But she wouldn't say it out loud. No way would she add that to the list of things her friends had to feel sorry about. "I'll be okay. It's, well . . ." She gestured to the frozen frame where the video had ended. "Super embarrassing. All my dirty laundry for the whole world to see . . ."

"I got a call," Declan said. "From his agent."

"The one where she said I need to do better or the team won't pay for a babysitter who can't keep track of the baby?" Mia asked, managing a woeful smile. "Don't worry about it. I'm quitting anyway."

"That did come up. But he's also been ordered back to the hospital for x-rays after this little incident with Rob."

Unbelievable. Mia threw up her hands.

Lila sucked in a short breath, and it was flattering to see the Braddock boys looking so bummed. But Declan just nodded. "Nobody wants you to quit."

"Thanks. But . . ." Mia shook her head.

"You're welcome to stay here. You know that."

"I can't, Deck. I came to get my things."

"Or you can stay with me and Amelie!" Lila said.

Mia looked around, wishing not for the first time that these people were part of her family, too. "Thanks. But I'm going to go stay with my dad for a little while." She paused, wincing. "If he's not too mad at me."

Declan shook his head. "You're not the one he should be mad at."

She smiled sadly. "Dad's never been mad at Ace his whole life. I'll get my stuff."

Lila came with her but they did more talking than packing. Mia wished she could stay there, that they were *her* family.

Ace never had seen all the good things that he had here in Silverlake. Never had. Never would.

Mia heard heavy boot steps on the stairs, and Declan stuck his head into the room. "Look, I know you won't want to continue with Ace now. But why don't you go pick him up so that you can tell him that yourself? It seems to me that you have other things to say to him as well. Take my truck."

Mia nodded her thanks. Declan followed her out to the porch, where he stood looking troubled until she'd driven too far to see him in the rearview mirror.

Chapter 27

THE MINUTE ACE SAW DECLAN'S SILVERADO PULL into the hospital parking lot, he relaxed. Strange. This was what it felt like when your family was a source of comfort. He'd come to realize during his stay at Silverlake that he could've had a lot more of that feeling if he'd given Deck more of a chance to get his bearings after the accident. Ace made a silent vow not to take his brother for granted anymore, and then a second vow, to ask Declan—as close as he was to Mia—to help him show her he didn't take her for granted, either.

He couldn't wait to tell her about Rob. And part of him wished it was Mia coming to pick him up, only he was kind of a mess, still, after reaggravating his ankle fracture.

The nurse who'd been overseeing his x-rays poked her head in the door. "Your ride's here, handsome."

Ace gave her his signature grin, the one that made the baseball bunnies wild.

But she just kind of bit her lip and looked worried. "Mr. Braddock?"

"Yeah?" He let his grin fade away.

"Your driver just returned this. I guess it was on the floor of the car?" She handed him his phone. "Thanks!" he said, beyond relieved. Mia was probably worried sick. And Declan had probably called, too, on his way over. "But maybe wait until you're home before you go down that rabbit hole. You need your rest." She pointed to the wheelchair sitting by the door. "Have a seat."

Rabbit hole? What was she talking about? And then it hit him. All those people taking video at the airport. "Awww . . ." he began.

"Them's the rules," she said.

He turned on his phone and while it was loading, he got in the wheelchair and let the nurse take him for a ride. He smiled at the folks pointing and whispering as they headed to the lobby doors. Nothing new there.

He really needed to talk to Lucille about the x-ray results when they came in. Couldn't let himself think the worst. Had to believe everything was going to work out just fine.

He told himself this as the nurse handed him the clipboard and he signed himself out. He told himself this as she pushed the wheelchair to the exit and the automatic doors slid open. He told himself this as he realized that the person standing next to the open door of Declan's truck was not Declan.

It was the one person he wanted to see most in this world. Except she was looking at him as if he was the one person she wanted to see the least. Mia was leaning on that truck, staring at him as if he'd let her down six ways from Sunday.

Oh *no*.

That hurt worse than his leg. Worse than any pain he could remember. Ace glanced back at the nurse; she was watching him worriedly. Mia turned away, busy moving the front seat back to give him more leg room.

And that was when his phone started buzzing as a whole mooseload of delayed texts and voicemails came in. Ace realized just how Lucille had known about what happened with Rob Bayes.

He'd gone viral.

There he was, chatting with Rob Bayes in the airport. There he was, punching him out. And there he was, poking him down the escalator with his crutch and saying way too much. He'd unintentionally spilled Mia's private life to the world. No matter how you looked at it, it was awkward.

"Hey, Mia," he said, trying to make eye contact.

"Drew," she answered, trying not to.

"I don't think Rob's gonna be a problem anymore." He wasn't fishing for gratitude, but . . . *disappointment*?

"That was *my* business," she said tightly. She gestured for him to climb into the truck. She even offered her arm to help him out. She was 100 percent professional . . . and zero percent personal.

"Mia—"

But he was settled in now, and she slammed the door and walked away. She got in the driver's seat and put the key in the ignition, but she refused to face him.

"How *could* you?"

Ace sat there frozen, trying to sort through his actions.

"How *could* you?!"

"I wanted to help you," he said lamely.

"Help? If you think that was helpful, then you don't know me at all. At all!"

"I *do* know you . . ." His voice trailed off. He ran through everything in his head. Getting the call, not telling her, not getting her input, punching Rob, revealing to Rob that he and Mia had a relationship, revealing Rob's indiscretions and mistakes to the world . . . revealing Mia's secrets to the world.

He was a celebrity. He was used to a certain amount of his business being common knowledge. But this was Mia. She was private. And she was going through a hard time. And now everybody knew it, whether she wanted them to or not.

How could he not have seen it before? He did know her.

And so he should have known that doing what he did would be a terrible mistake. He cursed under his breath. "Aw, Mia, I wasn't thinking. I—"

"You *never* think," she snapped. "You just do whatever you want to do, never mind how it impacts other people. It's all about you. Always has been, always will be."

"Sweetheart . . ." he began quietly, meaning it with all his heart.

"I'm not your sweetheart. I'm not your *anything*."

Her words were a knife to his heart, and the pain scared him in a way he'd never before experienced. "Then what are you doing picking me up? Just want to give me a piece of your mind? Go ahead and yell at me. Don't leave anything out. I deserve it. But then, forgive me as fast as you can, because, woman, I am in love with you."

He meant every word. But he hadn't meant to just blurt it out. It should have been different, special, and instead, it felt all wrong.

Mia must have gotten the brake mixed up with the accelerator. First the truck surged forward, and then it stopped too suddenly. And then she pulled herself together and hit the gas again.

"You're lucky you have family waiting to take care of you," she said, her eyes focused ahead. "I'm sure it doesn't come as a surprise that I'm quitting."

Ace stared at her profile, his blood rushing. "Did you hear what I said?"

"Yes."

"That's it?"

"What do you want me to say?" Her voice was measured and her knuckles were white on the steering wheel.

"'I love you, too' would be a fine answer."

She didn't give him an answer at all.

"Mia, you're gonna break my heart," Ace said.

"I guess so," she answered tightly. "Must be kind of weird for you, since it's usually the other way around."

Ace slowly sat back in the seat. "You can't quit on me."

Mia's breath came out in a rush. "I can and I do. Your

stunt with Rob was simply . . . unforgivable. If you think that made me happy in any way, you're really confused about what love is. But then, I guess I knew that. A guy like you . . . you say it so often it doesn't mean what you think it means."

"I say it so often?" he repeated in disbelief.

"Oh yeah, I love you, baby. Thanks for last night, *blah, blah, blah*," Mia said, in what was probably supposed to be her best Easy Ace Braddock imitation.

"That's not true." Ace gripped at his shirt, right over his heart as she sat in the driver's seat and mocked him.

"The pay period ends tomorrow. Once I drop you off, I don't ever want to see you again."

Ace couldn't remember Texas ever feeling so cold. "Mia . . ." he tried.

She shook her head. "Please don't. We were always gonna be a mistake. I knew that, but I couldn't help it. Can we not talk anymore, now?"

The trip home was the longest of Ace's life.

By the time she drove him through the ranch gates and parked the car between Lila's Suburban and her dad's Chevy Tahoe—what was Coach doing here?—Ace was done making stupid assumptions that life was still going to go his way.

Declan, Rhett, and Jake stepped out on the porch followed by Coach. It was as if they'd all been listening for the engine.

"Oh boy," Mia said, straightening her shoulders. "There's Dad. Welp. Your biggest fan still has your back."

Ace looked through the window. Coach Adams didn't look like his biggest fan anymore.

Chapter 28

COACH HAD FROWNED AT ACE BEFORE. HE'D SHOUTED at him to get his crap together. He'd lectured him on technique, strategy, and staying in the right frame of mind. He'd spotted him, talked trash about opposing players, and even screamed about political issues.

But Coach had never, ever looked at Ace as though he were a maggot. He had clearly seen the video, along with the rest of the world, and joined everyone else in judging him to be irresponsible. Again.

As Mia got out of the driver's side of Declan's Silverado, Ace found himself wanting to crawl under the seat, crutches and all. Letting down the man who'd devoted years of his life to making him into a success was almost worse than alienating Mia. Almost.

But at least Ace had faith that Coach, her dad, would be on his side in persuading her to give him another chance. Coach always had his back.

Through the window of the Silverado, he saw Mia cast a miserable glance at her father, saw Coach extend a hand toward her, and then saw Mia ignore it to run back inside. Coach's face fell, then settled into craggy, furious lines as he turned back to Ace.

In three strides he was at the passenger-side door, flinging it open. "WHAT IN THE HELL MADE YOU THINK YOU COULD MESS WITH MY DAUGHTER?!" Coach thundered. He grabbed Ace under one arm and yanked him bodily out of the truck. Shocked, Ace hopped and wobbled on his good leg, scrambling to hold on to the swinging door.

"*Hey*," Declan said, in dangerous tones.

"Let go of him," Rhett warned.

"Coach . . ." Jake began.

"Back off," Coach growled. "Young Andrew and I are gonna have a talk." He glared at all of them, challenging them to come any closer.

Ace hung over the truck door like a wet towel.

All three of his brothers looked at him for direction. They clearly would step in if he asked. But Ace shook his head. "Can we have the porch, please?"

Just then, Lila stepped out with their father's shotgun in her hands.

"PUT THAT DOWN!" All of her brothers, including Ace, yelled.

But Lila stood her ground. "Not until I know Coach isn't gonna hurt Ace." She squinted at Coach. "I know how to use it, even if some have complained about my aim."

"Okay, we're gonna need to stand down here," Deck said, stepping forward to remove the gun from her hands. A brief tug-of-war ensued, which he won easily. "Lila, get inside, before we all hang you in a laundry sack from a live oak again, just for your own protection."

Lila gave him a mutinous look. "I'm only going inside because Ace asked for privacy," she said before she marched inside, casting a worried glance behind her at Ace and Coach.

Ace did his best to offer her a reassuring smile.

Finally his brothers all exchanged a glance, then followed her.

Coach glowered at him.

Ace swallowed and reached for his crutches. "There's a big misunderstanding here," he said.

"No misunderstanding," Coach said in lethal tones.

"Please sit down," Ace asked, jerking his head toward the hand-hewn wood bench and rocking chairs on the porch.

"You sit down. Before I fell you like a tree, you little punk."

"Coach—"

"Shut the hell up. I have given you everything: my sympathy, affection, expertise, encouragement, knowledge, time, and trust—at great cost to my daughter, by the way. You think I don't realize that?"

"I—"

"I just don't know what to do about it. How to fix it."

"Mia—"

"Don't you even dare say her name! You aren't worthy, you piece of— *This* is how you repay me, for believing in your sorry butt? For taking you under my wing? You take advantage of *my daughter* while she's down and vulnerable?" Coach's face had turned purple.

"I love her," Ace blurted.

"You don't know the meaning of the word!" Coach roared. "You spoiled, arrogant little twerp. Rutting isn't love. You'd make it with a week-old bagel! A hunk of Swiss cheese! You think I'm some country bumpkin who doesn't read the morning papers or know how to spell *Internet*? You think I don't know what a supermodel is, or an actress? You think I don't notice how every woman in Silverlake— and a lotta men—fall all over you? You think I'm *stupid*?"

"Coach—"

"I *made* you! I gave up darn near everything to help a talented kid hold on to something in the wake of great tragedy. Give him something to *live* for, so he wouldn't fall down a black hole of guilt and misery—and that's where you were heading, mark my words."

The truth of that statement almost knocked Ace breathless. "I know—and I'm grateful, and—"

"Grateful," Coach spat. "Another concept you can't wrap your brain around. Gratitude requires respect, boy. And you have not only disrespected my daughter, you have disrespected me. You made a mistake when you tangled with Mia. *She*, not you, is the most important thing in my life, and the person who makes me the proudest. She gets up every day of her life to make the lives of others better. She never stops. She never complains. She never asks for help. She doesn't need thousands of fans to validate her, or a buttload of money. She doesn't need some fancy agent to fight her battles or get her out of trouble."

Ace didn't even know how to respond to that. He just hung his head.

"She also doesn't need some *jackass* to air her dirty laundry to the entire world or knock her ex down an airport escalator!" Coach bellowed.

Ace sighed. *Do I even try to defend myself?*

"Did it ever occur to you that I had it taken care of?" Coach continued. "That I and Vic and Pudge and Schweitzie had plans to meet up with that dirtbag and take him apart?"

Ace stared at him.

"But you had to insert yourself where you don't belong—" Coach's bushy, reddish-gray eyebrows drew down ferociously at his unconscious double entendre, and he coughed and choked until Ace reached out to slap him on the back.

"Get away from me," Coach growled. "You and me— we're done."

Done? What did he mean—done? That hurt worse than his ankle. "Coach, please hear me out."

"Ain't nothin' to hear."

"Give me a chance!"

"Done givin' you chances. You went too far."

Ace closed his eyes. There seemed to be no salvaging this situation. This was going to be the end of his relationship with the man he'd loved like a father. He couldn't change Coach's mind if he wouldn't even let him speak.

But he could still stick up for Mia. He could still try to make this mess up to her, if only in part. Coach's words ran through his mind again.

I have given you everything: my sympathy, affection, expertise, encouragement, knowledge, time, and trust—at great cost to my daughter, by the way. You think I don't realize that? . . . I just don't know what to do about it. How to fix it.

"Coach," Ace said heavily. "I wish you'd let me explain. But I realize you don't want to hear me right now. You're too mad."

"Darn straight, I am!"

"So let me say one thing. You don't know how to fix things with Mia? Well, for starters, why not tell her exactly what you just told me. About how you love her more than anything else in the world. About how proud you are of her. About how you respect her for not needing anyone's help . . . and also about how you had plans to help her anyway. I have a hunch she needs to hear all of that. Mia needs to know she's not alone. That she's got her dad back."

Ace's voice cracked on the last two words.

Coach Adams said nothing, only squinted at him balefully.

"I guess that's all I've got to say to you, then." Ace gripped his crutches. "Except that I love her, too. Whether or not you believe me, or think I understand the meaning of the word."

❧

Mia's open window overlooked the porch, and the sound of her father's angry voice easily carried on the breeze and up to her ears.

You made a mistake when you tangled with Mia. She,

not you, is the most important thing in my life, and the person who makes me the proudest.

The words she had dreamed, most of her life, of hearing. That her dad loved her more than Ace. That she was more important to him.

And yet the euphoria she'd always thought would accompany the words was missing. Because while she was furious with Ace, she didn't want his relationship with her father destroyed. She knew exactly what it meant to him— and also what it meant to her father.

And because . . .

Mia sat on the bed with her face in her hands. Because deep down inside, she'd always known that her dad loved her. She'd never truly been in any doubt. But she *had* wanted more of his time and attention. So she'd been hurt.

And maybe, just maybe, she needed to admit that she'd contributed to the situation by being a little stand-offish with her father, too. Out of pride. Maybe she needed to look in the mirror and assume at least a little of the blame so that they could resolve the issues between the two of them.

That was a painful and unwelcome realization.

You and me—we're done, he'd said to Ace. It was an outcome she'd actually prayed for once or twice as a kid.

And instead of cheering, she felt like crying.

She could hear the pain vibrating in both of their voices. She could hear the regret in both voices: that her father felt obligated to choose between them, and that Ace understood.

But worse, it half killed her when Ace refused to defend himself (*week-old bagel, Dad, really?*) but immediately went to bat for her.

Story of her life: Just when she hated Ace the most, she couldn't. He'd turn around and do something kind.

And just when she thought she might love him, she couldn't do that, either. Because he'd turn around and do something stupid, something cavemanlike, something that got caught on camera and went *viral*.

What did a girl do about a problem like Ace Braddock? Kiss him or kill him?

She sure wasn't going to kiss him, not ever again.

But she couldn't let the relationship between Ace and her dad end this way. It just wasn't right. They'd been a pair for too long.

So Mia pulled her face out of her hands, wiped her palms on her jeans, and stood up. She barreled down the stairs to behold all four of the other Braddock siblings shamelessly eavesdropping near a big plate glass window, along with Grouchy and Cat. She shook her head at them and barged out the door.

"Mia!" exclaimed Ace and her father at the same time.

She put both hands out, palms forward, giving them both the Heisman.

"Do not speak to me," she said to Ace.

To her father, she said, "You cannot stop speaking to *him*." She followed these words with a head jerk in Ace's direction.

"But, honey," her dad began.

"I won't have it," Mia told him. "*I* stopped speaking to him first."

Coach's forehead wrinkled.

So did Ace's.

Equally perplexed and out of long habit, they exchanged a glance with each another.

"And Dad, while do I love you for it, you don't need to fight my battles for me, either. But thank you. By the way, Ace was . . ." Her face heated. "Ace did not disrespect me."

"I was very, *very* respectful," Ace murmured.

She shot him a fierce, unforgiving look. "Shut. Up."

"Yes, ma'am," said Ace. "It's just that—"

"Which part of 'shut up' was unclear?" Mia asked Ace. "You do not speak to me. I do not speak to you. But you DO speak to my dad. I refuse to be the cause of a rift between you. Clear?"

"Uh," said Coach, rubbing the back of his beefy neck.

"Got it?" Mia asked. "Is this math too difficult for you, gentlemen?"

"Uh," said Ace, dragging a hand down his flushed face.

"Because although I'd love to knock both of your heads together, you'd just end up concussed. And what I'd really like more than anything is to drive back home with you, Dad, and do some serious talking—maybe followed by a big, fat bear hug."

Coach got to his feet. "That just might be in the playbook, sweetheart."

She smiled at him, tears welling in her eyes. "Good."

Then she turned her back on Ace and stepped off the porch.

Chapter 29

ACE WATCHED COACH AND MIA GET INTO THEIR RE-spective vehicles. Any trace of humor in him vanished completely as he realized this was goodbye. He watched them driving toward the ranch gates, watched the dust drifting across the tire tracks. The emptiness in his heart nearly took his breath away, and he could remember only one other instance when he'd felt this bad. As if everything that mattered in life had just been taken away.

Both times were his fault.

"Hey."

Ace looked up, trying to focus on Declan's face.

Declan's hand clamped down on his shoulder. Not too hard, just firm and in control. "Hey," his brother repeated. "Everything's going to be okay. We'll stick together."

"I think that's what you said the first time," Ace mumbled.

"The first time?" Declan looked over his shoulder. Rhett, Jake, and Lila all moved forward.

"Let's go inside," Lila said softly. "So you can sit down."

Ace didn't have any fight left in him at all. He let his family help him over the threshold and into the living room, where he sank into the sofa cushions. The sense of loss was so strong, so painful, that he closed his eyes, wishing he could disappear if he couldn't make it all go away.

"Are there some painkillers you're supposed to be taking?" Lila asked.

Mia would know.

"You should elevate your leg," Jake said.

Mia would have made sure of that, too.

Rhett sat down next to Ace on the couch. "We need you to care, Drew. You're kind of scaring us right now."

Declan walked in with a mug of coffee. Ace hadn't realized he'd even gone. He looked up as his oldest brother put the mug down on the coffee table and then crouched down at Ace's side.

"What are you thinking?" Declan asked.

"I told Lila when she drove me to Austin that I was lucky to have her as my sister . . ." Lila's hand gave his arm a little squeeze. "The same goes for the rest of you." Ace hung his head. "I'm so sorry I ruined everything."

"What are you talking about?" Declan was still kneeling on the floor beside him. "You didn't ruin anything for me."

Ace clenched his jaw to stop his emotions from getting the better of him. "I've ruined things with Mia. I've ruined things now with Coach. I ruined things for all of *us* . . . and I never stop letting you down, do I?"

"What? Ace, what do you mean?"

Maybe he couldn't fix anything, but the time had come to talk.

To explain why he'd gone away and never come back. To apologize.

To beg forgiveness from his brothers and sister, even if he'd never, ever forgive himself.

As he looked up at the portrait of their parents over the fieldstone fireplace, memories of that awful night flooded him. The argument: Ace insisting that Mama or Pop take him to the game.

"*You're not even slated to play, Drew,*" Mama said, wearily.

"*It's my team. I want to be there.*"

"*It's been a rough week, son. Can't say as I want to drive all the way to San Antonio for no good reason,*" Pop said, dragging a hand down his face.

"*You drove Rhett to his stupid math thing,*" Ace groused. "*And Jake to his football game.*"

"*Rhett is trying for a scholarship. Jake was actually playing.*" Mama dug into the freezer, trying to find something for dinner.

"*It's not fair! Why do I always get shafted?*"

"*Nobody's shafting you, Drew,*" Pop retorted. "*You don't need to be there. Give us a break.*"

"*You won't take me? Fine. I'll ride my bike.*"

Mama slammed the freezer closed. "*You most certainly will not, young man. It's too far, and it's dangerous. You'll get run over in the dark by some driver who's not paying attention!*"

"*Then I'll walk.*"

"*You will do no such thing.*"

"*You're impossible!*" Ace shouted. "*I hate—*"

"*Drew, that's enough,*" Pop ordered. He set a soothing hand on Mama's shoulder. "*Beverly. Honey, tell you what. We can drop him at the game and then grab a couple of pizzas for everyone on the way back. That way you don't have to cook. How's that sound?*"

"*Fine. Declan can keep an eye on Lila.*"

And they all climbed into the minivan, Ace feeling triumphant because he'd won. He was getting his way. But the triumph was short-lived.

Mama and Pop would never return.

If only he could take back his words that night. Take back the snotty attitude and the pressure he'd put on them. If only he hadn't been the reason his parents were on the road that night. But he was.

Ace tried to choke down his guilt and shame, not entirely successfully. He gazed at his siblings all gathered around him, looking as though they cared more than he could have ever imagined. And he finally took the burden that had been resting on his shoulders for thirteen years, took it right off, and set it down. He spoke to them of the things that had made him run from home, the things that made him stay away for so long.

"I was the reason Mama and Pop were driving that night," Ace said, his voice hoarse to his own ears. "The saying goes *wrong place, wrong time*. But I didn't have to play that night. I was being recruited. Nobody wanted me to get injured, so I wasn't playing. It was one hundred kinds of stupid. The game didn't even mean anything. We weren't going to regionals. We weren't going to nationals. I was just going to see my friends that night.

"They didn't want to go back out, but I was a brat. I threatened to ride my bike or walk. So they drove to yet another field and another set of bleachers. And Mama got so tired when we went to extra innings that she couldn't even knit that ugly orange afghan she was making. She just sat there with it in her lap, totally glazed over. For me."

He finally saw in his siblings' faces that they understood exactly what he was talking about.

"I knew they were exhausted," Ace continued. "Sick and tired of driving me to baseball. But I wouldn't let it go. I badgered them until they said okay. And at the end of it I go off for a burger or some crap, getting a ride home with *Coach* . . ." Ace laughed, a bitter sound. "I didn't even go back with them! What a jerk, right?"

Lila shook her head. "No."

Jake cocked his head, his eyes full of pity.

Rhett sighed deeply.

And Declan . . . Declan, who'd gotten the shortest end of the stick after the accident that killed their parents, went stony-faced.

"Listen to me," Declan said. He'd said the same words a million times in the aftermath of that night when he was trying to keep it all together. *Listen to me*, he'd had to beg. *Please listen to me.*

It didn't sound the same in Ace's ears as it had when he was a kid. Now that it was too late, he desperately wished listening to Declan was a real option. One that could fix all his adult problems.

"The accident was nobody's fault. It sure wasn't yours. You weren't even in the car, Drew. You weren't anywhere near it. So much of life has to do with things we simply cannot control. None of us blame you; we never have."

Declan looked at the others. "I don't recall anybody ever saying to me that it had anything to do with you at all." He managed a rueful smile. "And I sure remember who was blamed for what."

"I'm so sorry for that," Ace said, still full of misery and regret. "I owe you an apology. You were actually as good a stand-in father as anyone could have been under those circumstances. I'm sorry we all gave you such a hard time."

Ace shook his head and looked at his brother through damp eyelashes. "No, wait. I gotta own it for myself. I'm sorry *I* gave you a hard time about trying to lead this family after Mama and Pop died. My part of it's on me."

Rhett cursed softly and elbowed Declan's shoulder. "I've said it before, but I'll say it again," Rhett said. "I'm sorry about what happened between us, too. Our story was complicated, but I didn't do right by you all these years. I didn't handle things the way I should have."

Jake snorted. "Well, Declan's already heard *my* apology—more than once." He elbowed Declan's other side. "You wanna hear me eat crow again?"

Deck expelled a breath. "No more crow. It's not that tasty."

"The point is, nobody blames you for anything, Ace, and we've all made our share of mistakes," Lila said. "Well, I am mad at you all for leaving me alone with Declan for so long. His cooking is really awful."

"You're one to talk," Declan retorted. "Anyway, I know you're free to go, Ace, but you should stay." He shook his head suddenly, ruffling his hand through the front of his hair. "Maybe that sounds like I'm trying to tell you what to do, but that's not what I'm—"

"It doesn't," Ace said. "It's okay. It doesn't sound like that."

Declan blinked, clearly surprised.

"I don't know what I'm gonna do. Mia . . ." He shook his head.

"Don't run just to run," his older brother said.

"I won't. Not this time." Technically, the clock hadn't quite wound down on his "rehab." More than that, Ace knew that if he left Mia like this, he'd stay away for even longer next time.

Declan shrugged. "I'm just sayin' that you never really get anywhere, in the end."

Ace didn't have to answer, because his phone rang. He grabbed for it, praying for Mia's name to light up. It wasn't Mia. He sighed and took the call, bracing himself for what was to come. "Hey, Lucille," he said wearily.

"It's like this, Braddock. Management is not happy, but they're willing to give you a shot at an official workout as soon as you're ready. So no more public stupidity. Focus on healing that ankle, because if the results of the workout and stress tests aren't stellar, you're done with the Lone Stars. If you show you're one hundred percent, they aren't going to drop you, but you'll still have a serious PR load to deal with when you get back. Looks like being an upstanding citizen is going to be your second job."

She went silent, maybe waiting for a response. Ace looked at his ankle in its ugly surgical boot with barely suppressed fear, and thought this might be as low as he'd ever been in his life. Yet, as much he was going to pray that his body wasn't broken beyond repair when the boot came off, he was going to pray harder that Mia's heart could be put back together.

And even harder still that she'd find a way to believe in him.

Chapter 30

MIA LEFT HER STILL-UNPACKED THINGS AND FOL-lowed her dad's truck in her little blue car, all the way back to her childhood home. Since his defense of her, the bill of his cap tipped up a little higher, his broad shoulders were straighter, and his elbow rode out the rolled-down window, his sleeve billowing in the breeze.

She couldn't change the past. She couldn't change the unfortunate maroonish shade that he dyed his hair to stay looking young. But the way she viewed him *had* changed—forever. Today, her dad had been her hero. He'd chosen her over Easy Ace. And as the little car bounced along the gravel and then over several potholes on the route, her heart did, too.

In fact, it swelled—and not from the bruising it had taken. Mia's heart swelled with more love for her father, maroon-tinged hair and all, than she'd ever thought possible. By the time she pulled into the driveway alongside him, her eyes stung.

She jumped out of the car and ran toward him with open arms.

Coach looked a little alarmed. "Hey, baby girl! What—"

Mia hugged him, hard.

He wrapped her in his beefy arms, squeezed her tightly, and lifted her off her feet. "Hey, honey."

Her tears spilled over and ran down her cheeks as she inhaled his familiar scent: peppermint, piney aftershave, and the overpoweringly sweet brand of fabric softener that infested every one of his shirts. It was signature *Dad*. She could imagine it marketed as a cologne, distributed in Christmas stockings across America.

"Th-thank you," she managed. "Thank you, Daddy." She hadn't called him that since she was a child.

"For what? What's this all about?" he protested.

"You *stood up for me*. To Ace. Don't think I didn't hear everything you said."

"Why . . ." Coach seemed at a loss as he put her down, set his hands on her shoulders, and gazed into her eyes. His own were troubled.

"It meant so much to me," Mia said, helplessly sobbing. "It meant everything."

"Honey . . . oh, honey." Coach took her into his arms again, kissed her hair, and rubbed her back.

It made her cry even harder.

"What can I do?" he asked. "How can I make it better? Make it all up to you?"

"S'okay," she choked, her words muffled by his shirt.

"It's not," her father said, in gruff tones. "I know that now."

"It is . . . because it's gone. After only a few words today. All those feelings of . . . hatred . . . competition, that I had for Ace—they're *gone*. And all of the resentment I had toward you. I just needed to know that you love m-m-me, too. At least as much as you love him."

"Mia. Mia, sweetheart. I'm so sorry. So sorry." Her father rubbed her back again. "I'm not much for psychology, baby girl. But my best guess about all of this is that I couldn't stand missing your mom. It hurt. Real bad. Loving her and having us not be enough for her big heart. So I guess I closed off my heart to you because I couldn't stand it if I loved you and lost you, too. Stupid, maybe. Nobody's ever gonna give me the Nobel Prize for fathering . . ."

She chuckled weakly at that.

"I let your grandmas step in and parent you, do the job I should have done. And then there was Ace, who'd just lost his own folks. He was frozen and in such a world of hurt. My heart went out to him. Couldn't help it. And he did love him some baseball, that kid . . ."

Coach shook his head. "He was good before. But after the accident, he was phenomenal. Now I know it was probably that he didn't let anything else into his head. He just practiced and practiced and avoided anything and everything *but* baseball. He just couldn't face what happened that night. He blamed himself for putting his parents on the road; he's *always* blamed himself for their deaths. Couldn't ever talk about it, though. Just played ball."

Mia processed this information. Ace blamed himself for his parents' deaths. It certainly explained a lot of things . . . why Easy Ace lived so much on the edge. Got into so many fights. Had deliberately taken the blame for his teammate's mess. Did things like punching Rob and pushing him down an escalator.

Oh, Drew. Crutches and all, you had to go looking for a fight on my behalf? When it easily could have been you *thrown down the escalator?*

Suddenly Mia's anger at Ace dissipated. He might be a troublemaker and a jackass, but he was a jackass with a heart of gold. She recalled his words on the porch of Silverlake Ranch only an hour before. Even after Coach had renounced him.

You don't know how to fix things with Mia? Well, for starters, why not tell her exactly what you just told me. About how you love her more than anything else in the world. About how proud you are of her. About how you respect her for not needing anyone's help . . . and also about how you had plans to help her anyway. I have a hunch she needs to hear all of that. Mia needs to know she's not alone. That she's got her dad back.

He did know her.

And, oh, how his voice had cracked on the last two words.

As if he'd wished, more than anything, that he had his own father back.

Easy Ace Braddock hadn't really had it so easy in life.

And even when the man who'd been a substitute father had rejected him for "going too far," for "messing" with his daughter, Easy Ace—of all the people on the planet—had displayed *grace*. He'd been concerned for *her*, Mia, not for himself and the wound that was being inflicted upon him. Ace had not only relinquished the dad he'd stolen from her, he'd also gone to bat for her—again.

I guess that's all I've got to say to you, then. Except that I love her, too. Whether or not you believe me, or think I understand the meaning of the word.

Did Easy Ace Braddock really love her? Was that even possible?

Her father interrupted her musings. "I need a cold beer. Want one?"

It was a classic male peace offering. A way of saying that all of this uncomfortable emotional stuff needed to be washed back down into the gut, where it belonged.

Mia looked at her watch. "Sure, Dad. I'd love to have a beer with you." She had to get Mrs. Dooley settled for the evening, and then check-in at a new client's, an elderly gentleman. But one light beer with her dad wouldn't incapacitate her.

He moved a little stiffly these days, favoring his right hip. His formerly muscular frame was padded by fast food and middle age. And that hair dye . . . Mia felt a rush of affection for him anyway. And concern.

They sat down on the couch together, Stetson bounding from one lap to the other, wagging his tail and wriggling in excitement. Celebrating.

"I know you don't want to be the cause of a rift between me and Ace," Coach said, rubbing absently at the condensation on his beer can. "But I'm mad as all get-out. Of all the gals in Silverlake, he had to mess with you?"

Mia sighed. "Dad. I know this is hard for you to wrap your head around, but . . . it was my choice, too. I'm a consenting adult."

Coach tried to repress a shudder and shut his eyes tightly, as if to block out any unwelcome mental images.

Mia laughed softly. "I knew it was a mistake; nothing serious. Maybe I needed to wash Rob out of my hair."

"About dang time," her dad muttered.

"And Ace was right there, convenient. He can be a tool, but he's all right." She kept her gaze slightly averted so he couldn't see how much of an understatement *he's all right* really was.

Coach opened his eyes again and peered at her. "You defending him? After he's embarrassed you in front of the entire world?"

Mia took a sip of her own beer and washed her own feelings back down into the depths of her body. Where she hoped they would just pass on through. Like Ace Braddock, whose time in Silverlake was always planned to be limited and low-profile. "Yeah, Dad. I guess I am. He's not a bad guy. He just has a swelled head from all of his fans, and that makes thinking things through a little challenging."

"You make it sound like a medical condition," he said.

She laughed. "I'm pretty sure it is."

"Well, I want him to stay away from you." Coach snorted. "Told me he loves you."

"He said the same thing to me," Mia said sadly.

"He did?"

"Yup."

"And . . . ?"

She shook her head, looking down almost fiercely at her beer can, glad it was gathering more condensation and crying for her. She refused.

"Aw, baby girl . . . tell me it isn't true."

"What?"

"Tell me you haven't fallen for Ace," he said gruffly.

"Dad." Mia raised her chin and gave him the most level look in her repertoire. "Dad, do I look like an idiot?"

❧

For someone who definitely was not nursing a broken heart, Mia certainly had trouble wanting to get out of bed the next day to face the world. But she'd made an appointment with her boss, Phyllis. Now she sat waiting for her, staring at that same beautiful framed Mediterranean scene with the cobblestoned streets and little café tables arranged next to blooming pink bougainvillea that climbed the walls.

It climbed the walls a lot more gracefully than Mia did herself mentally . . . but then, she hadn't been born a plant. That seemed unfortunate at the moment, since plants didn't fall in love with the bees that pollinated them, no matter how sweetly they buzzed or how much honey they made or how hot they might look in their little black and yellow striped uniforms.

As Phyllis bustled in, Mia decided that she was officially losing her mind. Who fantasized about being a plant?

"Hi, honey! Welcome back to Mercy," said Phyllis, enveloping her in a hug that smelled of menthol, old paper files, and hair spray.

I am looking forward to some mercy. I know I'm supposed to learn a lesson from this mess of a life I'm living, but please, God, enlighten me as to what it might be? But Mia hugged her back.

"Thanks," she said, producing a smile. Telling herself she looked forward to snapping on some latex gloves, taking blood pressures and temperatures and patient notes. Dealing with cantankerous old patients like Kingston Nash and his contemporaries. There were a lot of sweet and uncomplaining ones, too. And the ones in serious, long-term pain, who needed her compassion, care, and comfort most of all. They needed her a lot more than a guy like Ace.

"So," Phyllis said, settling behind her desk and gesturing for Mia to sit as well. "When I urged you to take some time off, I didn't envision you using it to babysit Easy Ace Braddock." She laughed, but the humor didn't reach her eyes, which still held concern as she scanned Mia from head to toe.

"Oh, you know," Mia said vaguely. "It was a well-paid, plum assignment. Couldn't turn it down."

"Uh-huh. Especially when he's pushing people down escalators with his crutch on your behalf," her boss said wryly.

"Ace does have his . . . idiosyncrasies," Mia said carefully.

"Sorry," Phyllis said quickly. "It's just that everyone, but *everyone*, shared the video. I really should mind my own business."

Mia sighed. "It's okay. Ace had a misguided notion that he was helping me. As you can see, he didn't. So I'm done with that gig. Ace has brothers and a sister who can help him out. Our patients here need me a lot more than he does."

"Well, I won't deny that I'm thrilled to have you back," Phyllis admitted. "But I can't say that you look rested. Is it true that he stole a tractor and drove it to Schweitz's?"

Mia took refuge in humor. "I'm pretty sure that HIPAA rules prevent me from discussing the Grand Theft Tractor incident, among others." She winked.

Phyllis laughed and shook her head. "Okay, fine. Keep all the juicy details to yourself. But just so you know, there are a number of nurses here at Mercy who'd jump at the position if Ace is hiring again. They don't care if he's incorrigible, demanding, and entitled."

To her own disgust, Mia defended him yet again. "He's really not so bad. And despite his nickname, he hasn't always had it so easy."

She didn't like the way Phyllis was evaluating her. Mia got up. "So . . . want me to start again next week?"

"Sure. And Mia? We're really happy to have you back."

"Thanks, Phyllis. I've missed you."

Chapter 31

FUNNY THING. WHEN MIA WAS HERE AT SILVERLAKE Ranch with him, Ace spent all his time running away, trying to escape. Now that he didn't have the urge to bolt, she was gone and he'd have given anything in the world to have her back again.

Ace sat on the floor of his bedroom and let his head fall back against the wall. Sunlight streamed in from the window, forming patterns on the floorboards. He stared at his toes poking through the open boot and tried to make sense of his life. Across the room, a lone wax baseball candle sat under the bed.

Loss. Bone-deep loss. He missed Mia so much, and it sure didn't help that he'd repeated history with her. This feeling of loss, accompanied by the realization that he hadn't appreciated what he'd had when he'd had it, was something he'd struggled with since the day his parents had died.

Except Mia was still out there, vibrant, alive, smiling. Just not smiling for him.

Ace couldn't think of a thing to do except watch the dust motes swirling in the light. Jake and Rhett made phone calls from work, but Lila and Declan were around. They kept popping their heads in, giving him sad-puppy looks and bringing him coffee that tasted like AstroTurf. So wallowing in self-pity and heartbreak for his remaining time in Silverlake was definitely an option.

Ace used a crutch to recover the baseball candle that had rolled under his bed. He tossed it in the air a couple of times. Since he was alone, he brought it to his nose and sniffed to see if Mia's scent was on it. It didn't smell like her, but it sure brought back the memories of making candles together. It sure brought back the memories of all sorts of things they'd done together.

Despair threatened once more. Ace swore under his breath; he knew from experience that only time could lessen this kind of pain. But it wouldn't lessen the regret. He'd have that forever, knowing that he'd let Mia Adams get away, and it was entirely his fault.

He practiced tossing the baseball a couple more times. It felt good. He could almost imagine being back on the field, in his comfort zone.

"Bottom of the ninth," Ace murmured. "Bases loaded . . ." Playing in the major leagues was an exercise in managing stress, believing in yourself, and getting the job done. Ace didn't choke in tough situations. Until all hope was gone, he played every moment as if the game could still be won. No matter how many runs behind they were, no matter how bad things looked. He never gave up. That was what Coach Adams had taught him.

Ace stopped tossing the baseball and stared at it. *It's not over until it's over. Did you give it your all, Braddock? Did you try your hardest?*

He needed to take action.

There were all kinds of words out there, a lot of BS. The reporters mangled his quotes and printed half stories, plus there were all those lies he'd told to help Pete. He'd said all kinds of seductive nonsense to baseball bunnies over the years. But words weren't going to work in this situation. He was in love with Mia in a way he'd never been before; he hadn't known this kind of love existed when he'd used pillow talk so carelessly in his past. So he couldn't use the same dusty words on her. He'd devalued them. He had to *show* her.

Even if she still couldn't find it in her heart to believe, maybe it would lessen the pain *and* the regret he felt to know that he'd done his best to help her find happiness.

Even if it wasn't with him.

Ace tossed the baseball candle on the bed and grabbed the crutches. He hopped to the window, opened it, and stuck out his head: "Declan, are you down there? Hey, big brother . . . I could use a little help!"

❧

Ace, Declan, and Lila sprawled on the floor of the great room at Silverlake Ranch, surrounded by piles of glitter tissue, boxes, mailers, and all the baseball candles and spa products Declan could find that were left after Founder's Day.

Ace wore sweats and an ancient Longhorns tee, Deck was clad in his usual denim and a shirt with the sleeves rolled to the elbow, and Lila . . . Lila sported her typical peacock wear.

Today's ensemble included a chunky, multicolored necklace of natural stones over a funky gray designer top, which she'd paired with black jeans and black cowboy boots. Her hair was swept back in a messy side-ponytail.

Ace had signed every single baseball candle and was now propped up against the distressed leather couch. He pored over a yellow legal pad, writing and crossing out, writing and crossing out. He'd already made a list of where he planned to send everything: the stadium stores and upscale souvenir shops in major league cities, every member of every team's WAG committee . . . the list went on and on. The nice thing about being a social butterfly was that you knew a lot of people. He'd never asked for favors before, so Mia had a good shot of getting some interest, courtesy of using his name.

Maybe if he'd used his brains, she'd be using his name for the rest of his life . . .

"You okay there?" Lila asked. Her face, hair, and clothes all showed traces of the glitter as she filled the gift boxes with Mia's products, expertly arranging the fancy tissue to avoid damage and show off the goods.

"I don't know yet," Ace said glumly. "I really have no idea if this is going to mean anything to her."

"It'll mean something," Declan said. He didn't look up when he said, "When it's from the heart, it means something." Ace's brother was done stacking mailers and had switched to cutting lengths of striped gold and white twine.

Ace went back to his attempt to wordsmith the letter he planned to slip in with each sample. But it was no use. Instead he doodled his vision of Mia from Founder's Day; she hadn't stopped smiling for hours.

"We're just about ready to seal everything up; are you almost ready with the pitch?"

When he didn't answer, Lila looked up and appeared to read the frustration on his face. "Oh, I guess that's why they use you at second base," she quipped. "Maybe start with bullet points. Make a list of everything you want the people receiving your products to know. Stuff that will make them want the candles and soaps and stuff even more. Once you've got everything out of your head, you can craft the message more carefully."

With a groan of frustration, Ace dropped the pad and pen on the floor next to him. Both of his siblings looked up. "Maybe I could just draw a cartoon," he grumbled. "It's the words. I can't get the words right."

"What do you want to say?" Lila asked. "I mean, you could just send a standard sort of PR pitch. It's your name that's going to get her stuff in the door. It's your name that's going to get these people to try out the soaps and light the candles. Short and sweet is fine."

"I was thinking of making it more personal. Helping them understand why the products are special. Why they should stock them. There's more I want to say than just, 'Hey, I'm Easy Ace Braddock and you should buy my girl-friend's . . .'"

He trailed off as reality hit him like a sledgehammer. "My . . . *friend's* . . . stuff."

Are we even friends anymore?

It was crazy to have to ask himself that question. He was in love with her! He took one of the candles out of Lila's pretty little boxes and fought the temptation to throw it as hard as he could out the window. "Mia put her heart and soul into these products. There are things to say, and I just can't figure out how to . . ."

Ace covered his mouth with the back of his hand. This was embarrassing. He was gonna lose it in a minute.

"Hey," Declan said. He leaned over and put his hand on Ace's shoulder. "Close your eyes."

"What?"

"You heard me. Close your eyes."

Ace exchanged one of those *is he crazy?* looks with his sister, but he did.

"Now, think about everything that made you care about her," Declan said. "Think about what makes you not want to live without her. Think about the way your heart beats faster and your eyes can't stop following her."

Lila's jaw dropped. "That's the most romantic thing I've ever heard. How are you still single?"

Ace's eyes popped open and he grinned.

"I'm getting really sick of people asking that," Declan groused. "Ace," he ordered, "Close your eyes again."

Ace rolled them first, but he followed orders. There was a silence as Ace filled his mind with thoughts of Mia, bringing her smile to the forefront of his mind.

"When you're ready, open up."

Ace opened his eyes. Declan handed him the pen and pad. He began to write from the heart, as Lila chatted on to

Declan about what sort of letter *she'd* put in with Mia's samples.

Finally, he put down the pen. "It's kind of long—"

"Just read it," Declan said.

Ace began to read.

> *This is a personal appeal on behalf of a dear friend. I have never lent my name to marketing anything other than the Austin Lone Stars . . . until today, when I urge you to give these handmade, artisanal products a chance.*
>
> *They are created from natural, sustainable ingredients (home-harvested beeswax and honey, fresh goat's milk, and garden-grown herbs) by an incredible woman whom I wish you could meet in person.*
>
> *How do I even begin to describe Mia Adams?*
>
> *Mia is beautiful, inside and out. She's kind. She's a healer. She's creative, dedicated, and hardworking. You'd be lucky to have her as a friend, a sister, a mother, or an aunt.*
>
> *Mia is also generous to a fault. Generous enough to have shared her own father with a kid like me, when I was devastated and hurting after the death of my own parents. Because of Mia's graciousness, I was able to grow into the player and the man I am today. I will never be able to thank her enough.*
>
> *And so I enclose her handcrafted products for you to sample.*
>
> *It's my sincere hope that You & Mia will be a significant part of your life and your business.*
>
> *Thank you.*
>
> *Sincerely yours,*
> *Ace Braddock*

"I can't send this with the baseballs. It's not a marketing pitch." His voice was hoarse and his heart pounded.

"Sure you can. It's more than a marketing pitch, but it'll work beautifully . . . I knew you had it in you."

"How?" he asked his brother.

Declan didn't quite meet his eyes. "Just because you go away doesn't mean you're forgotten."

Lila inhaled sharply and looked between her two brothers.

"I can't use this for marketing," Ace said. "It's too personal."

"Yes, you can. And you can use it to try and get Mia back. Have Lila write some additional marketing copy for the individual products."

Lila snatched the letter out of Ace's hands. She read it again and at the end, she sighed. "Wow."

Declan merely picked up his abandoned work gloves and put them back on. "Let me know if you want more help." A small smile flashed across his face when he added, "Shocked the bejeezus out of me when you asked. In a good way."

Ace and Lila stared at their brother as he made his retreat. "Talk about shocking . . . did *you* know Declan was such a romantic? 'Close your eyes . . . think about the way your heart beats faster . . .'" She shook her head. Then she loaded all of the boxes of candles and spa sets into the Suburban and drove them off to the post office.

Chapter 32

SINCE MIA DIDN'T HAVE THE ENERGY TO EVEN THINK about milking a goat, swiping honey from a bee, or scrubbing her dad's kitchen for him, she allowed Charlie, Jules, and Lila to kidnap her and drag her to Schweitz's Tavern. It was her one night off—she didn't have any elders to look in on, either. And frankly, a margarita sounded pretty good right now. Especially one of Otto's, made with Cointreau.

The familiar hammered-copper tabletops and picnic seating comforted her, even though her appearance in the horseshoe-framed mirrors was haggard. To avoid them, she decided to sit at the long, polished bar.

Otto grinned and waved at them all with his bar rag, a pencil shoved through the dirty-blond curls behind his ear. "Ladies! Welcome. It's been only kielbasa in here all day."

"And what exactly are you saying *we* are, Otto?" Jules inquired. "Sauerkraut?"

"Gorgeous. Sexy."

"Who you callin' kielbasa?" yelled Mick from a corner. "I'm spicy Italian."

"Actually, you're a good old-fashioned Irish banger," noted Grady, who was with him. "So am I."

"I'm chorizo," said Rafi, with a devilish grin.

Otto rolled his eyes. "Right, right. All sausages, which was my point."

Mia smiled. It was good to be in Schweitz's. It had been a while. It took her a moment to recall the last time she'd stopped by . . . and then the smile fell off her face as she realized it had been the night she'd chased Ace here when he'd driven the tractor and they'd had their showdown.

Why couldn't she stop thinking about Ace? She refused to be in love with him, no matter what her dad said. No matter how mixed up her feelings toward him got. Anyway, he had publicly humiliated her, and there was no fixing that. She wouldn't be human if she hadn't smirked a few times at Rob's little escalator excursion. Still . . .

"Girls, what'll you have?" Otto asked, interrupting her thoughts, to her relief.

"Ice water for me and the bump," Jules said. "A round of margaritas for the others. It's on me."

Mia demurred. "Jules, you don't have to—"

"Rhett can afford it," Jules said. "I haven't even begun to spend all of his money yet." She gave a mock-evil laugh.

"I heard that," Grady called.

"And? You gonna run and tell him, or get a little more revenge on him for hooking up with your little sister?" Jules smirked and tossed her head, the rooster-feathers of her hair waving.

"Make 'em strong, Otto," said Charlie. "Mia needs some cheering up."

Otto nodded but cast Mia a sidelong glance. "Seeing Bayes take a backward ride down the escalator didn't make your day?"

Mia bit down on her smile. It was not appropriate to approve of what Ace had done, and certainly not to gloat publicly about it. She was still too mad. Wasn't she?

"Otto!" Lila glared at the bartender.

He shrugged. "Sorry. It sure made my day! Rob walked on his tab the last time he came in here. Not cool." Within moments, he set a giant margarita in front of Mia and several smaller ones in front of the others.

"That is *ridiculous*!" Mia said. "If I drink all of that, I'll—"

Bridget, Kristina, and Amelie chose that moment to walk in.

"Jeez, where's the fish for that bowl in front of Mia?" Bridget asked. "I think I'll have what she's having."

"Me too," Kristina said.

Amelie ordered a French rosé that Schweitz's only had because Jean-Paul stocked it by the case and had sent them a couple of bottles in case anyone "civilized" came into the tavern.

"So is your tool of an ex going to press assault charges against Ace?" Bridget asked Mia.

Charlie, Lila, and Jules all made simultaneous slashing motions across their necks with their index fingers behind Mia. "Because if so, I'll defend Ace for free."

Mia took a large gulp of the margarita. "My guess is that he wants to forget it, because it made him look bad, and he wants everyone else who saw the video to forget it, too," she said.

"True." Bridget looked as if she wanted to say more but took the cue from the other girls to drop the topic.

Charlie began talking to Amelie about her wedding dress and to Kristina about a wedding cake.

"How are the candles and spa products going?" Jules asked Mia, to change the subject.

"Orders are up," Mia said. "Way, way up. I'm actually a little nervous that I won't be able to fulfill the demand."

Lila's expression got a little peculiar. She excused herself and wandered over to where the Silverlake Fire and Rescue guys were sitting, laughingly protesting when both Rafi and Mick ordered her refills at the same time. "I'm not done with my first, guys!"

Ace's deep, sexy growl came from behind Mia. "You'd better not be trying to get my sister drunk, guys."

When had he snuck in to Schweitz's? As Mia whirled, her face heating, Grady scoffed. "We all know your sister can drink most of us under the table, Braddock. But I wouldn't allow these peckerwoods to take advantage of her."

"Good to know," Ace said, casting a sidelong glance at Mia, which she pretended not to notice. She slid behind Jules and her bump.

The bar went silent as multiple pairs of eyes moved from Ace to Mia and back again. "Hoo boy," Otto muttered. "Time for some music?" He cast Ace a meaningful glance.

❦

Ace looked at Mia again. She was still ignoring his existence. He nodded at Otto. "Got any quarters?" He pulled a couple of one-dollar bills out of his pocket and slid them across the bar, receiving a handful of change in return.

Then he walked over to the old-fashioned jukebox in the corner of Schweitz's, which was within spitting distance of the new mechanical bull. He eyed the selections, smiled, and chose one.

Within moments, a Texas oldie but goodie came over the loudspeakers: "You Take the Medicine (I'll Take the Nurse)."

Ace relished the moment when Mia registered the lyrics, choked on her giant margarita, then sputtered, casting an outraged look in his direction. He winked at her.

She glared back, as if to say that he wasn't getting *this* nurse.

He went over to supervise Lila and the boys. Mia, looking mulish, covertly got change from Otto, too.

Ace grinned. It was on! She wouldn't disappoint him.

When the last strains of his song faded, she sauntered over to drop her quarter in . . . and he found himself swaying to the tune of "If the Phone Doesn't Ring, It's Me."

Ouch.

Indignant, but not giving up by any means, Ace countered with "I Can't Live without You."

Maybe it was a little cheesy, but it said what he wanted to say.

Whereupon Mia consulted with Jules and then let him have it. Her second quarter called forth "If You Can't Live Without Me, Why Aren't You Dead Yet?" by Mayday Parade.

Now that was just cold. Colder than a witch's tit, as they said in Texas. Ace formed an imaginary gun with his hand and mimicked pulling the trigger at his own head.

A pig snort escaped Otto behind the bar, and other people started paying attention to the musical duel.

Ace resorted to Elvis: "Can't Help Falling in Love."

"You're such a juke-off!" Lila called, laughing.

He grinned and affectionately flipped her the bird.

Rafi and Mick started yelling musical recommendations, none of which were particularly kind.

But Mia didn't need their help to crush Ace. She selected "You Give Love a Bad Name."

Ace clapped a hand to his heart and pretended to stagger.

Bridget and Kristina shouted more recommendations to him. At least he had a couple of people on his side, too.

Ace volleyed back with "To Make You Feel My Love."

Mia clobbered him with "Tainted Love."

Ace went for "Love Her Madly."

Mia shot back "Victim of Love."

He tried "Whole Lotta Love," "Sunshine of Your Love," and "When Love Finds You."

She decimated these selections with "Love Stinks," "Love Is a Battlefield" and "Love Is a Losing Game."

Both of them couldn't help laughing now . . . it was hard not to, with the whole bar joining in.

So Ace went for something sexy: Bad Company's "Feel Like Makin' Love."

Mia hesitated before responding to that. She put on "Can't Buy Me Love," which at least wasn't actively hostile. It was upbeat.

Ace felt a smidge hopeful as he chose "Why Can't This Be Love?"

Mia stared across the bar at him as Van Halen played out the song. Then she finished her giant margarita, swaying a little on her feet as she joined him at the jukebox with one last quarter.

He could feel her body warmth as she carefully chose her song. Tom Waits. "I Hope That I Don't Fall in Love with You."

Everyone in the bar sighed wistfully and audibly.

"Why not?!" Lila yelled.

But Ace put up a hand, palm out, toward his sister. Telling her that this wasn't her business. He moved closer to Mia.

She seemed rooted to the spot as he approached and didn't stop until they were almost touching. He could hear her heartbeat, see the pulse at her throat, and sense the longing that she fought against.

Ace slid a hand into her hair and was rewarded with a sharp intake of her breath. He tenderly cupped her cheek as they both leaned against the jukebox.

She stared mutely up at him with those beautiful brown eyes of hers.

"Why not?" he asked.

Mia's mouth trembled. Ace pulled her away from the jukebox, into the dark hall leading to the back of the bar.

He wanted to kiss every hesitation, every wobble, every doubt off those lips of hers. The entire bar slipped away behind them, vanished somewhere into the moonlight, leaving just them and the aching music and his question. His hand, still in her hair, cupped her scalp as tenderly as he'd ever held anything in his life.

Ace slid his other hand into her hair and fell headlong into the desire he saw deep in her cinnamon-brown eyes. He bent toward her, mesmerized and yet afraid to do anything to spook her.

He touched his lips to hers in a whisper of reassurance.

Mia made a tiny sound in her throat; her pulse—he could feel it under his right thumb—kicked up wildly.

Ace deepened the kiss.

She kissed him back for half a second . . . then a full one. And then she pulled away, hand to her mouth.

"I think I just fell in love with you," he murmured, echoing the final lyric of the Waits song.

Mia shook her head, her bright, coppery hair obscuring her face.

Then she looked up at him, something desperate and self-protective in her gaze and shook her head: *No*.

She took his right hand, pressing it against hers just as they'd been in Mrs. Baxter's house that one day. "You're not even supposed to be in a bar, Drew," she said softly.

"You don't still believe I've really got a problem, do you?" he asked.

She smiled sadly. "No. I don't."

He looked at their hands, her fingers slightly entwined with his. Then she pulled away, and standing in that shadowy hall, he watched Mia walk away.

Oh, he still had a problem, all right.

Chapter 33

SITTING ON HER DAD'S COUCH IN A PAIR OF CUTOFFS and a tank top, Mia stared at her computer in wonder and, truth be told, some dismay. With all of the orders coming in, it was as she'd first thought. Demand was going to outstrip supply if she didn't do something about it. Fast.

On the plus side, she'd made a shocking amount of money very quickly. On the minus side, customers were expecting what they'd paid for, and the baseball candles required Easy Ace Braddock's signature. She hadn't thought about that when she'd asked Ace to sign the first group.

And now they were sold out!

Lucky for her, she wasn't still working at Silverlake Ranch and had a little more time before she was due back from her "vacation." Yeah, lucky . . . except being away from Silverlake didn't feel so lucky anymore.

She pushed back from the computer and swept her fingertips across her lips. She could almost feel Ace's mouth on hers. She could still see his smile, and that one-of-a-kind swagger as he tracked her across Schweitz's was not an image she'd forget any time soon. Even now, she could feel her heart beating faster just thinking about that moment, leaning on the jukebox, his hand in her hair.

It was kind of hard to focus on candles and lip balm and sales numbers when she was still processing the possibility that she might have broken her own heart by letting Ace Braddock slip away. Did he know what that kiss meant? Did he— A pounding on the door jolted her out of her reverie.

Stetson flew off the couch, letting the intruder know at high decibels that he was prepared to defend her to the death.

She put the laptop down and went to the door. When she opened it, Ace nearly fell inside the house; he was leaning so hard on the door he'd lost his balance. Declan's truck idled in the driveway.

Stetson went crazy but then subsided, recognizing the scent of Ace's toes in the surgical boot. He wagged his tail.

Ace took a moment to scratch him behind the ears. Then, breathlessly, he said, "Listen, Mia, I came as soon as I found out. Lila told me."

Mia stared at him. "Lila told you what?"

"About your orders exploding. Here's what happened. I sent the baseball candles and spa goods out as samples to a bunch of people. I hoped you'd get an uptick in business; you said that even though it wasn't your full-time job, you loved it. That's why I did it. I swear to you, it wasn't anything . . . I wasn't trying to do anything . . ." Ace swore, looking about as stressed out as she'd ever seen him. "I wasn't trying to control things or make things harder for you. I did it for your business . . . for you. *Please* don't take this the wrong way."

Ace looked so distressed, so virtually crazed, that it was comical.

Stetson gazed from one to the other of them, and then put his paws up on Ace's knees.

Mia crossed her arms over her chest and started to laugh. "And suddenly it's all starting to make sense. So where did you get all of these samples the order e-mails are talking about?"

Ace looked like he might be sick. "Um . . ."

She tapped her foot and narrowed her eyes, just to stick it to him a tiny bit more. "I sold out at Founder's Day, which was pretty surprising. I wasn't about to look a gift horse in the mouth, but it was *pretty surprising* to have to make a second batch of those baseball candles so soon. Well, those weren't as good. They didn't have your signature."

There was a pause. Ace cleared his throat. "I signed 'em all before Lila packaged them up for me," he said in such a low voice it was a bit hard to hear.

"Wow. You signed all of my stock?" Mia raised her eyebrows, trying to look severe. She was, in fact, absurdly touched.

"Yes, I did," Ace said, his voice getting a little stronger as if maybe he detected he might not be in as big a mess as he'd thought. "I underestimated the popularity of beeswax baseballs, I guess, and so now . . ." He gestured a little wildly.

"You underestimated *your* popularity," Mia said softly.

The stress on his face eased up a bit. His gaze dropped to her mouth. He moistened his lips and looked away. "Well, whatever it was, I came to apologize"—he shook his head at himself—"*again.* For getting in your business and . . . dang it, Mia, I know what this sounds like. I can hear it. It sounds like I'm interfering and taking control of stuff I shouldn't. But it's—"

"Different now," Mia supplied.

Ace nodded. "Not that you have any reason to believe—"

"Maybe I do believe," she said softly. "You are who you are, Drew Braddock. You're larger than life, you go for what you want, and you don't do it by halves. It's taken me a long time to realize that there is a big difference between somebody doing something *to* you and somebody doing something *for* you. So thank you for doing whatever it was you did to sell all those products of mine. That was a true kindness. I have no right to complain if the business is doing too well."

Ace's face lit up. "I thought I was going to leave Silverlake with you hatin' my guts."

Mia's stomach dropped. *Leaving Silverlake?*

"What the heck are you doing here, Braddock?" Coach Adams yelled as he came around the side of the house.

Ace tore his gaze away from Mia's only when he had to. "Coach, I—"

"*No.* I'm sorry. You don't get to come here yet. I'm not ready," he said. "Why don't you go on home. Wait for me to come around. I've still got thinking to do."

"Dad," Mia pleaded.

"No, baby girl. We don't need to rush anything. My first priority is making things up to you. Ace and I will talk in time."

"*Dad,*" she repeated, her eyes on Ace's devastated face. In that moment, she wanted nothing more than for her father to choose Ace instead, whatever it would take to make his pain go away. How ironic was that?

"I understand, sir," Ace said. He looked at Mia. "Listen, I, uh . . . well, I guess I said what I came to say. If you need any help with your wax—"

"What?" Coach yelled. "Braddock, get on home to your own family now, you hear!"

Ace flinched.

A door slammed and Mia turned. Declan strolled up as if Ace had just called in the cavalry. "Everything okay?" he asked.

Mia's dad looked thoroughly ashamed and a couple of shades redder than usual, and thankfully he didn't keep yelling.

"Everything's fine," Mia said. "We're done here."

The way Ace looked at her when she said it took her breath away. But he didn't speak. The Braddock boys turned, heading back down the driveway to Declan's truck. Mia had the horrible feeling that she'd missed out on something that had been hers to grab for the longest time.

But too late was just that.

Too late.

Chapter 34

Lucky I've been working out. Ace sat in a pair of boxer briefs on the examination table in the Lone Stars training facility. Besides his agent, Lucille, there were about six or seven other team representatives and medical professionals in the room. It didn't faze Ace to be almost naked in front of so many people. None of them seemed to mind the view. There was even a lawyer who was openly appreciating what Ace had to offer beyond a signature.

Ace winked at her, and she blushed, then quickly got down to studying some briefs of her own.

The last few weeks in Dallas had been 100 percent worth it. Lucille had set him up with a couple of professionals at a training facility not far from Rhett's city pad, where he'd been living. His agent had made sure he'd been given every creature comfort a man could want to go along with her admonishment that he'd better get "that Silverlake girl" off his mind so he could focus on his body.

As if. He'd proven an amazing capacity to multitask by thinking about Mia the entire time he was working out his body. And now, he'd passed his fitness tests and stress tests with flying colors. He was baaaack!

They allowed him a moment to get dressed as they all trooped out to the vast room outside that was lined with red lockers and royal blue padded benches. The white walls were studded with the Austin Lone Stars logo.

The team manager popped a bottle of champagne and they all toasted Ace's physical and moral rehabilitation.

Oh. Not champagne. Ace downed his cup of apple cider and rolled his eyes at Lucille. She smiled and shrugged.

Lucille wore a red dress that clung to her like plastic wrap and zipped all the way down the front. She also wore a triumphant smile. She was in a very good mood. Ace had just re-signed with the Austin Lone Stars for another year—they'd wanted more, but he just didn't see himself putting up with the wear and tear on his body for much longer. This injury had been a wake-up call. Besides, he had other things he wanted to do in life. Like Mia Adams.

The Lone Stars president popped her head in. "We hear congratulations are in order." Ace shook hands with her, and with everybody else as they started filing out of the room.

Lucille tossed her blond mane and smartly spanked the team doctor's butt as he was leaving, causing him to almost strangle on his own stethoscope.

"M-married," he stammered, waggling the fingers on his left hand.

She shrugged, blew him a kiss, and enjoyed his rear view for a moment longer before turning back to Ace.

"That was highly satisfactory," she said. High praise from Luce . . . or was she talking about the doc?

"Yeah, I'm psyched to play ball for another year," Ace said, checking his phone in hopes of seeing a message from Mia there. *Nope? Okay. Fine.* Well, getting to the World Series wasn't easy, either. So what if he still had some work to do? He smiled to himself. He wasn't giving up. Mia ought to know that about him by now.

Lucille studied him from her full height, atop four-inch heels. "You know, Braddock, most guys who sign a contract for millions of dollars are a little more in the moment about it."

"I've got some stuff going on in Silverlake," Ace said.

"Mmm . . ."

"You should come out there sometime. It's really something special."

She raised an eyebrow. "You've gone once in about fifteen years."

"Well, that's gonna change. I've been missing out."

"It's that nurse."

Ace knew his grin was about a mile wide.

"Don't mess it up," Lucille said.

"Working on it. I'm heading back to Silverlake in the morning." He stuck out his hand. "Thanks for making this contract happen. Thanks for keeping things together when I was all over the place."

She took his hand and they shook. "We really should have slept together when we had the chance."

"Oh well," Ace said with a smile.

"Oh well," Lucille echoed. Laughing, she escorted him to the limo waiting downstairs.

❦

Ace took the car to the huge house on Lake Travis that he shared with his teammates and was soon back at loose ends. Where was everybody?

His only companions were the putrid dirty socks under the coffee table that Harley always left there, a pair of leopard-print panties dangling from the dining room chandelier—really? And a pizza box ringed by beer bottles.

Out in the front yard was a stone armadillo coated in grackle guano and a big bronze Longhorn that several drunken Texas Rangers had once tried to steal. They hadn't reckoned on just how heavy it was.

Out in the backyard was docked a sailboat, a Hobie Cat that Pete Bergsen had managed to pitchpole on their last outing. The thought of Pete soured Ace's stomach.

He sat on the couch and played a video game for a while. He had no desire to watch daytime television. Evaluating training footage only depressed him and made him wonder when he'd ever get back out on the field again.

Actually, this whole place was kind of depressing. Ace tossed the game controller aside and looked around, wondering how it was possible that this house he'd called home for so long suddenly felt like a way station—and Silverlake Ranch had become something he actually missed. "This isn't my home," he said under his breath, testing out the words.

I know where home is, and it's waiting for me. It's waited for me all this time.

The doorbell rang, and Ace pulled himself out of his reverie and headed for the front of the house.

He threw open the big oak door to find a skinny kid with oversized ears, a shaggy platinum crew cut, and royal blue glasses. They'd slipped down his narrow nose, and he was grinning like a maniac. The little dude's picture had to be next to *dork* in the dictionary.

"Holy cow, it's true! Andrew 'Easy Ace' Braddock is back in Austin," he blurted.

Ace took in his T-shirt, which said WORLD'S TALLEST LEPRECHAUN. "And you are . . . ?"

"I'm an intern! With the *Austin American-Statesman*!" The dork stuck out his hand.

Ace looked down at it. "Congratulations. What's your name?"

"Stuckey. Stellan Stuckey."

He had to be kidding. *Stellan as in Skarsgård?*

"Oh, man," the kid squeaked, "I can't believe I'm actually meeting you!"

Ace suppressed a sigh, took the kid's hand, and shook it. *Will he ever wash it again?*

Stuckey did indeed look down at his hand as if thinking about cutting it off, bagging it, and storing it in his freezer for posterity—all because it had touched Ace's. This was truly the most uncomfortable kind of fan. And it was a little creepy that he'd just popped up on the doorstep.

But all Ace said was, "Pleasure to meet you, too, Stellan. How can I help you?"

"I didn't interrupt anything important, did I?" the kid asked apologetically.

"My daily calisthenics routine," Ace said dryly, gesturing at his couch and the TV.

"Oh, jeez. I'm so sorry . . ."

"Joke," said Ace. "Joke." It would be hospitable to invite Stuckey inside, but not only was he a baby reporter, but Ace wasn't sure he'd ever get rid of him. So Ace stepped outside and shut the door. He pointed at one of the rocking chairs on the porch and sat himself down on a bench. "What's up, kid? Why are you here?"

"Well. There've been all kinds of rumors. And then that video . . . and I said that it would be great to track you down and get a comment, you know? And next thing, all the other interns have a betting pool that I can't do it. Which ticked me off. So here I am, and . . ." The kid suddenly sucked his entire upper lip into his mouth and chewed on it, looking even more like a bad cartoon character.

He was so odd and pathetic that Ace felt sorry for him. What could it hurt to give Stellan Stuckey a comment for his amateur intern column? It wasn't as if Ace had anything better to do.

"So you've tracked me down," he prompted the kid. "What kind of comment would you like to get?"

He was rewarded with frozen silence, since in order to respond, the dork would have had to release his entire upper lip from between his teeth, which he did not. He just blinked at Ace from behind the crazy blue glasses.

"O-kaaay," Ace said. "What is it that you'd like me to comment *on*?"

Stuckey's eyes rolled a bit wildly. Then he pointed at Ace's ankle. "Does it still hurt?"

"It aches. Some days more than others."

"And it's from the . . . you know . . . the accident? With the Maserati?"

"Yes."

"And just how fast were you driving?"

"I wasn't." The words slipped out before Ace could swallow them. "I mean, I don't remember. Fast."

But the intern wasn't a total loss as a reporter. His eyes widened behind the blue frames. "You weren't driving?"

"I didn't say that," Ace revised hastily.

"Yeah, you did."

"I didn't mean it."

"I'm pretty sure you did."

"Then it was off the record," Ace snapped.

Stuckey shook his head. "Nope."

"Look, kid, I'm being nice to you. Work with me here. Strike it, forget I ever said it, and I'll give you something else. Something good. A real quotable quote."

Stellan Stuckey's eyes narrowed as his glasses slid almost all the way off his nose. He hurriedly shoved them back up to the bridge of it. "Okay. But I'm holding you to that."

"Or what?" Ace asked. "Don't think you have the advantage, here."

"But I do," Stuckey said, albeit cautiously.

Just then Bevo the Beagle appeared, streaking across the front lawn. Bevo was a community pup, shared by Ace and his roomies with three tech moguls who had a similar living situation next door.

"I'll sic my vicious hound on you," Ace growled.

Bevo galloped all the way to the porch, right up onto it, and dropped a dazed chipmunk at Ace's feet, wagging his tail wildly. He turned to Stuckey, barked once, and then turned back to Ace, panting and waiting to be told what a good boy he was.

"Good boy," Ace told him, feeling more than stupid. Some vicious hound.

Bevo tried to pick up the poor chipmunk again, but Ace held him off, reached down, and grabbed the little critter. It emitted a squeak of terror.

"Okay," Ace said. "Thank you, Bevo. I'll . . . eat it for dinner. Now, go chase a cat or something."

Stellan Stuckey raised his eyebrows.

"Aw, c'mon," Ace said. "That's off the record, too. I don't eat chipmunks. I'm going to take the little guy to the vet, I guess. Make sure he's not punctured." What in the Sam Hill was he going to do with it in the meantime?

"Stellan," Ace said, with a winning grin he'd used on thousands of fans and A-list reporters. "I'll be right back." He went inside and grabbed a colander he and the guys used for draining pasta.

Soon the chipmunk was installed under the colander on the porch, where it appeared to calm down—though Bevo was not amused. Ace shooed him away.

"Now, where were we?" he asked the intern.

"I'm not really sure. You want me to forget that you said you weren't driving the Maserati and believe that you don't eat chipmunks. And you said you'd give me something better." The kid's gaze was razor-sharp. Dorky he might be, but he was no fool.

"Hmmm," said Ace.

Stuckey asked, "Are you still going to be able to play major league baseball?"

"Yes," Ace said. He didn't elaborate.

"So why were you hiding out in Silverlake?"

"To hang out with my family. And I wasn't hiding."

"The family you haven't visited in over a decade?"

Ace glared at him. He'd done his homework. "How would you know that, punk?"

Stellan Stuckey just looked at him.

"Fine. I had a sudden urge to . . . get to know them again. Reconcile."

"Was there some kind of ugly breakup, way back when?"

"What? No. I just left for training and sort of never made it back there."

"Too busy for your family?"

"You know what? You're starting to piss me off, kid."

"I'll leave once you give me something good. Otherwise, I'm running with the Ace-wasn't-driving headline."

Stuckey pushed his glasses back up his nose and shot him a small, smug smile.

Ace had the urge to shove the kid's blue glasses where the sun didn't shine, but he reminded himself that he was now reformed and didn't indulge in gratuitous violence, no matter how provoked he might get.

He also had the urge to go ahead and let the cat out of the bag: tell the world that it had been Pete driving. His onetime friend and "brother" . . . who was so full of gratitude for what Ace had done for him that he now wouldn't give him the time of day. *Jerk.*

But Ace didn't play dirty that way. He never had, and he wasn't about to start now.

"So . . . ?" the kid prompted him again. "You were there for the Hill Country barbecue? To hide from the media?" He produced that snarky little grin again.

Ace started to feel as trapped as the chipmunk under the colander. It wasn't a good feeling. Why had he even opened the door to this little creep?

His knuckles began to itch again, the way they'd itched when he was pursuing Rob in the airport. "I told you, I wasn't hiding," he snapped.

"Then—you fell in love?" Stuckey's smirk widened. He thought he'd come up with another good line.

Ace froze. His brain started spinning deliberately. What if . . . ?

The kid homed in on his pause.

"Yeah," Ace said. "You got it. I did. Still am. I am one hundred percent, irretrievably in love."

Stuckey's jaw dropped open. "What's her name?" he asked breathlessly.

"I can't reveal her name. She'd kill me. But she's the most beautiful girl in the world; a knockout. And the bravest. And the most giving. And the hardest-working and most tolerant of crazy people. I want to buy her a diamond the size of a baseball, but she's not exactly speaking to me right now. So maybe you can help?"

Stellan Stuckey had produced his phone and his thumbs

were a blur as he took down all of this verbal gold. "Oh, man," he said. "Oh, man!"

"Think that'll get you a byline, kid?"

Stuckey's blue glasses had inched down so far during his manic thumb-typing that they actually fell off. He scrabbled around on the floorboards for them. "Holy moly!" Then he jammed them back onto his nose and scrutinized Ace suspiciously. "I'm going to hit *record*, repeat the sentences you just gave me, and you're gonna give me verbal permission to use them."

"Sure."

"Holy cow. You're not jerking me around."

"No."

Stellan hit RECORD, then babbled an intro to provide context, stating Ace's full name and the date and time. Then he looked up and asked in a carefully professional tone, "Care to tell me why the woman you love isn't speaking to you?"

"You're pushing it, kid."

"Yeah, yeah, okay." Stellan's faux-professional voice slipped back into to its naturally higher register. "But does it have anything to do with you poking that tool Bayes down the escalator?"

"Uh, maybe. She doesn't condone violence. By the way, I don't, either," Ace added, "when I'm . . . uh . . . not engaging in it, anyway. I'm very sorry for my actions. I want to stress that to the youth of America in general and baseball fans in particular." He produced his most professionally sincere smile.

"Of course," Stuckey said, nodding. "Of course."

Just then company arrived, in the form of a burnt-orange Jeep Wrangler stuffed with his teammates. Harley, Doug, Scooter, Bates, and—speak of the devil, Pete—they all climbed out and trooped up onto the porch. Pete, looking sheepish, trailed the rest of them when he saw Ace.

"Yo," Harley said, eyeing Stellan Stuckey. "Who's this?"

The kid seemed to have been struck dumb by all the baseball testosterone and fame surrounding him, so Ace answered on his behalf. "He's an intern, trying to get his first byline in the *Statesman*. He stopped by to ask a few questions, and I decided to be nice and not drop-kick him into Lake Travis."

While the rest of them exchanged greetings with Stuckey, Pete stood back with his hands in his pockets and, after nodding at Ace, looked anywhere and everywhere but at him. Pete seemed to want to disappear, in fact.

Ace's mouth twisted.

Finally Stellan turned to Pete and stuck out his hand. "It's such an honor to meet you."

Pete reluctantly shook it. "Yeah."

Ace had to give the kid credit: He had stones.

"So . . . heh. Do you miss your Maserati?" Stuckey asked.

Pete shot a wary look at Ace. "Sure. It was a sweet car."

The kid jerked a thumb at him. "Was it hard to forgive Braddock here for wrecking it?"

"No, no. Not at all," Pete mumbled. "He's my teammate, my friend. You know, my brother."

Like hell. "You're *not* my brother," Ace shot at him, unable to help himself. It was one thing not to betray Pete. It was another to pretend everything was fine after the way Pete had treated him in the aftermath of the accident.

Pete winced.

And Stuckey noticed, his gaze homing in on Bergsen's face and the way he turned away from Ace.

"I've *got* three brothers," Ace said. "And go figure . . . they actually return my calls." He turned away as Bevo the Beagle came racing up with a filthy tennis ball in his mouth and dropped it at his feet. As Ace bent down for it, then lobbed it for him, Little Blue Glasses went in for the kill.

"So how fast were you driving?" he said, stepping in front of Pete and looking him right in the eye.

Pete opened and then closed his mouth. "I . . . wasn't," he said, unconvincingly.

"That so?" Stellan pressed him. "Because several witnesses at the party sure said you were."

Aw, hell. Much as he no longer felt like it, Ace stepped in again to shoulder the blame. "We switched places, once I realized how much Pete had had to drink."

"Yeah." The kid's eyes were stony, behind the blue glasses. "After he hit the tree. Isn't that right, Mr. Bergsen?"

Bergsen whirled on Ace. "What the hell did you tell him, Braddock?"

Ace shook his head. "Not a thing."

"But *you* just did," Stellan Stuckey said. "Ace took the fall for you."

Pete's face darkened three shades. "Listen, punk, you write a word of that garbage and I will make you sorry you were ever born!"

"You threatening me?" the kid asked. He held up his phone . . . which was recording.

Stones. Ace was impressed. Looked like a goofball. Had nads of steel. Good for him.

Pete blustered, "I will sue you and your paper for millions—"

"No," Ace said, giving him a level look. "You won't."

If looks could kill . . . but they couldn't.

So Ace slung an arm around the kid. "I'll walk you to your car and we'll take a selfie, okay? Take it a little easy on ole Pete. Focus more on my other deep, dark secret."

"That Easy Ace Braddock is off the baseball bunny circuit?" Stuckey asked.

Ace nodded.

"Hearts will break all over Texas," the kid said. Then he added, "She's a lucky girl."

"Thanks," Ace said, pulling some cash out of his pocket and forking it over. "How'd you like to drop off that poor little chipmunk at the nearest animal hospital on your way back to write about my permanently lovelorn state?"

Chapter 35

MIA STOOD BAREFOOT IN HER RATTIEST JEANS AND a shirt that had once been her dad's, painting the red stitching on another batch of wax spheres, doing her best to think about anything but Ace Braddock even as she was elbow-deep in baseball candles. They perched along a six-foot foldable table in front of her in an assembly line.

Declan and Lila had decided to turn one of the rooms at the ranch into Mia's business headquarters, based on the premise that the baseball candles had to do with Ace, which meant that Silverlake Ranch was all in for whatever Mia needed. Besides, he had to sign them. Far from finding this presumptuous, Mia found it heartwarming; more and more she felt like the Braddocks were her family, too. She told herself that was why she missed Ace so much.

On the plus side, his absence meant she was actually gaining ground with those recent orders. Too bad her heart didn't care about orders and money; given a choice she would have traded a million orders just to have Ace come back.

She put down the baseball she was holding, a little shocked by the intensity of that thought.

"Wow," said a female voice from the doorway.

Mia reflexively tried to wipe the splodge of wax off her cheek and only succeeded in getting more of it in her hair. Her fingers were covered with smears of red paint.

Bridget stepped inside, wrinkling her nose as she dodged buckets and pots and piles of wrapping. She had on a very short, pristine blue pastel shift dress, and her high heels looked too expensive to be near this much paint. In her hand was a monogrammed white leather portfolio sandwiching a very fat, rumpled orange manila envelope affixed with a string.

"Hi!" Mia sucked in a nervous breath.

"It's good news," Bridget said.

"Ooh," said Mia. "Do you want to wait in the living room while I get cleaned up?"

Bridget nodded, her face the picture of relief.

Mia headed into the bathroom and washed her hands and face, picked the wax out of her hair, and double-checked that there was nothing sticking to her backside before she went into the living room. Her heart pounded.

Back in the Braddocks' living room, Bridget was peering at Ace's cartoons on the mantel, a big grin on her face. "Trust Ace to get my measurements right," she said. And then she sat down at the coffee table in front of her portfolio and got down to business. She opened the manila envelope and a big sheaf of papers affixed with a gold binder clip thunked down on the table. Mia sat down, her heart pounding double time.

"You'll want to read these," Bridget said, "but I'll give you the short version. I am happy to report that though 'poor Rob' will forever be missing his decency, he *has* managed to find both his sanity and some communal funds. He will pay back the loans and credit cards he took out in your name. And he has been found responsible for the mortgage situation. It's all in there." Bridget tapped the paper stack.

"I-I'm sorry?" Mia said.

"What about?" Bridget asked.

"I don't think I understand. It sounds like you're saying Rob is making everything right. I'm not going to owe nearly as much money."

"Well, that's not quite correct."

Oh, here it comes.

"This was determined by the judge. Since you've already paid so much, with no in-kind contribution from your spouse, you're done. It's all on Rob now, especially since the judge did not look kindly upon the fraud and forgery."

Mia sat there in shock.

"Uh . . . wasn't that what you were going for?" Bridget asked.

"Just like that? Where's the long, ugly fight?"

Bridget looked around the room like maybe she was hoping for a drink. "You already had that, seems to me. And Rob doesn't want to go to jail. It's over, Mia." Her gaze settled back on Mia's face and she frowned. "You don't look happy. What am I missing?"

What am I missing, Mia thought.

Drew.

"Why did Rob make it so easy?" she asked faintly.

Bridget sat down on the sofa next to Mia, looking a bit out of place against the rustic furnishings. She ran her hand across the plaid wool blanket that was resting on the top of the sofa back, presumably waiting for a colder season. "You know, I dated Jake for a while. I still kick myself for letting him get away."

"Oh, jeez, Bridget, please tell me you're not about to give me some after-school special advice," Mia said. "Honestly, I don't think I could accept it with any sort of grace."

The women laughed.

"Nah," Bridget said. "Not exactly. I was just going to say that the Braddocks have a way of getting things done." She shrugged.

"Rob really did sign off on all these things because of Drew," Mia said.

"Yeah." The lawyer put up her palm. "I wouldn't recommend his techniques as a matter of course, but when he uses them sparingly, Ace Braddock can be quite effective."

"I gave him such a hard time," Mia said. "I basically told him that he ruined my life."

"He won't hold it against you," Bridget said.

Mia slumped back against the cushions. "It doesn't matter now," she said hoarsely.

"I haven't seen him in the tabloids with any baseball bunnies since he left Silverlake," Bridget pointed out.

"I know. I've been reading them every day on the off chance there'll be an article and I'll find out how he's doing," Mia said, feeling herself turn red. "I miss him that much."

"You shouldn't read 'em. Don't torture yourself."

If it hurts to read about him with someone else, it's only what I deserve.

Chapter 36

*L*OVE IS HARD FOR EASY ACE BRADDOCK, BLARED THE headline in the *Austin American-Statesman* rolled up in Ace's hand. Ace himself chuckled at it. Stellan Stuckey had done him proud.

He stood in the doorway of Sunny's Side Up and gave himself a moment to soak in the feeling of well-being he was getting from this small-town tableau.

Quite a few important people in his life sat in this diner today . . . reading the newspaper.

Declan, sitting in what had come to be dubbed the Braddock Booth, choked on his coffee when he saw Ace and waved him over.

Ace headed toward him, hiding the pang of regret in his heart when he passed Coach Adams reading *his* paper at his customary spot at the diner's bar. Ace slid into the booth across from Declan and looked over his shoulder at the older man.

Coach put his palm on the story, then folded the paper. He looked like he was working himself up to something.

Ace hoped that something wasn't a public confrontation. He considered going over, but he only had to think of Mia to force himself to exercise a little of his newfound restraint.

Sunny gave a shout; she'd dropped the entire paper onto her griddle, where it sizzled over several strips of bacon. She pulled it off before it caught fire and trotted it out to their table, a piece of bacon still stuck to the greasy page.

"Who is Stellan Stuckey, and why would you tell him you're in love with Mia?" she demanded.

"I didn't say anything about Mia," Ace said.

Coach got down from his stool and turned toward Ace's table, paper in hand. The diner fell silent as the man slowly made his way past the tables until he was standing in front of his former protégé. "You didn't say anything about Mia?"

Ace sensed Declan's protective instincts ratchet up a notch, and he gave his brother a warning look. "No, sir, Coach, I did not. You can see for yourself."

Coach's hands shook a little as he unfolded his newspaper and opened it up. All Ace heard was the clattering of plates in the kitchen and the bell going off to let Sunny know she had to get her butt back there to pick up orders.

"Well, it says right in this here newspaper that this girl you're talking about is the most beautiful in the world. A knockout. The bravest. The most giving. The hardest-working and most tolerant of crazy people." Coach looked up, his gaze meeting Ace's.

"That's right," Ace said.

"Well, that sounds exactly like my Mia."

"Yes, sir, Coach, it does, doesn't it?"

Coach didn't look away, and Ace saw the older man's eyes well up a little. Which was conveniently when he looked back down at the newspaper and continued to read. "It says here that you want to buy this girl who sounds like my Mia a diamond the size of a baseball."

"More or less," Ace told him.

Declan, who'd just finished choking, wiped his mouth on his napkin. "Subtle."

"It's one of my best qualities," said Ace.

Coach nodded. "Andrew Braddock, are you truly 'one hundred percent, irretrievably in love, with my girl?" he asked quietly.

"Are the Red Sox the greatest baseball team in history?" Ace asked Coach.

There was a pause and then Coach—very slowly—smiled.

He started to laugh and then slapped Ace hard on the back. "Well, then," he said. "Well, then. I guess I have my answer." The two men only had time to meet eyes once more in a moment of understanding before cheers erupted throughout the diner and Sunny had to skedaddle to pick up some hot plates.

Every breakfast-snarfer with a paper in Sunny's Side Up had now walked up to stand around Ace's table.

"Hey, y'all." Ace nodded at them. "How ya doin'? Didja hear the rumor going 'round about butter? *I'm* sure not gonna spread it." He winked to the chorus of groans.

Declan read aloud dryly, "You're extremely sorry for your actions? You don't condone violence? You want to stress that to the youth of America and to baseball fans in particular?"

"That's brilliant PR there, son," said Coach Adams.

Declan rolled his eyes.

"What about stressing it to Mia?" Sunny asked pointedly, back at the table with a fresh pot of coffee in her hand.

"Sometimes a man has to defend the woman he loves," Ace said defiantly.

"Only if she's in danger," Sunny retorted.

"Oh, yeah? Well, just for your information, Mia was in plenty of danger. That SOB left her in a house with no back walls and no money to build them. And a coyote almost ate her one night."

"Say *what*?" Sunny grabbed her coffeepot and held it aloft like a weapon.

"She said there was a plumbing issue and they were fixing it," Coach mumbled, looking ashamed.

"She lied to you. Declan—back me up," Ace demanded. "She's been milking his goats and his bees to make money."

"You don't milk bees, Drew," Deck said, with a weary sigh.

"Whatever!"

"But yeah." Declan gripped his coffee cup. "Mia's been really on the ropes. Why don't you forget about a baseball-sized diamond and let's grab Jake and the Fire and Rescue boys to throw some walls up for her?"

"She gets both," Ace said stubbornly. "I'm designing plans for the McMansion, too."

Just then, Lila came flying into the diner, waving her iPad. "What *is* this!?"

"Last time I checked, it was called a news story."

"Ace, Ace, Ace," Lila said despairingly. "You don't propose in the paper. You announce an engagement or a wedding, but you don't *propose*."

"That wasn't the proposal. Why is it," complained Ace, "that I have thousands of fans, but I can't do anything right for you people?"

"It's that they admire your brawn so much that they don't usually notice your lack of brains," his little sister told him.

"Thank you." Ace glared at her and took a slug of his coffee.

"What are we going to do with you?" Lila moaned.

"Help me. Love me."

A peculiar expression dawned on Lila's face. "*Oooooh*," she said. "I thought of something that might just work."

"What?" Ace narrowed his eyes on her.

"For me to know and you to find out. You clearly suck at handling your own business, so I'm gonna have to step in."

"No, Lila." Declan aimed a stern glance at her. "You've got to stop meddling in people's love lives."

"Why? I have been extremely successful . . . even *triumphant*," Lila exclaimed. "I got Jake and Charlie back together. I got Rhett and Jules together. And now . . ."

"*No*," everyone said in unison.

Lila sniffed. "Fine."

Chapter 37

MIA FOUND MRS. DOOLEY ASLEEP ON THE TOILET, as usual. And as usual, she bellowed about her bowels and then Mia helped her get a warm bath before dressing her in a fresh nightgown and suggesting a prune smoothie. Mrs. Dooley shouted that the very notion was appalling.

Mia made one anyway, disguised with plenty of strawberries and blueberries, with whipped cream and a cherry on top. Mrs. Dooley drank it and pronounced it delicious. Then, still at awesome decibels, she pronounced Mia a national treasure, wondered at even greater decibels why that overtanned twerp Robert Bayes would be stupid enough to leave her, and said she'd greatly enjoyed watching him go headfirst down the escalator. Finally she asked Mia again to help her with Tinder . . . while her cat gazed on mockingly.

At last, still avoiding her emotions and telling herself that she was not the kind of moron to fall for Easy Ace Braddock or his cheesy lines about love, Mia drove to the new client's house.

Mr. Andrews was Vic the plumber's ancient uncle, widowed six years and wrestling with dementia. He loved bluegrass music, which usually warred with a loud cable television news program and tequila—not necessarily in that order.

"Hiya, missy," Mr. Andrews said, welcoming her inside and evaluating her body a little too freely and frankly. "I've been waiting for you."

Mia extended her hand politely. "It's nice to see you, Mr. Andrews."

"Call me Mack, darlin'." He didn't ask her name.

"Okay then, Mack." Mia dug into her satchel and produced some paperwork. "We should start by filling out these forms for the agency . . ."

"Never mind that. They know I'm good for the money."

"Ah . . . excuse me? Well, Mack, it's not really about that. These papers provide basic information on—"

"What'll you have to drink, missy? Fact is, all I got's tequila. Cuervo." He turned and limped toward a little rolling bar, stocked with glasses, a big bottle of the golden liquid, a lime, and a knife.

"Mr. Andrews, I don't drink on the job," Mia said. "Look, I'm going to go check on your food situation, all right? Do you have meals in the refrigerator or freezer?"

Mack rubbed his withered hands together and leered at her. "Ah. She's hungry, not thirsty."

Feeling more uncomfortable by the second, Mia retreated to the kitchen.

She heard the sounds of Mack pouring himself a drink. Probably not the best thing to mix with his dementia, but . . .

There were several frozen dinners in the freezer, cans of soup in a cupboard, and a carton of eggs long past their expiration date in the fridge. Mia tossed them so that he couldn't poison himself. She also transferred some dirty dishes into the dishwasher and wiped down his sink with disinfectant.

"What's taking so long?" Mack hollered.

"I'll be right with you." Mia washed her hands, picked up his paperwork, and reluctantly returned to the living room.

She froze in the doorway.

Vic's uncle was reclining on his plaid couch with an iced-tea glass full of tequila . . . and he was stark naked.

This was not Plumb Awesome. Not at all.

Stunned, Mia backed away.

"I'm so glad the agency sent a redhead!" Mack rasped, leering again.

Her eyeballs were scarred for life.

"C'mon over here, cutie, and give ole Mack some sugar."

She ran into the kitchen, fumbling in her pocket for her cell phone.

Mack sprang up, withered equipment and all, and pursued her, cackling, delighted by the chase. "Oh, it's like that, is it? I'm not too old to catch ya . . . though next time I'd like you to wear the old-fashioned nurse's uniform, 'kay? The one with the cute little white hat an' all."

Horrified, Mia sprinted around his kitchen island, trying to dial and run at the same time. Mack streaked after her, his eyes alight and something else disturbingly aloft.

She hit a random phone number in her recent-calls log and flew back into the living room, around the sofa this time, the crazy old man in hot pursuit.

"Mia?" said Ace's deep, sexy, male voice. "I was hoping you'd call—"

"Help!" she shrieked into the phone.

"What? What is it? Are you all right?"

Mack scrambled over the sofa as she yelled, "No!"

"What's going on?" Ace's voice held panic.

Mack caught hold of the back of her scrubs.

Mia tore out of his grasp and hurtled for the drinks cart, stumbling, dropped her phone, and grabbed two slices of lime. As a cackling Mack caught up with her yet again, she squeezed them, whirled, and ground them into his eyes.

He howled.

"Touch me again, you old pervert, and I will use this paring knife on you!"

"Why you gotta do me like that, darlin'?" he moaned, rubbing frantically at his eyes.

Ace was yelling something indistinguishable from her phone on the floor.

"Call my agency!" she shouted. "Call Bode Wells. Just get someone over here, please. I'm at Mack Andrews's."

Her heart still pumping adrenaline, Mia took a deep breath.

"Are you going to behave now?" she asked her patient.

"Aaaagh . . ."

"I'm not a hooker. Got it? I'm a *nurse*."

He moaned again, rubbing at his streaming eyes.

Mia sighed. Then she led poor, demented Mack into the bathroom, stuffed him into a bathrobe, and helped him flush his eyes with clear, cool water.

❧

Blue and red lights flashing on his car, Sheriff Bode Wells pulled up outside the Andrews place at the same time that Ace arrived, jammed into Lila's Suburban with the rest of the Braddock clan. His heart was pounding as he threw himself out of the passenger-side door before his sister even got the vehicle into park.

He ran up the cement steps, nearly breaking down the door when he threw it open and let it slam against the wall. "Mia! *Mia!*" His voice was ragged and rough to his own ears. "Mia—where are you?"

She emerged from the kitchen in her blue scrubs, looking white and shaken but also bemused.

Ace lunged for her, pulling her tightly into an embrace. Bode took one look, and seeing that Mia was in good hands, he headed toward the back of the house to make sure all was well otherwise.

Mia didn't break away from the circle of Ace's body. She let him hug her, which was incredible. *So* incredible to feel her, flesh and blood in his arms again. And safe. Safe now that he was here . . .

"Is he back there waiting for you?" Ace snarled. "I'm gonna—"

"He's in bed with a cold, wet washcloth over his eyes," Mia mumbled, her face pressed into the crook of his neck.

Ace finally understood why some of his fans claimed they'd never again wash a body part he'd autographed, because the feel of her mouth on his skin was heaven.

"He's eighty-seven years old," Mia continued, "and you're not going to do anything to him. I almost blinded him with lime juice."

"Say *what*?"

Mia pulled her face away from Ace's body and looked up at him, her eyes still troubled. "He's also got Alzheimer's and he didn't know what he was doing."

"Mia," Ace said hoarsely. "If anything ever happened to you . . ." He cleared his throat and pulled himself together, every inch of him readying for the warpath. "I'm not going to *let* anything happen to you ever again, you hear?"

The corner of her mouth quirked in amusement, but the look in her eyes went soft at his white-knight words. *Please, please let that mean that I still have a chance with her.*

"You can't protect me from everything, Drew."

The gentle palm she placed against his cheek nearly undid him. "I can sure as heck do my best," he answered.

Bode Wells returned, and Mia took a step back from Ace, blushing a little. The sheriff gave her a long, serious look. "You okay?"

Mia shrugged. "Yeah. I managed to defend myself. And he's—" She twirled her index finger at her temple.

Bode nodded. "I know. Well, he's asleep now."

"The dude needs to be locked up!" Ace said tightly. "He tried to—"

Mia set a hand on his shoulder. "But not in a jail cell."

"But—he could have *hurt* you."

She sighed. "He was having a . . . flashback, I guess. To a happier time in his life."

"Flashback, my left nut!"

"He needs to be in a facility, Ace. I'm fine. He's not."

"Why isn't he in one already!?"

Bode cleared his throat. "They're expensive. Vic makes a good living, but not that good."

Ace dragged a hand down his face and slumped onto poor old Mack's plaid sofa with his crutches in hand. "Fine. You know what: *I'll* subsidize him. But Mia's never coming back here. Not *ever*."

"I think we can all agree on that," Declan said, as the rest of the Braddocks suddenly trooped into the house. "You're a lot safer milking my evil goats."

Bode threw up his arms in surrender. "You Braddocks all just standing out there with your noses pressed to the glass?"

"Well, yeah," Rhett said, as if that was a crazy question. "Ace mighta needed some backup."

"Where else would we be?" Lila asked, with a befuddled expression on her face.

"Anyway, I'm a first responder," Jake said, as if that said it all.

Mia had to laugh.

Ace didn't find any of this so funny. Not at the moment. "I'm sick of this," he said furiously. "I'm sick of watching her kill herself to make pennies."

They all turned to him, Mia included.

"I'm sick of watching her work three, four, five jobs!"

"Ace," Mia said mildly.

"No, Mia. I've *had* it."

"You have?" Her voice quivered with amusement.

He caught himself. "I mean, *you've* had it. And you should . . . you should have me instead."

The whole room went silent.

"Ace?" Lila asked. "What are you—no, no, no . . . Ace, there are more graceful ways to—"

"Fine," he said, waving off his sister. She was right. He was too mad about finding Mia in trouble. He was too happy that she was giving him signals that said he was gonna get another chance to make things right.

But he was just plain *too* amped up to do that right at the moment, and no way was this woman he loved with all his heart and soul getting second best. Mia needed to know that when he asked her to marry him, he'd put thought into it. Heart into it. Everything he had into it. Fancy words, diamonds . . . every bit of love he possessed. The works. And maybe, if he was very, very lucky, she would say yes.

"Ace," said Mia. "It's very sweet that you came to my rescue, and that you're trying to solve my problems for me, but—"

"Damn it, woman. Which part of 'I love you' do you not understand?"

All of his brothers stood stock-still.

"Oh," said Lila softly.

Mia flushed bright red and said nothing.

"Is Spanish better?" Ace demanded. "Then *te amo, te amo.*" He pressed his hand to his heart, looked her square in the eyes, and repeated, *"Te amo, Mia amor."*

It went positively silent for a moment as they all absorbed the power of his words.

Mia's cherry-red color deepened to scarlet.

But she didn't say it back. Ace took a deep breath and exhaled.

"Mi-a Amor. Nice, Ace. Suave." Bode winked at him. "Keep going like that." It broke the tension of the moment and everybody laughed. With that, Bode gestured to the others that they should all wait outside.

After a moment's pause, Ace's entire family trooped outside after the sheriff. Ace's gaze never left Mia's face; he only had eyes for her.

"Mia, I've never been so scared in my entire life as during the ride over here," Ace said, brushing her fiery red hair out of her face, beyond relieved when she moved back to him and wrapped her arms around him of her own accord. "First, I just want you to know how relieved I am that you're okay. Second, I apologize for the whole Rob disaster. You're right: I didn't think. I'm so sorry. Third, I may be a jerk, but I love you more than anything, and I will publicly eat a wooden bat soaked in barbecue sauce to prove it to you—I swear."

Mia laughed at that. "Not necessary." She tilted her head

and looked deeply into his eyes. "But *that* would go viral, Ace."

"Yeah," he admitted. "It probably would." He'd never seen anything so beautiful as her smiling face under that dusting of cinnamon freckles. He'd never felt anything like the love and affection shining out of her eyes—with just the right amount of tolerance and amusement and understanding of who he was, deep down inside. Not just a celebrity. Not a uniform. Not a gravy train. She saw him. Really, truly saw him.

Mia knew the kid in him who had to call Jake and know every Braddock was safe before every game, who loved Apple Jacks without milk for dinner and cold canned ravioli for breakfast. She knew how much he'd idolized her dad. She even seemed to have forgiven him for stealing Coach away from her.

He leaned down and gently pressed a kiss against her smiling mouth, reveling in the way she melted into him. "What are the odds that you might take me on for life?" he whispered.

"Oh, Drew . . ." Mia buried her face in his chest.

He tipped her chin up and gazed into her eyes. "I've never been more serious about anything in my life—and that includes baseball."

Mia's eyes filled. "Really? Well, the odds could be worse," she admitted with a grin.

"That's a start," Ace said. "I'll take it!" He picked her up and spun around with her, while she shrieked and laughed. Finally he put her down, breathless.

Ace had come up against some formidable opponents during his career. He knew all about odds and what it took to overcome bad ones.

His next move, to win her, would be bigger than the World Series. It would be . . . everything.

Their audience might have stepped outside, but they were all once again rubbernecking without shame.

Ace stuck his head out. "Get enough of an eyeful? What are you all still doing here?"

Declan raised an eyebrow. "To give you a ride back to the ranch."

"Oh right." Ace flushed.

"You done being romantic and cheesy?" Jake asked, a smile playing around his mouth.

"No, not really—"

"Yes." Mia overrode him, clearly embarrassed by the audience and the whole scenario.

"Aw, jeez—what comes next, Romeo? Poetry spouted from a balcony?" Rhett gave Ace a noogie.

"What comes next is that I need to go find a ring," Ace said.

"Yeah, yeah, the size of a baseball. We'll help."

"Not that big," Mia protested.

His brothers proceeded to muscle Ace, against his will, back out to the Suburban, while Lila followed, laughing.

Ace looked back as Bode folded his arms across the chest of his uniform, his eyes glinting with amusement.

"*I'm* still here," he said, "to see if Miz Adams wants to press charges for excessive lovey-dovey." He lifted an eyebrow at her.

Mia shook her head, laughing. "That won't be necessary, Officer."

"All right.

"But thanks for your concern."

Bode nodded. Then he sighed. "I also have an incident report to fill out. Mack can't stay here any longer."

"No," Mia said softly, regret in her tone. "This can't happen again."

She turned and called after the siblings, "And thanks, all you Braddocks, for the rescue. I've never had a whole posse at my back before."

"Better get used to it," Lila called.

Ace watched Mia put a hand to her heart and smile.

Bottom of the ninth, bases loaded . . . Yeah, I got this.

Chapter 38

MIA WAS PRETTY SURE YOU WEREN'T SUPPOSED TO picnic on a baseball diamond when the warm-up season was in full swing, but Ace was adamant that second base at Silverlake High was the spot where he wanted to eat. Mia chalked it up to one of his superstitions, so she just laughed and started unpacking the picnic basket while her dad tried to keep Stetson from diving headfirst into the goodies.

They'd spread a red and white checked blanket on the ground; it turned out that base markers were good for keeping drinks from tipping over, important given that Ace had splurged on champagne for this outing.

The three of them ate and chatted together like a family, and if Mia was a bit suspicious that the food in the picnic basket that the boys had brought along was a lot fancier, prettier, and better organized than she'd normally expect out of these two, well, she certainly wasn't going to complain. And champagne!

After they'd eaten their fill, Ace poured Mia a second

glass, and they watched the sun set over the bleachers. She wriggled her toes in the fresh-cut grass, leaning against her man—Ace, of all people . . . she was still trying to get used to it. She'd never felt finer.

"Somebody's restless," her dad said, getting slowly to his feet. He snapped his fingers and led Stetson (dressed in his Austin Lone Stars gear) across the diamond to home plate to play fetch, leaving Mia and Ace on their own.

Mia gazed fondly after her dad, the weird maroon tinge of his dyed hair turning almost purple in the glowing light of sunset. One of these days, she'd tactfully take him to Edwynna at A Cut Above and make it a more natural color. Definitely before her mom came home . . . for good. She'd decided to retire.

Ace cleared his throat and pulled, of all things, a catcher's mitt out of the picnic basket.

Mia lifted an eyebrow. "What's that for?"

He looked almost nervous. "Try it on."

She smiled. "It'll be way too big."

Ace nodded. "Yes, it will be. Try it on anyway."

"O-kaaay." Mia slipped her hand into the glove, mystified. There was something inside it. Something completely unexpected. She lifted her gaze to Ace's. "What . . . ?"

He looked as serious as she'd ever seen Easy Ace look. "Don't leave me in suspense."

She pulled out the object and stared at it.

"Monty, the jeweler, got it in from Dallas," Ace said. "I hope—"

"It's incredible." The massive diamond sparkled madly in the red-gold sunset. The stone wasn't quite the size of a baseball, but it might as well have been. "Gorgeous. Ace . . ."

"I didn't know how to do this, exactly," he blurted. "I'm a proposal virgin."

A peal of laughter escaped Mia. "A *what*?"

"Seriously," he said, his blue eyes going almost navy with emotion. "I've never done this before, and I want to get it right."

Mia hushed up as Ace took a deep breath, the most tender expression settling over his face. "What I want to say . . . what I'm trying to tell you . . ."

She waited, breathlessly. Unbelievably touched that this wasn't easy for Easy Ace. Smooth talker extraordinaire. King of blue-eyed charm.

"To tell you that . . ." He dragged a hand down his face. "Dang it! I had this all worked out in my head. It was gonna be *perfect*."

She pulled his hand away from his face and whispered, "It's just me, Drew."

"Yeah. That's the thing. It's *you*. You're the one. Mia, I was so lost. I didn't even know how lost, until I saw in my heart what I *could* have with you in my life. You're a whole new beginning, and I can't wait to get started. When I said you were everything to me, I meant it. One hundred percent."

He took a deep breath and looked down at the mitt. It seemed to center him, soothe him. "So what I want to say is this: Mia Adams, if you'll say yes, then you'll be the single greatest catch of my entire life."

Her breath halted; her pulse stuttered. The ring continued to sparkle, casting pinpoints of white light everywhere. But it wasn't what held her attention.

Ace tugged on his baseball cap, suddenly awkward again. "Wait. That came out backward. First I meant to ask you if you'd *marry*—"

"Yes," whispered Mia. "Maybe I didn't want to fall in love with you, but I couldn't help myself."

His heartbreaker-blue eyes lit with relief. "You couldn't?"

She shook her head and took a deep breath. "Andrew Braddock, there were times when I thought if I never saw you again it wouldn't be a moment too soon. And then came the times when I was scared I'd run you off forever. I'm lucky, you hear me? I'm so lucky that you stuck it out in spite of those times when I couldn't see you for the man you really are.

"You're the man who showed me that there are second

chances in life. That whatever mess you've made for yourself in the past does not have to mean the end of your hopes and dreams. That you can make anything happen if you want to. I was working my hardest, that's for sure. But I never believed I would find happiness again, and love—the kind of love you give me. You show me every day that I'm not alone. That I have something to offer. That I'm precious to you, and that you'll be by my side, have my back *and* be waiting right up ahead whenever I need you. And there is no diamond ring that is worth more than that."

Mia slowly ran one hand through Ace's hair, her eyes searching his. "I love you. I love you more than anything in the whole world."

He actually blushed. Ace Braddock, of all the men on the planet, still had a blush in him. It was completely and utterly adorable. He seemed mortified by it, too, which made it even more endearing. He kissed her then, the feel of his lips on hers backing up every sweet, sweet word they'd exchanged. When they finally took a breath, Ace grinned. "So, you gonna put that on?"

"I thought I'd let you do the honors," Mia said softly.

"Oh. Right. Guess I'm making a total hash out of this." Ace took the wrong hand, then the right one (which was the left one), and slipped the gargantuan diamond onto her fourth finger, where it glittered like a disco ball at a New Year's party.

"Hardly," Mia said. "Your proposal is perfect because it's not perfect. And I love you for it."

Ace swallowed, hard. Then he leaned toward her, cupped her face in his hands, and kissed her again, so tenderly and thoroughly, as if he'd never let her go.

It was a bark from Stetson that broke them apart. And Coach, clearing his throat awkwardly.

"Mind if I marry your daughter, Coach?" Ace asked, with a goofy grin on his face.

"Not at all," her father said gruffly. "You've always been like a son to me."

Mia dashed tears of joy out of her eyes.

For the very first time, the words didn't trouble her at all.

"Did you know that some guys call a home run a 'moon shot'?" Ace asked her. "Makes sense, 'cause I sure hit a home run with you," he continued.

"And I love you to the moon and back, Mia Adams."

Epilogue

MIA STARED IN DISBELIEF AT THE WINDOW OF THE white plastic stick in her trembling hand.

It couldn't be. This was impossible, especially after the horrible, humiliating, heartbreaking failed IVF cycles she'd gone through with her ex.

She unwrapped another plastic stick, went through the motions, and waited. The same result appeared in the window.

Shaking her head, she did the test a third time.

Mia was pregnant.

Pregnant!

The normal, natural, non-test-tube-with-strangers-and-drugs way.

She grabbed all three sticks and ran whooping out of the bathroom to find Ace.

"Drew! Drew! Look! I'm-I'm-I'm—" She broke into unintelligible sobs of pure joy.

Ace came running. "What's the matter? Who hurt you?" he said wildly. "I'll—" His eyes focused on the bouquet of plastic sticks in Mia's hand. *"Really?"* he whispered, as if they were in church and not in their now-completed house—which had all its walls and no wildlife in it. He slipped his arms around her and hugged her jubilantly.

Mia nodded, tears still streaming down her cheeks. "How . . . ? I didn't think it was possible," she said, in tones of wonder.

Ace pulled away and puffed out his chest. "You never tried with *me*," he said proudly. *"My* boys are winners. They bat a thousand."

She smiled through her tears.

"Of course. Of course they do. You're Easy Ace Braddock."

Ace grinned and nodded. "True."

"I still can't believe it," Mia said, in tones of wonder. "We're having a baby."

"We're having a baby!" Ace shouted. "Hey, he can play with Rhett and Jules's little tyke."

Mia touched her stomach and wondered if Mrs. Baxter had used some of her magic on them. Who knew?

Ace grabbed her and swung her around like a very happy caveman. "Let's make another one!"

"Only one at a time," she protested, laughing. "Put me down!"

Reluctantly, he did. Very carefully. "I love you beyond reason," he said. "And my boy in there"—he pointed at her flat belly—"is gonna win the World Series, you mark my words. He's gonna be Silverlake's *next* hometown hero."

Or heroine. But Mia just smiled and kissed him.

ACKNOWLEDGMENTS

A huge thank-you to the entire team at Berkley Jove for being a delight to work with and for your care, support, and enthusiasm. We are so very lucky to work with you all!

And to Christina Rudisil, for sharing the real-life experience that became Mia's encounter with Mack. You home-healthcare workers are brave, hardworking, and invaluable . . . thanks for everything you do to ensure your patients' comfort and safety.

Don't miss the first book in
the Silverlake Ranch series, available now!

Walk Me Home

Keep reading for a preview.

Y*OU CANNOT PUSH ANYONE UP A LADDER.* THE WORDS echoed in Charlie Nash's head as she stared at the aluminum Everest in front of her. Someone famous had said that . . .

Charlie eyed the ladder cautiously, as if it might run toward her on its orange rubber feet and knock her down. "You want me to climb up on that?"

Eight slippery silver rungs: They winked coldly at her, daring her to brave them. Just one step at a time—up into the air—with nothing solid underneath her.

She was already feeling shaky enough just being here, in the Old Barn at the Silverlake Ranch. Days early for a wedding, of all things. She'd rather be buried alive than be here. But it was her cousin Will's big day, and Charlie was a bridesmaid, and her longtime friend Lila needed her help. Now Charlie had to balance on something? In these boots?

God had a sense of humor.

The ladder also made her think of a fire truck. Like the one at the local station . . . where Jake Braddock lived. It was just down the street from Griggs' Grocers. She'd had to stop by yesterday to stock up on vanilla pudding for Granddad.

Charlie hadn't ducked her head into her T-shirt like a turtle, but she *had* deliberately worn oversized sunglasses and a baseball cap, idiot that she was—everyone in Silverlake, Texas, knew Granddad's classic green 1954 GMC pickup. Who else under the age of fifty would be driving it?

Lila Braddock raised her dark eyebrows, so similar to her older brother Jake's. "Yes," Lila said. "I want you to climb up on the ladder. Unless you can levitate and hang those floral swags for this disaster of a wedding without it."

Charlie grimaced. "Funny." Her cousin's wedding, so far, *was* a disaster, for more than one reason. Will's formerly normal fiancée had morphed into an epic Bridezilla.

She had invited, disinvited, and then reinvited fifty out-of-town guests, who had to be housed somewhere in this town of less than five thousand people. She had ordered a custom wedding gown from Amelie on Main Street, then tried to return it. When this proved impossible, because of that whole "custom" concept, she had bought another off the rack in L.A. and hadn't yet decided which one to wear. Amelie was furious, and she was the most even-tempered, tolerant woman Charlie had ever met.

Add to that the cake catastrophe . . . Bridezilla had also changed her mind three times in the last three months about her wedding cake. Kristina Robbins at Piece A Cake was ready to hand her a five-gallon tub of ice cream instead and tell her to have a nice life. It was a good thing Bridezilla wasn't planning to actually live in this town after her big day.

And Charlie hadn't even *told* Lila the latest piece of nuptial news. She simply couldn't find the words—even though she needed to.

Lila checked the time. "We've got to get these decorations up. I have the ladies' knitting circle coming in at noon for their regular meeting. We can't be working on top of them."

Charlie nodded and moved forward to grasp the ladder. It was harmless. *It's much more stable than you are. With nonslip feet.*

The metal frame was unyielding and chilly in the early October morning air, which had seeped inside. She dragged the ladder over to the rough wall of the old boardinghouse's dining hall, where the reception would be.

She loved this old place, though it was bittersweet being here. It had started life as a hay barn for the Braddock farm back in 1839, then been converted into a boardinghouse for the ranch hands around the turn of the century, when the Braddocks had begun raising more horses than crops. The horse stalls had been closed in for separate bunk areas; the tack room was converted to a kitchen; and the "nave" of the barn became the central dining hall.

The rough wood on the outside had weathered over the years to a silvery dove gray, and it still retained the scent of cedar and straw.

The rich red golden interior walls soared to large windows that lined either side. At one end was a massive flagstone fireplace whose chimney shot straight up to the apex of the roof. Wide oak planks, beautifully finished, made up the floor.

Lila had brought in fine Oriental rugs and dotted them with hand-hewn rustic tables, comfortable oversized chairs, and glazed ceramic pots full of tall ferns and palms. She'd managed to make the place both elegant and cowboy-comfortable: a cross between palace and hunting lodge. While Charlie was a professional stager, she didn't have the interior design skills to have pulled this off. It was, in a word, stunning.

The fact that the Braddocks had hung on to the land over the years was amazing, considering the blows successive generations had been dealt. But hang on to it they had, following the family credo: Thou Shalt Not Sell Land. Even if thou must doeth odd and dirty jobs on the side. Even if thou must liveth elsewhere and get basically adopted by another family.

Oh, Jake.

Charlie swallowed hard as she went to the long folding table where Lila had set out three dozen swags made of grapevines and adorned with white silk gardenias. Charlie tucked one under her arm, turned, and set one foot tentatively on the bottom rung of the ladder.

This is nothing, Charlie. Just do it. Jake had helped her climb up to the high hayloft over on the opposite side of the barn a couple of times before, in high school. Once she'd gotten past the climb, he'd made it plenty worth it.

Before. Before that awful day back in high school. Before she and her family had left town in the wake of a devastating fire that killed her grandmother and burned down all the good times along with the Nash family home.

"Why is there a funny look on your face?" Lila asked, appearing beside her and folding her arms across her chest.

Charlie took two steps up—not that skinny jeans were easy to climb in—then three and four. She looked down, wobbled, and clung fiercely to the sides of the ladder. The swag under her arm crackled in protest as she shoved it upward into her armpit, where it poked her painfully through the thin cotton of her black sweater. Small bits of leaves and twigs caught in the fabric. "What funny look?"

Lila tapped her foot on the flagstone floor. "That one," she said, pointing at Charlie's face. "Hey. Easy on the gardenias. They need to be unsquashed. Perfect. She said she was sure this time, and we can't give Bridezilla any excuse to switch them out for calla lilies or roses. I am so done with her."

"No kidding," Charlie said with feeling. "And *you* don't have to be her bridesmaid." Charlie and Felicity weren't exactly friends, but given that she'd introduced her and Will to each other at a college party, they'd insisted she be part of the wedding. Even if she sometimes regretted that introduction, she wouldn't dream of turning down her cousin's request. She took two more steps up the ladder, looked down at the stone floor again, and felt nauseated. She clamped the swag even more tightly into her armpit. The hook it needed to hang on was a foot away from her face. *Easy. No problem.* Except that she had to let go of the ladder with one hand in order to hang it. *Yikes.*

"Charlie? Are you okay?" Lila called.

"Yeah. No . . . I have to tell you something." Charlie eyed the hook. She clutched the ladder. She did *not* look at the floor again. She refused. *Hook. Swag. Simple. Let go of the ladder with your left hand, and hang the swag.*

Except she really needed to let go of the ladder with her right hand first, in order to pull the swag out from under her left arm and rescue the silk gardenias. They probably didn't bloom well if saturated with Secret antiperspirant.

"So tell me."

Charlie sighed.

"And are you going to hang that swag or yourself up there?"

"I'd break the hook right off the wall," Charlie said. "I've gained back the eleven pounds I lost, even though I swore off chocolate."

"You look great," Lila fibbed. "Now hang the swag already and spill."

Charlie uncurled her stiff, reluctant fingers and slid her sweaty right palm off the ladder. She tugged the swag out from under her arm and set it on top. *Yes. Good.* Except there was something white fluttering down. A gardenia. It hit Lila on the head and then fell to the ground.

"Really?" Lila said, narrowing her eyes. "Come down from there so I can fix that. And tell me what's going on already."

On the one hand, Charlie couldn't wait to get off the ladder. On the other, maybe it was good there was some distance between herself and Lila. "Geoff is being sent overseas on a military assignment. So he just dropped out of the wedding," she said. "They're going to need another groomsman." The words hung in the air between them.

"*What* did you say?"

Charlie looked down at Lila's stunned face. "I'm pretty sure you heard me. And Bridezilla is freaking out about the lack of human symmetry in her big show. Somehow, I'm supposed to pull a groomsman outta my—"

Lila was shaking her head. "No."

Charlie sighed. "Got any ideas?"

"No. This is not happening. I'm an *event planner*. Not a magician."

"Lila? I really hate to tell you this. But you'd better grab a top hat and a rabbit, as well as a groomsman. Because Bridezilla is having a meltdown of epic proportions, and she can't take it out on her groom . . . so she's taking it out on us. I spent two hours listening to her rant and cry last night. And she'll call you next, because you're her wedding planner by default; you come free with the site rental."

As if on cue, Lila's cell phone started ringing to a barking dog theme.

Forgetting her fear of the ladder, Charlie covered her involuntary smirk with one hand.

"I'm out of battery," said Lila, looking at her phone as if it were a snake. "I'm on another call. No, I'm on another planet."

Bark, bark, bark.

"I have supplied porta-potties, pink doves, and even a stand-in wedding ring," she continued. "But I cannot pull a groomsman out of my behind. It's not possible."

Bark, bark, bark.

Charlie put her hand back on the ladder and inched down it step by step until she safely reached the ground.

Lila bent and picked up the silk gardenia. She stared at it as though she expected it to speak, to give her a solution. And then a very peculiar expression bloomed on Lila's face. Charlie watched it grow as a bad feeling grew parallel to it, in the pit of her own stomach.

Lila pursed her lips as she took the swag back from Charlie. She efficiently reattached the wayward gardenia with a snippet of floral wire. Charlie's unease grew as she nodded with satisfaction. When Lila pursed her lips like that, it meant she was determined. And when Lila was determined, she got what she wanted. No matter what it was.

Lila had pursed her lips back in elementary school when she wanted a purple bike with a pink sparkly banana seat. Check.

She had pursed her lips in middle school when she'd wanted to go on the end-of-year trip to New York City and had been told there was no money for such a trip. Check.

And Lila had pursed her lips in high school when she'd wanted to date the quarterback, even though she was a somewhat dorky sophomore and he was a supremely cool senior. Check.

Charlie glanced toward the ladder, feeling a weird urge to climb back up it in order to escape from Lila and whatever she was about to say.

"Add magician to my résumé," declared Lila. "I can supply a groomsman after all."

"Give me that." Charlie snatched the repaired swag from Lila and scurried back over to the ladder. Up she climbed the first step, the second, the third. "You're kidding, right?"

"Nope."

Up the fourth rung Charlie went, and the fifth. "You have a spare man in your back pocket? I need to get a pair of those pants for myself."

"As a matter of fact, I do." Lila looked as if she were about to purr.

Charlie eyed the hook again. *Simple. Remove right hand. Take garland in it. Drop it on the hook.* Basically, the same as staging an apartment. A little design sense, a little elbow grease. Nothing to it.

"The Silverlake Fire Station does a lot more than just fight fires, right?" said Lila.

Charlie's heart hurled itself into her esophagus, and she choked on it.

"They always have. It's part of their mission statement. It's tradition, helping out the town. If you think about it, it's . . . it's . . . an *obligation.* They have to help the community wherever help is needed, so . . ."

No. Don't say it, Lila. Do. Not. Say. His. Name. Charlie extended the swag toward the hook, clutching the ladder for dear life with her other hand.

"Yeah, *Jake. He's perfect!*" exclaimed Lila. "He helps out everyone else in this town. Why not his own sister? It's about time we had a real conversation anyway. Jake will *totally* do it. He'll be perfect. What d'you think?"

Charlie made a strangled noise.

"Oh, come on. You can't avoid him forever," Lila said in a pragmatic tone. "It's too small a town, and being in the wedding means you can't just do your usual flyover. Imagine if you and Jake could finally get past the weirdness once and for all."

"Are *you* past the weirdness with Jake?" Charlie asked pointedly. "He's *your* brother."

Lila flushed. "No, but I'd like to be." That old Lila gleam appeared in her eyes, and she pursed her lips again.

Uh-oh. Lila had given Charlie her friendship in Charlie's darkest hour after that damned fire, when the Nashes blamed Jake, and the rest of the Braddocks were pressuring their little sister to close ranks.

"Maybe this is the thing that could finally do it. Charlie, I need this. Jake's the perfect solution. Please say you'll roll with this."

Lila didn't have to spell it out.

Charlie owed her friend . . . especially since she was the cause of the rift between Lila and Jake. But the thought of being in a wedding with him?

Charlie stared at the hook. It was a very sturdy one, its screws embedded in solid wood. Never mind the swag. Never mind the extra eleven pounds. She was going to hang herself on it after all.

Ready to find
your next great read?

Let us help.

Visit prh.com/nextread